PAPER DAISIES

ALSO BY KIM KELLY

Black Diamonds
This Red Earth
The Blue Mile
Wild Chicory
Jewel Sea

'colourful, evocative and energetic' – *Sydney Morning Herald*

'impressive research' – *Daily Telegraph*

'Why can't more people write like this?' – *Canberra Times*

KIM KELLY

PAPER DAISIES

Jazz Monkey
Publications

First published 2015 by Pan Macmillan Australia
This edition published by Jazz Monkey Publications

Copyright © Kim Kelly 2015

The moral right of the author has been asserted.

A CIP record for this book is available at the National Library of Australia.

Design: Alissa Dinallo
Cover image: Hill End fence, Kim Kelly; daisy stencil recreated from original watercolour by Adam Foster, 1848-1928

Author photograph: Dean Brownlee
Printing: IngramSpark

Publishing services provided by Critical Mass
www.critmassconsulting.com

For the crushed
For a little revenge

I cannot be yours or any man's. I am my own and God's.

Louisa Lawson, 1848–1920

A good method of preserving all kinds of everlasting flowers is to take a box of moderate size, with a moveable base. Have some perfectly dry sand ready; if dried in an oven, the better. Pour in about three or four inches in depth of the sand, in which plant the flower stalks. Then gradually fill up the box with sand till all the flowers are covered; taking care to keep every leaf and flower in its natural position.

Australian Town and Country Journal, 1887

HOOROO

Become who you are!

Thus Spake Zarathustra

BERYLDA

'Time, gentlemen,' the examination supervisor calls from the top of the room, but my pen already rests, my physics paper completed four minutes ago. I dare a glance across to my right: Doug Jefferies is scribbling out a last answer to the final question on magnetism, even as he is closing the booklet, pretending he is not still writing. Bert Hughes in front of him runs his hand through his hair, breathing out the tension with a cocksure snort, stretching out his legs beneath the desk. I barely breathe at all; I keep my hands flat to the desktop, either side of my work, for I am not a gentleman.

I am the only one of my kind in here, and the supervisor, a fusty old frock-coated curmudgeon, reminds me of this with a sneer as he whips away my paper; as swiftly as he manages an avuncular nod of, 'Good luck, Jefferies,' for my neighbour. Only fitting, I suppose, as Doug is the nephew of one of the members of the professorial board.

The door is pushed open and thirty sweaty gentlemen rush out as bright summer midday rushes in, a stream of light piercing this dark-panelled tomb.

'Miss Jones.' A straggler reaches across me to hold the door. Clive Gillies-Wright. He grins his certain medal-winning grin. 'How'd you go with all that, eh?'

'Fine. Thank you.' I step past him and into the sun. My examinations are done. Literature. Latin. Biology. All fine. I can't wait to shove my results in Uncle Al– Don't think about him.

Look into the sky, brilliant blue above the chimney pots, and breathe in all my small but certain achievements thus far. Enjoy this moment: here, now. Today, the fifth of December, 1900. I am a student at the University of Sydney, and next year I will be admitted to Medicine – at last. I shall not fail. *Nearly free* ... my sister Greta whispers to me on the breeze, across the miles between us.

And now, across the quad lawn, only a few yards away, in the cool shade of the cloisters, here is Flo. My friend. Waiting for me. But she's got lost in her book, sitting there on the stone wall, getting a numb bum.

At the clatter of the sweaty thirty heading towards her, she looks up and sees me; she waves, shouting out, 'Bryl! Oi – over here!'

Her voice rings around the pillars and flags and I laugh. Flo, darling Flo McFee – medal-winning indelicate. Fabulous.

BEN

'Mr Wilberry – sir? Excuse me?'

It's Gregham, at the door of the herbarium, assistant to the chair. I suspect he's come with another instruction from Dubois himself. What does our esteemed Head of Botany want now, perchance? That we deem wattle a weed? Or perhaps the eucalypt – all five hundred of its species? Sheep don't fatten or fleece well enough on it so let's dig it up and burn it, *oui*? I should like to send Gregham off with a message for Dubois: Bugger off. Go back to where you came from, Professor Jean-Pierre bloody Continental trespasser.

I rub my eyes, take a moment before I turn around. I blink down through the looking glass on the bench, set above the native specimens of *Viola betonicaefolia* and *hederacea* I've just pulled out – examples for my end-of-year general extension lecture on differentiating indigenous species from those introduced, such as the common European *odorata* – which actually is a weed. Dubois has already made his annoyance at this lecture known: *What is this knowledge for, should I venture to ask? Flower arrangements for the Christmas holiday, oui?* No, it is knowledge for the floral record, for posterity perhaps – if the sheep should damn well eat them to extinction. It's been a battle all this year, since he arrived. A battle which *conservation fanatics* such as myself will possibly lose in the long run; but I'm going down fighting, in my way.

Gregham clears his throat behind me.

I clear mine too; can't keep the man waiting.

I turn around and see he's holding out an envelope. Perhaps Dubois has finally gone above Professor Jepson, our faculty dean and my ally, and had the chancellor agree to my sacking – which I will have overruled. He doesn't know how things work in this country – not at all. This continent may be large, but its principles are simple. One doesn't sack a Wilberry – you arrogant little Frog.

'I'm sorry, sir,' Gregham says, and he does look sore.

I'm about to tell him not to worry about it, it'll soon enough be sorted out, but he adds: 'I'm sorry – I read it. By accident. The telegram, I –'

He leaves his stammering there as I open it. And I know what it is. I see it in Gregham's sorrowful eyes as clearly as I see it typed out across this page in my hand:

RETURN HOME A.S.A.P. IF YOU CAN. YOUR MOTHER IS DYING.

Mama. My dear Mama. So this is it; her time has come. This telegram is from her doctor, Doctor Blaine. Not unexpected – it's been her particular battle all this year, a slow battle for her life – but the blow is not easier for knowing that. The cancer is finally having its way. And I've got to get to Brisbane to her – now. Got to get home to Queensland. And I am here in Melbourne, a thousand miles away.

I push past Gregham at the door, and I run.

BERYLDA

'Here – look.' Flo opens the flap of her tote to reveal the amethyst glint of a half-pint flask. 'Gin.'

'Oh no you don't,' I warn her off. Post-examination fatigue is coming quickly upon me, beginning at my knees: I'm not sure I'll make it all the way across the grounds of University Park back to Women's College without a feeble feminine rest. I'm not getting up to no good tonight.

'Oh yes we do,' Flo insists. 'We've got the Wonderland party – for Clive. Don't you remember?'

'Oh. Yes. Now you mention it.' Clive Gillies-Wright, who will undoubtedly win the Physics prize and probably the Higher Maths prize too, is having a going-away party. Really going away – to the Transvaal. Deferring academic excellence for a year on the veld hunting Boers with the Scottish Horse Regiment, doing his duty for Queen and Country.

'You can't rat out, you're Alice.' Flo elbows me and I'd fall over my feet but that she scoops me along, that same elbow now under my arm, her hand squeezing mine conspiratorially.

'I won't rat,' I say, as if she'll hear anything else. Her shoulders are broader than mine and she's half a foot taller. But I won't rat, as I usually do with ra-ra rugby boys' things; I'd usually rather stare at the wallpaper, alone in the common room. Clive's all right, though; I should say hooroo, fare thee well. I ask her: 'Where'd you get the booze?'

'Hoddy.' She leans into me, pressing me with her warmth for her youngest elder brother, Hodson, who's articled-clerking now at the family firm, McFee & Packhorn, in the thick of the Phillip Street legal fraternity. She's adored and indulged by all three of her brothers, all lawyers, wanting their little sister to join them at the profession too, and jealousy pricks at the thought. Her family is perfect; mine is – Don't think about that.

'Hoddy is a very naughty boy,' I say. 'What if you get stupid on the hard liquor and someone takes advantage?'

She pulls a maniacal, cross-eyed face at me: 'I should be so lucky!' She laughs at herself: even tipsy she's intimidating to boys – perhaps especially then – and she doesn't care. Her laughter fills the distance across the park and winds around the squat, square convent-like tower of Women's. For a moment I am scooped up and away along a string of her tight golden curls escaped from under her hat. She is as curly as I am straight.

'Besides,' she says, leaning into me again, but serious now, 'Hoddy just told me the cadavers in the Legislative Council are most definitely not going to consider the bill again before the summer break.'

The Women's Franchise Bill. I'm not much surprised but Flo is taking it personally, as she does these sorts of things. She glowers over at St Paul's as we pass it, as if the boys who reside there are responsible, as if we're not attending the Wonderland party there for Clive tonight. She rails the rest of the way back to our digs, about the attorney-general, misnamed Wise, having killed the bill last Wednesday before it got a proper hearing in the Upper House: 'Is New South Wales going to be left the only colony where women have no voice at all – in a *Federation*? In less than a month we'll be a state, a proper *state* – with no women's *vote*.'

Like the entire rest of the world, bar New Zealand, and South and Western Australia, and I must suppress my ambivalence: voting is the least of what I want for women; for me, and for my sister, Gret. But I can't tell Flo half of any of that. Not now. Not yet. One day I shall confide in her, though, speak of the depths. When I am sure of her confidence. Maybe next year –

'We can't lag Victoria – my God,' she rails on up the path. 'What if they get female suffrage in Melbourne before here? What disgrace would *that* be?'

'I'm sure they won't get the vote before us.' I laugh, uncaring of that ever-enduring inter-colonial sport, the Sydney–Melbourne tit for tat, and my laugh is such a distant bell it can hardly have come from me. A cloud swoops across the sun and I can only see Uncle Alec smashing down the women's vote, should he win the Bathurst seat in the New South Wales parliament next year; he will smash it down with a blithe and easy wave amongst the men, behind closed doors, stepping out of the House with a rueful smile, pretending his hands were tied. Resentment swoops through me, a black crow's wing. I would not have had to endure this first year of Arts – the humiliation of compulsory literature, of Shakespearean sonnets and snide Pope, soppy Keats and femicidal Browning – if he hadn't forced me to. Alec Howell: stamping me with the suggestion of some kind of failure before I even set foot in this university. No one does a year of Arts any more before admission to Medicine – no one capable of sitting the Medical entrance exam, at least. No one like me. I will be twenty by the time I return here to begin my future properly in the new year, my sister's future, too; I am too young to vote, should that ever be permitted, but old enough to strike out along the path that must be ours: free of him. *But Berylda, you must be sure you are up to the challenge*, he said, in holding me back this year. He always sounds so reasonable. Don't think about him. Don't let him intrude. Don't let him spoil this day.

'Oh Bryl, listen to me going on and on,' Flo squeezes my hand again. 'I must need a drink.'

I squeeze back. 'Me too.'

BEN

'Welcome aboard, sir. Ah –' The crewman looks at my ticket; he might be the captain for all I know or care. 'Mr Wilberry, is it?'

'Yes.' I just want to get past him, get on, get going. Get this steamer on its way. Mama: the very thought of her stops time altogether.

'One of *the* Wilberrys?' the chap is asking.

'Yes.' There's only two of us: Pater and me, and it's infamous Pater this chap is referring to. He must be a Queenslander, I suppose; this is the *Arawatta* to Cooktown. I've taken it a dozen times over the years, at least, and I was fortunate to get on it this afternoon, with only an hour to spare.

'Well, I'd better make that a special welcome aboard then.' The chap touches the brim of his cap. Hands me back my ticket, with some other load of waste paper.

I keep pushing past him, up the gangway to my cabin. As though I might make this ship go faster, if I keep moving. I throw my bags on the bunk in the room, a room to myself, thank God. My heart is belting around like a lost dog. Wait, Mama, wait for me.

'Sir.' Another chap behind me, a soft rap at the open door. 'Dinner is served at seven thirty, if that is suitable for you. Will you join the captain or do you prefer to eat alone? And, um – roast beef or fish pie?'

I look down at the wad of paper still in my hand, half crushed: my ticket and, behind it, shipboard information, what appears to be the cargo list above my fist, should I care to know that we are carrying: *137 cases of beer, 423 bags of onions, 73 cases of cheese, 42 kegs cream of tartar, 191 bales of chaff, 730 bags of rice, 215 cases of starch, 55 cases of currants, 60 cases of naphtha, 48 bags of oats, 27 packages of drapery, 30 cases of soap, 10 cases of brandy, 25 packages of tobacco, 30 reels of barbed wire, 7 horses, a quantity of circus gear* ... A quantity of circus gear?

'Sir?'

'What?' I ask the chap still waiting at the door, but I don't turn to him.

'Dinner?'

'I'll eat here, please. Just a cheese sandwich and bottle of beer – nothing else.'

'Right you are, sir. Stout or –'

'Not concerned – you choose.'

'Of course, sir.' He leaves, closing the cabin door behind him.

I pull open the curtain at the window above the little writing ledge and stare out at the docks, at the confusion of steamers and punts, of business going on and on. It's a cold, grey summer evening as we move out of the Yarra and make for the sea, a wind blowing up from Bass Strait, from Antarctica: a Melbourne specialty. This city that is still so foreign to me, even after ten years: an imposing stonewall of a metropolis built with gold rush cash, long gone now, which manages to be both grandiose and bleak at once – like the weather.

It will take three days, weather willing; three days to get into Brisbane. Round the broken bows of Victoria, up the interminable coast of New South Wales – this continent is far too large. Mama, wait for me.

BERYLDA

Flo is at the kitchen table, her back to me, a white powder puff pinned above her tails – Hoddy's tails. She is a living, breathing outrage. Her powder puff is bobbing, as are the long white ears she has made from an old petticoat and wire, as she chops away at a cabbage.

She glances over her shoulder, all painted whiskers and pink-carmined nose, ringlets swinging, and I'm already laughing as she says: 'Can you hurry up and start shelling those peas, Alice, or we're going to be late.'

Who could argue with that? I tie my apron on over my blue dress and at least my costume is complete too. I'm Alice mostly for my size: the smallest.

As I sit to begin rapid shelling, I ask Flo: 'What dreadful thing are you making tonight, then?'

'Oh, just ordinary cabbage noodle stew,' she says, *chop chop*. 'But with peas, for something different.' Her ears bob emphatically.

I laugh some more. 'Mm mmm.' As if she doesn't frighten boys enough, she's also a strict vegetarian, on conscientious grounds – her whole family are. Exuberant, gin-swilling, vegetarian Christian Socialists. Is there anything more outrageous? She's been trying to get a Vegetarian Society going on campus all year, but so far I am her only acolyte, and that's just for loyalty's sake.

'No one else will eat that gloop except for you, Flo.' Margie swishes in, her auburn tresses piled high in an impossible pompadour: our Queen of Hearts. 'You should be banned from contributing to supper – forever and always – never mind occasions at St Paul's.'

'Oh!' Flo pretends offence and shrugs, 'Each to their own,' before brandishing her knife at the bowl of oranges and limes at the other end of the table. 'Margie, hurry up and start on the fruit, will you – for the punch.' Which will be lethal, with the addition of Hoddy's contraband – don't even think it too loudly lest our strictly teetotal Miss Macdonald, our dear principal, suspect the no good we are up to. Miss Macdonald will not be joining us this evening, though: as a Master of Arts in Archaeology herself, she has a faculty dinner on, oh stroke of fortune, and she's put Margie, third year honours in Logic and Mental Philosophy, in charge of us all in her absence – madness. All twenty-one of us here at Women's.

Soon our little communal kitchen is full of swishing and bustling and laughter, all girls together, and I do so love it here whenever it's like this, so full of colour and fun. Jayne is a vision in purple and yellow braided bathing costume, black whiskers and ears – the Cheshire Cat; Phylly, in a vast, bright red crinoline, spotted all over with discs of brown paper, is the magic mushroom. Jen starts playing her guitar somewhere amongst us; she will win the French Medal this year. I could stay here in Women's College forever, sit here at this table pulling pod strings forever, if I were allowed. But a terrible wave of longing and dread sweeps through me at the notion: that I might not return to Bathurst one day. How could I ever think such a thing, of abandoning my sister there, to deal with him alone? I must book my train ticket – I'll do that tomorrow. I must.

'Berylda Jones, how beautiful you are as Alice – stand up.' Jayne is grinning over me, turning to Eva Marie to say: 'Isn't she? Look at her.' Faces look at me, towering over me, even as I stand, and Jayne is asking, 'How on earth do you cope being so pretty, Berylda? Do you even come from this world? Your complexion, your eyes – you are an unusual thing. Where did you get your loveliness from?'

The longing and the dread sweeps through me again. I feel the blood rush to my cheeks, but I am stone. I cannot reply to Jayne. But I don't have to.

'Keep shelling those peas!' the White Rabbit shouts above her noodle soup, and my smile returns at her command.

Soon enough Margie is herding us all across the lawn towards St Paul's, with our pots and trays and punchbowl, and the boys are thrilled to see us, all whistling and carrying on. I have two cups of punch – it's delicious. I even let Clive Gillies-Wright kiss my hand when he finds me. He says something to me about this morning's exam having been full of tricks, but I'm not listening; I'm hoping he doesn't get shot on the veld, or get dysentery. He is a nice boy. He's dressed as the Hatter, a rainbow of ribbons wound all around his topper, but with green tights and gold brocade tunic he's at least half Romeo. If I were a nice girl, we might have something to talk about, reason to dance.

But that's by the by, and I am tired now. Well and truly tired, right inside my brain and in my bones, the tricky physics of exhaustion has me. As the piano starts thumping for a song and all the sweaty ra-ra in the room starts up in earnest, I make my excuses. I don't need to be here, I know how things will go: there will be fantastical tales told of Mafeking and Her Majesty's gunships, unanimous envy of Clive's impending adventure, uproarious jokes told about sending over a football team instead to sort out the enemies of Empire over a beer-guzzling contest, and Doug Jefferies, who is already eating one of the brown-paper discs off the bottom edge of Margie's mushroom, will soon be up on one of the tables, smashing a plate or two, before stumbling outside to fall into the lake, or some similar thing – upon which the college warden will call the occasion to a halt five minutes before curfew at ten p.m., reminding us all that such casual frivolities as this will be banned in future if students do not comport themselves appropriately and respectfully as young ladies and gentlemen.

'Hooroo, fare thee well, good luck.' I tap Clive on the back of his shoulder, and I flee, as Flo mouths to me through the crowd: 'You rat.'

I am. Single-minded, and necessarily so. The night is my only chaperone as I tread back across the lawn. I shall read myself to sleep, as usual: finish the chapter on the circulatory system from the copy of *Braithwaite's Surgical Anatomy* I smuggled out of the undergraduate med library in my skirt a week ago. *Just browsing*, I told the librarian's doubtful glare: *I'm hoping to get into Medicine next year*. Just 'borrowing' a book I'm not allowed to have.

BEN

'So you bothered yourself to come home after all, did you, son?'
Mama smiles at me from her bed, in her elfish way. She is a
small sweet bird; she can't be dying. But she is. She is too small
against her pillows. I can see that her breath pains her even as the
opium tonic is easing her way. 'My dear bear.' She holds out her
hand to me, and I fall to my knees beside her: relief that I am here;
guilt that I was not here all this time. I haven't been home since
winter break, since June; she wasn't so bad then; yes she was. 'Ben,
please.' She holds my head to her smallness. 'Don't cry.'

I wasn't, until she said the word. Now I cry like a small boy, into
her pillow.

'Hush.' She pats my head. 'My Benjamin bear, it's all right.'

I struggle to regain my senses. In June, we went riding out along
the line of Capricorn, out from Eleonora at Jericho, as we do every
winter break, when the weather is best there. We ride out along the
dusty ochre plains, towards the Jordan, her hat flying off the back
of her head as she brings her horse up to a gallop, daring me after
her. Every year, since I was a small boy. She can't be dying. Eleonora
Trenton Wilberry: my mother. Ellie. Mama. But she has been dying
all the while since June; since before then. She told me all about it
that day, and the certain prognosis.

'Ben,' she says into my hair now. 'I'm very pleased that you are
here. I'd like you to do something for me, on your way back down
south, if you can.'

'Whatever it is, consider it done,' I tell her, but I can't yet look up.

'There's a bloom,' she says, and she pauses, the pain too much. I would tell her not to talk, but she must tell me what she wants me to do. I wait for her to continue, and after a moment she does. 'It's *Helichrysum* – of some kind, I think,' she says. 'I don't know what species. It's on the farm, at Mandagery. I would see it every January, when I was a girl, by the creek. It was the first paper daisy I ever saw, though I didn't know what it was back then. Go and find it for me, will you, Ben? And bring some back for the garden here. I always meant to …'

She is half-dreaming through the opium, but she must tell me more. I ask her: 'What does it look like, Mama, this bloom – what colour is it?'

'Oh, you won't miss it, Ben,' she says and I can feel her smile radiating through her hand on the back of my head. 'It's red, a little pompom of flame at the centre; rows and rows of raylets all around, spearheaded. Like small red suns. Woody stipes – a bit like *elatum*. But so red. Get some, will you? I don't think the farmer will mind, do you? Who owns that property now? Do I know that? Or have I forgotten? I wish John hadn't sold the farm when Father died. Oh Ben, but I'm looking forward to seeing Father again, and Mother too. In a little while. Don't worry, my sweet bear, they will look after me. They always have.'

Have they? They married you off to Pater, didn't they? And a man called Bentley has the Trenton place at Mandajery Creek, although for all my rambling across the country I've never been there myself – it's somewhere in central New South Wales. Where the female breeding stock is better, apparently: less chance of accidentally marrying someone with a bit of black in them, than in Queensland. And still I can't look up at Mama. Anger has me for this little while, at all she has had to contend with; at all she has been denied. By Pater. Who is right now out at our property, at Jericho, breaking in a new manager. Because that's what you do when your wife of thirty years is dying. Eleonora: name a cattle station after your pretty wife and tame her, and forget her. When he bothers to get here, I will tell him what I think of him, once and for all. Tell him what I should have long ago: that he's a selfish bastard. He's the reason I live in Melbourne and only come home twice a year; when Mama – when there's no longer a reason for me to come home, I won't come home at all. Not for him.

'Promise me? Promise me, Ben?' she asks.

'I promise.' I will find her bloom and bring it back here for her, and then I'll –

'Don't disappointment me, Benjamin. And heaven knows, you've been such a disappointment to me.' She tugs at my hair, to make me look up: she is having a joke with me even now, with her wry smile, one I can't help returning. She loves that I am a botanist in Melbourne; she is as proud and pleased as a mother could be at that. She places her small bird hands either side of my face and adds: 'A perennial disappointment, you are, my son – every time you fail to bring a girl home. Aren't there any girls down south? None at all?'

'It would appear they have somehow failed to see me in their midst,' I try to joke, for I am a large and lumbering person, not easy to miss. I try to laugh but it's a strange, dull noise that comes from me. Because I am a disappointment to her: she has been asking me this question for the past two years, yearning for grandchildren, any children, to fill this empty house. I am twenty-seven years old, nearing twenty-eight; I have no excuse for this disappointment, except that it seems I am not equipped for that part of life. I only have to look at an attractive young lady and I become an imbecile.

'I'm sorry, Mama,' I tell her. I am sorry in every way.

'Hush with sorries, Ben. You have nothing to be sorry about. I made you. You are perfect. Your time will come. She will be perfect too.' Mama closes her eyes. She seems to sink further into the pillows; shrinking before my eyes. She murmurs something else, but I don't understand her.

'What is it?' I ask her. 'Tell me.' Tell me every last thing you must.

She sighs; a shallow, rasping sigh. She doesn't open her eyes, but she murmurs along a breath: 'Don't argue with your father, Ben. Walk away from him, as you have always done. Walk away ...'

She doesn't speak again. She sleeps, and she doesn't wake. I watch over her, but she will not wake.

I watch her breathe.

'Nothing more to be done, Ben.' Doctor Blaine is at the door. 'If the pain should disturb her again, I can administer the drug by hypodermic syringe. She will feel no more pain if I can help it, let me assure you.'

Assure me? I cannot be sure if any of this is even real. I know all of the facts of the matter, of course: that Blaine had thought for so long it was only a stomach ulcer, as had Mama, and by the time the tumour was detected, it was considered too large, too risky to operate. They had a go at the X-ray treatment, to no avail; I had a go at researching this far-fetched cure and that, to no avail. Blaine said it would be a matter of months, or perhaps a year, maybe two; it was never easy to predict, except in its ultimate result. But now that the inevitable is occurring, I am lost to these facts. All facts but one: my mother is my light, and she is leaving me.

I sit with her and watch her breathe. I hold her little sparrow hand all through the night and into the dawn, until she breathes no more.

'She is at peace, Ben,' Blaine says as he checks to find it true. 'She is with God.'

She is gone.

I walk out into the garden. Her garden here at Indooroopilly, in lush, evergreen Brisbane. My mother's beautiful creation, of poinciana, jacaranda, her melaleucas by the river, and her drifts of *Helichrysum* there – *elatum*. A host of small white angels swaying on the warm breeze against the wide green river. In full bloom. They fill the house, they are the stars of all of her arrangements, her beloved paper daisies, her everlastings. They will fill the vases at St Andrew's too; every summer they do, by her hand, and now they will appear on altar and casket for her.

No. She cannot be gone.

She should have been a botanist. *Oh but you can't be a botanist north of the border, wouldn't matter who you were*, she'd wave away the suggestion. *No such silly thing as botany in Queensland, dear, you know that.* No such thing as a university in Queensland, either.

19

I plunge my hands into the cool of the river as though this might cool my pain, hush the sound that is breaking from me now.

Another sound belts through it anyway. Pater's team of four careering up the drive for the stables. The bastard has bothered to come home.

BERYLDA

I wake with the bell for prayer: it's seven forty-five. But I stay in bed, pretend I'm asleep for a little while longer, not that anyone goes to prayers with any regularity, except Margie and Jayne, and they're not here anyway. They've gone home; one to Tamworth, the other to Caboolture, somewhere north of Brisbane, far, far away. And those who haven't gone home yet have all left for the river, at Lane Cove, for the boat races.

All but Flo, who remains here with me. She's not attending the races on protest, because the women's rowing club remains debarred from competing. Darling Flo, I can hear her turning the pages of her newspaper, propped up in bed, sipping her morning cocoa. She remains here because I remain here, I'm sure. Her family only lives a short ferry trip away across the harbour, at Waverton; she resides at college because her parents want her to discover her independence, on her own. Her parents actually *want* her to. Such an incredible, foreign idea to me. Perhaps one that might not have been so odd, had my parents not – Oh God, don't stray there.

I open my eyes and look up at the curtain, at the sun streaming through the muslin, pale gold light, shimmering hot already. I should get up or it'll be a sticky old walk across to Grace Brothers at Broadway, to the bargain table sales: the reason I've given for my hanging about so long after the exams. So that I can buy Greta her Christmas present, something as dear as she is to me; something as sweet as she is, but womanly, too. She is twenty-two; how did

21

she turn twenty-two this past year? In all my delaying, how does anything happen? But it's true enough that I must also wait for the Grace Brothers sale, quite genuinely, because I am running out of my pitiful allowance; I'll have to sell a book or two as it is: *A Study of the Novel* and the biblical *Anthology of English Verse* can sacrifice themselves. And I shall purchase that train ticket today, Greta darling, I really shall. If it's not too hot to walk all the way to the station, at Redfern – perhaps this afternoon.

'Oi sleepyhead – listen to this,' says Flo from her bed across the room. 'News from Hill End – that's out your way, isn't it?'

'Yes, it's not far from Bathurst.' Don't remind me: *Bathurst, Bathurst, Bathurst*, and Hill End is another cloudy dream in itself. 'What's news?'

She reads over a yawn: '*A Chinese herbalist, by name of Dr Ah Ling, has purportedly cured a man of a malignant tumour. The tumour, in the upper arm, of local miner, George Conroy, was said to have burst from the skin after the application of an herbal poultice, thereafter returning full function to the arm and relieving totally the man's previous agony. The cure was achieved without surgery or any modern therapy for the treatment of such cancerous growths. When asked about his condition, Conroy would only say, "It's a miracle! And he never charged me nothing but what you would pay for a draught of Woods Peppermint or a bottle of beer. Nothing!" Curiously, none who were approached in the town seemed to be able to say precisely where this miracle worker Ah Ling lives, except that it is in a thatched hut on a tobacco plantation, somewhere in the wilderness between the Hill and Tambaroora.*'

'Sounds interesting,' I say absently. I just don't want to think about getting on that train, of returning to that district at all. Oh bum – I spy on the night stand – I am yet to return *Surgical Anatomy* to the med library, too.

'Sounds amazing!' Flo scrunches the paper at me. 'You should try to meet him, over the break – go and ask him all about it. It sounds positively revolutionary!'

'Yes, Flo.' She has me laughing before I am properly alert. 'That's precisely what I'll do. Start a medical revolution over the holidays. In Hill End. With a mysterious Chinaman.'

Chinaman: the word clangs in my ears for a heartbeat before: 'Oh my!' Flo jumps up, looking at the time, aghast, ringlets flinging. 'Get up, lazybones – get dressed. We've got to be the first at the bargain tables if we're going to get the best stuff. Hurry up!'

'I'm hurrying.' I am laughing still more as I rise. 'What on earth do you want at the bargain tables?' Flo doesn't want for anything.

'I want the most dreadful stuff imaginable,' she says. 'A great big splashy hat, specifically, for Federation Day. Something that even Mother will disapprove of.'

I would ask her why but I know the answer: yesterday the *Evening News* proclaimed that at present we ladies are far more concerned about procuring charming hats and gowns from Grace Brothers than we are about the 'birth of the nation' or 'the women's suffrage question'.

I think I might just have to procure for myself something a little splashy, too.

BEN

'Cut your hair, son – you look like a sheila,' Pater greets me after he's finished conferring with Blaine about the particulars of Mama's death.

Don't argue with your father. No, I won't; neither will I have my hair cut. I walk away.

Into Mama's sunroom. He doesn't follow me. I sit at her desk and pull out her current notebooks: her calendar of the garden, address book, birthday book, correspondence folders, and her diaries, her pages and pages of observations, day after day:

The honeyeaters seem to have stayed long into the season, well into summer. Last summer. Lists for Christmas dinner and table settings, and: *Ben looks so very well. A little thinner than he should be perhaps, or perhaps that's a mother's imagination. He's big enough, as always. He seems sad, however. I cannot bear that he should ever be sad. But he's a human being, so there's nothing to be done about that, I suppose. He'll get along all right. They all do, don't they? God, please send him someone to cherish beyond me. A good match. Joyfulness. He was such a joyful child.*

Rain remains incessant …

Not a cloud in the sky today. I stare into the sky until I can no longer see.

Time is marked by the opening and closing of the front door. The undertaker and his assistant come and go, taking her away with them. Then comes Reverend Ainsley, the new vicar, whom I don't really know, so I don't move from Mama's desk to greet him. Then a cohort of the Queensland Parliament arrives – the hardest boiled Protectionist cohort. I hear their voices, possibly half-a-dozen of them. 'John, John, bad luck. So sorry to hear about Ellie, old man. So sorry.' And that dispensed with, the commiserations quickly fall to what will be the certain death of the colony after the first of January, when the newly formed Commonwealth conspiracy of southerners will rob Queensland of its trade tariffs and its Kanaka slave labour force. I can't hear Pater's responses; perhaps that's my imagination. He is never quiet on such issues: he is the Minister of Agriculture, self-proclaimed despot of Central Queensland, and you've never heard hypocrisy until you've heard John Wilberry decrying the injustices of the proposed Immigration Restriction Act. How else do you break a shearers' strike unless you can bring in black slaves?

Their voices rise, the drone of massive, overgrown wasps. 'What *is* this Australia for?' I hear one above the rest. 'We will never agree on taxation rates – we can't even agree on a standard railway gauge. The only state that we will become is one which is destroyed. We're still getting back up from the collapse of '93. It is insanity.'

Insanity. Whose fault was the collapse of '93? Melbourne bankers, who have only one goal in mind: to ruin Queensland, by withdrawing capital, provoking all manner of strikes, which only in turn encourage the nuisance that is the Labor Party, and push up the cost of wages. Whereas in God's country, shearers and stockmen and canecutters should work for free, because they are so bloody privileged to be allowed to be Queenslanders at all, and any such thing as a federal bank is satanic. I can't sit here a moment more. I shall go out to the greenhouse; I shall look over Mama's trays of seeds.

'Ben.' I am stopped halfway across the back verandah. 'Benjamin, isn't it? Sorry to hear about your mother. The worst.' My eyes are blinded looking back into the shade; I see the shape of the head, bald, and a voice I vaguely recognise, now asking me: 'Still at the roses and all that?'

'What?' Roses? For a second I don't understand what he's referring to, as I'm not particularly interested in roses, and then when I do understand him, when I hear the trace of mockery, I walk away, into the greenhouse, and I shut the door behind me.

'Ben – Ben, old matey.' I hear Cos, my old matey, at the window. Cosmo Thompson. My oldest friend. Bothered to turn up, good on him. But by now I can't speak at all. I am flicking through Mama's packets of seeds: carnations, coreopsis, cornflower … 'Come round when you're ready,' he says. 'We'll get nicely schnigged.'

I nod. Yes, I will want to get nicely, arselessly drunk soon. After the funeral.

One hour folds into the next until the sun is rising again and I am dragging on a suit. I am not much a part of the day; it's all more of the same, but with Protectionist party wives, and some Labor members of the Legislative Assembly, good on them for bothering. Faces, hats. Shaking hands I barely touch. I have more to say to the *elatum* in the brass vases. I stare at the casket: willow wood and silver plate; she'd have liked the wreath: Mrs Farenall designed it, she and Mama were friends, laughing over teacups and dividing boat orchids for winter. Cos whispers in my ear before I rise to give the eulogy: 'Doesn't matter what you say. Say whatever you must.'

A handful of words: 'Eleonora Trenton Wilberry might have been a brilliant botanist, but as it was, in her horticulture and floral artistry she was an inspiration to many, not least to me. A tireless worker for the church and for her community, had time and circumstance allowed her to do more in her own right, only God knows what contribution she would have made to the botanical record. I am certain it would have been an invaluable one. Her garden was the outward reflection of her soul: bright, all-embracing, and ever joyful. She was my mother. Farewell.' At least that's what I meant to say.

Whatever I have said, Pater waits until after the burial to get into me for it. He waits until all are dispersed, heading to their carriages. We are not ten yards from where Mama lies in the ground, when he says: 'You are a shame to me, son. A bloody embarrassment – you always have been.'

I look at him square on for the first time in I don't know how long. We are very alike in basic construction: large, heavy

26

muscled, bullish. But different in every other way. I might get into him, right here, right now, if it wasn't for Mama, and the more of her that is in me.

'You are not returning to Melbourne,' he says, and he's been wanting to offload this for the past two days. 'If you're not going to take an interest in the property, then you will at least do your time with the QMI – and you will do it this coming year. You are leaving in January.'

With the Queensland Mounted Infantry. No, I am not. I am not going to South Africa for this bastard's misguided sense of honour: where to kill, to tame, to press your will is to win, and winning is everything.

'I'm not making any more excuses for you,' he says, narrowing his eyes at me.

I narrow mine back: he doesn't need to make any excuses for me, it's a volunteer force, even if Queensland treats it like a compulsory sport – like the rugby. Got to be better than the New South Wales Lancers. Got to be the first ones on the troopship to Cape Town – pick me, pick me – that desperate to impress Mother Britannia. I want to tell him that I'm not surprised he's embarrassed. But that's just Queensland, isn't it. Terrified that Federation will rob them of their colonial army, and they'll all have to muck in under the one flag, with all those sheilas from the south, too – Jesus Christ, even Tasmanians. As though this land we're standing on right now wasn't called New South Wales itself forty years ago. As though Pater forged the boundary single-handedly in some bloody battle – one he is still waging in his permanently belligerent mind. I don't say anything: there is too much to say.

'What's wrong with you?' He does look bewildered now, and old. He is old: he's sixty-two. And I suppose he is lost in his own kind of grief – at my intransigence. 'You can shoot, you can ride, you can do both at the same time, making daisy fucking chains as you go. You are a Wilberry. You will do your duty. Fuck. You will do as you are bloody well told.'

Except that I am possibly more Wilberry than I will ever care to admit: no man tells me what to do. A strange feeling comes over me, a kind of deflation; perhaps it's pity for him.

He says: 'If you go back to Melbourne, I'll cut you off. I'll disinherit you.'

I say: 'Go on then.' And I walk away. He won't disinherit me; he can't anyway: I'll sue him for all he owes Mama, for all that is my legal right to her estate – to every Trenton penny held in trust. If he knows anything about me, he must know I'd do that, on principle.

'Coward,' he says at my back.

Because he doesn't know me at all.

'Don't you walk off,' he calls after me. 'I need you to sort out the staff at the house.'

Sort out which of the servants should stay and which now should go? Today? Wouldn't want to waste a penny there, would you. There is some desperation in his voice, some pain of his own. He can have that all to himself. I keep walking away.

I set off for Cos's place, only a mile from the cemetery, at Woolloongabba, and the weatherboard sprawl of the town through here numbs me again. It's a very pleasant area. Pleasant. Sleepy. Torpid. And my feet know the way, even if my mind doesn't know where it's going. Where am I going? To Cos's, to the Swamp, which is the name of Cos's place, for it sits by a marshy bog, stumbling distance from Brisbane Cricket Ground. He'll be here by now; he didn't come to the burial. And here I am now, too.

At the gate of the Swamp the callistemon are suddenly magnificent – ordinary *viminalis* but their screaming scarlet bottlebrushes are blooming as though they are also insane. They love this swamp. They are so prolific they almost conceal the house, consume it, except for the roof. What a sight they make. As does the house: a Brisbane original, built by his grandfather when there was nothing much else around and the old man was just a spud farmer looking for a brave woman and a more suitable crop. This is a place that Mama has never seen, though; I would never have brought her here, as much as she always found Cosmo entertaining. I wonder if she sees me now.

'Wilber, is that you?' Susan's face appears by one of the verandah poles at the front door; she wipes her hands on her apron and beckons me in. 'Cossie's out back – he said you might come.' Her large dark eyes are full of compassion but she says nothing more, only leads me through the door and down the hall, not quite his wife, not quite his housekeeper, not quite black, not quite white, not quite his at all, but always his muse.

He is in the studio, the back room of the house, stuffing his pipe. He looks up at me from amidst the mess of his life: two easels on the go, a riverscape and a Susan, papers and books everywhere, paint splatters on the walls, the floor, the windowsills, his taxidermied native cat, Kevin, by him on the sideboard, standing guard over his brushes. Good old Kevin, curator of hanging offences here at the Swamp. And I feel my face smile for the first time since I got home. I breathe out. And in again: this house smells of the river; it's part of the river. I look through the row of windows at the back wall, to the mess of lilli pillies and black wattle and birdsnest fern that make no attempt to be a garden all the way down to the massive bunya pine, where the bog becomes a creek.

Cos presses a rum into my hand. 'Get that into you.'

I toss it down my throat, don't even taste it, and I reach for another.

The sound of small children is coming from the kitchen: Tildy and Ted, it must be, the twins, banging pots and pans: one of them runs in half-naked and giggling, and wearing a pot as a hat. They were babies in a basket the last time I saw them; the first time. 'Come back here, scallywag!' Susan calls and the little brown bottom wobbles back out.

I say to Cos: 'They've grown.'

He rolls his eyes. 'Not fast enough.' He scratches his beard and says: 'So. What do you want to do, apart from drink? What can I do for you, my old Wilb?'

'Not a lot,' I say, but there is something I must do and fairly quickly; all I want to do. 'I'm leaving in the morning,' I tell him, and then I ask him: 'You don't feel like coming on an expedition with me, do you? Bit of a ramble? I wouldn't mind having an artist along.'

'Where to?' He regards me warily, chewing on his pipe.

'New South Wales – out to Mama's old property, past Bathurst somewhere. Looking for a plant. *Helichrysum*. Possibly. A daisy, of some kind.'

He makes a face of disgust. Brisbane Cricket Ground is a long way to go for Cos these days, and I can see its telegraph wires from here. I shouldn't ask him to come with me; can't go anywhere with Cos without him making a mess of some kind. But I don't think I want to be alone on this ramble; and I've got to go. It's not only the promise I have made to Mama; I've got to get away from here. And he is my best old matey, and the very best botanical illustrator I know, when he can be bothered doing something for me.

'Hm.' He stares at me for a moment, over his pipe, before replying: 'Why not, hm? Embrace fate. *Amori fati*. Say yes?' He turns to Kevin on the sideboard: 'Say *yes*, hm?' And I've not got the slightest idea what he's talking about. 'We only go round the wheel once, don't we?' He turns back to me. 'Once and eternally: might as well make it interesting, and stop you from doing anything ridiculous. Keep you from harm.' He scratches his beard again, suspicion and sympathy in his squint: 'You all right, old chum?'

'No. No, not really,' I must admit.

He gives me a nod now and he asks: 'Read any Nietzsche yet?'

And I laugh, and I tell him: 'God, no.'

In my mind, I'm already back on the waves, on the steamer south. Where are we going? Sydney first, we'll stay at the club, at the Union. See where I am, where we are, from there.

BERYLDA

'It is not too late to stop this madness,' the woman at the lectern on the stage implores the crowd gathered here at Newtown Town Hall. A Mrs Ermington of the Anti-Female Suffrage League. She is being given a polite hearing by the housewives and shopkeepers of Newtown, and even some of their husbands, these workaday people who live up the road from the university and, as Flo said when we arrived, probably just want the vote so that they can get the Labor Party in, so their husbands might get better wages or some other nefarious socialist plot. They are not all that interested in charming hats and gowns, it would seem; neither are they much interested in Mrs Ermington, who is getting her pennyworth whether anyone likes it or not.

'Conserving our social fabric, the sanctity of our institutions, of family, of the right order of things, *is* a woman's place *and* her power. To stand *behind* her husband is not a diminution of status, it is merely correct. It is right; it is as God intended. Amongst the small number of men who support this heresy of female participation in politics, most are happily careless of the consequences – "Why not let the ladies have the vote if they want it, what harm could it do?" they say – while others are intellectual types, distracted by abstract theories of justice and equality that are simply impractical – nay impossible – in reality.'

Intellectual types – she said that as if you wouldn't want to be seen in company with one of them.

I whisper to Flo beside me: 'Why's she been invited?' She has no obvious credentials of any sort, apart from being some city councillor's wife, and her words don't invite discussion: at what is supposed to be a public discussion of the womanhood suffrage question – one, I had presumed, to encourage pressure on the cadavers in the Legislative Council to pass the wretched law when it is presented to them yet again in the new year, however fruitless that presentation might be.

'Know thine enemy,' Flo whispers back.

I study Mrs Ermington again. She wears a superbly tailored suit of oyster grey, and she is so stuffed into it I don't know how she is drawing breath at all. Not very many years older than me and condescending to lecture women far more sensible than she is on how they should conduct themselves. Whomever she is, she is really quite awful.

'It is a woman's place further to provide quiet and stillness as a balm to such tumultuous, masculine affairs as politics – not to *add* to their chaos,' Mrs Ermington continues undaunted by the yawning and blinking before her. 'And woman *will* only add chaos to men's affairs. To be quiet and to be still is the woman's supreme power, for in this she holds the key to the civilisation of all men, the ability to quell base desires and create in their stead peace, tranquillity. Order.'

Order. The bolt of dread at getting on the train this afternoon shoots through me again at the word – and with yet another thought almost as dreadful: wouldn't you know it, I have forgotten to return *Surgical Anatomy* to the med library, haven't I. Now *that's* incredible. I've dallied here in Sydney almost a week past the bargain tables, with yet another excuse in attending this awful 'discussion' with Flo, because it worked in well with the catching of the Thursday evening Western Mail instead of Wednesday's, as if any day's wouldn't do, and I've left my intellectual contraband once again on the night stand, when I meant to drop it back first thing this morning – a week ago. I'm going to have a tough time smuggling it back in there now without being seen, aren't I. What's the time? Ten past eleven. My train goes at three fifteen. I'd better do it now.

'Flo – I've got to go,' I hiss. 'Stupid library book. See you back at Women's.'

'Oh!' She is appalled at my oversight, that I am prevented from standing here being revolted by Mrs Ermington a second longer. She waves me out the door: 'Go – go.'

I go as fast as my legs will carry me, back out into the searing sun on King Street, a madness of cartwheels and hooves and the whistle of a suburban train choofing through to Stanmore, so loud that I almost don't hear the man leaning on the corner of the Town Hall building spit at my feet: 'Tart.' I imagine Mrs Ermington installed him there herself to spit at every female going past. I have no time to think of him. I begin to run, like a tart, up the length of shops that line this road, all the way back to the college. How I love this road: its jumble of colours and sounds and smells. The Italian fruitshop, the discount drapers, the book dealers, the bakeries, sweet little hotels and groceries on every corner, cheap and cheerful Christmas decorations going up all around. Flo is determined to convince some unwitting entrepreneur to get a vegetarian café going somewhere here next year, and I hope she does, not only because she is a terrible cook but to give us an excuse to be here in this street more often. Incredible that I won't see it for six long weeks.

I scurry down the narrow lane of Little Queen Street, short cut of flat-faced workmen's terraces no lady should be seen near, and then I sprint across Carillon Avenue, past the university gatehouse, across the lawn and into the college, where I take the stairs two by two, up to my room. This room I share with Flo. The beds are stripped down to their mattresses, our luggage piled on the floor in between them, and as I catch my breath I close my eyes and I say a little prayer: Please. Please allow me to return here next year.

And then I grab the book, stuff it into the deep pocket of my skirt and comport myself in a tranquil and well-ordered if moderately speedy fashion out the other side of Women's, past St Paul's and right across the campus grounds to the Medical School. Oh dear, I'm puffed by the time I reach it, by the time I see its broad front of lancet windows, all the stately tracery of its Gothic revivalist façade, so lately revived it's less than a decade old, and it's so deathly quiet inside, even my heartbeat is too loud, echoing amidst all the cool and so recently hallowed stone. The door to the anatomy room is open as I make my way, and in there, in the gloom, I spy the skeleton standing by the plaster torso of Man and hear the voice of some other phantasm warning me: *You'll never be a surgeon, Berylda.* And I don't listen to him. I find the library door is open too – oh splendid, marvellous luck – and I spy the librarian in there, and he's in conversation with a man. A large man, taking up all of his attention. I scurry in, shove book on random shelf, and scurry out again, chirruping: 'Oh dear! Wrong room – silly me. Happy Christmas – hooroo!'

And that's that. Resume tranquil and well-ordered comportment, back across the grounds.

BEN

What was that? I look behind me and I imagine I see a hat disappearing round the doorway, a woman's hat, the edge of a skirt. Someone that might not have been there at all had I not distinctly heard a voice. Then again, I've been imagining I can hear Mama's voice at all sorts of odd moments; a glimpse of something, who knows what, at the edge of sight.

I rub my eyes and look back at the librarian, remember where I was, and I tell him: 'No. No, I am not looking for pharmaceutical texts – any botanical records, preferably ones that show the plants in illustration. Native plants. I'm looking for a particular plant, a daisy, found in central New South Wales.'

He looks at me dully, screws up his face in wonder that anyone might want scientific illustrations for anything that can't be cut up for experimentation or distilled into a drug. I had thought it might be pointless coming here, that's true, but I do want to see if I can find any record pertaining to Mama's bloom and its location before I condemn Cos to wandering the hills with me in search of it, and I am annoyed by this librarian's attitude.

I must have made that a little bit apparent, as the librarian attempts now to be helpful. 'Have you asked in at the Science faculty? They'll have botanical types of things there.'

Yes, I'm mightily sure they do, but there's no one there. Of course, that is where I went first: shut up like fortress.

'Not to worry,' I tell him, and I leave. The books I asked for from the Royal Botanical Gardens should be delivered to the club sometime today. And, hopefully, I've a few things to pick up from the New South Wales Wildflower Society chap I spoke to yesterday – an amateur of course, he's otherwise a Castlereagh Street solicitor, but he seemed confident of finding whatever they might have on indigenous *Helichrysum*, or any other similar plants, amongst their records.

I set off back towards Broadway, to the city. Perhaps I should return to Cos first – have lunch, if he's awake yet. I feel sorry I dragged him along with me already. I'd forgotten how much he hates Sydney; but he's enjoying reminding me, at least.

BERYLDA

'How about I try to come and join you in Bathurst – after Old Mac's had enough of us and gone back to the office. What do you say?'

Old Mac is what Flo calls her father, with such affection it makes my brain bleed with jealousy. But I am also absorbing her suggestion: that she come to me, in the holidays, come to me and Greta. I couldn't think of anything I'd rather have happen. 'Do you think you really could?'

'I don't see why not. Towards the end of January, when we're back from Woy Woy, unless Mother comes up with a compelling objection. I'll write to you and let you know – all right?'

'All right.' I smile, and my smile meets hers. Uncle Alec won't be happy that I have invited a friend to stay, but he won't be able to say no, either. Not to an illustrious, impeccably well-connected McFee, who has in fact invited herself. I grin.

And then she embraces me with the full force of her exuberance, here on the crowded railway platform at Redfern. 'Oh Bryl! It'll be 1901 when I see you again – a whole new century! When we return to this place, you'll be at the Medical School and I'll be taking my first subjects in the Law – Torts and Government Institutions – can't wait. Who knows what incredible things we might do!'

She swings me around in her arms now, almost knocking over a porter with the centrifugal force of my boots. He shakes his head at us but he smiles a merry hooroo, too, as he wheels his baggage trolley through the crowd.

'Change is in the air, my fabulous friend, my comrade.' Flo promises revolution in her laughing green eyes, still yet filled with excitement and optimism at the way things turned out at Newtown this morning: someone called out 'Will you get off!' in a most unladylike manner to Mrs Anti-Suffrage Ermington, another joining in: 'Go home! Go home to your ivory tower – go and be quiet and still in there,' which prompted a chorus of booing from the gathered, and a slow hand clap that continued until she left the stage. I'm sorry I missed that.

Flo hugs me to her again. 'We're going to get the vote next year, see if we don't. I can *feel* it. Just as surely as one day you're going to be the tiniest physician that ever existed and I'm going to be the first barrister with bangers!'

I am in hysterics as she holds me out from her again, shaking me by the shoulders: 'Changes is ours!'

Change. Yes. It surely shimmers and crackles around us in this Christmas heat. Little do they know in this bustling, overbusy city crush that Flo McFee and Berylda Jones are in their midst. Corsetless, young and free, we shall change the world. Or at least be permitted to practise our professions. How could we not?

But now the whistle blows. The Western Mail is steaming. It's time for me to board.

'Oh no!' No. I so dearly do not want to go. I reach for her hand.

'Oh yes!' Flo gives me a last cheek-smacking kiss before pushing me away up the steps of the carriage. 'See you soon!'

She has her train to catch too, in half an hour, on the Northern line for Woy Woy and her parents' summer retreat on the water there. A train to catch back to her perfect life. She waves now, still dancing on her toes on the platform, and that wave carries me out from the station, all the way out over the jostling tin rooftops of Sydney.

Out past Parramatta, in the dairy fields that unfold from there, I see a black and white cow leaping about with the gold dust of the late afternoon sun sprinkled along her back, showing off to her sisters, and I laugh out loud for the inexplicable gaiety of it.

The desiccated dowager in the seat opposite scores me with a thin-lipped once-over again. I know what she's thinking: *Vulgar girl.* And I laugh at her too.

It's not until the train emerges, huffing and creaking, from the steep Lapstone Rat Hole at the foot of the mountains that my mood begins to switch properly for home. A little further on, as we wait halfway at Faulconbridge for the extra engine to take us the rest of the way up, I look out into the first of the pine trees beyond the station here, and as I do, the dread does not so much stir as manifest somehow solidly, as physical presence. It always does at the sight of these pine trees, their cool, dark shapes against the dusk, boughs outstretched like the arms of some pleading, hungry horde, and my dread gathers and gathers with them, all the way to Katoomba. Where home should be. My pulse thumps in time with the straining of the engine here along the ridgetop, every single time. For what my life and my sister Greta's life would be if home were still here, in these mountains, if our parents were still here; if they were waiting for me at Katoomba Station now. If we didn't have to live with Uncle Alec.

Dismiss him from your thoughts; push him away. There's still three hours before you must see him. Make the most of it.

In the fading light, I open my copy of the *Evening Times*, to distract myself with whatever featherheaded silliness might be in it today. How will Womanly Virtue rescue Civilisation this Christmas? Will she ever go in for fish at the festive table? Or is it really best to stick with poultry? On the rural news page, I read a funny story about a farmer from Cootamundra who, when being taught to drive a motor vehicle, kept yelling at the engine to pull left, before smashing the disobedient contraption into a tree at his right. Then I spy the name Hill End again, in a small paragraph below:

> *A girl of thirteen was reported missing on Monday, having failed to return home to her family's orchard outside the township of Hill End the day before. It is presumed she is lost, and all attempts to find the girl have so far come to nothing. A timely reminder, with the holiday season upon us, of the dangers of straying into the bush.*

No name. Just a girl. Lost. I close the paper. As the sun begins to sink, I close my eyes to the twilight and I am thirteen once more. And I am not lost: I am safe at home, with my perfect family. Greta and I are home from school for the holidays, home in Katoomba, our picnic rug spread across the lawn of our garden at Echo Point, at the cliff's edge. Mother has packed us a basket of jam sandwiches and a flask of lemon cordial: *Don't go beyond the fence, girls.* Papa is laughing, clutching at his heart: *You'll fly away one day anyway and leave me to weep forever – don't go yet!* Aunt Libby is visiting from Gulgong with Grandpa Pemberton, ancient and crooked over his cane, and she has left him on the verandah to join our picnic. *Good afternoon there, my favourite sisters.* She nestles between us, her rosy bergamot scent warm as the sun as she looks up through the pine needles with us, making up stories about the Three Sisters, the three rock pillars down in the misty valley below. *Do you fancy they get chilly down there in the night? Shall we make them some woolly hats?* We lie there giggling, under the smiling sky.

I wake at the screech of brakes. And when I open my eyes again the world is black. Downhill, speeding black.

BEN

'**B**loody savage! Get your hands off me!' Cos bellows, with not the slightest irony, drunk off his head, as I drag him up the steps of the club – to lock him in our room.

'Mr Wilberry.' The doorman nods to me, unseeing as the doorman of the Sydney Union Club necessarily is. It's nothing to him that Mr Wilberry is wrestling Mr Thompson up the hall and up the stairs, for this is a gentlemen's establishment and I'm sure these walls and a long succession of doormen have seen far worse. But it's no less embarrassing to have this one witness this particular spectacle. It was probably him who received the messenger lad from the pub over at the Rocks, too, and had the butler quietly find me in the library downstairs, to whisper in my ear, *Mr Thompson is in need of your urgent assistance at the rear of the Australia Hotel, sir*, the discreet means of informing me that I had better rescue Cos from the brothel located there – before he caused any more damage to that establishment, or to himself. He is that drunk. Well, he has been hard at it since lunchtime; didn't bother to wait for me to get back from making my enquiries at the university before getting stuck right in. He ordered a Bordeaux with his breakfast, apparently, and then took off.

It took me almost an hour to find him, down a back lane between Cumberland and Gloucester Streets. Although Cos and I spent six long years at school here in Parramatta, I don't know Sydney very well at all these days and I've never known its brothels, but the publican at the Australia was most helpful in directing me to where old matey was corralled in a little terrace down that lane, and when I got to him he was well into picking a fight with the police sergeant holding him there. *New South Welshman can't play cricket*, he was slurring and swaying, and giving his best impersonation of *Homo idiotus*. Fortunately, the police sergeant, who'd been drinking at that same pub, was reasonably schnigged himself, and quite good humoured: *I'm sure he's a fine fella when he's himself but he's frightening the ladies – you gotta take him home*. Home is precisely where I should have left him, isn't it, and for good – for one day our names and my relative sobriety will not get us out of trouble.

'Do you have to carry on the way you do?' I mutter to him pointlessly as I shove him in the door of our room. Couldn't stuff a pipe, let alone walk, though he's attempting both at the same time.

He falls onto the bed, my bed, spilling his tobacco pouch across it and moaning, 'I'm bored, Wilby. You leave me alone all day. In Sydney. It stinks here.'

'What, unlike you?' I shouldn't speak to him at all when he's in this state.

'I want to go home,' he moans some more. 'There are no women in this room. Where's Susie? I hate this place. I hate clubs. Savages!'

'Shut up, Cos. Please,' I ask him, as pointlessly. And promise him: 'I'll book you a passage home tomorrow – first thing.'

'No! I'm not going back on that ship, God's bollocks, no, I am not,' he says, and before I can say *I'll see about booking you onto a saga of trains then*, he gives me his best old matey look, full of sincerity; pathos. 'I won't leave you alone, Wilber. I don't want you to be lonely and sad. I love you.'

And I'm glad he does. When he's sober, I am glad he is here. Grateful. I don't know how I'd be faring without him.

'Can you get me drink?' he asks, trying to prop himself up on an elbow; failing. 'Just one more?'

'No.' Prudent to leave him now; he'll talk himself to sleep. Eventually. He won't be so bad as this when we're on the road. Out of Sydney. When we head west after Christmas. Out into the fresh air. Countryside. Greater distance between pubs. Our train out to

Bathurst can't come too soon; perhaps I'd better get us out of here quicker, though, find somewhere to stop in the mountains on the way through: restorative climate, and coral ferns, scribbly gums …

'Please?'

I lock the door.

He shouts for the entire club to hear: 'But I love you, Wilby!'

Someone chuckles from behind another closed door, calling out, 'Half your luck!' and I return downstairs to the library, to the books and papers spread in disarray across the desk there, just as I left them – the records I've borrowed from the Wildflower Society, and the unexpected abundance of material from the elderly but enthusiastic curator at the Botanic Gardens. I should tidy it all up now, in consideration of the other guests.

I pick up the old and faded Wildflower Society illustration of *Xeranthemum coronoria* that I was looking at before I was interrupted. Stare at it under the lamp as though it might show me something different from the last time I looked at it. It's not what I am looking for; it's not what Mama described. The bloom is possibly the right shape and formation, and its location is near enough, recorded as Canowindra-Cowra, somewhere in the central western districts of this colony, but its stipes are fleshy, its foliage glabrous, smooth and strappy, and it's the wrong colour – yellow and cream, and distinctly bicolour. It's definitely not red. It's been incorrectly named, too – it's not *coronoria*. It's most probably *bracteatum*. I could write a small narrative for it in the margin: 'this specimen was discovered by an amateur botanist-solicitor, and fancifully sketched by his mistress one stolen week away in the woods'. Half the botanical record wouldn't be with us if not for enthusiasts such as them. But I doubt this one is even indigenous. It looks most like a European strawflower, or a cultivar escaped from someone's garden bed. Or it doesn't exist at all.

Like red native daisies, perhaps: I've never heard of such a thing, apart from *bracteatum* cultivars, and even they are more orange than red. But then I've not seen much of central New South Wales, have I. Only Bathurst really, and only once, during school, rugby against St Stanislaus, midwinter, didn't know where I was …

Ben, go to bed yourself, I hear Mama say, and with her voice comes that disorienting rush of grief.

I pour myself a port instead, my vision blurs, and I look into the bloom I'm not looking for again. Astounded that she is gone.

NEW YEAR'S EVE

This world is the will to power—
and nothing besides!
And you yourselves are also this will to power—
and nothing besides!

Thus Spake Zarathustra

BERYLDA

The label on the bottle is so very slightly crooked. The label on this bottle of Jicky perfume. This little something splashy from Grace Brothers I had to buy for myself. This bottle of Sydney from some other elsewhere called the Rue de la Paix. This scent of away I had to have. The velvet box. The satin lining. It cost almost a pound. Nineteen shillings nine pence for a stupid, stinking bottle of –

A thud against the wall now, from my sister's room; my mirror shudders with it, and the bedsprings stop wheezing for a moment.

What is Uncle Alec doing to her in there? I think I might know, but I can't believe it. And yet I do. He is molesting Greta. He is raping my sister. I know little about sexual connexion; too little, apart from the anatomical mechanics of it lately gleaned from a book; suggestions of it strewn through a handful of metaphysical poems; boys sniggering at the back of the lecture hall, at Marvell, at Donne. I put it all together now, and I am paralysed. No, this can't be.

I keep staring at my bottle of Jicky. You'd think Monsieur Guerlain might have had his label stuck on with a little more care, for the price.

'Please. No.' Greta's whisper slips under the door between us and the wheezing of the springs resumes.

My results came this morning, in the mail. One credit, in Literature, two distinctions, Latin and Physics, and I have won the Biology prize. Unexpectedly. I have exceeded my hopes. I am accepted into the School of Medicine: *one of twenty-five fortunate candidates*. I am congratulated by the board. Is this why he attacks my sister now, in this way? Is this some sort of revenge?

I hear him grunt, again. Louder. Does he mean for me to hear him? Animal, rough, cruel. And there is something in Greta's small, quiet cry, something striving for stillness, that makes me hear also that this is not the first time he has done this to her.

Oh God.

What can I do? What must I do? I want to slam through this door between our rooms and into him, scratch his face to shreds for what he does. For every evil he has committed against us. And now this. Oh, my sister. But I cannot move. I am petrified. I am so frightened of him, of what he does here, and of my own confusion. I cannot quite absorb –

'Right,' I hear Uncle Alec say now. *Right*. A favourite word of his, when he has made his point, and now, I can only suppose, a signifier that he has satisfactorily completed this degradation of my sister, this ultimate humiliation of all the humiliations he inflicts upon her. *Right*. It's half-question, as if he were a bored and weary country physician feigning interest in some persistent case of dyspeptic hypochondria, when he is in fact District Surgeon of Bathurst Hospital.

'Be in the drawing room and presentable by seven thirty,' he commands her, raising his voice just enough to command this of me too. He is so sure that I am listening, I can hear the smile in his voice; I can see the sour moue of his lips. He murmurs something then about the Gebhardts, a chuckle with it, lightly snide: 'Damnable Germans – always five minutes early for dinner. Mustn't be caught unready, must we?'

'Hm.' Greta's assent is barely a whimper beneath the clip of his footsteps. I hear her snuffle and whimper again. He has hurt her; he so often does. But this hurt is the worst of them. I can hear it loudest of all: a soft groan as she moves, I imagine she is curling around it, onto her side. Why don't I rush through the door to her: why do I continue to wait? Staring into my pocket watch, its hands too quick and too slow and too gold across the blank white face. I am stunned with my own guilt – at my inaction. At my every delay.

Staring into my copy of *The Dawn* on the edge of my dressing table, these thirty-six pages of elsewhere, hand-me-down cast-offs from Flo, December's covers flopped open to a page of advertisements: P.D. Corsets. The *GRAND PRIX* of feminine constrictions of straight-front style, *avoid inferior imitations.* The sixteen-inch pinch of the illustrated waist pinches at me, though I've seen it a thousand times. How can a premier women's publication conscience this obscene condonation of slavery in their journal? Because there would be no publication at all without it. Buy Holbrooks Worcestershire sauce, while we're here. The best you can afford from Connery the Expert Hatter. Pinch your sixteen inches' worth of lies however you can get them. What good are feminist ideals to me here? Now. It is as if Flo and all the colours of hope have disappeared.

I stand up and stare out of the window. Our every breath is a bargain, and yet each one is as unstoppable as the last. I am breathing. The river snakes along indifferent at the edge of the road beyond our garden here, and I breathe. The turrets of the hospital remain indifferent sentinels at the edge of the town behind us, at the edge of the bush, at the edge of each breath. And the hills all around us are as blue as corpses. Chloroformed.

'Ryldy? Ryl, are you there?'

'Yes, I'm here, Gret. Of course I am.'

I rush to her now. How do I ever conscience not being here all the time, every moment, every breath, for her? And yet I lingered in Sydney with Flo that full fortnight longer than I had to, making excuse after excuse to myself to avoid coming home. What did I bring Gret for it all? What did I get her at the bargain tables? A parasol, which she adores, a sweet and womanly broderie anglaise parasol, but it's just a stupid, pretty thing. I am so ashamed that I have failed my sister in this way. I have failed to protect her. How have I failed so despicably?

We turn the handle of the door as one, my darling sister and I. Five years, it's been. Here. Five years he has subjected her to his constant contempt. And now this new attack. This progress of his violence. Her eyes are wild and wounded, her voice trapped in the aching sinews of her throat. Five years. How many more? Before …

I do what?

I hold her to me. 'Gret – Greta – tell me. Tell me what he has done.'

BEN

'It's getting on,' Cos complains. 'Do you have to climb *every* mountain you see?'

I ignore him and push on, up towards the homestead ahead of us at the top of the hill, more heap of dirt than mountain. I want to look back over the floodplain from there. I don't remember Bathurst being this interesting to look at, geographically; but then, that school rugby trip was over a decade ago, I was seventeen: it was all mud and scrummages and possibly a mild concussion.

'Yes, you must,' Cos mutters. Then he sighs, in that extravagant way of his, and stops on the road. 'I'm having a pipe – right here, Wilber. And then I'm returning to the pub.'

I shake my head at his predictability, and tell him as I do daily now: 'I will forgive you should you decide to go home.'

'Couldn't possibly do that.' He calls after me: 'Someone must bear witness to your descent into madness.'

'Ascent.' I correct him and keep on. And I smile to myself: he is concerned for *my* health? So much for the country air having any effect on his temperament. But I remain glad he chooses daily to remain with me, not least because he can make me smile. If complaining were a sporting event, he'd be the champion of the world. He's been hard at it from the moment we got on that steamer from Brisbane, over two weeks ago now: the air was too cool, the sea too choppy, the food terrible. All this way and not even a decent match on at the Sydney Cricket Ground to compensate, and who

51

could ever want to live in that city anyway? A boil on a bloom, he called it, and sketched it in wrung-out mood the day after his near arrest: the view from the club, from Bligh Street, back towards Circular Quay, a crowd of chimneys disgorging their filth of fast money and even faster smog – bursting out of the centre of a flannel flower. He really is an exceptional artist, in any mood; the sharpest eye I know. Stopping the past two days in Katoomba, he kept to the hotel while I made my explorations of the Jamison Gorge and the Three Sisters, and when I returned he'd made a drawing of the button grass I'd collected earlier from some falls at nearby Leura – such exquisite accuracy, such life in all he captures on a page, and he made that drawing for me without my even asking.

Most accurately, though, Cosmo Thompson is a lazy bugger; always has been. Look at him: lying down there in the grass on the verge above the road. He's a potbellied wallaby stretched out in the last of the sun, smoking his pipe and reading his little book of Nietzsche, his new philosophical fascination, gospel according to Zarathustra, whoever he is. Cos is at his most content half-grogged and freshly serviced.

There is smoke coming from a rear chimney of this homestead ahead, I see; I imagine a family inside it, contentedly dressing for church, for this New Year's Eve. It's a grand-looking house, though not all that large. Bluestone and iron lace and roses climbing about the verandahs, set high behind a white picket fence. I look south, back towards the town, Bathurst, though there is no view of it from here, not much for the untrained eye to see at all but the occasional clump of stubborn and stunted prickly wattle, a distant stand of candlebark: the wind must surely belt across this place, across the marshes of the wide river flat of the Macquarie below, and right up to this homestead. Isolate, like the town itself, it's as suddenly here as not, amongst these cleared hills of tussocky wire grass that tumble out from the forests of the Great Divide.

I follow the fence line round towards what appears to be a cherry orchard, just over the leeside of the hill. Now, that is something delightful, I suppose, in a chocolate box kind of way. Cherries, roses, bluestone and iron lace atop a grassy knoll, with this great blue sky arcing over all.

I'm about to call out to Cos, tell him that he should come up and have his pipe here. Or rather, we could make a raid on the orchard. There must be at least twenty trees and they are heavy about their business, I can see even from here. But then, just beyond the last of them, on the fore edge of a dam, I think I see something of far greater interest to me. No, it couldn't be – the silvery sheen of the foliage, the scatter of white blooms. A drift of *Helichrysum elatum*? That favourite native of Mama's garden at Indooroopilly. Here? In the ranges of mid New South Wales? Surely it's too cold here for them; the spring frosts would be too harsh; I think it even snows. Of course I am imagining I see Mama's *elatum* here. This is only an hallucination, a trick of my grief. I am mad: daisies on the brain.

I am reminded that Professor Jepson will have received my letter by now, informing him that I must delay my return to Melbourne and the work I am commissioned to continue with for the Agricultural Board, and most directly for Dubois, as I wish to undertake a period of personal field study, on *Helichrysum*, and I don't how long I'll be. *I shall inform you of my progress* – that's what you say to the Dean of Natural Sciences, isn't it. Ally or not, Wilberry or not, grief-mad or not, I might well lose my job for this one; it's not the first time I've wandered off. Dubois will want my head on a platter. I can hear him going on: *Daisies? What is this outrage for? What is the use of native* Helichrysum *but to give bloat to the cattle?* I'd better return with some fairly incredible daisies then, hadn't I.

Plenty of daisies in the world. Ninety-four genera of aster on this continent alone, of which there are many, many hundreds of species, and of which *Helichrysum* is but one of twelve suborders, with many, many varieties in each of them, and I've looked at so many daisies over the past few weeks, a cornucopia of *Compositae*, so many illustrations and interpretations of Mama's humble and beloved *elatum*, too, no wonder I'm seeing a mirage of one now.

And it is getting on, isn't it. We should go back to the hotel. Get a good night's sleep. We're going out to Manildra in the morning, then on to Mama's old property, for what it's worth. I have not found a single red daisy in any of the literature at my disposal: nothing in *Flora Australiensis*, nothing in the crate-load of chief colonial botanist's records, no hint in any scrap of enthusiastic scribble; no forgotten glimpse retrieved from any of my experience, either, and I've seen a few daisies in the field throughout my not insubstantial rambles, from the northernmost tip of Queensland, to the southwest foot of West Australia, and as far southeast again across to Bruny Island. But we have to go and have a look. I do, anyway. Mama said it bloomed in January, so if it's there along Mandajery Creek, I'll find it. The creek in its entirety is about seventy-five miles long, a week's exploration; perhaps two. Perhaps what I'm looking for is not of *Helichrysum* at all but of rare *Helipterum* or *Xeranthemum*, and never recorded before; or perhaps a new subtribe altogether. Something to discover, in a part of the country I've never studied before. And therefore not very mad at all for this botanist to be going after. Not just some glimpse of Mama's last dream, spoken through an opium haze.

A few steps further on, though, as the pickets give way to post and rail, I'm sure it's Mama's common subtropical *elatum* I see here by this dam in subtemperate Bathurst. Dappled by the branches of a pretty spectacular old melaleuca, too. Like a corner of her garden has somehow ... I blink but they remain: the familiar habit of the stipes, straight and woody tough and yet so supple they sway with the breeze. The blooms float; tiny angels. Unmistakeable. It must be *elatum*. Or some cooler climate species very near to it, and one I've never heard of. I'll just hop over the fence for a closer –

No, perhaps I will not.

A great unchained staghound bounds out through the orchard, decidedly against this idea.

BERYLDA

He licks his finger of the velouté, draws it out with a kiss: 'Mary, that is perfection.'

The entree. Creamed chicken tartlets with truffles, it will be, and served at precisely eight forty-five.

Mary titters behind her hand like a girl, although she's hardly that. 'Sir.'

I stand at the kitchen door, watching them. Watching his back, the expansion of his ribs at a breath as he says something else to Mary. And I want to kill him for what he has done. I am here for the wishbone, though, for Gret, at her behest. We are fond of a secret wishbone, my sister and I, small rituals of hope; and we need one now: she remains lying wretched on my bed, refusing to speak of what just occurred, except to say: *I'll be all right in a little while, Ryldy.* Because he has done this before and so you know how it goes? How many times? When did it begin? I think I might know, and the picture I am assembling in my mind is a horror worse than anything I could have imagined. *He's been odd in his temper since October – you know, with all the goings-on with the Liberal League.* With his election as treasurer of the Bathurst branch of the Free Trade Party; yes, I know: his self-admiration must have swelled with his success, and with it comes sharper cruelties: that's always been his way. *Don't worry, Ryldy. He'll soon go back to ignoring my existence, you know what he's like. He frightened me this time, that's all. I'm only so sore and moaning around now because my whatsits are so late, I'm all emotional and tender inside.* How long since your menses should have come? *Oh, three weeks, four ...* I'm sure that she does not know what this might mean. And I'm not going to explain it to her. Yet.

The fowl carcass is sitting in a dish by the stove still. Good. I could step out from this threshold and snatch it. But I am transfixed by Uncle Alec. Leering at Mary. She's a gristly old boiler, our housekeeper, but not unattractive. He's a small neat man made large by his own vainglory and the like dimensions of this town. Purportedly handsome, in appearance and character. What a man he is to take such interest in the running of his household, what taste, what style; what a man he is to have such affable relations with his underlings. How very modern. How very liberal. Our Man for the New Age, the electioneering pamphlet will say. He smooths his moustache, leaning over a pot on the stove, peering down the muslin at Mary's décolletage as he does. Does he make connexion with her, too?

Don't worry, Ryldy, honestly. I'll be all right. My sister's ability to disconnect from the facts is even more advanced than mine. What is this black dream we live inside? When will we wake?

Prince is barking incessantly outside, and has been since I left Gret a minute or two ago. It must be the fellow come with the fireworks, waiting at the gate. What a man Alec Howell is to treat his guests to the spectacle of a firework display for this most special of New Year's Eves. Twenty-eight sky rockets, no less, so the entire district cannot fail to know about it.

'And what is for the main course?' he is asking Mary now, sampling the anchovy paste for the late supper canapés, continuing to flirt with her. He knows very well what is for the main: he instructed it down to the last crumb a week ago.

'The lamb, Mr Howell.' She flutters her eyelashes. She makes my stomach turn. 'With the 'aricots and my special roast parsnips and taties – and the minced tongue croquettes of course. All just as you like 'em, sir.'

'I had better like them, Mary,' he teases and grins: a small, neat wolf. 'Or I'll mince you.'

I'll mince *you*. There's a knife lying by the mutton tongues on the table behind them. I could pick it up and drive it into his back. Would I have the strength to get through? Possibly not. *You'll never be a surgeon, Berylda*, he reminds me at every opportunity, not merely to state the obvious that women are not permitted into that field, but to belittle me, gratuitously, because he can. I will never be a surgeon as he is. Slight of stature he may be, but he's strong as a rat trap, lost count of the femoral shafts he's sawn through, the skulls he's drilled into, along with the occasions upon which he's boasted of such skill. And I am slight as air beside him. No, I don't think I'm strong enough to push a blade through those muscles, through his ribs – through to his black fetid heart. Moreover, I am too cowardly to try.

And Prince is still going at whatever poor fellow he has bailed up out there. Uncle Alec appears deaf to it as Mary pretends to scold: 'No, sir! You may not have any more of my anchovy paste! Get away with you and your naughty fingers.' She shoos him and then snaps out an order at the maid, little Lucy, who's just coming in from the laundry under the load of napery she's pressed for the event, but the master remains un-shooed, poking now through the chicken carcass by the stove.

That forces my hand. Don't you touch my chicken. I step through into the kitchen and take the dish from him, announcing as brightly as long practice will allow me: 'Well, doesn't all this look and smell wonderful, Mary. We're in for a feast tonight, aren't we just.' I wriggle the breastbone free of the wing it's caught round and wrap it in my handkerchief, and so quick I am about it, I've already turned to leave before Mary can say: 'A feast indeed, thank you, Miss Jones,' as Uncle Alec commands: 'Ah Berylda – see who that is at the gate.'

Can't have the master opening his own gate, can you. He's not that modern. Why do any such thing when you can demean your niece by sending her instead? What am I compared to a kitchen maid?

Not halfway to the front door along the east hallway, it seems Prince has stopped his barking anyway. I stop to listen. Silence, except for the ticking of the mantel clock in the drawing room.

Perhaps it was only someone going along the road on their way down to the river bend with a rod, taking the scenic route. I almost return directly to Gret, to my room, but I decide to take a moment to calm myself down first. I need to take a moment to release the violence in me. This compulsion to fly at him. Kill him. Make him gone. My steps pound out my hatred up the hall.

How can I make *us* gone? *Now*. Not some time in the future but today. Stop this hideous dream. This dream that has been unfolding and unfolding, shock upon shock, since we arrived here. I was almost fifteen; Gret seventeen. One moment we were on summer holiday at Bathurst, with Aunt Libby and Uncle Alec, here at Bellevue; they had just returned from their honeymoon, Aunt Libby still unsure how she would decorate the rooms in the gleaming new home he'd had built for her while they'd been away; it would be a jolly time of choosing fabrics and papers. A time not to be. A black curtain fell. It falls now. It falls and falls and I am breathless. Mother and Papa would not be joining us, we were told. Their carriage had come off the tracks in the mountains, the engine brakes having failed at the zigzag above Lithgow. A tragedy. No. It was preposterous, and remains so. A few months later, a few minutes later it seemed, Aunt Libby became ill and left us too: typhoid fever, we were told; a broken heart we knew. And our lives have been his to play with ever since.

Five years. How will Greta endure one day more of this? How can I possibly leave her to go back to university? How can I get us out of here now? The questions spin me round and round and round. He will not stop; he will never stop. He will only become more vicious. *What an excellent year 1901 will be, Berylda*, he clapped his hands at me this morning when my results arrived. Clapped them right at my face. No word of congratulation for me, but something else. A threat. Holding the threat under my nose, tight between his clasped palms. A threat that vibrates through this house; it always has: along the tightrope I dare to tread, to remain his favoured one. The one allowed to return to school when Greta was denied her final year. Allowed to attend university, while Greta is imprisoned here. Allowed to remain unmolested, while Greta is –

Damn him to the furthest pit. If there is a child growing in her now, this will ruin her, in every way. She doesn't have my will, my single-minded resolve, my ropeway to the outside world. He has blasted her will, addled her with his brutality, his relentless sneering, his insults, his dismissals – *stupid girl; cretinous thing; yellow mongrel; are you listening to me, you vacuous little bitch? Do you have a brain at all in there?* So that she is more child than I am, though she is the elder by more than two years. But what can my will do for her now? It seems I am watching a precious ornament fall from a shelf but I am too slow to prevent it smashing. Too slow inside this dream.

Wake up!

And then what? Kill him. Kill him tonight. How? Chloroform. Arsenic. Drench him in paraffin and set him alight.

And have Gret see me hanged. No.

What alternative is there but to keep to the plan we already have? No matter how bad things get, Greta will insist that I do. That I continue with my studies; that I become a doctor and – *You'll never be employed in a hospital, Berylda. No board will ever permit women to practise on the wards, you know that.*

What do I know? That he will string me along with my studies, only to interfere with my prospects when I qualify? Make sure I will never be employed? I try to close my mind to him, to his threats, to his games, but they are everywhere here in his domain. I don't know if he will even allow me to return to Sydney. I will have to fight him so hard to get there: charm him, cajole him, perform for him, manipulate with games of my own. And even then, it will be five years, if I commit myself well, before I even complete the degree.

Five more years. No. Greta cannot be subject to this. Five more years at the barest minimum. Uncle Alec's interference aside, no woman passes the final in Materia Medica first go – the pharmacy examination – that professor is a notorious misogynist and has not let one woman straight through in the five years we've been allowed to sit for it at all. Five more years is impossible.

Impossible as us ever being able to wrest any of our parents' estate from Alec Howell, damn the blindness of that law – the one that says it was remiss of Aunt Libby to not die before our parents.

I have asked the 'hypothetical' of Flo inside half-a-dozen different guises, and the answer has come back from Hoddy and Old Mac the same. Everything that should be ours – Papa's share in Hartley Shale, our home at Katoomba, Mama and Libby's small but tidy fortune in old gold from their parents' prospect at Gulgong – it's all with Uncle Alec, our legal guardian. And isn't he doing such a wonderful job of looking after us, all society says; and now look, the younger is even off to medical school, they'll toast him tonight. What a man. The trap is tight-laced around us. We can't fight him on this issue, not at all. We will need not only women lawyers and women voters but women legislators to be able to do any such thing. And money: we are essentially penniless but for the scraps he throws us.

We must be made free now. Gret must be freed. Please. How?

If anyone will do it, Ryl, you will do it, she said to me when I left for college at the beginning of the year. *It will be all right. Don't worry about me. You'll be a doctor one day and we will leave. We can return to Echo Point.* Simple as that.

I stop at the front door, touch my forehead to the cool timber. Breathe …

Prince barks again, just the once, chasing a bird, perhaps. A happy enough sound that returns me to myself somewhat, and turns the handle in my hand. I must find Buckley before I think or do another thing, have him chain Prince at the stables. I don't particularly like the Gebhardts or Reverend Liversidge or, for that matter, the majority of those invited to the festivities this evening, but neither would I see any of them torn to pieces. I open the front door.

Prince looks up at me from the gate at the bottom of the garden path. Tail wagging. Tongue lolling. The late sun dancing across his brindle coat, he is as beautiful as he is savage.

And there's a man patting his head. How very odd. It's no man I've ever seen before, here or anywhere, though there is something curiously familiar about him. Long flaxen hair like a travelling minstrel, tweed breeches and haversack, he's travelled off the pages of some great strapping Walter Scott adventure and up to our yard. And he appears to remain in possession of both hands, unmolested by Prince.

The man straightens and smiles, a heartbeat of déjà vu. 'I beg your pardon, young miss.' He points towards the orchard. 'My apologies for the intrusion, but I was hoping I might take a look at a shrub, ah. The daisies, over by the ...'

BEN

I lose my way in the words as I look back at the girl again and see that she is not a child at all but a young woman, compactly made. She is wearing a blue dress, a gown of pale blue; she is a piece of sky drifted down onto this chocolate-box verandah. A displeased one. Not surprising, I suppose: I just addressed her as *young miss*.

'You would like to look at what, where?' Her frown is severe, her hand raised against the sun.

'The daisies ...' I look again down the lee, into the heavy boughs of the cherries, searching for something appropriate to say in such a circumstance as this – incidental conversation with the fairer sex, of which I am generally – no, absolutely – lacking. 'I am a botanist ...' I offer and then, unable to think of anything else to say, I determine to make my departure swift and immediate. 'I beg your pardon. Miss. Ah ... I do apologise. I am sorry to have disturbed you.'

'Ha!' The girl waves me away for a nuisance. 'Disturb me? Prince finds you a good enough fellow. Go and look at your daisies.'

She turns and walks quickly away, around the western side of the verandah, stopping briefly to speak to a workman who is approaching the rear of the house with a barrow of wood. Then she disappears into the shade of the awning; a door creaks open and then closed again.

I look back down at the dog. Prince. Good name for him – a proud beast. And a distrustful one: I thought he might actually jump the fence for me. Teeth bared and snarling. Intimidating, and I am not easily intimidated, not by animals at least. And then he just as suddenly stopped. Sniffed the air, propped his paws up on the fence, as though in welcome, then bounded up towards the gate here, as though asking me to follow, and I did.

The dog licks the back of my hand now as I reach down to raise the latch. Funny creature. I must have confused him somehow; some smell about me. There might be a fair smell about me, too, or a foul one – I realise that I haven't had these strides properly laundered since I left Melbourne. Perhaps the girl caught a whiff of me as well. That's almost a month's worth of whiff, and more. Strike me, but it suddenly seems I've been on the road a long while. Wandering. Years, not weeks.

I look behind me as I open the gate and see Cos there where I left him, down by the verge of the road, still drawing on his pipe, book open on his chest. I assure him mentally that I shan't be long, but as I do a sense of uncertainty slips through my mind. Shan't be long.

Ahead, I look to the white blooms, under the good care of the old melaleuca by the dam there – *linariifolia*, just like Mama's, its broad canopy in full flower, too, as though dusted with frost. Are these Mama's *elatum* beneath its shelter? They are exquisite, whatever they might be, floating on this gentle breeze, as though over the surface of the water, against slow ripples of molten bronze.

I really have no idea how long I shall be.

As long as this farewell takes me, I suppose. My chest tightens at it: Farewell, Mama. Where is she now? Wandering pleasantly through some celestial garden, I hope; a small child capering along beside her, asking her the names of the flowers.

I am that small boy still. I shall always be.

Just as these are indeed her white everlastings here, so improbably, on this hillside in Bathurst.

Yes, it is *elatum*. Joy blunders through me. Here they are. The fineness of the leaves, the tall, elegant hands, each stem topped with their inflorescence of bell-shaped bracts, with their multiple rows of snowy rays, holding deep golden discoid flowerheads swelling at their centres. And they are profuse; thriving. I look into the sky as though I might see the way this piece of my childhood garden floated down six hundred miles to find me here. The dog beside me barks once in concord. Yes, it might well appear I am not mad.

BERYLDA

'I wish for that stranger you found to carry us away.' Gret smiles at last, closing her eyes for the silly game as we snap the bone.

'Ha!' She has the greater half too: 'You win.'

'I did.' She regards it, still clenched in the crook of her little finger. 'What did you wish for, Ryl?'

'The same.' I smile with her as I lie beside her on my bed. You don't want to know what I just wished for. I can't clear the violence from my mind. I want to take out his eyes with a fork and feed them to the chickens.

'Really?' says Gret. 'Well, that'll make it a powerful wish then. Hopefully. Both of us wishing for exactly the same thing, that will double our chances of it coming true, don't you think?'

'Yes.' She snaps my heart to pieces. She is so very hurt but she will not scream it. She can't. And I play along: 'Why don't you sit up then now, darling, and you might see him at the window.' I want to see how physically injured she might be, too; see if she winces with it again. I press her a little: 'We should get you dressed for dinner anyway. Are you up to it?'

She nods and sits easily now, perching on the edge of the bed; no flicker of pain now, but ... God, I can't believe what he has done to her; but I believe it more and more.

'Are you sure you are up to this?' I press her again. The consequences of disobedience will be harsh and unpredictable, but she is not going to suffer this dinner if she can't sit without discomfort. I shall forbid it with all that I am. I shall announce it to the guests: Greta sends her apologies and hopes you all understand that our dearly devoted Uncle Alec raped her this afternoon. And I shall do no such thing. I am too sick with this myself; sick with not knowing what I should do. What can I do?

She stands and assures me: 'I feel quite a bit better. Really. I'm all right. And Mrs Weston is coming – I couldn't miss seeing Mrs Weston. She's always so lovely to me.' Mrs Augusta Weston, wife of the District Medical Officer, inveterate bush nurse and general force to be reckoned with, and in fact always lovely to Gret.

'Yes.' I assure her: 'And she wouldn't ever want to miss seeing you either.' Could I dare to tell Mrs Weston? Would she help us? What could she do? I can't even get Gret to admit to me what he has done. *Are you sure he didn't hurt you anywhere down here?* I gently pressed her tenderness. *No, of course not.* She made a face. I can't ask her more; I can't ask her what I must: what was he doing to you on the bed? I can't force that shame on her.

She smiles again at me over her shoulder as she steps towards the window. 'You are lovely, Ryldy.'

I rage inwardly at every terror my sister has endured and every terror yet to come. I pray this silent scream might shoot into him and through him and shatter all his bones.

'Oh – is that him?' She points out the window, to the edge of the orchard, where the dam meets the fence. 'The man there. He's making a bouquet – look.'

I stand beside her and see the strange man is in fact cutting himself a bunch of those daisies. Drab things; no perfume to them. Natives of some sort. Buckley would get rid of them but that ducklings hide in amongst the stems each spring. The flowers look like wet feathers to me – flung around the plant as if the fox has had some fun in there. I say to Gret: 'He's an odd one.'

'He looks strong enough to carry us away, doesn't he?' she says, as if she might actually be calculating the matter. 'And look at Prince sitting by him – he loves that man.'

I slip my arm around her waist. 'Yes, he seems to, doesn't he.' The dog loves the man. Love. If I were one to shed tears, I would surely shed them now, for all that most basic of commodities is denied us.

She turns to me: 'Invite him to dinner. Can't we?'

Just like that.

'Gret.' I don't say no, but my tone says *Don't be dense*. There is fantasy and there is foolishness. Uncle Alec wouldn't even hear the question – invite a vagabond to dinner? – never mind such a sudden alteration to his plans. The table is full, and it is his table. I say: 'Look at the time,' not looking at it at all. 'I should fix your hair.'

She sits down at my dressing table, but she continues to watch the stranger past the mirror, wishing onwards. 'Wouldn't it be good to gad about that way? Go wherever you want to – into the hills and far away?'

'Hm.' I take up her hair and begin to brush it: black, lustrous. Chinese hair, we whisper it between ourselves, and if you look closely, you can see. Our thick dark hair and our noses barely there. We are our grandmother: we are Chinese. But Gret is a whisper more so than me. Her hair a little shinier, straighter; her almond eyes as brown as mine are blue. *You are an unusual thing. Where did you get your loveliness from?* Our beauty is noted regularly, but the question never answered. Uncle Alec knows precisely who we are and where we come from, though. Another of his special barbs for Gret: *Choo Choo Chong, go back to Hong Kong,* muttered privately, of course, as every insult is. You wouldn't want anyone to know you were harbouring dirty Orientals under your roof. I am sure he brings his worst upon Greta because she is this fraction too Chinese. A certain breed, we are, and not so rare in these parts: littered across the Gold Country like black poppies.

And it's as deep in my blood as it is in hers, urging me now to go and visit that Dr Ah Ling, that Chinese herbalist out at Hill End, not for his miracle cures, but for a poison, a fatal opiate to slip into Uncle Alec's tea. Damn that I didn't choose Organic Chemistry over Biology this past year, or I might have learned something useful about herbal potions myself; but I was only allowed to choose the two scientific subjects, and I'll do the chemistry subjects next year anyway. If I'm allowed. Ah Ling. Uncle Alec knows of him. When I arrived home from university, he'd only got back here himself the day before, from Hill End. He'd had to go out to the little hospital there to trephine a broken skull, drain the blood, some fellow who'd come off a horse. Alec Howell described the performance of his surgical miracle to me in every self-congratulatory detail, and added, *Can't do that with herbs or snake oil, can you – although there's a Chinaman out there who claims he does all sorts of impossible things.* Dirty, lying Celestial, was the sentiment conveyed.

That brings me to some decision now. Some defiance at all I cannot do. I shall go out to Hill End, and I'll take my sister with me. We shall make an excursion of it, just me and Gret, into the hills and not so very far away. Buckley can take us. We will picnic by the Turon in that pretty spot where it crosses the Bridle Track, and we'll stay over at Wheeler's Hotel, that one with the mermaid calliope whirling out all those funfair tunes, those songs that made Mother laugh, so long ago … Songs I can't remember now except for the rhythm of Papa's riding heels dancing me round by the hearth, that precious last time we were all together there … I kiss the top of Gret's head with the secret surprise. An excursion for us. For her and her box of paints; she lives happiest and brightest there, in her watercolours. She will paint the river, the mermaids, the poppies. I will demand it of Uncle Alec tonight. Somehow I will make him say yes to me. Somehow. Beg; bluff; smash a vase. Find the right appeal to his vanity. And I will indeed then visit Ah Ling while we are there, and I will ask him for a potion all right – one for Gret, something to expel the child safely, quietly, now, before we even have to whisper a word to each other about it. Before we must decide there is a child there at all.

She is still looking out of the window, watching the stranger. I watch him now too. He looks up into the tree above his drab daisies, looking into it for an age. Prince still by him, tail wagging.

'What's he doing, do you think?' Gret asks me.

'I don't know. He said he was a botanist – I suppose that's what a botanist does. Looks at trees.'

'And flowers,' she says.

'And flowers.' I begin to pin up her hair. I take my prettiest silk camellia and hold it by her face, seaweed pink against the raven sweep, and ask her opinion: 'Hm?'

But she doesn't see it. She will not be distracted from the man in the garden. 'He would need to look at the grass, too, wouldn't he?' she says, from some other elsewhere. 'There are lots of different types of grasses. A botanist would look at all of them.'

'I'm sure he would,' I say, struck by a deeper memory at her words, her abiding perceptivity, the quiet intelligence that once was loud as mine, in her own way. Visions of the days my big sister led me, and not I her. I am chasing her through the foggy edges of our garden at Echo Point, cold, damp mist licking up from the valley through the fat pine trunks, and I am small and scared, but her strides are bold, her laughter bolder: *Come along, Ryldy.* Fleet fingers at the piano: *Come along, Ryldy.* So quick at any rhythm or rhyme: *Come along, Ryldy.* And ever insisting I hurry up the vast mountain of Katoomba Street in the blazing sun, for the sweetshop near the station, hands on her hips, tapping her toe: *Come along, Ryldy.* Aunt Libby consoling me, puffing too: *Big sisters – ha! Always such bossy boots.* What would my sister be beyond this prison, given the chance? Bossy? I wish for that. I wish she will become the bossiest sister that ever lived. I wish that I will find a way for us to leave before her spirit is extinguished altogether and forever.

I follow her gaze back to the stranger and I watch him again with her. Daisies in hand, he starts making his way back up the hill. Perhaps Gret sees some like kind in him: there is certainly something distracted about this fellow too. He appears to be chatting with Prince as they walk; then he stops in the midst of the orchard and we can just see him pilfering the cherries, deftly cropping a branch-load into his haversack.

'A thief!' Gret is thoroughly delighted by him now.

'A thief he is.'

He buckles his haversack and sets off again, past the verandah's edge, past our view, and away.

BEN

Two steps back down the front path, I am embarrassed at my greed: denuding almost half that shrub of its blooms. For what purpose? To place in a jar on the counter of a random bush cockies' pub before moving on? Mama would not look approvingly on such waste. And so I turn back towards the house. I shall give most of these *elatum* to the young lady there; surely she would want everlastings for her table.

I ring the bell at the door and wait, my face already hot with the effort of wondering which foot I might place in my mouth first this time. I wait several moments, staring into the brass plaque by the door, mind tracing round the *B* of *BELLEVUE*, before deciding that the belle inside has had a good look at me through the glass and chosen not to answer, and so I divide the stems, leaving myself just the one, just a sample for the herbarium, a hand of three blooms and a bud, which I thread through the straps of my satchel, before I bend down to place the rest on the step.

Just as she opens the door. I'm sure it is she for I am looking at a pair of dainty shoes, ivory slippers bound with silk ribbons, ivory ankles beneath the pale blue skirt. Strike me, that's a fine pair of ankles …

'Yes?' She is demanding an explanation for my presence here now and I needn't look up to see that severe frown dividing her brow. I can hear it well enough. 'What is it?'

I pick up the flowers and offer: 'I thought, perhaps ... these ... you might like?'

She looks at them as though I am offering her a bunch of eels.

I start to back away. 'Once again, my apologies. Inappropriate – ah ...'

But now she thrusts out her hand and grasps the flowers from me, saying: 'Not inappropriate at all. What a thoughtful gesture.' She smiles at me, but there is some arrested sigh of forbearance in it, the smile one might give an imbecile. Fair enough too. She says: 'My sister will delight in these, thank you.'

'Oh. Good,' I say and lose my way again as the frown leaves her face. It is a flawless face. The face of a porcelain doll. Astounding symmetry.

She thrusts out her other hand. 'Berylda Jones.'

'Oh?' I look at her hand. Porcelain hand. Belonging to a girl called Berylda. She doesn't expect me to take her pretty hand, does she? In my grubby oaf's hand?

She does, it seems; still holding it out to me: 'And you are?' Greeting an imbecile.

'I am ...' At the touch of her fingers against my palm I'm sure I have not the slightest idea. Her hand is so tiny, petal soft and so white inside mine as I bow over it, we cannot be of the same genus, let alone species. My hand has never appeared so large, and it is a fairly large one.

'A name will do,' she says impatiently, frown threatening again. 'Whom shall I tell my sister gave us a present of these flowers?'

'Yes.' *Benjamin*, I hear Mama sigh with her perennial disappointment. Give the girl your name – it's not a hard task. Just a name. Just a girl: they comprise half the human world. 'Of course. I am Benjamin – Ben Wilberry.'

'Of course?' She laughs, lightly yet derisively.

I think she is about to say good day and shut the door when a man appears behind her, an older man, considerably older than me, hair silvering above his sideburns. Unquestionably the master of this house.

'Who is this?' he says, protective, and well he should be. There is some military straightness about this fellow; the father, I presume.

'Sir.' I recover my senses enough to afford him the expected and conventional courtesies. 'Good afternoon. I am Ben Wilberry – botanist. Miss Jones was kind enough to allow me to inspect a shrub of interest to me on your land, just by your dam. I saw it only in passing ...'

The man responds with a blank stare, as though to tell me that my explanation is not satisfactory.

'I'm from Melbourne University,' I add, searching for some more convincing justification for my being here. 'I am from Queensland, actually, originally,' I say, very unhelpfully. 'Er. Conducting a study of a particular plant. Presently. Here. I apologise for the intrusion. Yes, ah ...'

The girl looks up into the curve of the tin roof above us; and that's about right – that's about how quick it usually is before I lose the attention of a girl. But she hasn't lost mine: there is something curious about the shape of her eyes, an accentuation to the curve of the lid, a petal there too. Something curious about the shape of her altogether. Sylphlike. Slip of a girl ...

'Not at all.' The man thrusts out his hand, suddenly, confusingly. 'Alec Howell, how do you do,' he introduces himself, and he is *Howell* not *Jones*, not her father? And he has one of those overly eager grips I always find disconcerting, for I can't return it. If I did I'd have left a trail of crushed hands behind me. 'Now, Wilberry,' the man says, eager as his handshake, 'I suppose you must be one of *the* Wilberrys of Queensland cattle fame, are you?'

Queensland cattle fame. Must that be my perennial calling card? 'I suppose so. Yes.'

'Aha!' he says, pleased at his guess. 'Eleonora Station, isn't it?' He either wants to be sure, or he's the type who's sure he might know how much pickle I had with my lunch.

'Yes,' I reply. 'Eleonora.' Whether Mama liked it or not. Fifteen thousand Shorthorn out of Jericho, what woman wouldn't want her name emblazoned over that? I suppose he must have loved her once. Did he? Ever? Who would have thought Pater's renown had travelled so far south of the border, though – small country, for all its enormity. I must admit: 'My father is John Wilberry, famous cattleman.' Amongst other things. As well as the second most compelling reason for me having wandered onto your property just now to look at a flower – *bloody embarrassment – you always have been* – and why I've spent the better part of this past decade in Melbourne's School of Natural Sciences, as distant from him as practicable.

'Well, well. What about that.' This Alec Howell is pleased to make this connection; I'm not sure I've ever met one quite so pleased. A small man, he rises up on his toes with his pleasure.

'Oh, but we must invite him to our dinner, Uncle.' The girl is suddenly animated and insistent, a blush on those porcelain cheeks. Strike me all over again, but she is an extraordinary creature. There is a quick, sharp glance that passes between her and the man, though, some misgiving, something I have indeed interrupted. I open my mouth to decline.

But he is eager still. 'Splendid thought, Berylda,' he says with a quick, sharp licking of lips, muddy grey eyes set again on mine, ready as a needle-grass skink. 'Unless you have other plans, of course – it is New Year's Eve, after all.'

'It is, yes, and no,' I reply, 'we've no other plans this evening. But we wouldn't want to intru–'

'We?' The man rises up on his toes again. If he were any more eager he'd spring up and hit the tin above us.

'My friend Cosmo Thompson,' I tell him, searching for an excuse to extricate myself from this awkward, unsought invitation. I shan't tell him Cos would most likely get drunk and insult one of his guests, or all of them. I say instead, 'The artist travelling with me on my study. We're staying at the Royal Hotel in the town, just for the night. And we have an early morning tomorrow,' ah, there's the tidy excuse, 'taking the train to Manildra, we're for Mandagery Creek, hoping to find some specimens of interest there.'

'Right,' Alec Howell says, and he appears not in the least bit interested in my own pursuit. 'Well, you and your friend Mr Thompson be back here for eight and you'll be most welcome. Not a terribly large affair,' he says with a smile of modesty so false it's carrying a beacon. 'A few colleagues from the hospital – I am the surgeon there – and a few other good people from our fine town.

Let off a few fire crackers at midnight, eh? Nothing overly formal in this house. What do you say?'

Curiosity puts me in two minds about this now. Alec Howell is a grasping little specimen, I'd say, presumptuous, and nothing sincere about him at all. Those muddy grey eyes want something; the kind of man who always wants something. I'm sure he will very quickly become a bore. I am sure I do not want to share any table with him.

But the girl, she entreats me with her smile. 'Oh do say yes, Mr Wilberry.'

Oh yes, I would like to see the girl once more. Yes, even if it means I must blunder my way through each course for Cos's amusement. Do I mean to do that to myself? Surely not.

'Thank you,' I say to her – barely – and look to her uncle, clearing my throat. 'Thank you, Mr Howell, for the invitation ...' and I only make the decision in this breath: 'Yes, we would be most happy to accept it.'

The girl, she seems most happy at the idea, doesn't she? She suggested it; she entreats me. She nods over the bunch of everlastings in her hands: 'Wonderful.'

And I doubt very much I've made a wise decision. I can hear Cos laughing himself arseless already.

BERYLDA

'Tell Mary,' Uncle Alec commands me as he closes the door. 'With relish,' I hiss under my breath as I walk away from him, towards the kitchen. Mary won't be pleased, she'll have to bring in a pair of chairs from the drawing room, a tragedy of mismatching woodwork and china to upset the order of her world, but that is of no concern to me. I lean my head around the door and address the colander hanging above her at the basin: 'The master has invited two more guests – see to it that they are accommodated at the table.'

She complains: 'Oh but they'll have to put up with the tarts what have got the cracked pastry, there's no other –' Et cetera. She can complain to the maid, poor Lucy; she will anyway.

I must return to Gret, to tell her about our visitor, share this news that she will love, but as I make a dash across the rear parlour to do just that, I find Uncle Alec there, and by no accident: he is waiting for me. Hands behind his back, he is peering over the mullioned panes in the doors here, as if inspecting them for smudges, as if he's not in fact checking to see that his own reflection is as agreeable to him as it was the last time he looked.

'Berylda,' he warns as he turns to me, stepping into the centre of the room, blocking my path. 'You do not walk away from me as you did just now. That was very rude.'

I stand before him, staring at the chiselled wedge of his nose. I do this unthinkingly at the beginning of a remonstrance, and

75

his face vanishes around it. Behind him, the day is fading; buttermilk clouds spatter up from the hills: altocumulus, such formations are called, if I remember that lesson in atmospheric physiography correctly.

'Is this how you intend dress for dinner?' He detests that I have cropped all of my hemlines; he has told me this every day since he collected me from the station.

I say nothing: obviously I am dressed for dinner. I love this evening dress, its simplicity. It is my Wonderland dress. My prettiest dress, mantel of organdie set over silk marocain, and prettier for the cropping of its train during term, too. I wonder how Clive Gillies-Wright is going; if he's packed for the Transvaal yet.

'If you must wear such an ugly gown, at least have the decency to wear appropriate undergarments beneath it. Enough of this adolescent rebellion. Put a corset on. Immediately.'

Rage fills the space before me and I cannot hold back these words, this defiance: 'I will not wear a corset this evening. I am decently dressed as I am now.'

'What did you say?' The voice scritches with instant infuriation, shocked by my insolence, as am I.

And yet I can't step back from this rage. You have injured my sister; in ways I can barely understand. I inform him: 'No woman of intellect wears a corset beneath her dress.' Or not unless she intends to continue in Arts – and no one at Women's College wears a revolting Gisbon Girl straight-front. No one serious would.

'A woman of intellect?' He laughs. 'Is that what you are? You look stupid. You look slovenly. Like a gypsy tramp. Loose. You will only make a fool of yourself.'

'Then there's no reason not to let me, is there,' I retort. Blindly. I am not a fool. I have won the Biology prize for First Year, I remind myself; I have been accepted into medical school. I am Bryl: Flo calls me Bryl for brilliant. What would she do, what would she say if she were here, in this moment? I do not know; I have never confided a hint of any of this in her, or anyone.

I walk past him. I walk away from him with my heart drumming out thunderclaps of fear. I have never been so bold with him. But I am angry bold now. I have reached my limit this day, for all that he has done to us. His insatiable need to beat and tether everyone and everything to his will. From the moment I wake in this house, his relentless litany of criticisms begins: I butter my bread too thickly; my perfume is too strong; my hair too tightly pulled back from my face; and my skirts are too high above the ground: *Your stockings may be glimpsed when you walk, Berylda. It's unseemly.* Well, let the ladies faint with outrage then and the men tremble with desire, but let me get about them freely. What's *unseemly* is a man having any opinion whatsoever on women's undergarments. A man? A rapist. Is that a man?

'Berylda. You do not defy me.'

I do. God help me, but I do now.

I close the door on him and his rising ire before he can grasp my arm to brand me with it. Exhale as the latch clicks at my back, keyless and useless against him, but he doesn't force his way. He will have too many other vastly petty details to attend to at this time. He'll be needing to petrify little Lucy over the state of the silver next, line up the labels of the wine bottles, pluck his eyebrows.

'Shall I wear this dear old thing again, Ryl?' Gret is here, in my room. Of course she is, where I expected to find her. She is at my long mirror with her own favourite gown held to her, of delicate fawn voile, tulle-ruched, lovely in every way but for the Chantilly train that trails behind it like Miss Havisham's regret. I'd like to tear it off and burn it. 'I think I shall,' Greta answers herself and asks another question: 'Cinch me in for it, will you, please?'

Cinch her into her straight-front? There she is with it already fastened to her frame, waiting for me to pull in the laces. 'No,' I snap back into myself and at her. 'Don't wear that corset tonight – don't wear a corset at all.'

'What?' Greta looks at me in the mirror, wide-eyed, as if I have lost my mind.

Perhaps I have. I am still holding the stranger's daisies; alien things; why do I have them? I have quite forgotten. I toss them on the chest at the foot of my bed as I repeat to Gret: 'Don't wear the corset. Don't wear one any more.'

'Why?' She is wary at my bizarre demand.

'I want you to be free in this way, if we can be in no other, that's all. Now. From this moment. Please.' That's all? I am demanding that my wounded sister provoke her tormentor more?

'Ryldy, I'm not as brave as you are.' She shakes her head and looks down with such defeat, such sadness, my anger only rises up again and higher.

'Yes you are,' I demand now. 'You are braver than I am, Greta. Every single day.' Every single day that you spend alone with him, when I am not here. I cannot leave you alone with him again.

'Ryl ...' She remains wary. 'Uncle Alec will not like this ...' But I have begun unfastening her, and with the pop of each stud down the busk, I promise her silently: He will not touch you again. I don't know how I will achieve this, but he will not touch you ever again.

'A woman ought to be able to be both beautiful and unshackled, oughtn't she?' I twitter on outwardly, pulling the obscenity from her, and she groans, knowing her protest is useless, as I button her into her gown. 'A woman ought to be able to go about in the world undeformed by the apparatus of torture. She ought to be deemed right as she is made. You are excellent just as you are made, my sister. Now here.' I fluff the tulle cloud of her mantel about her shoulders and then take a pink chiffon sash from the drawer of my dressing table, to match the camellia in her hair. I tie it loosely around her waist and deem it: 'Grecian chic – direct from Paris. You heard it first in the *Sunday Times*, direct from Mullumbimby. You are lovely, you are perfect – you are slim enough, my darling.' She is so slim, so small, we both are, the absence of corsetry is more noticeable for what it doesn't pretend to plump; how can it not be more right, more modest to go without? I kiss her on the cheek: 'You are excellent. See?'

'Hm.' She smiles slowly, swishing one way and then the other. The bodice of the gown drapes softly down to her waist without all the boning and banding beneath; there are few women who could say they make such a fitted piece look more beautiful without help. Of course my sister is excellent, in every way.

I stand beside her in the mirror, and we grin together for a moment with the scandal. And then I shudder at myself, at my own absurdity. What *am* I doing? Both of us corsetless at dinner:

Uncle Alec will most definitely be furious, disinclined to grant me the favour of any excursion to Hill End. But some switch has been thrown today. I will match him for fury. If he attempts some retribution, if he lays so much as a whisker on my sister again, I will fly at him. Be in no doubt. I will scream this whole town down. I will scream until we are free. Or until I am locked up.

'I'm not sure.' Gret brushes a hand across her abdomen, still wary, but playing along with me now. 'I might be a little bit too free here – I feel as if I might float off.'

'You won't float off,' I quip, convincing us both we can pull this off. 'You are no longer duck-shaped.'

'Oh!' Gret laughs, really laughs. 'You are too funny.' Tossing her chin up with that sudden burst of who she really is. 'Quack.' She flaps her elbows. The loveliest duckling that ever there was.

'Quack quack.' I put on my eminent physician voice to make her laugh more: 'And I'll have you know that it has been scientifically established as a fact that you'll enjoy your meal a whole lot more without your belly being pushed back to where your bum should be.'

'Oh!' She pretends dismay at my coarse language, hand to brow. 'You do learn awful things at that university.'

'I do.' I can only agree.

'And oh again but what are these?' Gret says suddenly, not laughing now. She has seen the flowers on the chest by the bed. I stare at them with her and for a second I wonder, too.

She picks them up, and as she does I remember: our stranger. 'Oh them.' I pretend indifference. 'Yes. Well. Guess who's joining us for dinner.'

'No – really?' She has guessed.

'Yes. Our stranger. That's right. That was him at the door just now. His name is Ben Wilberry. Botanist and bringer of bedraggled daisies from our dam.'

She looks down into them, her face a picture of pure delight, of this small wish made true. 'Oh but they look gorgeous cut, don't they?'

I want a photograph of her holding them, gazing into them just as she is now. A bunch of these plain things made gorgeous in her arms. 'Yes,' I say. 'And I must report that Mr Wilberry has fearfully big strong hands, too. He might just cart us off yet.'

I am only jollying her along, of course, and she knows it, but she says, wistful, all her sadness returned: 'I feel so light without my corset, I think I might be very easy to carry.'

I hold her around the waist, tight to me, tight around the wrongness of what that monster has forced inside her, and I promise her and all that hurts her as I kiss her cheek once more: 'My Gret, you will always be easy to carry. You are a thistle wisp.'

Please, God, fate, whoever, if anyone is listening yet, give me the strength. I close my eyes with this one endless wish: Give me the strength to carry both of us. Carry us away.

THE FESTIVITIES

Disobedience—that is the nobility of slaves.

Thus Spake Zarathustra

BEN

'N̲o.' Cos is not amenable to the idea, glancing back towards the house. 'Forced march up that hill again? For what? Some dead-boring dinner with some farmer you've just met? So I can spend the evening listening to you go on ad infinitum about your shrubbery? No.'

'He's a doctor, not a farmer. And you didn't go all the way up this hill the first time,' I reply. 'Hardly a hill at all, and in any event, I'm sure we can arrange a cab.' Though it's barely three miles back to the Royal from here; or not much more, at any rate.

'I'm not so sure about that, Wilber,' he grumbles, trudging sullenly on. 'Oh look – another hill.' He points ahead to, indeed, another small round knoll, but one the road winds around, and as it does the town begins to re-emerge from windswept bushland with the appearance of the hospital: monumental building that speaks of monumental aspirations – ones that tumble into a sports oval down the other side of the rise.

'Oh look,' I say to josh him as much as to laugh at where we find ourselves. 'And now here's the ubiquitous cricket pitch. I could just leave you here for the night, couldn't I? Leave you to graze the wicket?'

But the only response I receive is an emphatic, scornful snort and a continued dragging of heels. I'll have to work harder at this. Could I be bothered? *Wonderful*, the girl smiles at me again and again, and I am bothered more than is reasonable. I beg a little:

83

'Come on, Cos. Please. What's the difference between a pub full of people you have no interest in and a house full of people you have no interest in? Come on, it's New Year's Eve.' As though I care for that.

Just as I say this a gang of oiled-up young louts swagger out from a lane and onto the street over the other side of the oval, pushing and shoving each other along towards town, possibly shearers or miners or similarly enthusiastic groggers, possibly on their way to the Royal for the dance they're putting on. I try again: 'Look – not only will there be cabs tonight, there'll possibly be an ambulance or two.'

Cos grunts, still dragging his feet. 'But I don't want to trim my beard,' he whinges, determinedly churlish.

And that annoys me: 'Since when has an untrimmed beard stopped you from partaking of free feed and water?' Never. I look over at him as we cross the road into the main street, an enigma to me as ever. We've known each other fifteen years, since our first journey from Brisbane to Sydney, to school at Kings, at Parramatta. We were both thirteen; he complained the whole way on the steamer even then; and every single time. If he's not being entertained as he wishes to be entertained, he's not happy. Misanthropic. Mercurial. Spoiled. Never challenged to be anything else. But he's not entirely his own creation. If the Wilberrys command a sizeable tract of Central Queensland, the Thompsons have great swathes of the coast, under cane, purchased dirt cheap in the 1860s, and two elder sons to squabble over its skyrocketing profit. He doesn't need a challenge, a gainful occupation, so he doesn't have one, despite his not inconsiderable talents. He shares none of my restlessness. For all the years I've been away in Melbourne, in the Shallow South or the Bog Smoke, as he calls what, in a few hours' time, will be our national capital, he's never bothered to visit me: too much trouble. And yet, here he is, troubling with me now ...

Looking sideways at me now, through his scowl: 'Do you reckon they'll have a decent Scotch at this place?'

I do believe I might be cracking him. 'I reckon the grog and tuck will be fairly decent, yes,' I promise him. 'The host is eager to impress.' And I must warn him: 'Nearly fell over himself at mention of the Wilberry name. A fan of Pater's, I'd say.'

Another sideways glance: 'Why do you want to have dinner with him then?'

'Ah. Well …'

'What?' He's interested now.

'Well, there will be … hm. Of course there will be others attending the party.' I've already given myself away. 'There is, ah –'

'Oh God, man, it's not, is it? No. Not a *lady*.' His laugh, at my expense, is already arseless. I want to see a girl, and like some callow youth, I cannot go alone. 'That settles it then, doesn't it, my old matey.' He sets off now at a potbellied wallaby trot through the town. Ludicrous fellow, my stalwart friend. 'Reckon that nice bit of barmaid'll press me tails at this short notice?'

Nice bit of comely redhead at the Royal. 'I'm sure she will,' I say, although his question was rhetorical. Cos has little trouble with convincing maids of any kind to do anything at all for him. And I remember only now that there's a stain on the left knee of my dress-suit trousers. White sauce delivered by a rogue chunk of stewed carrot, three evening ago, back at the club. What am I doing to myself here? I'm sure I won't even speak to the girl. Berylda. Even her name is daunting. Amazing.

'Chop chop, Wilber.' Cos is shoving me along now. 'We don't want to be late.'

And I imagine Mama is laughing, too.

BERYLDA

'A pair of sluts.' Uncle Alec flicks his eyes across us with disgust as the doorbell clangs, angry that we are not dressed to his satisfaction, and that we are late to the drawing room. Too late for him to order us back into our own rooms to make ourselves respectable: the Gebhardts are here, a good ten minutes early. Set your clock by them.

As he marches past us, I squeeze Greta's hand and whisper: 'We will have some fun tonight.' Regardless, and despite him. We might as well attempt to. I make a face at his back, sticking out my tongue like a tiki carving, and Greta has to cover her mouth to keep the laugh in, keep her decorum as we stand here, waiting, in our place, by the piano.

He stands in the entrance hall as Lucy heaves the front door open, before she disappears into its shadow, a sliver of a shadow herself, barely there at all.

'Good evening!' The master's arms are open wide to receive his guests. This festival of deceit has begun.

Mrs Gebhardt swooping in towards us, always a slightly threatening rustle of taffeta ahead of her pronouncements; this woman cannot speak in anything but pronouncements: 'Good evening, girls.' Her hawk eyes slide over us and then settle on me, her tone almost accusatory. 'Berylda, I have read in this morning's newspaper that you have come first in Biology. Congratulations to you. This is a good result.'

'Thank you,' I reply with a smile as difficult as her manner. Mrs Gebhardt means well, and I am grateful to be congratulated by someone other than my sister and the distant professorial board. I look over at Uncle Alec: busy shaking Dr Gebhardt's hand as if he didn't hear; as if he didn't see Dr Gebhardt this morning on his rounds. He heard Mrs Gebhardt, I'm sure, and he's making a point of continuing to refuse to congratulate me, when normally he would be boasting of my academic successes as if they were his own, just as he did last year, with my matriculation results. I drill my hatred into the back of his head with a blunt-toothed and rusting trephine, as Mrs Gebhardt pronounces on: 'I see you reform your dress also.' She looks Greta and I up and down again. 'Both of you. This is unexpected and very good.'

Very good observation, barely thirty seconds in; won't the master be pleased. Greta looks down into the fawn mist at her breast, unsure for a moment, his words having struck there, staining her. I can feel what she is thinking: *Do I look like a slut, really?* But when she raises her eyes again, she has found something of a smile, too: 'Thank you, Mrs Gebhardt.'

A thankyou overrun by Mrs Gebhardt's next pronouncements: 'In Bavaria, I must tell you, young women are discouraged from wearing such cages of the lungs nowadays. The corset is detrimental to good posture, good breathing and muscular strength.' She really could lecture any learned professor under the table, given half a chance. 'One third of young women, at least, will not wear this garment any longer. Not in Munich. Men will not marry a girl who wears one. The effect of the corset is provocative on the one hand, such a display of form and flesh, and *vanity*, while on the other it –'

'Interferes with Fräulein's capacity for chopping wood,' Dr Gebhardt adds behind her, chuckling at his own wit, Uncle Alec joining him. In open contempt. Ho ho ho. 'The woman's place is in the yard doing all the hard work for us, ja!'

'Ho ho ho.' I fling my own contempt lightly into the space between them, and I am ignored. Still ho-ho-hoing together, Uncle Alec has his hand on Dr Gebhardt's shoulder now in that way of masculine conviviality, but I know he is pointedly refusing to acknowledge me – us. He is so incensed by our disobedience, he is straining for jollity, too. I can see it in the clench of his jaw; the hint of perspiration on his forehead. Good. But my breath catches. For fear. And for my own disgust. I see them for what they are, these men: mutually repugnant; mutually parasitic, too. Uncle Alec despises Max Gebhardt, hates his foreignness, his German know-all-ness, and he hates his forthright wife most of all, but as dispenser at the hospital, Dr Gebhardt serves a purpose other than keeper of the keys to the medicine cabinet: he's an oily, sycophantic fool who possibly couldn't get a job mopping floors in a German hospital but thinks he might be district medical officer one day if he stays in with Alec Howell, for whom he would take strychnine if it would aid his own cause.

'Aperitif, Max?'

'Well.' Mrs Gebhardt rustles away indignantly, back towards the entrance hall, and breath returns to me, with force, at her shrill call: 'My shawl, girl – where is the girl?' She swoops off to startle Lucy out of her wits with a demand for the shawl to be redeemed from the closet.

'It is a little chilly now,' says Gret. She stares into the ebony gloss of the piano case, her aloneness palpable to me. 'The sun has gone right down. Hm.' She is fading with it.

And the evening is already unbearable. Fun? Vain promise, that was. We are lilies on the dustbin of time here, Gret and I. Saying desultory good evenings to our guests as they arrive: Reverend Liversidge next, who is always faintly appalled at seeing us, as if we might have stolen one of his ribs; and then come the Wardells, a mutually torpid howdy-do to and from Dulcie for the year it's been since we last saw one another; and then the Dunnings arrive, heralded by the commotion of their motor vehicle up the stable drive, which sets off Prince chained in the yard out there and a debate over the contraption in here.

'I'm not yet convinced of its efficiency. Seems faddish to me,' says Uncle Alec.

'It will be no passing fashion,' Dr Gebhardt assures as only a supreme know-it-all can. 'The Kaiser commissions engineers for its adaption as warhorse now.'

'Did someone mention the war?' Major Harrington struts in, lately back from his turn in the Transvaal, full of the swagger of winning. 'I tell you what, them German Mausers are a good gun. I'll say, they are a topnotch machine. I'll drink to the Kaiser!' The major pats Dr Gebhardt on the back, as if these German guns aren't being used by the Boers and their rabble of mercenary militias to shoot at the New South Wales Corps right now – and as if the British and German Empires aren't just a little bit suspicious of each other generally. It's all just a boys' adventure, a game: shooting at each other.

'To Mausers then!' Uncle Alec shoves a glass into the major's hand and I wish there were a way to force him to go off to this African war. Have the marauding Boer guerillas murder Alec Howell: hang him from a tree and leave him for the crows. He holds the rank of captain in the Corps, after all: he should take his turn and go. But Dr Weston, the District Medical Officer, will not allow it. Alec Howell is too indispensable here, it is said. Alec Howell is too cowardly to go, more likely. He might tear a fingernail. Look at his hands: more meticulously kept than mine.

Where are the Westons? I ask the mantel clock. It is ten past eight. They are late. Several eternities pass. Gret leans into the bow of the piano, slumping a little in her unbound state, the noise of the party rising around her, but she is not here amongst us, and I am racked with a worse fear: she is leaving, without me. The facts are before my eyes: if I don't find a way to free her from this prison now, soon, she will break loose in her own way. She will simply break. *Smash*. Wake up. I take a step towards her and whisper: 'Watch out, duckie, you're slouching – smudge the polish with an elbow next and there'll be trouble for you.'

'Save me.' She smiles back, just, a subtle flutter of the lashes that seeks to assure, *I'm all right, Ryl*, as her words thump into me. Save her. Will anyone here help me? Anyone?

'Mrs Weston!' Gret straightens at a dash for the door, enlivened again. Mrs Weston is here. Thank God. She'll at least save the evening.

'Ah! There you are.' Augusta Weston embraces my sister with her generous arms; her voice is warm, rich velvet. 'It seems an age since I saw you last. Where have you been hiding, my sweet one?'

'Only here.' Gret smiles, indeed sweet at the small rescue she finds there inside this woman's arms.

Augusta Weston surveys the room at a glance to find the more precise answer as to why Greta Jones is so rarely seen in town except to attend church or Mrs Hatfield's salon on William Street for gowns and gloves at the change of season as propriety demands. 'Good evening, Alec.'

He squirms a little under her gaze. 'Mrs Weston, happy New Year.'

And I find this brief flash of discomfort in him immensely, disproportionately satisfying. Mrs Weston does not know what Uncle Alec does to us, to Gret, what he has done to her today, no one does, of course, but she knows she doesn't care for him. She is the District MO's wife and medically specialised in her own right, in the dark arts of midwifery, delivering half the population of this district while producing seven sons of her own – she doesn't have to care for Alec Howell. She does not reply to his toast, either.

She turns to me, a blast of fresh, bright lavender air. 'Berylda! Come here and let me look at you as well, dear.' That enlivens me now too. 'You are lovelier with each passing year – no, each minute. Both of you. Aren't they, Anna?' Mrs Weston turns to Mrs Gebhardt for agreement and all the women in the room are as figurines come to life, cleaving off from the men, making our own circle in this bow of the piano.

'Oh!' But Mrs Dunning appears horror-struck as she joins us, looking at me, and Gret too, peering round each of us one way and then the other. 'Oh my dears, but where are your foundations?'

Our corsets. This is unreal. Honestly. No one in Sydney notices, too much else going on at any one time to pay attention to the underwear choices of others. But this is Bathurst where the tiniest anomaly must take on gargantuan significance. A city desperate for social relevance grasps at anything.

Mrs Dunning remains agog; scandalised: 'What have you done with your corsets, girls?'

'Chucked 'em in the dustbin,' I tease her, and not very kindly. She's a hypocrite, and particularly dimwitted about it. Yes, one can get along in a thoroughly modern motor carriage, extravagant as it is filthy and bought off the bent backs and poisoned lungs of those who work in your mines, but woe betide society should women want to get about corsetless. What in heaven's name would you want to do that for anyway? Why would you want to be able to move your torso as you wish? Mrs Dunning is goggling at me uncomprehendingly right now.

'Yes, the corsets are in the dustbin – where they belong,' Anna Gebhardt pronounces, unashamed anomaly herself, and Mrs Weston, professional rescuer that she is, commences to steer the committee on it immediately: 'Anna, I must say I am coming around to that idea myself. Well, halfway at least. I've been lately contemplating the establishment of a Young Women's Physical Culture Society, for the promotion of natural health and wellbeing. If a corset must be worn in any way other than therapeutically or remedially, it must be worn *safely*, don't you think? This fashion for tight lacing is not good. Not good at all, and never has been.'

'Oh but I don't know.' Dulcie fondles the locket at her throat worriedly, as if we're discussing the tragic plight of Boer orphans starving to death in Her Majesty's concentration camps. Dulcie Wardell has lately returned from a sojourn in actual Paris, and Rome, and New York, touring with a maiden aunt, where clearly she's thrown herself into her studies in vapidity. She's ever been ace at it. And I shouldn't be too jealous that she has travelled: it's about all she's got going for her. Plain as she is simple; as I am caustically mean tonight. Smile and listen respectfully, Berylda. God, am I even here? The twentieth century is dawning and I am *here*? With Dulcie Wardell sighing regretfully, moronically: 'I don't know that I would be able to stand upright without my scaffolding.'

'And *that* is the very problem, my child.' Mrs Weston blinks at Dulcie as if surprised that one might be so wilfully ignorant. 'That is all your spider waist will do for you – limit oxygen to the brain.'

The laugh that bursts from me at this is so loud the sound bounces off the top of the piano and round the chandelier, shocking even me.

Mrs Wardell, Dulcie's mother, is goggling now too, at a loss as to how she might respond, Mrs Dunning still open-mouthed beside her. Perhaps they'll faint simultaneously; that'd be fun. As police magistrate's wife and mine owner's wife respectively, they are most unused to being put in their place, and by one so expert as Augusta Weston, who now tightens the circle to include them absolutely: 'How are things out at Magpie Flat? I've heard there's been no end of trouble with the miners – what are they after this time? Accident insurance or some such thing, is it?'

Who in heaven's name would want that, either? Working a mile inside the irascible belly of the earth. What could go wrong? Why penalise the good and virtuous mine owners for their dirty workers' inability to plan ahead? Should be damn grateful to have jobs at all. *Should be damn grateful to have good and honest workers*, I hear Papa say; and I am sitting outside the office at Hartley Shale, with Gret, playing knuckles, waiting for him to finish his business. I don't know why we're there; perhaps on our way to Gulgong. But I know he was a miner himself before he was a prospector. He was arguing with his partners about not putting wages down: *Trade depressions don't last forever*. Nothing does. Please. What would Papa do if he were here? He'd shoot Alec Howell for what he has done. Shoot him dead with the pistol he kept in the drawer of his desk.

If Papa were here, we would not be forced to endure this at all. My sister would not be shrinking behind Mrs Weston right now so that the man who rapes her cannot see her across the room.

I have shrunk from the conversation now. I stare into the sturdy girth of Mrs Weston's shoulder: it's almost the same circumference as Gret's entire head. Augusta Weston would make a fine surgeon. She could chop a bit of wood. She could chop down a tree. I glance over my own slight shoulder at the men. Yes, Augusta Weston could put an axe through the lot of them. These besuited apes who control Bathurst. Control the world. There is Reverend Liversidge stroking his cloven chin, as he stands shoulder to shoulder with Justice Victor Wardell, who would convict the working poor wholesale if it would more quickly earn him the Sydney posting he craves, and on the other side of him, lighting his cigar, is J.C. Dunning, proprietor of Magpie Flat copper mine and chief political puppeteer of the district – he'll be supreme master of Uncle Alec, should he achieve his ambitions in the new state parliament. Alec Howell, honourable member. God help New South Wales.

And God help me, please, for I am diabolical in my hatred of him. *You ungrateful little stain*, I hear him and hear him. *What are you thinking now? You do not presume to tell me what you want. You are lucky I don't throw you into the street – under a train.* How often has he spewed his disgust at me? Sometimes without any reason at all. My face is warm with every sneer, every threat, and the more urgently I will my blood to cool now, the warmer it becomes. I stare hard into the piano case. The lights of the chandelier are reflecting off the gloss. Pretty orbs of light hovering in the piano case that I might still my mind around – until the wires beneath crash discordantly through me for what happened here, in this room, at this piano, only the night before last. *Play 'Yeller Gal'*, he demanded of Greta with a clap of his hands: *Play 'Yeller Gal' for me.* He laughed, a little after dinner laugh, to ridicule her, privately, intimately, as he sang the words to this half-breed coon cartoon loud in her ear: *Oh! I'll gibs ya all mah money, won't ya be mah honey, my red-hot little orange yeller gaaaaal – faster, Greta, faster*, laughing at every stumble of her fingers at the keys. Sadist. How many nights does he make her sing that song? What other humiliations does he subject her to when I am not here? His evil pervades every corner of this room. Infects every speck of dust in this house.

See him now: so controlled, so aware of his audience, he is reptilian. He is peering over Justice Wardell's shoulder to see where Mr Dunning has got to. Ever on his toes; ever looking around himself, no matter whom he's speaking with, for there might be someone more useful along any moment. How shall I be useful? The answer creeps up my spine and across my scalp. If I am diabolical, let it be so. Let me act. Tonight, when all the guests are gone, I will let the gas run from this chandelier above us. I will close all the windows. I will wake Gret; we will scurry out into the night. I will strike a match as we leave. He will be gone. In a wild conflagration of my hate, looking around himself in desperation at the gathering flames.

A terrible accident, it will be. A terrible, terrible accident. That acetylene gas, such an innovation for the country home, installed at such vast expense, too. And so very dangerous. What a tragedy.

My pulse is racing now. I need air.

Breathe.

I need to get out of this room. Out to the verandah. Subdue this compulsion. This violence. Ice my blood. Before some wild conflagration bursts from me.

As I move to step past Gret, Mrs Wardell leans towards her, saying: 'I once boasted an eighteen-inch waist, you know, but wore it out to twenty-two. Don't tell a soul.'

She runs a hand down the stiff busk of her straight-front and I want to scream. *Don't tell a soul? Don't tell a soul what lies in my sister there.* I am putrid with disgust at it. Shame. Hatred. Despair. Defiance. All sin. I am sin. But I force a smile upon my face as I say: 'Excuse me, please.'

My smile is a shimmering steel blade as I step towards the drawing room doors, through the men.

To see the stranger beyond them. Mr Wilberry. Mr Wilberry has arrived to join us for dinner. I'd quite forgotten he was coming.

BEN

'Good evening, Mr Wilberry, and – excuse me.' The girl darts past us. Though she is small and sparrow-swift, her steps shake the boards; the roses on the table in the entrance hall tremble as she makes her way – right out the front door.

'Er,' I reply as she disappears. This was not a good idea.

Cos belches under his breath beside me: 'That the one?' Indifferent: 'Little thing, isn't she.' Couldn't be less interested as he strides into the house, thumping his chest, sniffing the air. 'I take it all back, Wilber – this place looks entertaining after all. A real rib-tickler, this'll be.'

'Hm.' I look back out through the open door, after the girl, but there is only the night there.

'This way, sirs,' the maid is urging us to enter the drawing room ahead. 'Please.' A note in it that says she'll be in trouble if we loiter too long at the threshold. So young, this maid; she is actually barely more than a child, cheeks plump and rosy, her hair is slipping from her cap. A weird house, this is. As pleasantly arranged inside as out, a perfect dollhouse set above its imitation Yorkshire dale, and yet – what is it? The pictures on the walls too straight? The parquetry too polished? Pretentious, I suppose, and adamantly so: silver card dish on the hall stand so buffed you could trim your beard by it. Which is why it looks entertaining to Cos. Who are they expecting might call here? And yet there is something else about this place. A feeling; an incongruity. Which is most probably just me, being incongruously me. I wonder where Mama's *elatum* have found themselves in this –

'You're late!' Howell has his hand around mine before we're quite through the drawing room doors. 'I'd just about given you up.'

'Given us up?' For what? Is he dinkum? It's barely gone twenty past eight. 'Late?'

'Never mind.' Howell smiles, but there's a pained expression in it – we have put him out somehow. Have we? He is still gripping my hand, pulling me in with it, as Cos assures him: 'We'll try not to mind. But you might in a while – you haven't tried to get rid of me yet now, have you.'

Howell laughs thinly, uncertainly. 'You must be Mr Thompson?'

'Yes. One and the same.' Cos offers Howell no hand – he's gone straight for the drinks tray, on a cabinet just inside the doors, as though he needs another one so soon, tossing back the last rum chaser getting into the cab.

I'm sure Howell would like to remark at my friend's fairly conspicuous lack of manners; perhaps he's thinking what rough Queenslanders we are and making the necessary allowances, but he does not comment. He has no doubt made a rough sum of our worth: we barbarians could probably buy out this room with change to spare. As we step fully into it, I look over at Cos, helping himself to a malt, and strike me once more but this house is very weird: all this show of splendour, of finely turned mahogany, of heavy gold drapes, of sparkling crystal, and I'll bet that whisky is the mellowest old Scotch – but there is no butler to serve it, just as there was no man at the door. Nothing wrong with serve-yourself, of course, I'm all for it, but it just seems ... what is this uneasy feeling?

Howell has his hand on my arm, and he's leaning to his right, speaking to a man with his back to us: 'J.C. – Mr Wilberry has arrived.' The man turns: a well-stuffed piece, the turgid flesh of his neck spilling over his collar and sweating lard. Howell introducing us now: 'J.C. Dunning – meet Benjamin Wilberry. The cattleman.'

'Botanist,' I correct him, futilely, I'm sure. I am no more cattleman than I am familiar with J.C. Dunning, but I won't be avoiding the charge of either in this place, it seems.

'Mr Wilberry,' this Dunning bellows like a bull, and the male portion of the party turns to me as one. 'Very pleased to meet you.' What for? In anticipation that Pater might gallop in behind me, stockwhip cracking? I can never quite guess what men like these are after, but if they wish to emulate Pater, whatever it is they want, it will never be enough. I press Dunning's fleshy hand just hard enough to be unpleasant. He smiles, exposing a blackened tooth, as though to say, *Go harder, feller.*

I look behind me, back through the drawing room doors: nothing but the dimness of the entrance hall there. I look over at Cos, who's made himself butler to the ladies by the piano, convincing them that they all need a pre-dinner drop, too. 'Oh go on, it's never too early to start. Not now I'm here – you'll need a drink in a minute, trust me.' The matrons are already hypnotised, one of the older ones going all girlish up to him: 'Oh, I don't suppose one would hurt, would it?' No. I shall need little convincing myself.

'To all here now and to the new year!' one of the gentlemen toasts.

'I'll drink to that!' another answers – the elderly one in military dress, a caricature of stiff-legged brass, twirling a waxed moustache. 'God save the Queen! Her Glorious Majesty!'

My collar bites into my throat. Claustrophobic: now *that* best describes the atmosphere of this house. Chokingly claustrophobic. The smell of roasting lamb seems to have been piped into the room, too, mingling stickily with some overly sweet potpourri, promising that dinner, like everything else here, will be of the finest quality, and as predictably inedible as it will be insufferable, for me. A dog barks somewhere outside, just audible under the hollow bleating of voices in here. It's that brindle staghound, Prince, I imagine. I would prefer his company and his conversation.

'Don't you agree, Mr Wilberry?' Howell is asking.

Possibly not.

'Wilber?' Cos holds up a decanter to me, and as I nod I almost startle. Is that the girl there by him? No. It is not her. Very like her, but not her. A softer line to the jaw, a rounder face, and something else. Her gown is not blue but the colour of ripe sorghum, a pale rust, of some softer line too. Must be her sister. She is staring off into some place above the noise, as though pondering a question, and then, as though sensing my own stare, she glances at me, no more than a blink, before stepping away, out of view, behind a tall, broad-backed woman.

'This Federation of ours, our *nation's* big day tomorrow.' Howell has me by the arm again. 'You are not in favour of our Commonwealth?

Couldn't care a fig, personally, if truth be known; my position is decidedly New Zealandish: distant and wary.

'Commonwealth?' Cos pricks up across the room at the very idea, though. 'Did someone say *Commonwealth*?' And now in spluttering impersonation of his famously belligerent sugar baron grandfather he announces to the party: 'You bloody Southerners wanting our Kanakas out is what your Commonwealth is all about! Who's going to cut the bloody cane now?'

The room falls silent but for my groan.

And Cos, holding glass aloft in one hand and decanter in the other, like some crazed messiah, shouting: 'Joke!' He explains to the stunned: 'Just a little *joke.*' Then he grins, before stunning them again: 'Shoot the Kanakas! That's what I meant to say. Shoot the blacks! Shoot them all! For Federation Day! We're all one big family now!'

The fat man, Dunning, is the first to respond, erupting – enthusiastically: 'Aha! Now there is a toast *I* might drink to!'

All the men are falling about laughing; all the women are horrified. And we haven't been here five minutes.

Cos has conquered the room; he almost bows: '*Joke,* ladies – my ladies, that was a little joke too.'

'I'd say you're a little drunk, sir,' the tall matron observes, and not too unkindly. She is rousing on a naughty boy.

Cos is not that drunk, yet, though; and Howell is not at all amused – he is most put out now, and not unjustifiably so. 'A joke is a joke, sir, but there will be no obscenities uttered in this house,' he warns, referring, I'm sure, to Cos's use of the bloody *bloody* adjective rather than his call for the slaughter of blacks.

'My ap –' I begin.

'Oh, have another drink yourself, Alec,' Dunning cuts me off, and Cos's opening insult to our host is in every way complete.

I look behind me again. If the girl has not joined the party within the next five minutes, we shall be leaving, too.

BERYLDA

'You right there, Miss Berylda?' Buckley's voice rolls under the cicada hum, rough as brick dust, scouring through the confusion in my mind. Buckley is a good man. A true man. Such things do exist. 'Miss Berylda?' he asks again, my name gentle on his gravel rasp. He calls me Miss Berylda still, for the child I was when we first met, a girl just turned fifteen. He is a kind man. A kind of comrade in this awful dream.

'I'm all right,' I reply. 'Only taking some air.' My voice is like some ragged wraith of a thing dragged up from a dungeon. 'Stuffy in there.'

'Take your word for it,' he says. I can hear his crooked smile of sympathy.

And that's all he has, my word, as he's not allowed past the kitchen. Wouldn't want a manservant sniffing round your chattels indoors now, would you. Alec Howell says in hushed tones and often that Roo Buckley is not to be trusted, the gardener has 'a past'. Some kind of felon once upon a time, is the suggestion. Does old Buckley a favour keeping him on, so thoroughly modern is Alec Howell, so liberal, so Christian. What a saint. As if he doesn't keep Buckley on because he's cheap. As if Alec Howell is not the real criminal here.

Buckley says: 'You've been out here a while, miss – sure you're right?'

'I'm sure. Thank you.' With my forehead pressed to the verandah post for who knows how long, I'm sure he presumes that

I am ill. I am, I suppose. I see him now as I raise my head from the post: he's at the edge of the garden bed a few feet below me, here at the back of the house. He is the colour of brick dust too, in the day; in the night he is near invisible.

'Where the devil has she got to?' We hear Alec Howell now, harassing Mary in the kitchen, looking for me. His demand, carrying through the window behind me, is a full brick hurled into my back.

'I don't know, sir – she hasn't been in here.' Mary's sigh contains a little whimper, the exasperation of too many pots on the stove.

'Ten minutes for service,' he warns her, and taunts her as he leaves: 'Those tarts – hm, very pretty indeed.'

'Oh, Mr Howell – sir!' Set your clock by that too.

My senses snap back into me. I can do nothing against him here, now. I can do nothing for justice for my sister tonight. But I can play him. At some point this evening there will be a toast to me, for my success this year at university. It's unavoidable. Alec Howell will be forced to raise his glass to me, because it will be *unseemly* not to. He won't be able to resist the opportunity to congratulate himself for my results; his vanity will break him at some point. And when it does, I will make my appeal to him to let Greta and I take that excursion to the Hill. This small escape will be ours. It must be. I begin to make my plans for it now as if this might ensure my success.

'Buckley?' I ask.

'Aye, Miss Berylda?'

'Could I ask you a terribly big favour?'

'Course, miss – whatever you wish.'

'Would you forgo your holiday tomorrow to take my sister and me for an excursion?'

'Nothin' I'd rather do, miss,' he chuckles. He's an old man and alone in the world: there's possibly nothing else he has to do apart from weeding the beans. And he is our friend, however distant he is from our lives, our predicament. 'Where you thinking of going?'

I smile. 'Out to Hill End,' I say to him. 'Stopping at Wheeler's Hotel. Perhaps over two nights?'

'Now that's an excursion.' Buckley chuckles again. 'Wild Wheeler's at the Hill – you sure about that?'

101

Uncle Alec will say no to it, is what Buckley is sure of. I am too. He will find every reasonable objection to the idea. Hill End is too rough a town now the big money is gone and the rest ever ebbs away, now that the gold gets scarcer there, too expensive to extract. Too many strangers; drifters. Desperate escapees. Not a place for ladies, or corsetless sluts, as we are. But I will make him say yes. Somehow. I will find my moment, my ploy, just as I did to be allowed to attend university in the first place: *But it will be such a reflection of all your good care of me – I will work so very hard, Uncle Alec. I will make you so very proud.* I'm going to make him say yes. In front of his audience. I will accept no rebuff or compromise; I will shame him into it, and I will enjoy it. *Poor Greta hasn't been anywhere interesting for months*, I shall say. *Not even out for an afternoon's drive in the buggy, you've been so very busy, Uncle, haven't you?*

And should he threaten us in return, I will threaten him back. I will threaten to tell Mrs Weston. And I *will* tell Mrs Weston what he has done. I will tell her what he has done to Gret, what he has put in her. I will tell Mrs Weston tonight. I will.

I must.

And I can't do any such thing. For Gret's sake, I can't tell anyone – not when she refuses even to tell me. I can't entirely trust that Mrs Weston would believe us anyway, or even if she did, that she would back us. Would Mrs Weston put her reputation on the line for ours? No woman can trust another woman to do that. Can she? The whole town will say he does not molest Greta; the whole town will say how difficult it has been for him since his wife died, since he took on the care of two ungrateful orphans. Gret will be called a harlot; and me with her. Sluts. I will lose my place at the university. On a word, his word, my future, our future, will be snatched from us forever. I have been around this circle of reason a thousand times before; that he increases in his degeneracy makes no difference to our situation. I can trust no one with this, not in this town.

But tomorrow, I can take Gret to Hill End, and I will. There I will find the Chinese doctor, Ah Ling, and I will ask him for a purgative, something to expel a child, if one exists in her. Some concoction of oil of pennyroyal or tansy or bitter apple to induce convulsions of the uterus, any of which might be bought from any chemist, any of which I would give to her myself, except that I don't know what dosage might be safe – they don't write instructions for abortion on the packets of these pills. A Chinese herbalist will know, though, and when the convulsions come, I want my sister to lose this pain in a whirl of merry-go-round calliope tunes, remembering Mother and Papa, too, and fizzing with too much ginger beer, merely her whatsits come and gone. And, brief though our journey will be, it will afford me precious time, precious clarity, away from him, to think. To plan more and thoroughly: to move our future forward. Quickly. Perhaps a telegraphed message to Flo, some kind of SOS to compel her to come to us straightaway. And then what? What would Flo make of all this? Would she understand? I love Flo so dearly, I so want to tell her everything, but I cannot be sure. It's one thing to trumpet for justice, another to take a personal risk to see it done. I'm not sure that she has seen anything of darkness but her own bright and happy sleep. With Flo or without her, I must find a way to make Gret safe from him.

However I manage it, Uncle Alec will say yes.

'Yes,' I reply to Buckley. 'Yes, I'm quite sure. We'll set out at dawn and along the way we'll picnic, at that place where the Turon meets the Track. You know it?'

'Aye, miss. Aye, I do.'

BEN

'Here she is!' the German shouts, pointing as though he might win a prize by finding her. 'Miss Berylda! Alec, here she is.'

Berylda. I turn to see her. Yes. Here she is. Slipped in through the side door behind me. A piece of sky slipped into the room. A porcelain face making off with my mind. I am staring at her but I can't help it, and she doesn't notice anyway, doesn't notice me at all as she moves through the party. I notice everything about her. The tremor along the boards beneath her feet meeting mine. Her frown twitching as she speaks with her uncle, stepping away from him hurriedly as though they might have had a disagreement earlier. Perhaps that's why she charged out as we arrived. She glances away, back towards me, but still she doesn't seem to see me. Her eyes are cast downwards, frowning into the carpet as she walks through the room, and that line between her brows is an entire country I wish to explore. Why does she frown so severely? This beautiful country of porcelain sky.

A gong sounds from the dining room beyond, shaking me from my stupor a little, and more fully with the shout of, 'Dinner, my friends!' that follows. Howell. That's quite a voice he has in him. The man is expansive now, arms stretched wide in invitation; he appears to have recovered his pride with his control of the house.

So that Cos must shout in return: 'Bonzer!' Rubbing his hands together: 'Lead us forth to the trough!'

And I groan again. He will have Howell for his sport tonight – effortlessly, teasing the cat with string. Dunning, whom I've gathered is some kind of industrialist, some kind of parochial big hat, is still wheezing and wiping tears from his eyes at Cos's call for a celebratory black-shoot. Cos will have this fat man for the first course, and that may well be worth waiting for too. But we can't possibly stay for dinner. What excuse might I make for our exit, though?

Howell attempts to counter: 'Well, if you eat the way you drink, Mr Thomp –'

Cos doesn't give him a fraction of a moment: 'Never mind, Mr Howell – or Doctor, what are you? In any event, never mind. Wilber will make it up for me. He eats nothing – bloody vegetarians.'

This silence is a dreadful one. The directness of Cos's assault on Howell is too much. Howell has stopped in midstride, pressing the back of his hand to his mouth. The hand forming a fist. I must remove Cos. Remove him before Howell does suggest some violence and Cos then takes out the man's front teeth with one lazy jab. Don't push this wallaby to it. He's not grogged up enough yet to miss.

My hand is an inch from grasping the back of his coat. 'Cos. Enough.' And I mean it: he may well be immune to embarrassment but I am not.

'What?' He turns to me, eyes huge with cherubic malevolence. 'But you *are* a vegetarian.'

Yes, I am. And laughter again fills this room, this awkward void, but there is another sound inside it now. Some melody, or the sound that a star might make in shining; a shower of such stars. It is her; I know it is the girl who is laughing. I turn to her and she is leaning against her sister; they must be sisters, they are so alike. 'Oh Gret.' She can barely stop her laughter to speak, bent over it, holding her middle as though she might burst. 'Vegetarian. Oh dear, won't Mary be appalled.' And I hear now it is not one sound, but two. The sisters laughing: what a sound. Chimes entwining. Enchanting.

'Doctor Howell.' Even Cos appears to be tamed a bit by it. He holds out his hand to our host. 'I sincerely apologise. I go right over the line when it comes to a joke, spirits too high – enough is enough. I shall be a lamb for the rest of the evening. My word.' He holds left hand to heart: 'I promise.'

He promises nothing of course, sniffing the air, already composing lamb jibes in his head, and Howell is still bristling. But he accepts the handshake, and with it he says: 'It's Mr – Mr Howell. I am a surgeon.'

'Are you *really*?' Cos will let him have his pride and his party back, for now. 'I'm doubly sorry then. I had no idea you were a medical man, such a noble profession.' Such a liar, such a master at it, and the party moves off again towards the dining room.

'Yes, a wonderful surgeon, Mr Howell is.' One of the matrons is certainly impressed by him. 'A saver of so many lives and limbs.'

'And he will be greatly missed at the hospital when he's called upon to take up a seat in the new state parliament next year, as he should be – our man for the New Age,' the Reverend fellow enlightens us, with that arch air of one who believes he owns some territory on the ear of God.

'Oh is that right? And what party will you be running for?' Cos asks the entire room, because he's just put together why we've been invited – and tolerated. So have I. These sort of people are looking for the support of the biggest hats in the land, such as Pater; they're after a national union of conservatives, and possibly financial assistance as well. Of course. And not a chance on this earth. I almost laugh. As Pater might say: *I will eat my own next steaming turd before I'll put my hand in my pocket for some wet-head from Melbourne – the next two if the bastard is from Sydney.* He's only slightly less averse to those in Brisbane who dare to exercise their parliamentary rights to speak in his presence. Howell must be naïve – or mad.

'Free Traders, of course,' Howell replies, pride fully restored, fully on the tips of his toes, and he is bang out of the solar system mad. Even if we were on speaking terms, Pater is a Protectionist, a farmer before he is even Minister of Agriculture, with a natural inclination to want to protect the price of his beef from grasping little tax-thieving nonentities such as this. Federation for him will be just another set of laws to be circumvented. 'We'll be making a stand against the labour movement in this district, keep them well out, before they ruin the place,' Howell adds, as though that shared political aim might make a blind bit of difference to the pastoralists of Queensland. 'We're all with the Liberal Reform League here.'

'Hooray! Hear, hear!' We have a chorus, like a mass delusion. A coalition of farmers and industrialist free traders? These people are so much of a New Age they must be out of the millennium.

'You don't say,' Cos drawls with such exaggeration I don't know how anyone could fail to hear the roguery in it.

The girl is still laughing, arm in arm with her sister. She catches my eye now as she passes ahead of me. She smiles at me, differently, somehow into me, with some faint and cryptic conspiracy, drawing me along. Still smiling, turning away again, she says: 'We'll find you something suitable to eat, don't worry, Mr Wilberry.' Discarding the words behind her as so many crumbs.

I cannot find a reply. But I know I will wait a thousand years and more to see that smile, to have her smile at me again.

BERYLDA

Greta winces as she sits at the table. Only slightly, there behind her eyes, but I see it. She chatters over the discomfort, settling next to Mrs Weston. 'I'm so hungry tonight – I really am going to fly away if I don't eat something soon.'

'Dear, I wish I could eat as you do,' Mrs Weston replies. 'I only have to look at half a pea to grow this girth half a yard these days.' They chatter away about nothing; the happy chatter of playing at being featherheaded around a dining table.

As Uncle Alec's admonishment of me just now replays and replays: *You delay dinner for some more attention, do you? Be careful or I will give you the attention you deserve.* Pinching his thumb into the back of my hand, digging his nail between my bird bones there.

I glance at him now, ho-ho-hoing over himself, directing guests to chairs, and my reply burns through my glare: *Why don't you just die?* This minute. Spontaneous expiration by vanity-induced cerebral haemorrhage. BANG. Give us all a proper thrill tonight.

'What does a vegetarian eat?' Dulcie sends her own inquiry up this side of the table. One really wouldn't guess she'd travelled further afield than Mediocrity Flat, honestly.

I could begin laughing again. Mr Wilberry is to be seated at the foot of the table, the honoured guest. Great lump of gristle in Uncle Alec's teeth now. An unexpected vegetarian, and his flagrantly misbehaving friend. Most excellent. Greta could not have wished a more perfect stranger into our world.

Mr Wilberry smiles and clears his throat, tucking that unfashionably long hair behind his ears. Oddly nervous manner for such a large man; a strong man, lifting out the chair for Mrs Dunning beside him with one hand. Not so much choosing his words as discovering them and addressing some particular stripe in the wallpaper above the sideboard with his answer: 'Oh, I eat anything, really. Just not those things which have a brain.'

'Why's that?' Dulcie persists in her genuinely brainless way and her mother growls across the centrepiece: 'Dulcie, each to their own.'

'I'm not offended, please,' Mr Wilberry assures them both, and then to the wallpaper once more, he says: 'The experience of farming cattle, I suppose, it can send one either way.'

How neatly put.

He adds, looking down at the table: 'Very pretty menu card, though.'

It is. Gret made the cards this morning, fourteen of them, and two more no less pretty ones this evening just before the guests arrived; she lingered over those as we kept to my room, making ourselves late for muster. Mr Wilberry holds his menu card in his enormous hands, looking into it as if finding his focus there, and he is sincere in his appreciation of it, as anyone should be. Each one possessing a splash of New Year fireworks, they come from that mysteriously well-fortressed place of joy in my sister's heart, her paintbox place of refuge.

'I'll say it is a pretty card,' Mr Thompson agrees, brandishing his in the air.

'My sister's doing,' I say. 'She got all the artistic talent.' My words are keen, as I always am, to push to the light Greta's gifts that so few ever have the opportunity to see, but my voice is squashed tight by my myriad conflicting feelings this night. I sound dismissive, superior; I don't mean to.

'Miss Jones.' Mr Thompson overlooks me anyway, just about diving across the table at my sister: 'I want mine framed. You'll let me keep it, won't you?'

109

'Oh? But of course you can keep your card.' Greta is shy and uncertain at his compliment, edging yet a little further behind Mrs Weston's sleeve, but I see the sweet pleasure in the corners of her smile as she looks away.

'Even though I am lying,' the man says now, and the table holds its collective breath at what dreadful thing he might say next. I blaze a glare at him: *Don't you dare embarrass my sister.* But he doesn't take his eyes from Greta's card; he declares: 'It's not a very pretty card at all, Miss Jones. It's very clever, is what it really is.' And he is not as drunk as he seems; he is sincere, assuring her, respectfully: 'It is no easy thing to do, effectively – fireworks. Making light from dark from nothing on the page. And in watercolour. Bonzer stuff.' He raises his glass: 'To Miss Jones's exceedingly clever cards.'

And her face colours exceedingly beautifully as everyone else toasts her too: 'Clever Greta!' and 'Magnificent menu cards!' She is the centrepiece, a rare moment for her, and she shimmers with it even as her wounds would rather send her into the sideboard to hide. At least, from where she sits, she can't see Uncle Alec using his card to blot the bottom of the decanter, having poured J.C. Dunning another drink, ignoring this small celebration of her altogether – and there's nothing unusual in that. He would never praise Greta. Not if his position in the Liberal League depended on it. Never.

Fury threatens, more urgently still, and I stand abruptly: 'Speaking of menus, I should go and horrify the housekeeper with our brainless vegetarian changes to it.'

I sound rude and horrible and leave as abruptly, my own face flushing through one hundred degrees of rage and shame. I am appalled at myself. I am appalled at what this house does to me, shrivelling my own spirit, making me mean, not just this evening, not just for this new low Alec Howell brings us to, but always, and I promise Mary silently as I make my way to the kitchen that I will not be rude and horrible to her too. I will not be like *him*. She will be upset enough as it is at our surprise culinary problem. There's nothing on the menu apart from dessert that isn't full of brained things, even the soup – beef.

But still my tone is jagged, clipped and rushed as I descend upon the kitchen: 'Mary. We have a problem. Mr Wilberry eats no meat.'

She gasps: 'What? No meat?'

'Yes. Have you spare rounds for the canapés?' I ask as gently and helpfully as I can, but she whimpers in response.

'Rounds?' She looks over at her hors d'oeuvres, her regiments of anchovy rosettes, identical sprigs of dill topping each. Lucy, about to carry a tray of them out to the table, stops statue still with dread panic. Mary cries: 'There's no meat in there, it's only anchovies, and Mr Howell said –'

'It's all meat to a vegetarian,' I snap. Impatience takes over me at her dithering, her terrible need to please her master. She adores him and I hate her so very much for it. I'll make the wretched canapé myself. I find the little pile of Mary's discarded, not quite perfectly circular toasted rounds by the piping bag on the table between us. I slice a tomato from the bowl at the window end. Sprinkle it with salt and pepper. Garnish it with a sprig of parsley from the jug by the cutting board. Not quite as elegant as Mary's own efforts but: 'There's your vegetarian canapé.' I push the plate across the table at her. 'Make a mushroom soup au lait for Mr Wilberry, and a potato gratin for entree. It's not hard, Mary. I'm sure he won't mistake the lamb for pumpkin with the main, and I'll warn him there's tongue in your croquets.'

'But –'

'Just do it, or Mr Howell will be most displeased.' I wipe the knife and stab it back into the block.

'Yes, Miss Jones.' She is duly cowed.

And cruelty's chain drags as I return to the dining room. Mary is an exemplary servant, really, when even a tolerable one is not easy to come by, even in Sydney, and she is an extremely fine cook. I have never acknowledged it. The best I can give her is this contempt. Cruelty passed down the chain from her beloved master and through me. Or it is simply me? Am I the one who is wrong here after all? Am I the cold, ungrateful jade he says I am? Does he in fact have a right to behave as he does? Is there a right order to things that I am resisting because I am – Oh God, no, stop – not that wrong thought. No. I am not wrong. I can't be. Can I? My questions, my confusions, run round and round.

And stop suddenly at the dining room door, at the sight of Mr Wilberry's back, filling the space before me, suspending the bedlam inside me, and eclipsing Uncle Alec altogether. In fact, Mr Wilberry eclipses almost the entire party from this view, for me. I am used to being quite a bit smaller than others but Mr Wilberry is quite a bit larger than most – as tall as I am when he's seated. I move around to my place between him, at the foot of the table, and Dr Weston on my right, and as I do I see Mr Wilberry is speaking to Reverend Liversidge, up from Mrs Dunning at his left. 'Ah no, I'm not a professor, no, nothing like that as yet. Merely a lecturer, in structural and physiological botany, mostly, with a research interest in native classification. But really I earn my keep with the study of the various suitabilities and unsuitabilities of cropping for stock feed, across various terrain. There's a push on at Melbourne now to bring agriculture into the School of Natural Sciences as a –'

Mr Thompson leans across the table from the other side of the Reverend. 'He teaches the hothoused youth of the shallow south that apples do in reality grow on trees. Gets them out in the field with gumboots, secateurs and all that. Extraordinary stuff. They grow beans on the campus too, apparently.'

'Thank you, Cos, yes we do.' Mr Wilberry indulges him, in that way of being both fond and irritated. A mismatched pair, Mr Thompson as darkly chaotic as Mr Wilberry appears fair and mild; they must be old friends. 'Thank you,' Mr Wilberry says to Lucy as she offers him the tomato rounds. 'That looks delicious.' And back to Reverend Liversidge: 'I am presently on a … somewhat of a break, undertaking a study of a particular species of –'

'Oh don't go on about plants, Wilber. Save us.' Mr Thompson is wonderfully awful, a crude and bearded Oscar Wilde exhumed for a tour of the Antipodes.

Reverend Liversidge is certainly not interested in botany, asking Mr Wilberry now: 'You did your undergraduate study at Oxford or Cambridge?'

'Neither – no,' says Mr Wilberry, with that nervous clearing of the throat. 'I went straight down to Melbourne. Biology and –'

'Melbourne?' Reverend Liversidge is shocked, as if Mr Wilberry said he'd gone straight down to hell; shocked in that way so many of the previous generation are: How is it possible one might be entirely educated in Australia? He's a Cambridge man himself; don't we all here know his wife died after a diabetic coma rather than be subject to another lecture upon his St John's College glory days.

Dr Weston, opposite, is Oxford, but rather broader of mind; body too. He takes four canapés onto his plate and says to Mr Wilberry: 'You home-grown brains, it's you who will change this ragbag of colonies into a nation once the ink is dry.' Through a mouthful of anchovy paste he says to me: 'That's you too, Berylda. Haven't congratulated you on your results yet, have I?'

Mr Wilberry turns to me and Dr Weston, his eyes asking over his own mouthful of tomato: 'Hm? Congratulated?'

'This young lady is for the School of Medicine in the New Year, at Sydney.' Dr Weston tilts his glass in my direction and then swigs to the novelty, merrily remaining deaf, dumb and blind to the injustice that he and every other DMO in this rag bag of colonies will conspire against me should I dare to apply for a job on the wards once I qualify. 'Came top in Biology, too – name in the *Bathurst Free Press* this morning, and a prize to come from the board. Perhaps a scholarship.' A wink across the table to Uncle Alex: 'Such a credit to you.'

And here, thank you, Dr Weston, is my chance, my turn in the light, to strike for the one thing I might achieve tonight: to make Alec Howell agree to allow us to take that excursion to the Hill. I glance over at Gret, who's pretending fascination at whatever Mrs Gebhardt is pronouncing upon now, and my anticipation gleams: she will so love this surprise. Please, fate be kind and give it to us.

But before I open my mouth, Mr Wilberry, it appears, is clearing his throat again to speak, and by habit I hesitate. To find that, no, he's not clearing his throat at all. He's coughing. No – now he gulps. A strangled sound.

What in heaven's name?

The man is choking on his tomato canapé.

BEN

Even as I am dying I am a great blunder of the world, my destiny to leave it in this way, slamming fist to tablecloth, knocking fork onto floor. Choking. Medicine? Sydney University. Biology prize? What kind of hoax is this? Here is a girl I might bloody well come to admire. In fact, I think I do so now already. And I must die. In pandemonium: chairs scraping, ladies gasping. A fish thrashing about for –

Awfff.

The blow between my shoulders dislodges the bread in my throat and the air rushes in, and out again; croaking, 'S-sorry, I do beg …' as I turn to see who has saved me.

'Don't apologise.' She frowns. 'My fault, I'm sure. I sliced the tomato too thickly.'

She sliced a tomato for me. It is difficult to say which is more astounding: the tomato slicing or that belting she just gave me. I don't admire this girl, Berylda. No. I have fallen irretrievably into her frown.

BERYLDA

'Oh, well done!' his messy friend declares, sloshing claret across the table, deep red bleeding into the white cloth. 'The entertainments here this evening are topnotch – what!'

'Berylda.' Mrs Weston is on her feet too. 'Indeed that was well done. Are you quite all right, Mr Wilberry?'

He nods, cheeks flushed, tucking that long hair behind his ears, eyes downcast, clearly embarrassed. 'Thank you. Quite all right,' he rasps painfully. How unpleasant for him. It was exciting for me, though, for the discovery I have just made: I am stronger than I thought. Far stronger. The force of my fists on his back …

'Three cheers for Berylda!'

'Little Miss Dr Jones!'

'Hip hip hooray!'

Glasses are raised around the table, around my scalpel smile, and I glance the blade up the centre of it at Uncle Alec as all resume their seats. I am exhilarated by this power in me. If I could find the impulse, the passion that was in me just now to drive a blade …

God, arrest this thought and keep it from me. I have just saved a man's life; I am not about to do away with another, no matter how much I'd like to. Need to. Must. Hush. Keep my resolve wrapped tight around the things that might be achieved. I have a demand to make of dearly beloved uncle, don't I, and how can he deny my request for a few days away with my sister now? I have saved his party from ruination. I sit poised in my seat, to watch and wait for another moment, the best moment, to play my card for it.

'As I was saying, there will be some competition over the selection of a Free Trade candidate amongst the Liberals – fierce. But we will be in it.' He has resumed lecturing Mr Thompson on his political aspirations, lecturing over my feat as if it never occurred, still punishing me for my undergarment recalcitrance, of course. I am not to be forgiven for my insolence. I watch him, waiting for my opportunity to interrupt, and as I do I drill my own resolve into his face: *I will succeed in making you say yes to me.* He is seeking his own assurances from Justice Wardell at his right: 'We are shoring up the numbers amongst our League. We are the ones to protect the colony – excuse me, *nation* – from the socialists. It begins in New South Wales. We'll break the trade unions here, won't we, Victor. Break them before they take hold, and I am the man to lead the charge.'

As if empty slogans lead anywhere. Why does Uncle Alec despise the trade unions so? What is the workingman to a surgeon but largely irrelevant unless the company offers to pay his bill or he volunteers for unrestrained medical trial and error? Mystifying.

I am certain I see a flicker of unease cross Justice Wardell's face. 'We've a federal election to get through yet. Much can happen in these coming months, Alec. The Protectionists are strong and might yet throw their hat in with the Laborites – the worker and the farmer have more in common against the industrialist than not, and might make a new party of themselves. All is in flux. No counting of any sort of chickens for a while, I'm afraid.'

Yes. That was a rebuke, if a subtle one. Smashing the workingmen's co-operatives of Bathurst is rather a grandiose ambition in itself. Miners, shearers, timber cutters, a rabble of labourers five thousand strong in this town alone. And Uncle Alec does not have his selection as a state candidate guaranteed. That's almost worth remaining here for indefinitely. To see him thwarted. I see a great hobnail boot grinding his head into the dust of William Street, and a ploughshare dragging over the rest of him.

Lapdog Gebhardt springs to his master's side: 'Months?' The chemist shakes his jowly chops. 'But we must be working always against the socialists – now. Immediately. They are the plague of the federation in Germany. Constantly disrupting unity. Constantly disrupting industry. These labour parties in the colonies here are already too strong. Imagine what federation will do for this workers party? They will take over totally. They are tyrannical madmen waiting for this chance. They grow stronger and stronger every day we delay.'

'Shoot them. Shoot them now,' Mr Thompson insists with a theatrical wave of his hand. 'Chain 'em up with the blacks and the Kanakas and shoot 'em all. Ingrates! I'll cut the blasted cane myself, see if I don't. Australia for the White Man! Australia for the Fat White Man!'

'That joke is stale,' Uncle Alec admonishes, disdainful curl of the lip, not turning from Dr Gebhardt and Mr Wardell to address Mr Thompson directly.

'It's not entirely a joke, though, is it, Mr Howell?' Mr Thompson is suddenly sharply sober once more. 'It's what you'd really like to do, isn't it? Get rid of the lot of them that won't do as you want them to do. Aren't what you want them to be. Your skivvies, your vassals, your slaves.'

'What are you then, sir? A libertine? An anarchist? Nihilist? Some other inane fad?' Uncle Alec's shoulders shift in discomfort as he is forced to face Mr Thompson. Oh but this is fun now. I am on the edge of my seat; so is Gret, her eyes wide, napkin pressed to her lips to hide her own enjoyment of this turn.

'No. I am myself.' Mr Thompson's smile is open and smug. 'I am a fat white man.' Most definitely a handsome man; most comfortable in himself, and most definitely aware of the effect of it, too.

And Uncle Alec is writhing inside with the challenge of it all; rattled and raising the scritch in his voice just enough to betray himself: 'You think it fair and just that the unions stand over industry demanding their wages at threat of bloodshed? For that is what they do.'

Mr Thompson snorts, dismissively: 'You think it fair that industry stands over poor men and keeps them poor not at threat of bloodshed but with bloodshed in fact?' A slow nod over a wry and calculating smile. 'I'm fascinated by it all. That's what I am. Fascinated. You do realise that the Labor Party is more for the Fat White Man than anyone in this room, don't you? Dependent upon you as a lamb. And no one hates a coloured skin the way the worker does. You really should consider going in with them. You can all join fat white hands as the ultimate Super Party. It's the only way your empires will continue to survive this New Age, the only way you will ever be the kings you think you ought to be – make the workers your friends and go on a big, long black shoot together, Waltzing Matilda all the way. I'm not joking.'

'You're not, are you,' J.C. Dunning says beside him, fascinated himself; Dunning is a fat white bullfrog, and a little keen on Mr Thompson's wild ideas, it seems. Keen on his flagrant liberty. He says to Mr Thompson: 'But you have some cheek.'

'Not as much as you do, sir,' Mr Thompson retorts, patting his own ample stomach.

'Ho!' And Justice Wardell almost chokes on his canapé too, roaring: 'Jolly good!'

Jolly good, I'll say. The balance of power here is topsy-turvy now all round. Anything might happen tonight.

'I cannot apologise enough,' Mr Wilberry rasps at his napkin, pressing his fingers against his forehead, squeezing his eyes closed.

'Please, please, Mr Wilberry,' I admonish him, almost gaily, 'do not apologise again.'

'I'll say, we should do it as the Germans do, eh?' Major Harrington nudges Dr Gebhardt. 'Make military service compulsory. That'll sort out the lot. Conscription is the way!'

I wonder if perhaps that's not a bad idea – universal military service whereby all men would be compelled to go off and shoot each other – and that thought, as well as the wine I've just glugged down, makes me laugh.

Mr Wilberry looks across at me. He appears somewhat terrified, before he says: 'Your laughter is – er. Quite an enchanting sound, Miss Jones. Hm.'

I laugh again: enchanting? How curious; how thoroughly absurd. He smiles, a pleasant and gentle smile. A pleasant and gentle face, even his eyelashes are fair. I return his smile, but I am confused once more, and even more strangely. Is this man whispering sweet nothings to me? I'm not sure; I don't know men, not young men. I am best known for my avoidance of them. An odd sensation creeps up the back of my neck, warmth and chill at once, and I don't know this sensation, either. My heart drums wildly. I look down at the table. I look at his hands there, either side of his plate. Such large hands, Mr Wilberry has, they dwarf the plate. He could throttle another man with one firm grasp, and with this thought I see these hands tight around Alec Howell's neck, shaking him, bashing him into the mantel. What I might make them do, if I could. Oh God. I look away, into Dr Weston's left cufflink, my eyes blurring around its tiny enamel crest.

Breathe. Listen to the table talk, people merely making noise at each other, until I find Mrs Weston's voice amongst it. She is politely, reasonably attempting to subvert the natural order of Mrs Dunning's tiny mind, over the eternally stalled Women's Franchise Bill. 'Who else but a woman can take the issues that most affect us up to our administrators – deplorable rates of maternal and infant mortality, deplorable dearth of properly trained nurses in the bush. Men do not care for these things at the ballot box, Virginia, not even where they care deeply for their wives and daughters. It is not their care to consider. It must be for women to take it up to the parliament somehow.'

'Oh, Augusta, I suppose you are right,' Mrs Dunning concedes regretfully. 'But only to a point. Perhaps women – *married* women, mind you – *might* participate one day. But not the full franchise, surely. What lady would want to participate in the parliaments themselves? Not any lady, I would say. It's simply not right, not the right way of things. It simply wouldn't work.'

Like slapping the Virginia Dunnings of this world across the face with reality: futile. Like most overprivileged women of her generation, she can't imagine why or how others of her sex might want or need to do anything beyond producing children and afternoon tea parties. Like most determinedly feeble-minded women, she can't imagine how any of the limitations inflicted upon womankind might be overcome at all. And why would you want to anyway when your husband buys you mink and pearls?

No amount of reasoning, polite or otherwise, that South and West Australia haven't morally or economically disintegrated under their equal suffrage provisions will shift the unshiftable, make the thoughtless think. No amount of irony that our monarch remains a woman, a mother of nine, grandmother of everyone else and Queen over twenty British prime ministers thus far will make the blind see. No wonder New Zealand declined the invitation to join in our Federation.

But Augusta Weston understands the practicalities of justice, unfurling her rich velvet reason up the table now to the host: 'What do you say, Alec? Should a lady have the full vote here? Full rights of franchise? How would I go in the parliament?'

I look up as he chuckles, having been put on the spot, squirming in it, and like a true politician he refuses to answer the question: 'I am sure you would be formidable, Mrs Weston.'

'Will you push for it? My vote?' She presses him, bright lavender entreaty with a dare. 'Are you indeed our man for the New Age?'

And again he squirms away: 'For your vote, Mrs Weston, yes of course. I would be unwise not to push for your approval.'

'Yes, you would.' Mrs Weston sighs deep inside her therapeutic foundations, and as her husband makes some condescending jest about the necessity of his wife's approval in all things, she says, 'Thank you, Donald,' before rejoining Anna Gebhardt's discussion of Bavarian mental hygiene as the more engaging conversational option.

Alec Howell will not vote for our enfranchisement when the bill comes around again. Why in heaven's name would he? He is our guardian. What more could we want? Sir Henry Parkes reincarnate he is not, and he is proud of the fact. Liberal only in his ambition, his lust to command. To belittle. To deride. To control. If he is the new man for modern conservatism, what will the face of the party be? Monstrous.

'I believe in the full enfranchisement of women,' Mr Wilberry says softly beside me. Almost too softly. Clearing his throat, running a fingertip along the length of his soup spoon; such a tiny soup spoon under his hand. 'My mother was something of a suffragist, a supporter at least. She could never express the view openly. I believe she would want to now, for the younger ones coming up.'

'Would she? That's good,' I reply, brusquely, disconcerted immediately again, and I cannot look at him. This man, this pleasant, gentle stranger, who provokes this odd sensation, a prickling of my skin at the depth of his voice, a queer rush of feeling that is at once welcome and not welcome at all.

'Women?' Mr Thompson splatters himself across the table for a timely distraction. 'I say shoot them – Mrs Weston. Mrs Weston, you'll be in this, won't you? Bloody women – chain 'em up with the blacks and shoot 'em. Get rid of 'em once and for all. That'll teach 'em.'

'Yes, yes,' Uncle Alec tries condescension with our clown now, 'we've heard that one.' Above Mrs Weston's hoot of, 'Hooray to that, young man,' and Dulcie's, 'I don't understand what any of you are talking about now,' he resumes his discussion with Justice Wardell: 'I mean to say, what happens if a female parliamentarian is alone in the House – middle of the night, late sitting. What has she? One hundred and twenty-five chaperones or one hundred and twenty-five wolves about her?'

It is as if a black sheet is thrown across my vision at the words.

I know what Alec Howell might do. Are they all like him?

Wolves.

Mr Thompson turns on Mr Dunning: 'You'd have a hard time containing yourself, wouldn't you? I don't mean you personally, Mr Dunning, of course. Wouldn't have to be too quick on her feet to get away from you, eh, now would she?'

'What did you say?' J.C. Bullfrog can't quite grasp the attack.

But I can. And for the first time this evening clarity has me, at last, and with it comes an intuition. Whoever these strangers are, manic Mr Thompson and mild Mr Wilberry, they are our allies somehow. My plan coalesces with my courage. Now. My moment is now to make my demand. This chance for a little escape; and with it this chance for a little revenge. Quickly: turn the thought to words, and words to knives.

'Uncle Alec,' I call over Mr Dunning's slow boiling outrage. 'Speaking of chaperones, Buckley has agreed to hold off his holiday to take Greta and me out to Hill End tomorrow, out along the Bridle Track.'

'What?' There's a fascinating outrage. I'd like it photographed and mounted above the mantel. I might give him a stroke tonight yet. 'What is this?'

'Oh Ryl!' Greta exclaims, appearing half-thrilled at the surprise and half-horrified by my new provocation. Don't you worry, sister, I will not let him come for you tonight, I will not have you pay for my sins with a beating, or worse; but I cannot tear my eyes from Alec Howell's to let her find my promise there.

'Yes, remember?' I prod him further and twist the tip. 'I mentioned it just this afternoon – before ... Before you went to see Greta about ... whatever it was you went to see Greta about, when she was in her room. Remember?'

I am bolder than I have ever been. So close to the truth. So close. Shall I announce to the table what you went to Greta for this afternoon, Alec Howell? Do I bluff or shall I dare? I am pinning him to the board like a rat for vivisection: *Do not deny me.*

And yet he attempts to, of course. 'Hill End?' he scoffs. 'What would you want to go out there for, Berylda? To see a Chinaman about some snake oil perhaps?' He sneers under his smile.

'Perhaps.' I shrug, smug: if only you knew. 'He sounds like an interesting character, don't you think?'

'No, I do not. That quackery of the Celestials is not medicine, girl, that is newspaper sensationalism combined with village idiocy, and you will not be going to Hill End. I must forbid it. Never mind that the track is in too dangerous a state of disrepair. Never mind that the town is a den of vice.' He ho-ho-ho's over me, *stupid girl, whatever is she talking about,* but none join him. I have his audience for my own.

'Vice?' I laugh, savagely gay. My sister would be safer living in a brothel than here. 'There is vice around every bend, isn't there, Uncle? Wherever we may go there are dangers – why, a young lady is molested at Redfern Station once a month, isn't she, and I brave its Western Mail platform several times a year. But Buckley will keep us safe on this journey – you know he would do anything for Greta and me, if he could, if he ever *knew* we were in the slightest trouble. And anyway, I hope to travel with even greater guardianship – I thought that it might be just the thing to invite Mr Wilberry and Mr Thompson to accompany us. No one would dare accost us with these strapping fellows in our midst, now would they?'

I don't give Alec Howell or our guests more than half a blink to digest it. I press on wildly: 'Oh do say yes, Uncle. It's been so terribly long since Greta's been allowed *anywhere*, never mind that I deserve a little reward for all my hard work this year. And Mr Wilberry. Mr Wilberry, if you come with us, you'll catch the display of black poppies along the Bridle Track – the old scenic road there. I'm sure they are in bloom this time of year, and they are a sight, those poppies, a botanical treat. Might you delay your plans for us? What do you say? It'll only be a few days – perhaps three?'

'Black poppies?' Mr Wilberry looks completely boggled, as if I've slipped a drop of their opium into his glass, as Mr Thompson does exactly as one would expect of such a keen troublemaker, demanding of his friend: 'I think you are required to say yes in this circumstance, Wilber.'

As Mrs Weston weighs in: 'Those poppies truly are a glorious sight. It's all glorious out there. Down along the riverbanks – oh, you should plan a picnic for the journey, Berylda.'

'I was thinking precisely that, Mrs Weston,' I say, and I turn my blade into the centre of Alec Howell's forehead. 'I was thinking we should picnic at the Turon, where it crosses the Track, although Greta and I haven't been there for many years, of course. I have such happy memories of that place, our last excursion with Mother and Papa, that summer before ...'

Hell descended.

And I have bested the devil at his own game. I win. He can't possibly object now, not without betraying himself as the vile bully that he is. He certainly can't deny our esteemed guests their black poppies, and he can't threaten to join us, either – as he must attend the official Federation celebrations here in Bathurst tomorrow, gritting his teeth through it all too, at being snubbed for any invitation to Sydney, to the Governor-General's swearing in and the choir of ten thousand singing 'Australian sons, let us rejoice'.

He chuckles with Justice Wardell, feigning indulgence: 'Young and wilful – what can one do?'

We'll find out after the guests leave, won't we; and whatever evil retribution you devise, I will stop you. But you can't stop Gret and me from going to the Hill. Not now.

'Oh *dear*, but *who* will chaperone you?' No one is more confounded than Mrs Wardell. '*All* of you on *excursion – together*? A few *days*? In *mixed* company? But what if the road is very bad and it's more than a few days – *nights* – out *there* – oh *dear*.'

'Oh Ettie,' Mrs Dunning chides her to confound me. 'This is the twentieth century. Have a bit of faith in the youngsters to make the appropriate arrangements. They're hardly going to Peru. What a marvellous little adventure it will be, though – makes me wish I were young again.' What makes her turn so rapidly modern? She bats eyelashes across the table at Mr Thompson now. Oh, I see, and how very revolting. Never mind your reputation so long as you've got a good franchise-free foundation garment on.

And Mrs Wardell is clucking ever on: 'Well, I can't allow Dulcie to be part of such an escapade.'

Good, I smile sweetly, because she's not invited.

I look to Mr Wilberry again: *Say yes, you must say yes.*

He says, as if answering some other presence at the table: 'Hm. Well. I suppose Manildra can wait a few days, can't it?'

BEN

'What is it you must do at Manildra, Mr Wilberry?' she asks me.

Mama's elusive bloom unfolds its red raylets in my mind. I look over my shoulder: it's as though she remains with me somehow. As though she is just in the next room, pressing petals, the child with his chin on the edge of the table, at her side, watching; she's saying something to him that I can't quite hear.

'The specimen?' The girl's frown is impatient for my response. 'You said you were going to look for a …'

'Yes,' I say. 'An *Helichrysum* – a daisy, everlasting. Like the flower – ah, that grows by your dam here, and not quite like it. Or possibly not of that species at all – another perhaps. I'm not really sure what I'm going to Manildra for, actually. A promise I made, to find …'

She squints at me below the frown, impatient and now possibly disturbed by all my stumbling about with these words. She must be wondering how it is I manage to conduct lectures at the university, much less negotiate my way through the conversations necessary to getting about in the world; I sometimes wonder that myself.

'Find what?' she says abruptly: *Come on, come on.* She rubs the back of her neck, as though I might be giving her a pain there, or a shiver of disdain.

Come on, come on, Mama demands too, right at my ear now.

'A flower,' I say, looking down at the gilt lace border of the bowl set before me. 'One my mother remembered from when she was a girl, from her home, at Mandagery Creek, before she married. A native. Hm. She is no longer with us.'

'Oh?' I look up again at the sound, the softness of the chime. The frown has vanished to porcelain once more; her face so close, her eyes hold worlds of blue kaleidoscope jewels laced through with rays of hazel stars. 'A recent loss?' she asks.

'Yes.' God but it is, so freshly cut. 'Only a few weeks ...' What? Her perfume mists over what's left of my mind, sweet and yet ... what is it? Rosemary and new boot leather? And something lovely ...

'So. You're going to look for a paper daisy for your late mother?' she asks, and I am held by those eyes, the shape of the lids, petal-like and porcelain also.

'Yes.' I attempt a smile, for this beauty, this beauty I am sure I must pursue even as it is eluding me. What is this enchantment? 'I am searching for a bloom my mother once loved and I'm not even sure precisely what bloom it is, or exactly where it is. I'm likely only to find some good examples of lignum swamp or some other predictable thing. That is a bit mad, isn't it?'

'No. I don't think so,' she says, her expression unreadable. She turns away from me to say something to her sister over the table, something about picnics and a carnival calliope.

I don't absorb much else for a while. I couldn't say what was in the soup.

I will travel with Berylda Jones to Hill End tomorrow. Extraordinary. The most extraordinary thing that has ever occurred, to me. Even Cos behaves himself for the balance of the meal; even when the talk turns dangerously towards religion, something about getting around the Papists that have hold of this town, he says nothing, makes no interjection that God is dead and we shot him too. He only eats his dinner. Extraordinary. He must see that this is important to me, whatever this might be. This wanting to know Berylda Jones. He'll let me have a go without further ructions. I hope. He'd bloody well better. I've never wanted to have a go quite like this before. A go at conversation. With a girl.

I turn to her, trying to think of something not too idiotic to say, but she is turned away from me again, deep in conversation with Dr Weston beside her. They share a joke over of some text she read before Christmas, having pinched it from the medical library, keeping ahead of her studies in the New Year. 'I'll be struck off for breaking rules before I even begin!' She laughs and I'm sure that I can hear a trace of Mama's laughter through it too; a girl running down a hall, a hat disappearing around a door. She and Dr Weston talk on, discussing the subjects she will take next year: a course of further, cellular biology, medical physics, anatomy, organic and inorganic chemistry … I am lost in the licorice darkness of her hair; near black, not quite. What is this chemistry?

What have I done, agreeing to travel with this girl? I am mad. I help myself to another drink and think of poppies.

I have seen plenty of poppies in my time, of course. *Papaver orientale* across thousands of gardens; and fields of *somniferum*, grown for their latex, for their morphia soporific. Mama left me on a cloud of that stuff. North and south down the eastern seaboard, I've seen them: trails of pink along the hillsides northwest of Brisbane, and like tracts of summer snow from Bendigo to Ballarat. Only the day before yesterday I came across an interesting specimen at Leura, near Katoomba, pale orange petals and pollen of a deep indigo, randomly sewn amidst the dandelions between the railway tracks and the village. But in all my travels I've not seen a black one. I know they exist, as I know they are not black except in the rarest instances. They are generally a brownish purple; translucent plum cups. They are the colour of my wine.

BERYLDA

The bells of All Saints will be into their grim ringing by now, calling the faithful and the lonely to the watch-night Mass, the Catholic Cathedral of St Michael and St John answering in endless competition over the merry fiddles and drums thumping out of every other establishment in the town. I watch the clock on the sideboard here, willing time away as we scrape empty our dessert bowls. It is 10.32 p.m. *Tick. Tick. Tick.*

'So, what about these nasty cases of bubonic plague we've been hearing about up north then?' Dr Weston is asking Mr Wilberry across me, referring to the outbreak that has struck in tropical Townsville these past months.

'I'm afraid I don't know much about it,' Mr Wilberry replies, unceasingly apologetic. 'I'm in Melbourne for most of the year, and in Brisbane, lately I ... hm. I was a bit preoccupied with other things ...' A dying mother, I suppose, and he sounds as weary of this evening as I feel. He drains his glass. I yawn.

Time yawns and yawns but I am increasingly restless. For tomorrow. It cannot come soon enough, as if freedom might truly lie there at dawn, somewhere beyond Duramana at the head of the Track. I can hardly hold anything else in my thoughts.

Reverend Liversidge stands and gently taps the side of his glass for quiet. 'May we all be joined here now in prayer. Let us give thanks for this our bounteous ...'

He blabbers away and I pray for our freedom. I pray for absolution from whatever I will do in these days to come. I pray that I am not to blame, for whatever I will do. Must do. To keep Greta from further pain. I pray there is another way; I pray that this whisper of a child is taken from her tonight by some other will, slipping from her, never to be. That happens all the time, doesn't it? I pray that tomorrow, at dawn, I will by some other miracle have the power and the means to simply leave this place. To take my sister and leave. Leave to live our lives in peace, to live as our parents intended us to. I pray as if there is a God that listens to me. I pray as if the smear of custard in the bottom of my bowl is God: Hear me, hear my prayer.

'Thank you, Reverend.' Uncle Alec is standing now. 'Might I follow those elegant words of gratitude and hope with one toast that may match it?' He raises his glass and waits for all to stand with him, before he pours fourth: 'To my dear nieces, Berylda and Greta. In gratitude of the beauty and light that you bring to my world, and in hope that it may ever be thus.'

'Berylda and Greta,' fills the air; my throat fills with bile, acrid over sickly saccharine. And a lump of deeper shame: how many times over the years have I allowed these moments of praise to fool me, just for a second: make me believe that if I were good enough, if I worked hard enough, some love might come. Some change.

'Wonderful girls,' Mrs Weston's rich velvet reaches towards me but is as quickly lost. As Mrs Dunning calls shrill above all glasses raised: 'And here's to you, Alec. Such a wonderful man you are, taking the girls to your heart as you have. Sacrificing your own needs for theirs. And with such admirable, laudable results.'

'Hear, hear!' All hearty cheers.

Alec Howell is smiling his wolf smile amidst them. This congratulation society bestows upon him, in spades. Alec Howell is such a wonderful man, never remarrying, so devoted to his nieces is he, and they aren't even blood relations. Who has ever heard of such selfless charity?

'And last but never least, to my dear Libby.' He charges his glass now even higher to even heartier cheers. 'You are never forgotten, my dearest.'

Oh let's drink a cup of kindness for his poor dearest departed wife, shall we? Poor, poor Libby. Libby Pemberton, such a dear little thing she was, fine and fragile, the fever swept her up and away like a leaf, taking his heart with it forever. Look at her portrait there, smiling over Mr Wilberry's shoulder, on the wall opposite her husband's chair. Those dark eyes and all that lush raven hair, what a divine woman she was. You could easily mistake her for a Spanish señora with those looks; the eyes of a Welsh pirate princess stole him away, he says to any who ask of her origins, her uncommon features. How Alec Howell must miss her. Too young, she was, too swiftly lost, and yet she gazes at him every evening still and lovingly; and why wouldn't she? The man is a rock, a martyr, a model of moral responsibility and rectitude. He is superb. Browning should have written a poetic monologue for him.

And he is now smiling that wolf smile directly at me. The promise of retribution never more positively conveyed. Something is coming for us when the guests leave, be in no doubt, that smile is saying. Perhaps he will beat me; he will certainly need to when I bar his way to Greta with everything I have. He hasn't taken his hand to me for what seems ages; not since I returned home for the winter break and he'd discovered through a colleague that I had been seen too often unchaperoned walking across University Park, and once noted laughing raucously on King Street in Newtown – *cavorting* was the charge. He slapped me in a perfunctory way, at the end of the remonstrance; nothing out of the usual. If only he knew what else I get up to off the chain: consorting with socialists at suffrage demonstrations and drinking gin-slipped punch at St Paul's – before walking across the lawn alone in the dark. I return his smile now, raise my glass to him: *Cheers dearest Uncle, and may the new year bring you some charge of malpractice that will see you sent away to be surgeon at Townsville Plague Hospital.* But whatever you do, whatever you plan, you will not stop us from going to the Hill. Not now. You can't. You don't want our gallant strangers to see what you really are. Beat me – go on – but be careful about it. I gulp down the remains of my wine in anticipation. Was that my third glass? I really wouldn't know.

'And now, ladies, if you will please excuse us.' He gives us our command to leave the men to take smoke in one end and break wind out of the other for an hour – or, rather, fifty-five minutes it'll have to be, since we're running so recklessly over schedule.

I glance over at Mr Thompson as I turn to file out with the ewes, will him to do something upsetting, but he doesn't; he is busy stuffing a pipe.

And Mrs Weston is taking my arm as the door closes behind us, her voice low, keeping me to her side. 'A word with you, dear – about Greta. Perhaps it's time to start thinking about a suitable fellow?'

'Time for what?' I can barely conceal my shock, or my revulsion, at the suggestion: a suitable fellow? Greta, exchange one gaoler for another? And in this predicament? No.

'Yes, time to consider marriage, perhaps?' Mrs Weston persists. 'Is there a reason she's not in favour of the idea?'

'Reason?' If ever I might tell you. My sister is in no state to be married. I look around the drawing room for her, but she is not with us; taken the opportunity to sneak off to the closet, most probably.

'She seemed to avoid the topic with me,' Mrs Weston continues and I feel as if I might choke for all I want to say. For all I *must* say. But …

'Did she?' is all I can say. I pretend it's none of my affair. 'Greta knows her own mind about such things, I'm sure.'

My own mind turns inside out. Has Mrs Weston of her own accord guessed that something is wrong in this house? Is she *inviting* me to say?

She squeezes my arm affectionately, pats my hand in hers. 'I only mean to be of use, that's all, not meddlesome, dear. Greta is isolated here, or so I perceive, and she is too much a treasure to be shut away. While that uncle of yours seems rarely to notice any need other than his own, as is the way of most males. Hm?'

'Hm.' Can I dare hint at the truth of his ways?

'I suppose he is too busy to care,' she says, with sympathy. But does that sympathy extend to him, too? I can't take that risk. That she will not believe me; not support us, if she knew. He rapes my sister. Would she think it a regrettable right of men to do this? A burden to be borne with a sigh; quietly.

I pretend that I am distracted elsewhere, breaking from Mrs Weston to hunt through the music in the piano seat. 'Where is that song?' The lines and dots of the sheets swirl around before my eyes. What am I looking for? Where are our answers? I might crawl under the piano and stay there, if that were ever an option. I scrunch back the corner of some piece or other under my hand, a grasp of desperation, and it reveals some sort of reply: Elgar and Rossetti's 'Song of Flight' sitting there beneath it. A promise in it that we will fly, somehow, yes we will. Beginning with tomorrow, to the Hill. One step at a time.

'Ah, here we have it.' I straighten just as Greta returns to the room, and I hold out the sheet to her. 'And there you are – in time to entertain us.'

'Oh all right then, shall I?' She smiles, taking it from me, smiling again at the music I have chosen for her; of course she would love to play it but she hesitates for one moment to doubt herself. The question that has crept into her soul: *Do you really wish me to play?* Her gaoler's mark. She was not always this way, I would tell the room if I could. There was no sound Papa loved more, once: *Play Gretty, play – play the cares of the world away.* And she would, so sure of her skill she made me pout in envy. I want my sister back. I will have my sister returned to me. Whole.

'Yes, dear, please,' Mrs Weston insists. 'Play for us – you must.'

Greta sits down at the keys, clever hands dancing across the melody, free at last inside this song. I posted it home to her only in September but the sheet is imprinted on her heart, her eyes closed as her soprano soars, a summer breeze:

'While we slumber and sleep
The sun leaps up from the deep.
Daylight born at the leap!
Rapid, dominant, free,
A thirst to bathe in the uttermost sea.
While we linger at play,
If the year would stand at May!
Winds are up and away

Over land, over sea,
To their goal wherever their goal may be.
It is time to arise
To race for the promised prize,
The Sun flies, the Wind flies.
We are strong, we are free,
And home lies beyond the stars and the sea ...'

We are strong. We are free. I give myself over to this promise above all others. We will prevail. We will arise. We will fly to our rightful, natural home, one day. This is a race of endurance, not of speed.

'Ah,' Mrs Weston's sigh of delight carries over the final chords, and above the small applause. 'Ah,' she repeats the sound, because there is nothing more that can be said of excellence.

I close my eyes to stay with it a while. Stay a good distance away from Dulcie's turn at the piano now, her mother boasting, 'So many pretty songs she brought home from abroad, I can't keep up.' She clumsily gets on with some dreadful ditty, strangling a lyric about hearts and flowers 'a picture of what love should beeeeee ...' Perhaps Mrs Weston is right about spider waists depriving the brain of oxygen. Dear God. '... a candy-coated fantaseeeeee ...' Shut up, shut up. '... but in your soul I've found the one my soul can seeeeeee ...' Who writes this nonsense? Honestleeeeee.

A lovers' fantasy all right. I look up into the folds of the drapes; Aunt Libby's joyful golden drapes. And I hear our aunt screaming through this house, a handful of moments after her honeymoon, screaming this house down. Screaming, and screaming, and screaming as she did at the end: *No! Alec, no! Help me! Help me! Please, help me!* Her intestines rupturing, her mind fracturing in the fever, until it finally let her go. And she was gone. So cold she was as we kissed her goodbye that final time. That final debt of nature paid. There is nothing that love can ever do to bargain it back. Nothing. The bridge that love cannot cross. But if it could, I would ask our wonderful, funny, cherished Libby if there is such a place as hell, just so that I might know he will one day go there.

Dulcie can sing him into the fire. On and on she whines, until the music stops again abruptly.

I snap into the present once more as the dining room doors open again at my back, with a rumble of footsteps and Uncle Alec toasting himself: 'Sir Henry, I must admit, I am not. I mean what is the good of universal public education? What good does it do for those with little aptitude? Greta, for instance – should she have the same education as Berylda? Of course not. It would not have made a difference good or ill for Greta to never have attended school at all – apart from the expense to her parents, rest their souls. Why should we foot the bill then for those dull-minded types of the working classes and the racially impure? It is best for them to be made to be manually useful as early as possible – is it not best for the spirit to be useful at what one is best at?'

Manually useful. Is that what my sister is? I do not hear the replies of the men, some general hubbub of agreement as thin and as offensive as their cigar fug. I hear only that Alec's words are deliberately chosen. Spiteful: meant and timed for me and my sister to hear.

I do not turn around. I cannot believe he stoops to this public humiliation any more than I can believe that no one speaks against it. This is the point, of course: a reminder of who is in charge. If he stood over her right now, smacked his hands together in her face and demanded she play 'Yeller Gal', just as he did in this very spot the night before last, would anyone speak against him? Would anyone care? Perhaps privately. But none will speak against him. And I cannot turn around, for if I do I might well scream. I cannot meet my sister's eye for fear of the same; for the rush of desire in me: to kill him. Right here. Right now. I hold my breath. My vision dims and the room begins to disappear around me.

Until Mr Thompson dashes into it, coat tails flapping: 'Don't stop the music now!' Bounding through the hubbub, bounding through my rage, for the piano. 'Excuse me, miss, whatever you are,' he shoos off Dulcie, and seats himself with a cracking of knuckles. 'Let's sing! Let's sing until three!' He appears considerably more intoxicated than he was when we left the men to themselves; he is bashing at the keys and yawping discordantly: 'Ooooooooh! Do you like bananas, ladies, because my banana likes you. It's fat and sweet and succulent, so I've been told, and nicely bent.'

'Oh my Lord!' Mrs Virginia Dunning's shriek is almost as lewd as the song.

A mortified Mr Wilberry has his head in his hands, while everyone else has begun clapping theirs in time to the galloping music hall tune, whether they've caught the fruity innuendo in the lyric or not.

'It's Queensland's best, you won't regret this taste of sunshine once it's et!'

Gret's caught the gist and, hands clasped over her mouth, she's shaking with laughter at the filth and uproar both. But I cannot find my own fun in this.

I turn to Uncle Alec now instead. Numb. Beyond exhaustion.

He looks back at me with vacant, unseeing eyes. His smile is tight. A pinched smile. I once overheard Buckley refer to it in conversation with the ice man as *tighter than a cat's craphole*. That's precisely the type of smile it is and Uncle Alec holds it until he can bear it no longer. Thunder stolen by the clown, bested yet again.

He claps his hands against the gathering rhythm, shouting over it: 'Enough song, my friends! Enough! Come! Come out to the verandah. It is time for the fireworks display!'

A full six minutes early, too. *Tick. Tick.* Move along, everyone. We are so very nearly done with this evening's farce. *Tick. Tick.*

Mr Thompson smashes down a final dis-chord: 'Ba-ba-ba-ba-ba banana booooom!'

FIREWORKS

You must have chaos in you to give birth to a dancing star.

Thus Spake Zarathustra

BEN

'God save the Queen!'

The first of the rockets roars up and it is red. A red bloom exploding across the night, a shower of red stars.

There's your everlasting, dear son. See, it is here.

Her voice is so distinct this time, when I turn around I expect to see her. But she is not there. Of course she's not. And I'm a bit drunk myself. Quite a bit drunk. I should not have taken that second port but I couldn't stop myself – if I'd wanted to be trapped in a room full of self-important bastards outdoing each other for sanctimonious greed and bigotry, I'd never have left Queensland.

'Happy New Year!'

'Here's to 1901!'

'To the twentieth century!'

'God save old fat ladies hanging on!' Shut up, Cos.

Another whistle, another bang, and a bright lime chrysanthemum bursts out of the black above a bunch of whistling Catherine wheels, spinning out gold sparks. I laugh up into the night.

'Good show, hm?' Alec Howell directs my attention rather than asks me, then under all the spellbound *ohhing* and *ahhing* of his party he grips my left wrist and I bend to hear him direct me further: 'You will not encourage my nieces to undertake this journey to the Hill, I hope.'

I will not? There is no greater guarantee that I will disregard such a *hope*. Just who does this fellow think he is, telling me what

I might or might not do? With some West Country farmboy accent slipping further around his own one-port-too-many, he is no better of mine; he is not even a peer. He is an odious little turd, actually. I tell him: 'You need not be concerned, sir. Cosmo and I are far more reliable than we appear. I'm very much looking forward to seeing this fabled place of Hill End. Unexpected diversions can lead to the best discoveries, I've always found. An old gold rush town, isn't it? Tending more to ghosts these days? No?'

His eyes narrow right down to a squint and his grip tightens for a moment, as though he will insist, but then he lets it go again, silently. Still staring for a moment longer as though promising consequences. I laugh again: what consequences could this man promise? He is so very little, in all ways.

'Oh! Whoa wee, look at that one!' The sister points up at the next rocket, a huge burst of silver. A little childlike she might be, I suppose, a little reticent, but no more than I am. Waste of an education, the little turd said. Who would say that of any child? Even Pater insists that the children of the blacks out at Eleonora be schooled, under the lash as God intended, keeping his flock of stockmen faithful. But to say this of such a young woman, any young woman, when she is so talented – quite obviously. Cos will frame her menu card, too, I have no doubt; after intense consultation with Kevin the Curator, he will hang it somewhere in the studio. Greta Jones's watercolour fireworks will be kept and admired forever at the Swamp.

I look back at Howell now and down at him. 'You like to pick on girls, do you?' The question spills from me, but he is turning away. Don't think he heard.

Which is just as well. I should get myself and Cos out of here before either one of us opens our mouths again. Where is Cos now? I look up the verandah and find him: shirt front hanging out, champagne swaying, harassing that magistrate, Wardell. Hopefully belching in his ear. Over the port, that paragon of justice declared he was all for striking miners as they keep his conviction rate looking healthy in the eyes of the Attorney-General, before thanking Howell for arranging the latest round of quiet venereal checks for all the local prostitutes. *Good, clean town, this is*, he declared.

I yawn as another rocket whistles upwards, and then another: bang, bang, bloom, bloom, orange and then blue, and then Cos falls backwards off the verandah and into the agapanthus below. Absolutely arseless. It's time to go – immediately.

But I am yet to ask the girl what time she wishes us to return in the morning. I am yet to speak to her again at all. Why did I drink so much? I do not need further handicapping. Berylda. Where is she? There, at the opposite end of the verandah, outside the pool of light coming through the doors of the rear parlour; she stands apart from the rest of the party. She is looking up, as though at some point beyond the fireworks, beyond all this shallow frivolity, and she is indescribably beautiful against the night, her nose, her lips, her chin, a cameo in ivory on onyx; and impossibly serene with all the noise going on here, the explosions, the chattering, the incessant barking of the dog. Perhaps she won't notice I'm drunk, or care. That I am apparently now approaching her with the words: 'Er ... Miss Jones. What time should we ... Ah – and horses? Tomorrow, should we ...?'

'What?' The frown is as swift as her ability to interpret drunk imbecile: 'Oh. Yes – dawn. Be here just before dawn, please. And you may take our horses if you wish. They're in need of a decent outing themselves, anyway.' And the furrow deepens sceptically: 'You do ride, don't you?'

'Ride? Horses. Yes. Of course.'

'Good. There is no room for you in the buggy. All style and no substance, I'm afraid – ostentatiously small vehicle, just a one-horse.'

'No room in the buggy. Yes, good.' I am hers to direct as she wills; I will pull her buggy myself if she should ask me to. 'Dawn then. Just before.'

'Yes. Dawn then. Just before.' She mocks me with the trace of a smirk as she returns her attention to the night sky.

Mama's laughter trailing through it like the fading tendrils of these fire flowers above us: *Here is the study you will never return from, my dear wandering bear.*

Not an altogether attractive prospect, Mama. The girl is not interested in me. No girl has ever been interested in me, and why should this one be? Berylda Jones wishes us to come to Hill End with her and her sister as chaperones – that says enough right there, doesn't it? And as reward I might have three days in her company, in the midst of stupefying beauty; three days exploring the Macquarie and the Turon, the gorge there, which I have never seen but have certainly heard of: steeply clad with river gum and river oak, understoreys of grevillea, banksia, all in full summer inflorescence – and that rare alpine callistemon found there. When did I read that paper on it? Was it last year or the year before? I don't know what day of the week it is, never mind what I read when.

Cos looms up out of the dark of the yard. What's he been doing out there? Pissing into the vegetable beds, possibly. We must leave before the girl changes her mind about us, too. But before I can find an appropriate load of bumbling stupid to farewell her with, Cos has launched himself back up the verandah steps and is shaking me by the shoulder. 'I believe my work here is done, Wilby. And I'm tired now.' He yawns, a bellowing moan into the sudden quiet; the fireworks display is finished, too.

Thank you for small mercies, my friend. I turn to the girl; I say: 'Early start – yes, we should go. Hm.'

But I'm not sure she has heard me. She has closed her eyes, her face again upturned to the sky. She is absorbed in some meditation, somewhere else, out in the universe, not here, and I am interrupted by another: 'I say, we can motor you boys down the hill, if you like.' It's that Mrs Dunning, wanting five more minutes of Cos as much as this opportunity to show off the new wagon – 192 pounds it cost, so she's said at the table, twice.

'What, woman? We're not leaving so soon,' the industrialist husband corrects his wife, the blubbery neck shaking with it. He's still stung by Cos's Fat Man insults, rather kick him down the hill than drive him.

So would Howell; his hand is quickly outthrust to see the back of us: 'Good of you to come this evening, Mr Wilberry, Mr Thompson. A most colourful addition to, er, a most colourful event.' He chuckles, fancying himself a wit as well as master of this small and eminently forgettable universe. As I shake his hand with some sort of 'thank you' in response, I have the sensation of touching a slug. I do not wish to see this man again. I hope not to encounter him in the morning.

'Goodnight, Mr Wilberry.' The girl is suddenly here again, taking my hand. Berylda. Her small perfect hand in my great oaf's one. Again. How does this occur? She presses my outer knuckle and smiles *that* smile at me: 'Till tomorrow. Dawn then. Just before.'

The smile that drives right into me, seeing me. Could it be? Could she find something in me? Something beyond some pleasure at paralysing my mind altogether by taking my hand? She is dropping it now. Unreadable, exquisitely so. Turning away again …

I suppose I bid them all goodnight as we leave. Cos leans into me as we amble back round to the front path, and something touches my left hand through the dark as we reach the gate – something wet. The dog. The staghound, Prince. 'Where did you come from, boy?' I'm sure someone said the dog was chained. Well, he's placid enough now, anyway. I pat his head: 'Good night, Prince.' I hear him pant; his tail wags against my thigh but he doesn't attempt to follow us out of the gate.

'God's hairy eyeballs, Wilb, that was bloody terrible,' Cos says as soon as we're on the descent to the road; tripping into me over tussocks, belching into my ear: 'And that was mutton, too. The things I do for you. The things I do. And now we're changing course from Manildra, wherever that devil of a hole in the ground might be, for Hill End. Hill *End* – doesn't the name tell you something? End of the earth, Wilby, end of the earth it can only be in this place.' As though the place by the same name in Brisbane is famous for anything but flooding and, at three miles from Woolloongabba, being the western boundary of all his tolerance.

'You can go back to Swamp paradise whenever you wish,' I remind him. 'And I mean it. I'm all right now. Really. Drunk, quite successfully drunk, but in fair condition. You don't need to look after me any more, such as your looking after me ever is.' And it's true, I think; something's shifted. Mama is gone, but she is here. And it's all right. Nothing I can do about it anyway; it is what it is. 'Thank you, old matey of mine, thank you for keeping me company,' I tell him. 'But not for the banana song.'

'You loved it.' He belts a shoulder into me.

'No, I didn't – honestly.' I laugh. 'But really, all the embarrassments you've ever caused me notwithstanding, go home to Susan. Don't worry about me from here. You don't want to come rambling with me – and you never did. You don't want to come trail-riding to the End of the Earth with me now. Your effort on my behalf thus far has been valiant – well done. Epic.'

'Epic.' He grunts. 'Might as well see it through to its grisly end. I'm in no burning hurry to get home to Susan.'

'Why? Do you have trouble in paradise?' I ask him, surprised, and not only because he's been moaning so loud and often about being away. Susan and he are made for each other, in the way that flotsam and jetsam go together, and I realise I haven't much asked him about himself these past three weeks; too preoccupied, obsessing about daisies and being off my head with grief.

'Huh,' he grunts. 'She's more interested in the babies than she is in me. She doesn't care about me.'

'Aw, Cossie,' I mimic Susan, and the tender smile that is always in her voice, for what is really her third child, in Cos. He's jealous of the twins, I imagine, of the time they take up, taking Susan away from him. I see his last portrait of her in my mind now as we walk, full of worship: her coffee-coloured breasts, her full lips, and those huge dark eyes that come from another world – literally. She wandered into Cos's life looking for work, two years ago, scared that the Protection Act for the blacks would see her picked up off the street and shoved onto a mission. She's not that black, she has no tribe. She has no story, as she calls it. Just something in her past that has made her content to hitch up with a mess like Cos. There'd be plenty of story to Susan, I'd say. Susan Turner from Caboolture. I look at Cos, shambling along beside me, falling down. She was looking for a job: she found one in him. And she cares for him absolutely, despite his many faults. I am jealous of what they have, I suppose, even if the children don't bear Cos's name. But then I've never really known what I might want in that regard. Always been too shut up in myself, maybe too scared to embark on that sort of exploration. Too certain of failure.

Our way is lit by bonfires now, all the way into the town, blazing on every corner, drunks sing and stagger down the main street, the last straggling crackers let off in soggy, halfhearted afterthoughts behind a row of terraced shops promising a city and only delivering: 'Oi Bluey, you got another bottle at home, ain't ya?' We could just as well be somewhere in Brisbane right now. Anywhere in Australia. But we are in Bathurst.

And I have just met a girl called Berylda. I look behind me and see the half-moon is sinking behind the hills. Silver-frosted hills. What am I chasing after now? I'm not sure it's the sort of joyful thing Mama had in mind.

I ask Cos: 'What do you think of the girl, really? What do you think of Berylda?'

'She's pretty,' he says. He stops, unbuttons his fly to relieve himself again on the step of some shop: *BLUNT'S WATCHMAKER & JEWELLER*. 'Very pretty. Pretty. Tiny. Freak.'

'Freak? She's – what did you say?'

'What did I say?' He is a lot further schnigged towards oblivion than I am: cross-eyed with it. 'I'm sure I have no idea.'

'And me probably less.' I keep on towards the pub, the quicker to be asleep, the quicker for it to be morning. To see her again.

Cos laughs after me: 'I say, but that uncle doctor was mad enough to flog a cat, wasn't he? Reckon that's what he's up to now? Got all his little kitty cats in a pretty little line.' Cos shouts up the street: '*Step up now, kitties, step up and take your flogging! Roll up, roll up, get your floggings here!*'

'Happy New Year, gentlemen.' A constable nods, plodding wearily past, truncheon clasped at his back. 'Must be time for nighty-night bedtime, ay?'

Must be.

BERYLDA

Gret is wiping tears from her eyes as I climb in under the covers beside her, the best tears of laughter, fuzzy-brained, as I am, in some state above and beyond fatigue; past fear. Hysterical: 'Poor Mr Wilberry. He very nearly didn't leave here alive, did he!' Gret can very nearly not speak, recalling the tomato canapé debacle.

I lie beside her and tremble helplessly with it too. 'Poor Mr Wilberry indeed. What has he got himself into with us?'

'Trouble!' Greta squeaks. 'I can't believe you ...' She can't get the words out but I know what she means. She can't believe the poor man nearly choked; she can't believe I then practically demanded he escort us to the Hill. She can't believe I challenged Uncle Alec as I did.

I can't believe it, either. It's half-past one. God, but I don't know how I will sleep I am so far gone and fidgety inside. What a night. I thought the Dunnings would never leave, J.C. Bullfrog very nearly putting us into a standing coma on the verandah with all his overpickled blabbering about the *hard line we liberals must take with conservative values if we're going to win this thing.* Blurb, blurb, blurb. I tremble and snort some more at that: liberal conservatism, modern conservatism – isn't it all oxymoronic blabbering? If it wasn't so serious. So dreadful.

'And Mr Thompson.' Greta gets that far before squeaking and weeping again. 'Oh Mr Thompson.'

'Isn't he the worst?'

'No! He's the best!'

'You're only saying that because he flattered you,' I tease her.

'I am not. He's wonderful.'

'What if he turns out to be as depraved as he is outrageous?' I tease her again.

'He's not depraved.' Greta reaches for my hand to assure me, all silly giggling suddenly stopped. She stops my heart: for she knows what depravity is, even if she won't say what has happened to her. She squeezes my hand, and now she snuggles towards me and whispers: 'Thank you.'

'What for?' Leaving you to suffer alone as I do, all the long weeks I am in Sydney? I'm so sorry, Gret, for all you have endured.

'For our little trip away.' She pokes me in the centre of my shoulder: 'Thank you, Ryl. We're going to have a lovely time, I know it. Do you remember, when we went there before, and I wrecked my gloves with chocolate ice cream at that fair? Mother was so cross with me.'

'Hm.' We smile together at the memory, at the streaks of sweet sticky mud ruining new ivory silk. Careless. We smile together that Mother was never cross. I don't remember ever being truly scolded for anything, except for straying beyond the fence at Echo Point, too near the cliff edge.

Greta takes a strand of hair escaped from my plait and curls it back around my ear. 'Mother and Libby would have liked Mr Wilberry. He's a prince, a real one – that's why Prince likes him. And that's how I know Mr Thompson is a good sort of fellow, too. Mr Wilberry wouldn't have any friends about him he didn't really like.'

'That's inarguably true of Prince.' I grin and we dissolve into spluttering gusts of hilarity again. Oh how our Prince bailed up Reverend Liversidge just as Mr Wilberry and Mr Thompson left, went straight for the clergyman, springing up onto the verandah out of the blackness, nearly frightening the man out of his skin before Buckley caught him by the collar, just in the nick of time. Don't know how he got off the chain; perhaps Buckley slipped it accidentally when he was locking up after the fireworks. 'Our trusty hound saves his best for hypocrites, doesn't he?'

'The look on Reverend Liversidge's face ...'

'Berylda.' Uncle Alec wraps on the bedroom door, *bang bang bang*. 'Return to your room – now.'

Gret stiffens beside me and I call back: 'No. I am sleeping here tonight.'

'You will return to your room now.'

I dare: 'I will not leave my sister tonight.' *You will not touch my sister again.*

The door flies open. Alec Howell's face is made of stone. He says nothing. He drags me off the bed by my plait and onto the floor before I can take a breath. My scalp screams.

'No!' I try to scream with my voice but the sound that comes from me is too small. It is trapped inside this dream. It cannot reach Buckley in his room at the rear of the stables; it cannot reach Mary and Lucy in the cottage beyond. But still I scream and scream.

Alec Howell drags me across the floor by my hair to the door that adjoins my room with Gret's.

'You will never touch my sister again!' I wail with everything I have, my bare feet slipping on the boards, slipping on the edge of my nightdress as I try to stop him from dragging me.

Prince yowls outside; he cries for all that I can't.

Alec Howell barks into me: 'I decide what I do. You will do as you are told.'

'No!' I grab at the door frame and as I do I see Greta watching, silent in her terror and her pain, her face removed of all expression, as if collapsed, drained of life. I see the flowers on her night stand. Mr Wilberry's paper daisies, untidy featherheads shadowed large upon the wall. I whisper to them as if they might truly hear: 'Help us, please. Help us. Someone, please help us.'

Alec Howell kicks my hand from the door, pulls me up by the wrist and throws me into my room. Blue spurt of a match now as he lights the lamp on my table, then he slams the door closed behind him and stares at me. Steady. Cold. Dead-hearted.

He says: 'I have no need of Greta – not tonight.' As a matter of fact. *Not tonight?* How many nights do you need her? He says: 'Tonight I need you.'

And I don't believe he means he needs to thrash me. What does he mean then? What does he need from me? Oh – *this* is my punishment? He means to rape me too? Whatever it is, whatever he does, I am steel. Let me be colder and more dead-hearted than him. I will take his violence and I will show him nothing for it. No fear. No hurt. I will not cower or flinch. Whatever happens now, he cannot harm me more than he already does by terrorising my sister.

He continues to hold me in his stare. He can do whatever he wishes, and he will.

I hiss back at him: 'Well? What are you waiting for?'

He chuckles, brushes a piece of fluff from the lapel of his dressing-gown, and says, 'Hm. Right.' And now he smiles, and I gasp with the chill of it as he says: 'Berylda, you are capital.'

What? He is playing with me. His smile is one of such pleasure I am caught in its horror, caught suspended in anticipation of what is to come. What violence will it be? What will he do to me? How does it happen between a man and a woman? I have read the book, but I do not know. I am bracing, bracing, bracing.

He fondles the cord of his dressing-gown.

What?

He steps towards me. He brushes the side of my face with the back of his hand. And I immediately betray myself, recoiling under his touch. An almost gentle touch, I feel the scrub of his coarse hair against my cheek. I don't understand. He has bested me, I know this even now, but my mind is a leaf lost in a storm.

His right hand reaches around my neck, thumb caressing my throat, the tenderest threat: he can kill me if he likes. He leans towards me, his left hand at my back as he presses himself against me, closer and closer, his breath stale, rancid with wine, and he kisses my cheek, my ear, my neck. His beard flays my face; my whole body wails. Paralysed.

And then he stops. He releases me and smiles again. 'That's right,' he says. 'Good girl.'

'Good girl?' I hear myself ask him, my voice so far from me, so far from here. What cruelty is this? What does he do now?

He smiles, ever more pleased with himself. 'You mean you haven't guessed?'

149

What?

He chuckles again. 'Such a clever girl and yet so naïve. Of course you are the one I need, Berylda. You have always been the one I need. And now it's time these needs were met.'

'Do it then!' I snarl. 'Do it.'

'Patience.' He laughs. 'Marriage mustn't be entered into too hastily now, must it?'

'Marriage? What are you talking about?'

What?

What?

What?

'Our marriage. Yes, that's right,' he says mundanely, seriously – impossibly. 'I will announce the engagement when you are back in Sydney, give you a few weeks to come to terms with the idea. Put a smile on your sour little face, and you *will* put a smile on that face.'

'But you can't –' You are insane.

'Oh, but I can.' The wolf smile is a world of certainty, the reptile mind is made up, his words soft, slow and deliberate. 'There is no need to be so alarmed, Berylda. You will be permitted to begin your studies in Medicine – that's what you want, isn't it?'

'Yes, but –'

'Yes. Right.' He nods and rolls his right hand as if leading the dullest student. 'And when you do resume your studies, you will return from Sydney each Friday afternoon to be at Bellevue every weekend, such is your devotion to me, and to prepare for your wedding, which will be held at All Saints on the ninth of March; Liversidge will perform the ceremony – I'll speak with him about it next week. It is of the utmost importance, you see, that we do hurry things a little, as we must be married before the candidature for the party is decided. I want you with child preferably before these New South Wales elections are held, which I expect will be sometime mid-year. I must be seen to be more of a traditional family man; this is the element missing from my appeal to the public and to the party, I believe. After the child is born you may resume your studies once more. You will still receive your degree, of course – and this way I will be seen to be the modern family man as well, a supporter of women, women who will encourage their husbands to support me. You will be permitted to practise; you may even specialise, in either gynaecology or pharmacology; you may choose which, as you may choose rooms in town, on William Street or Durham Street. As you may choose to remain a good girl. Or not.'

He nods and gestures for me to answer him. For me to be pleased at this plan. I cannot even blink.

'You will see the sense, my dear.' He nods again, sure. 'I have considered this for some time, obviously, and now the time has come. Enjoy your frolic to the Hill, for it is the last you will be permitted. It is time for you to grow up and accept your responsibilities. When you return to Bathurst you will begin nightly congress with me. Indeed, you need not bother with your corset from now on, unless some strain upon your back might make you desire it. Optimally, I want you visibly gravid by election day.' He claps his hands and rubs them together; satisfied: 'Right. Understood?'

'Right,' I reply. I spit it through my teeth. 'Understood.'

He says at the door to the hall: 'Our children will be perfect, Berylda. I would like a minimum of four. Five would be ideal. It is all achievable and manageable – your sister will help raise the family, so that you may otherwise do as you wish in your … *career*.'

And I promise silently at his back: *I wish to see you dead.*

I will see him dead.

I will see him dead before this week is out.

My mind rages round and round and round this lead-sealed trap. My hand begins to throb where he kicked me. My shoulder hurts where he wrenched my arm.

I go to the window for air. I lean on the sill. I breathe. In. Out. It is moonless now, so black I cannot see a thing. No river, no hills. Nothing but black space.

And I am sure now.

Pharmacology? Be careful what you wish for.

I will find the perfect way. To end this.

He has left me no choice.

'Ryldy – Ryl, are you all right?' Gret is pressed against the door for me now.

'Yes, yes.' I rush past her, dash under the bedcovers. Cold, so cold; trembling.

'What did he do? What did he say?' she asks me through the dark, curling around me.

'Nothing of consequence,' I say to her. 'Just reading the riot act on my behaviour, laying down the law. You know what he's like. Don't worry about it.'

Because I will kill Alec Howell, and my darling sister will never know a thing about it. No one will.

THE TRACK

Man is a rope, tied between beast and superman—
a rope over an abyss.

Thus Spake Zarathustra

BEN

'Wilber, steady on – your legs are longer than mine.' Cos is puffing along the road, where the milkman's just deposited us, on his run home, a little way past the hospital – no cabs this hour on New Year's Day. I don't know why he's insisted on coming, but insist he has: *You can't go running off after a girl without witness – who would ever believe you?* Reaching for his tobacco before he was even awake. *And someone's got to make sure you don't hurt yourself in the pursuit.*

'It's not a matter of leg length,' I say, already leaving him behind. 'It's that pipe you have to have before getting out of bed.' Not to mention that generous gut he's been cultivating the past few years.

The sun is about to rise over the hills; the sky is bronzing with it. And it is cloudless, promising good weather today. I begin to run, as though she might not wait for me. My head pounds with last night's wine and worry at displeasing her. Displeasing her? I dreamed of her frown, all night long, falling into her frown, falling into a field of nettles. But still I'm running, for her.

Almost at the gate, just past the drive, I see the verandah is lit up by the lamp at the door, cutting out the iron lace below the roof in silhouette. I see her now, Berylda Jones: pacing round from the western side of the house, that sparrow-swift stride both dainty and belting the boards. I can hear her footsteps from here, a good thirty yards away, and the contradiction makes me smile, quite stupidly.

Until I see him, following. Howell. They are in silhouette too, black shapes in the yellow kerosene light. He is pointing at her back, beseeching, insisting, urgent words spat through clenched teeth, trying not to shout; something that sounds like 'stop it'. She keeps striding across the front of the house. He catches up to her, grabs her by the wrist; I feel the pinch at my own from last night, the slug trail it left, just as the dog barks and bounds up the front steps. Howell lets her go then, with a dismissive wave she does not see. He disappears inside the house with angry slamming of the door, and a strange rush of desire comes to me, to grab him in return, to break his fingers, crush him.

I jump the fence, like Galahad storming the white pickets, and put a giant boot into the flowerbed. *Ranunculus asiaticus*, white and double-bloomed, now scattered across the lawn, and the dog bounds for me, paws on my shoulders, almost pulling me to the ground with the forward momentum.

'Is that you, Mr Wilberry?'

Who else might it be? I look up, following the audible frown to the corner of the verandah; the movement of her skirt there.

She is already turning away: 'Come straight around to the stables, please.'

The dog gives me a grunt and nudges my hand with his snout: *Come on.*

I come on. 'Good morning, Miss Jones,' and it's only a few paces to catch up to her.

'It is.' She turns her head to glance at me, just as the sun flares above the ranges, and I see her more clearly now, striding into the day. I see the blush of her cheek as she turns away again. Energetic and confident, with her straw boater and that shortened style of skirt that shows her boots, she could be captain of the ladies tennis team. Pale grey skirt and black boots, charging across the crest of this hill. I am tied to the black band at her waist as she goes, somehow remaining ahead of me, though my stride must be twice hers. I imagine she would beat me at a game of tennis, soundly. And yet she is so small. *Petite is always the better adjective, Ben,* Mama would correct me whenever I referred to her as small. And I am smiling stupidly again.

'How capable are you on horseback?' She glances back at me once more. Was that a smile? Too quick to see.

'What?' What did she ask me? I am suddenly caught up again in wonder at her. Wonder what sports clubs she might actually belong to at Sydney, at the university. Strike me, again and again, she's a medical student, or about to be. I wonder if she's at all interested in botany, from a medicinal point of view; she was discussing something about chemistry with that Dr Weston last night, wasn't she? Not that I have ever been taken much by the chemical nature of things myself, but – that could be something to talk about with her today, couldn't it? A point of interest? What would I know? I've never spoken to a female university student before, except to say 'excuse me' in a corridor; they don't seem to enrol in botany past first year at Melbourne. At Adelaide there are loads of girls, but Melbourne, the sky would fall in if women began –

'Mr Wilberry?' Her tone is impatient. 'I said, do you ride well?'

Do I ride well? 'Yes, I suppose so,' I reply, although riding is one thing I can safely say I do well enough. Not that I have had a decent ride since – that last with Mama, out at Jericho, out to the billabongs, at the edge of Eleonora. Last June. Her absence catches me again, and I can't think. For a moment I can only see my mother belting up the trail ahead of me, her straw-coloured hair falling down her back. She was too young to die; too young to be gone. And I am small again; alone with Pater for some forgotten reason, and he's throwing me on the back of that massive bay stallion we had once, to get to church: *You'll keep with me, son, or you'll go to hell.*

'Good,' the girl says, pulling me back from all that. 'You can take Caesar then – he's a little headstrong and more than keen to be out.' She glances behind her yet again, and again only for a second, not long enough for me to see her face at all before she asks: 'Where's your friend? Mr Thompson, is he not joining us? Sore head, has he?'

'Yes. No. Yes – ah. He's on his way.' The gate creaks; it's him, shambling in up the path now.

'He can have Jupiter.'

'Jupiter? He doesn't sound much less headstrong,' I say, thinking of Cos, who is not much of a horseman, not by any measure.

But she laughs, that soaring chime of a laugh. Should I suppose she is laughing at my joke? I don't know, it wasn't much of a joke, but she looks at me now, directly, under an arched eyebrow. 'Our dear Uncle Alec – he does so love a tyrant. Loves nothing more than to keep these ones trapped in the top paddock too. They're mostly just for show, poor things.'

I have no trouble believing her; everything about Alec Howell seems false. But I don't answer her. The old workman is leading a pair of stallions from the stables. Alec Howell is fond of a good show, there is no doubt. These horses are nothing less than majestic. Arabians, one black, one roan. Hardly poor things.

'Which one is Caesar?' I ask her.

'The black one. My sister and I call him Jack, though. We had a stallion very like him once … some time ago.'

I laugh, for he is the one I would pick if I could choose. 'Jack. He's beautiful.'

'Isn't he just. And Jupiter is Rebel, to us – he's a little silly sometimes, something of a show-off himself. But we won't leave Uncle Alec entirely steedless – he'll have Neddy, our doddery old workhorse, to ride into town with.' She laughs again: into me. As though she is seeing me, recognising me only now. Her blue eyes are the sky awakening in this soft golden sunrise light. Beautiful is not the adjective, not the right adjective at all. 'Buckley – Buckley,' she says, turning away from me again, 'Jack is for Mr Wilberry, please.'

I take the reins from the old man and place my right hand on the top of the stallion's shoulder as he comes round to me. He seems steady enough as I look into his great dark eye, steadier than me as I sense Miss Jones touch the crook of my elbow, only for a second, but she is so close I catch the breath of her perfume, that fragrance of rosemary and something else; a glimpse of a bruise across the back of her hand that charges into me with the pain of whatever accident caused it.

'Test him,' she says. 'Make your adjustments, please, and then we'll be off.' She is in a hurry to be away, that is all her touch implies; her eyes imply it too – *come on* – and I will not waste time about it. My hand is reaching for the pommel already as she says: 'My sister and I will travel in the buggy with Buckley. You and

Mr Thompson will travel ahead – north over the bridge first, then straight on to Duramana for the Track – from there, you'll need to keep well ahead, see that the road is passable as we go.'

'Yes. Passable,' I manage to reply.

I will see that the road is passable. I will mend the road should it need mending; I will be the road, for Berylda Jones.

BERYLDA

'Good.' I watch Mr Wilberry's handling of Jack: quickly astride and taking him around the yard, quite obviously capable. 'Good.'

He is here. Mr Wilberry is here. I doubted a thousand times through the night that he would come; feared that my rudeness, my capriciousness at dinner would give him second thoughts. But he is here, and Alec Howell cannot now stop us from leaving – he would not dare. Mr Wilberry is here, and we will be on our way in a moment. Please. And I will not let go of my half of the wishbone, clutched inside my pocket, until we are out of the gates. It is only the short half, my half, the losing half, but I am clutching it so tightly it is digging into the flesh of my palm, the tiny but immutable shape of my resolve. Inside this shock that returns and returns to me, echoing through every cell that amounts to the material of me, making less and less sense each time.

Marry Alec Howell? Incredulity marries horror, searing up my spine and through to the ends of my hair. How can he think this will be plausible, to anyone, in this town or elsewhere? He is forty-two years old. I am not quite twenty. Why would I ever accept him? Much less want him? My departed aunt's husband. That is disgusting enough. Never mind that this is the same hideous animal who rapes my sister. This is delusion. Possibly a psychosis, if that's the right term for it. He could have any other woman; he could have Dulcie Wardell and all her purebred Caucasian wealth, connections, twenty years of unfettered childbearing in a snap of his fingers; her mother would throw her at him with the chequebook. Why does he want me? My skin crawls at the question. And my shoulder aches again from where he pulled me by the arm just now, chasing me halfway round the verandah, demanding that I kiss him as a token of my pledge to accept him. *You will stop this resistance, Berylda*, he warned, hissing the words at me from some realm beyond madness. *You will not continue this coldness to me, this wilfullness, you ungrateful little slut – stop it, stop it now.* Only leaving me be as Mr Wilberry arrived and Prince started carrying on – poor hound who will no doubt get a hiding on my account sometime today, because of my resistance.

Stop it. I will stop it. I will stop you, Alec Howell. There are no questions any more. I will simply find the way.

'Ryldy, I've just realised I forgot the jam.' Gret emerges from the stables, where she's been organising all of our baskets and boxes into the buggy. 'I'll go back in and ask Mary –'

'No. Don't worry about it, don't bother Mary – she's in full breakfast flurry now,' I almost bark at my sister. I don't want her to go back inside the house, as if he might hold her there until I kiss him, until I sign the marriage certificate, until I give him his child. 'We'll get some jam along the road.'

So blithe and twittery I sound, or at least I hope I do, but I cannot recall if there is a shop on the road before the Turon crossing at all. My mind is tattered and frayed, too fraught to remember. Will anything even be open on this New Year's Federation Day? How far is it to the Hill precisely? Forty miles? I know this answer and I can't think of what it is. Hysteria creeps along the back of my neck. Will our Sally be able to pull the buggy far enough and fast enough to get us away?

'Aye,' Buckley says, with that soothing, scouring growl of his. 'We'll call in on the Kings at Duramana, misses. Mrs King – she'll have some jam and she'll open a window for me, no matter the day.' Yes. Of course. The Kings live along the way, their little teashop a famous last outpost of civilisation before the Track; I know this, of course I do. And our Buckley won't take us anywhere but safely; he's packed the tent and more water cans than we could ever need, just in case; and he can sense my urgency to be away, even if he can't know the truth of why.

'Oh look, Mr Thompson's arrived.' Gret waves over my shoulder now. 'Good morning – good day to you!' She smiles into the sun; her lovely face is the sun.

But I am past pleasantries as I turn to Mr Thompson. 'You'd better make yourself comfortable in the saddle,' I instruct him abruptly. 'It'll be a long day in it.'

'Good morning to you too, Miss Jones.' He is out of breath from walking up the yard, but ever equipped with sarcasm. 'If I fail, will you have me shot at dawn?' Saluting me and winking at Gret: 'Your sister always such an awful sergeant major?'

'Oh Mr Thompson, are you always so awful?' she bats it back to him merrily.

On any other morning I would relish her brightness, to see her so gay and carefree, but I am too far past the pretence of laughing along at anything now. I look over my shoulder, back towards the house, expecting Uncle Alec to appear with the hunting rifle. No evil and no desperation seems beyond him; I am frightened as I have never been. The terror threatens to overwhelm me: slicing through the ligament strings that hold my body upright. My knees quiver; my bones are turning to aspic. If we don't leave now, this minute, I shan't be able to run. He will catch me. And I will kill myself and my sister with me before he does.

'If we're to make the most of the day, we must leave at once.' I attempt to sound cheerily keen, but my voice is so shrill it pierces my own eardrums. 'Hurry up, Greta, in the buggy – without delay!'

BEN

'God's nuts, Ben – you'll pay for any damage.'
He's sincere. It's been some time since he last referred to me by my given name. And I'm sincere too: 'You didn't have to come, you really didn't.'

'Oh yes, I did.' He glares at me, as his arse thuds into the saddle again. Predictably, he is not fancying this Rebel, this roan stallion, not that the horse is playing up. Cos is finding the cadence of the trot impossible to negotiate, can't find the beat of the rise or bring the horse to amble. Berylda Jones turns in the buggy ahead now, and she waves for us to overtake, giving me a dilemma: I am as reluctant to leave this view of her as I am to torture Cos further. One hand on her hat, the other in the air and her frown compelling me into the golden blue dawn, she is a petite but perfectly formed Aurora in her chariot.

'Come round!' she shouts, half-standing up out of the rear seat. 'Come round!' she urges again, leaning out over the back rail of the carriage as though our lives might depend upon it. What is this hurry? This constant charging, charging, charging of Berylda Jones? In her little chariot, more black pumpkin than buggy. Will we be turned into field mice if we're not out the gate before the sun is fully over the hills? 'Come round!'

I shout across to Cos: 'Bring him to canter and then ease him back a little bit.'

Cos shouts back: 'You bring him to canter if it's that easy.'

KIM KELLY

All right, I'll try. I ride out ahead, to encourage the roan, and he complies now, not too surprisingly, eager for the speed, eager for the downhill rush. He stays with me and we pass the buggy to the left, and as we pull in front along the drive this Rebel finally settles into the four-beat with my Jack. 'Well done.' I smile at Cos. He glares at me again: I shall pay regardless. I look behind us for her again as we meet the road, but she is bending now behind the old man Buckley, driving from the front seat. What is she doing? Perhaps tying a bootlace. The sister bends too, looking down at whatever it is they are doing, and as the buggy veers slightly with the camber of the hill, the crowns of their straw hats are twin discs of *Helichrysum bracteatum*. Golden everlastings opening to the golden blue day, just for a second, before the red mane of their mare flies across them with the winding of the road. The crest of Bellevue is an arc above us, against this dawn, the plump little maid from the house running now along it to close the yard gates behind us, the puff of her white cap the only cloud.

'Ben! Jesus, Wilber, look out – the bridge!'

I see it, and the great pothole crumbling into the drainage ditch this side of it. Just as Jack takes it, sure hooves stamping onto the timbers, needing no direction from me. This is a magnificent horse. So is Rebel, instinctively giving us room over the narrow span, dropping back. They travel well together, this pair.

I look over to Cos, half a length behind, and I can't help chiacking: 'Gee up, old matey!' A little bit of payback for all his champion whingeing.

He is still gripping the reins, white knuckled. 'Bloody mad,' he mutters, oblivious to the Macquarie scattering the day's first diamonds at his back.

If this is madness I'm happy to be mad. To be happy: a slightly foreign sensation of late ... of quite some time, I suppose. Years. And now it's getting away with me. *Yes*, Mama laughs along the wind, her old hat flying off behind her as we race over Eleonora's fenceless ochre plain. *This is happy, son, and so you should be.* Happy as a child in a puddle of pink mud, dreaming up through the branches of the bimble box gums around the billabongs. I was joyful then; I am joyful now.

164

The road ahead is the colour of fleece and the river in this place is overflowing with summer, the bank blushed with dog roses spilling through a veil of olive box leaf wattle, the water's edge thick with pin rushes, thick with life – midges and dragonflies, frogs and trout. Who wouldn't be joyful?

'You bastard, Wilberry!' Cos's complaint punches out of his lungs against the pounding of hooves. 'Slow down!'

And I can only laugh at him again: 'Go back to the pub! Go on!'

But I slow us down, back to a walk. We have pulled ahead too fast, it seems: we've lost sight of the buggy. But as the road leaves the river again, bending north across the flood plain, we soon see them coming on behind, and then not as the road bends west, and then north once more. I look out to the basalt-topped slopes that ring this wide valley like a great mounded barricade of mineral wealth: millions in it, as they say in San Francisco. A hamlet of rather more humble weatherboard homesteads and tin sheds is settled here along the flats, though, a dairy yard, a sheep run, another dairy, and then a paddock turned over to goats, no doubt to rid it of burrs, which the goats will only assist in spreading further. I hear myself laugh again now as a trio of kids, as white as the paddock is green, chase us along the fence line at the verge. Fearless. How can it be possible that they do not know their own happiness? Impossible as goats ridding paddocks of burrs.

Beyond the next bend the road stretches out as far as forever, cutting across a sea of pleasantly undulating pastoral idyll. Summer rains have been kind here: this sea is looking pretty green. But if I didn't know it would all lead into forest and soon, I would be disappointed. Dense wilderness lies patiently just at the backs of these blocks: I can see it; taste it in the air.

'Bloody hell.' Cos has had more than enough of it already and we're only two miles gone, if that. 'How long is it to the End of the Earth?'

I look past him to the buggy coming on behind us, a little above us on the swell of an easy rise. The girls' hats swaying in this cool morning breeze might be the only two daisies left to discover in the entire world, and I tell him: 'I don't care.'

BERYLDA

'Is it passing, Ryl?' Greta is still holding my hand, stroking the backs of my fingers with her thumb as we lurch about in the rear of the buggy.

'Yes.' I nod, although it has not quite passed: this urge to vomit, which has had me doubled over in the effort to suppress it since we set off. It is only the relief at being gone, I'm sure: surges of nausea rushing in over surges of panic. My head is still bowed, my eyes fixed upon the filigree of Gret's bracelet, our grandmother's bracelet, its pattern of minuscule fans slipping about before my eyes like snakeskin, but it is passing. I am calming. I can hear my breath, loud in the cave I have made of my chest, hear it above the churn of wheel on road. Listen to it, and insist that it slow, until it is slowing, at last, and I am returning to the present once more.

I look up, and find myself inside the pleat at the back of Buckley's waistcoat, trace it up to his leathery neck, to his Sunday best felt hat. Our Buckley: this sight of him is comforting to me; this firm shape of goodness travelling with us, gravel voice soothing Sal: 'Ten miles for a rest, girl, there girl.' He would protect us, truly, if anyone ever could. As I cool my senses around him now, I see in my mind his hand reaching for me, when I slipped on the ice on the back steps, last winter; his eyes alarmed, that I might fall, before he caught me by the elbow, and he laughed then, with me. A reflex of goodness – one that left a thumbprint on the inside of my arm. A kind bruise, a sparing bruise.

'Better?' Gret squeezes my hand and the injury there shoots slivers of glass through my veins, into my heart: restoring hatred with my composure. I see the toe of Alec Howell's slipper smash into the back of my hand, over and over. Why did you kick me? Why do you do these things? Why?

'What do you think it is, Ryl?' my sister is asking me again, my sister who knows far worse violence than this. 'Do you think it was something we ate? You were a fidgety-bug in bed all night long.'

'Was I?' I pretend ignorance, shake it off with all other questions and assure her: 'You're probably right, probably something I ate. But it's nothing now. I'm sure it's gone.'

'Hm, I hope so,' Gret replies. 'I didn't feel so well when I woke, either. I wasn't going to say anything to you about it, but when I went to wash I really felt quite queasy.'

'You did?' I look at her. 'Were you sick at all?'

'No.' She pulls a face, scrunching her nose, a grimace over a smile. 'Too desperate not to be, I think – I wasn't going to miss out on getting away today by being ill, was I? But I'm not sure that lamb was the best.'

'Maybe,' I say but I'm not so sure her queasiness has anything to do with bad meat. It might just as likely be *emesis gravidarum*, mightn't it? Morning sickness, find it in the fine print on a bottle of Lawford's Fluid Magnesia – and that's a sign of pregnancy, isn't it?

I ask her: 'Are you still tender, inside?'

'Only a bit – it's nothing. Bloated.' She puffs out her cheeks. 'When whatsit arrives, I'll be fine.'

I search her eyes again for any understanding that she might have conceived a child, but she only smiles and says: 'Stop worrying about me.'

How can I? And how could she know about the workings of her body in this respect? I doubt Mother would have taught her anything much; it's not a conversation to be had until one is engaged to be married, is it. Unlike me, Greta doesn't read packets of pills or pinched library books or poetry. And I am wholly returned to myself now. She will be purged of his abominations soon.

'I don't think Mr Thompson is very comfortable – at least not on a horse.' Greta changes the subject, tilting her head round Buckley now, her grin impish. 'See how his legs are jiggling about? Not like Mr Wilberry – he was made for the saddle. Look at him. Jack seems pleased with him too. See how fine they look together?'

I tilt my head to the other side and see that Mr Thompson's legs are in fact jiggling in the stirrups, quite comically, the brim of his Panama jiggling in time above them too. I can't see Mr Wilberry so well from my angle, but I can see how tall and straight he's sitting, the easy rock of his shoulders with the rhythm of Jack's gait that says perhaps, like Jack, he'd rather be out here, on the road, than penned. He seemed a different man last night, shoulders hunched too large above the party, constrained in tails at the table, uncertain, or not quite amongst us there. He is conversing with his friend now, pointing out something along the side of the road, the breeze catching the sleeve of his rustic hayseed calico shirt as he does so, and something about this easiness of his makes me want to hear whatever it is he's saying. And something else: an odd impulse, that I should be the one riding beside Mr Wilberry, hatless and free as he is. As if I've ever been inclined to ride before at all. As if I've ever been inclined to such silly romantic thoughts.

As if he might have heard this one, he looks over his shoulder now, and he waves. A small, brief gesture but it somehow traces his gladness across the air between us. He turns back to his friend, his face to the rising sun, and my cheeks prickle with that sensation I can't name – that warmth. The sun is in his hair, all through that too long flaxen hair. He is sun-like: bright and large and somehow necessary.

'If I could choose a man for you, Ryldy, I would choose Mr Wilberry.'

'What?' I snap from my own abstraction. 'Don't say such a silly thing.'

'Silly thing?' Greta is hurt by my sharpness, my scowl. 'Mr Wilberry is a nice man, and he seems very obviously taken with you. What's so silly about that?'

'Mr Wilberry is indeed a nice man and you can choose him for me all you like, but it's not going to happen and you know why,' I say to my sister, as I say to myself. It is fantasy, of course. A nice thought. About how things should be: nice men and nice women who get married and live together forever hatless and free. A nice ballad of mutual admiration and respect penned by an otherwise idle wife for *The Dawn*. Crochet it into a doily. It doesn't exist; certainly not for Greta and I; perhaps not for many at all.

'Well, there you are then, Ryl,' says Gret, moving her hand from mine. 'It's not going to happen if you don't want it to. I'm sorry I opened my silly mouth.'

Oh no, don't be cross with me, please; don't begin our journey this way. 'Don't be sorry, Gret. I'm sorry I snapped at you. I'm out of sorts. I –'

'Yes, you are out of sorts, aren't you.' She looks out over the fields, away from me; I know she's blinking back the sting of it. Of everything.

If only it wasn't such a silly romantic thought. If only this nice man could really carry us off and away. But it can't go that way. Not for me; not any more than it can for Gret. We are both defiled in our different ways and, together, spoiled beyond repair. There is no man I could ever trust, in that sense. Marriage? Never. One gaoler for another? Never. I look ahead to Mr Wilberry again, sharing some joke with Mr Thompson, deep warm voice carrying back to us, a trail of sunshine too. Yes, perhaps in another time, another life, it might make some sense, to imagine, to hope for such things as admiration and respect. In this one, I should never have suggested that these two accompany us anywhere. Poor Mr Wilberry, if he is in fact taken with me, caught up in my losing game. I must make things clear with him, be careful not to encourage him any further than I might already have done. I like him as much as Gret does. I truly do.

She shifts beside me, away from me, fiddling with the catch chain on her bracelet; looking over her shoulder, into the fields.

I look down into the bruise across the back of my hand, spreading like an ink stain, the stamp of Alec Howell's claim, his troth to me. 'I wish there was some gentle, easy way out for us, Gret. I do but ...'

There is not. The carriage wheels grind on over gravel.

'Hm,' my sister sighs. 'So much wheat in these fields,' she says, 'it's difficult to imagine there are enough people in the world to eat that much bread, don't you think, Ryl? But even more difficult to imagine that not every grain would taste the same if you could separate them out. All the bitter from the sweet.'

I look up and find myself inside her eyes, imploring me; my sister, my mother and my aunt all at once. 'Please don't let him take everything from us. I want you to be happy. I need you to be happy, Ryldy, even if I can't be. Perhaps because I might never be.'

Her hand moves to her belly, and I don't know what she is telling me by it, except perhaps some truth of how deeply she hurts. A thousand emotions grab me by the throat, and I promise her with my eyes: *This will be gone from you; he will be gone from us.* As I promise her aloud: 'I will be happy. And so will you. We will make our own happiness. Our own wonderful life for two. That's always been our plan. Yes?'

'Yes.' She smiles. Angel face. 'We'll say no more about unhappy things. Enjoy ourselves, enjoy today. Isn't it a magnificent day? Every colour has come out to meet us.'

'Yes, it has. It's a beautiful day, and I hope you paint every corner of it,' I say to her as I look over my shoulder now, into the dust kicking up behind us, fear clenching around my empty stomach for all that I must do, for our chance, not at happiness, but at some life free of fear. This relentless fear. I see the flicker of a black shape through the dust, some distance away, and panic surges once more. For a sliver of a moment it is him, come after us. But it is only a crow.

I look ahead. I must keep looking ahead, into the distance beyond Mr Wilberry, beyond all impossibilities imagined or real; I must remain fixed upon what might actually be achieved, what *has* to be achieved: tomorrow I will visit the herbalist Ah Ling, to discuss and procure poisons, and in three days' time, when we return to Bathurst on Thursday evening, Alec Howell will be dead, and so will all his seed.

But today, for Gret, let this be one beautiful, happy day. It is the very least that she is due. Try then – *try* – Berylda. Try to enjoy this day.

BEN

'You really do love all this, don't you?' Cos is making a study of me in this scene, resentfully. 'All this monotony of the bush. And for what? Destruction of the arse.'

He's still thumping around in the saddle, still winded at every word. I could tell him to shut up to conserve his energy, meditate to the rhythms of life, let go. Or I could just tell him to shut up and turn back for the pub, as nature intended. Both pointless options, and we're too far from town now for him to turn back on his own anyway. Only about five miles from town, in fact, and he is helpless. He's definitely not coming to Mandajery Creek with me after this. I'll lock him in his trunk and post him home.

'I don't know what you see in this sort of country,' he keeps on, because he's the epitome of commitment in this regard. He is also sobering from last night now, and badly. 'It's just all one giant bird's nest.'

'Perhaps that's because it is.' I laugh. We are in wooded terrain now, a forest of yellow box, full of robins and honeyeaters. A flock of bright green budgerigar rises up from the understorey as we pass.

'Nothing to look at – nothing.'

I keep on laughing at him; he's journeying entertainment of a sort, isn't he? Can't see the forest for the trees.

'Nothing?' I give him some mock astonishment. 'How can you say that, Cosmo? Open your eyes, man. See, under the tea tree there.' I point into the bush at the roadside, up to his left. 'There's a pile of wombat shit. Fresh, too – see how it shines?'

He cringes in disgust and says: 'It's only funny that I'd forgotten just how peculiar you are.'

'I'm peculiar, am I?' But I suppose I am. Under the shedding bark of the yellow box here, I see the clumps of spinifex that feed both wombat and budgerigar, and am reminded that Professor Dubois would agree – he finds my enthusiasm for indigenous ecology a waste of public money, never mind peculiar. I wonder if he's had his latest rant yet at my letter to Professor Jepson; convened a special meeting for Wilberry eradication. I wonder if Professor Jepson has finally given in; if I still have a job. Does it matter if I don't? Probably not, except that the bush will have lost its only advocate in the department if I go. I am what I am, I suppose. A mopoke blinks at me from a knothole now: *Yep*.

And I'm as quickly distracted by a spectacular ironbark up ahead, to prove the point. An old specimen, massive canopy spread wide above the road, its rough, furrowed bark glowing red out of blue-black, like some yet to be discovered source of light. Outstanding thing. At least I think it's an ironbark. What species is it, I wonder –

'Whoa! Whoa there, fellers!' Buckley shouts out to us from behind.

I turn and the old man is waving for us to stop, and as we do I am rather pleasantly caught between this probable ironbark and the Jones girls drawing near.

'What a place to be,' I say. It is astounding that I am here.

And Cos replies: 'You could try not looking so obviously blithered for her.'

That just as suddenly triggers panic. 'Do I look stupid?' I ask him, my pulse jumping at the idea of having to talk to her again, any second.

'No, not stupid.' Cos shakes his head slowly, eyes closed in sufferance; oh how I annoy him. 'Just don't be so –'

'Whoa, Sally!'

They are here; Buckley is pulling the buggy up level with us, and I am making a good effort not to grin too directly at the girls.

Not to look too obviously blithered, whatever that means. Berylda is not looking at me anyway; she is fishing about for something in her pocket. Keep your eyes on the old man; he's pointing up the road.

'House past the church, a way up on the right – that's the Kings' place,' he says. 'You'll see the sign for the teashop, see if we can get a pot of jam there for the ladies.'

'Never mind if we don't get any,' the sister says behind him, leaning forward to touch the old man on the shoulder, smiling at me and at Cos as she does so. Her smile is luminescent; there is something ethereal about her, something that is as enchanted as I feel. 'We have plenty of honey for our bread, and a whole great load of fruitcake.'

'We do, yes,' Berylda Jones says, impatiently, looking down at her watch, and then up at the road. 'We won't be stopping long, whatever the case.'

The frown determined to be on with the journey; the sister releases a small sigh at it, perhaps of impatience too, but of a different sort. And I wonder at Berylda again. She seems anxious to get away – still – when we are well away. What is worrying her? What is this sense of conflict that seems to shade her? Or perhaps, like Cos, she simply doesn't enjoy the travelling. I don't know her to say. Anything. I simply want her to look at me again. I follow her gaze up the road. What does she see? From where we are stopped, you wouldn't know there was a church or a house anywhere nearby. Not even an abandoned fence post makes its presence known; only that big red ironbark making the yellow box look a little disheartened around it. It's lonely country, I suppose, in a human sense. Not everyone is at home in the bush, are they. But there is something lonely about Berylda Jones. Something in her that I recognise, even if as yet I don't know what it is.

'Git up, Sal.' Buckley's off with the buggy, and she is gone before I can look back at her again. But as we follow now, the bush makes its fun with my assumptions as it makes fun of us all: beyond the last stretches of the ironbark boughs, only a few yards away, a drive appears through the yellow box, opening to a clearing on which sits a small timber chapel, not thirty feet long, with a couple of carts gathered outside it and a group of little girls running around ahead of the service, flitting about like cabbage moths, white ribbons amongst the waist-high feather-grass. It will be a special Federation service, most likely, and they'll be getting it out of the way early before the concert and some games and far too much jam and cake. A backblocks church on a public holiday, the same scene playing at Jericho, playing out across all the colonies, that is a kind of unwritten federation in itself, of God and sunshine, jam and cake.

'Jesus bloody James and John, I feel like wombat shit,' Cos picks up where he left off. 'Wombat shit under the shoe of Old Roger.' And I do have some sympathy for him now as I look over at him: he really is suffering from last night, sweating with it.

'Here.' I reach back into my satchel for my water bottle and pass it across to him. 'Get that into you.'

His head, I'm sure, is splitting, and not only from the grog – I don't think he's been conscious this early in the day since the housemaster at school used to belt him awake every morning for his limber-up. It wouldn't be eight o'clock yet, I don't think. My own headache has disappeared, probably with the pleasure of being out here, but I won't tell him that. Cos drains the bottle, hands it back and slouches into silence. I wonder if I might leave him at this teashop when we get there ...

It's only another quarter mile on before we come to the next clearing, the next gate, and an old weatherboard that's seen some more prosperous days. Its greying timbers, half-stripped of their white paint by sun and wind, look so tired of holding themselves upright they might sink back into the bush if you blink again. A faded sign across the front gable says:

KING WONG LEE
FINEST TEAS
QUALITY MEALS

In red letters six inches high. A restaurant, unfortunately misplaced, or bypassed. A Chinaman's gamble not paid off.

Cos groans. Not likely there is even a quick hair of the dog at this establishment.

There's a tap, though, by the water tank, and I'm about to jump down to refill my bottle when a woman appears on the verandah, and some warning in her stance stops me. Surprisingly, she is white, not Oriental, and aged as the house, hair wild and grey, like the bird's nest forest around us, and her apron grimed. She waddles up her scrappy path of broken brick and bindy-eye, and she's waving – but not waving us off. She's greeting the old man Buckley, calling out: 'Roo! Hey, Roo! Happy New Year's to you! Roo Buckley, fancy you turnin' up here today. What's goin' on, hey?'

'Happy New Year's to you too, Jessie.' The old man takes his hat off to her; old acquaintances. He says: 'Taking the Misses Jones to the Hill, love. Excursioning – with some visitors.' He brushes away slow, red bushflies with the brim of his hat by way of introduction to us. 'We're after a pot of jam, you got any?'

'Only plum left,' she says, and then she looks directly at me, face as pinched as her words as she looks me up and down: 'It'll be a shilling.'

It'll be highway robbery. Still, it won't be tinned stuff, I suppose. Real jam, probably made from her own plums somewhere in the yard. She continues to stare at me for a moment, rather unsettlingly, as though waiting on my shilling. All right, I suppose; I dig into my coin pocket for the money, only to find that she's turned away, gone back into the house. I look over at the buggy, at the girls; they are whispering to each other, looking up at the house, and then, only half a moment later, the old woman is coming out to us again, holding a tin of Perfection Preserves in her hand, its label almost as faded as the sign on the gable.

'Naturally,' Cos groans again at the well-aged, three-penny tin of jam, and so does the leather as he shifts in the saddle.

She steps up to him and says: 'Not good enough for you up there on your high horse, is it, mister?' and even Cos is stunned mute by the outburst.

'Now, Jess, it's all good.' Buckley is quick to step down from the vehicle to her, taking the jam tin from her and pushing the shilling into her palm.

But she won't be pacified now. She turns around to the buggy behind her, shaking her finger up at Berylda: 'Girlie, you tell that uncle of yours and all his mates around town, it's good enough for you – right?'

Who are you to shake your finger, you cranky old witch? I might say something to pacify her myself, but that Berylda seems unmoved by it. She looks down at the woman with that inscrutable stare of hers; withering. And then she smiles as quickly at her; that smirk, sardonic, under a nod: 'You are quite right, Mrs King, your jam is good enough for anyone. I shall tell my uncle exactly that.' Then the frown as quick again, concerned, as she queries: 'And how is Mr King?'

'Oh. Well, you know. He'd be better if he could ever get his licence back.' The woman's words are spat out no less tersely but her whole face wrinkles around the answer like an old rag. Some terrible misfortune has occurred here, it would seem, to make her a crank.

'What licence?' Cos asks her, hearing the sound of some injustice too; always an ear for a sad story, bless him.

'His minin' licence, his licence for his prospect,' the old woman says, surprising us again, and she explains, with the weariness of one who's done so many times, to anyone who'll listen: 'They took it off him, the coppers. Seven year ago. A trumped-up legality, it was. 'Cause he's a Chinaman is what it really was, and them company mines don't want the competition nowadays from them that just want to work hard. Don't want no one gettin' rich but the company bosses. Kick the Chinaman out, that'll solve the problems of the world, that will. All his spare money he put in the Duramana school, my husband did, in the church here too, and in our teashop that woulda brung some more life to the place, make it a proper village, make some money for everyone – what's he get for it? A slap in the face. Now all he's got is the ope – and that's all you'd have too, if you had his troubles.'

Opium. Poor bugger.

'That's some bad luck.' Cos nods and he couldn't be more sincere. This woman's husband has had his livelihood unfairly revoked by the authorities and now he's doing away with himself, slowly. 'I'm very sorry to hear that,' he tells her, and he is sorry, personally: it's rife in the cane fields his family owns, the evil ope, not unknown for blackbirded Kanakas to do away with themselves quite deliberately by it, for want of going home to their islands. Opium was also the big excuse behind the Protection Act against the blacks – its full name being the Aboriginal Protection and Restriction of the Sale of Opium Act. Apparently opium has been responsible for the black race dying out. Strangely enough, in all my travels, I've never seen a black on the ope. It is evil.

But the woman ignores Cos's understanding; her anger returned, pointing her finger at Berylda again. 'All 'cause of your White Australia, this is. Now you're gunna make that the law as well and kick him back to Kwantung? Over my dead body, you will. You tell that uncle of yours, I put a curse on him. I put a curse on your White Australia. It doesn't exist. Never has. Never will. You tell your Mr Howell that.'

Berylda holds the woman's gaze again; and she nods with something more than sympathy; a kindness, an assurance. 'Oh, I'll tell him, Mrs King. Don't doubt it. I'll tell him that for you.'

Oh how I want to know this girl, this woman, Berylda Jones. This strength, this thread in her that holds her back so straight. I want her to look at me. Now. She doesn't. She keeps her eyes on the tragic old woman; watches her go back into her house, slamming the door shut on it all.

'They've had a hard time,' Buckley says, getting back up into the buggy, as though it might need explaining for us. He says to me: 'Keep up ahead now. You'll see the fork. Take it to the left. That'll be the Track.'

'Can barely contain my excitement,' Cos mutters under his breath as I tell the old man: 'Righteo.'

As we turn back for the gate, I look behind me for Berylda again but still she doesn't see me: she's looking down once more, at her watch, and when she looks up, she looks only at the road.

BERYLDA

'Mrs King knows something of the devil then, doesn't she?' Greta says as the wheels crunch out onto the gravel once more. She speaks up through the boughs of the trees, to the sky, her own prayer that someone should know something of what he does.

'She would know him by reputation anyway,' I suppose. 'His opinions would be hard to miss through the district now, I'm sure.'

'I hope he doesn't get into the government.' My sister sends up another wish, but hushed and obscured, so that Buckley cannot guess what we are talking about. 'I hope every miner despises him.'

'If they really knew what he stood for – cutting all their wages and seeing children back at the coalface instead of at school – they would parade him through the streets for a thief and string him up. I think you can be certain of that.' I bump her shoulder with mine, and we share a smile, of a sweeter wish: our little holiday is working already, and Greta is unfolding something of her own feelings with the road.

'Do you remember how furious Papa was, about what happened to Mr King?' She unfolds into memory now, to that last time we were all together here. 'Under these very same trees we passed.' Gret looks up into their leaves again. 'We must have come this way, mustn't we?'

'Yes.' I return with her too. Here. I remember. It was such a hot day, we were pestering Papa for a cold drink and he teased us that there was nowhere to stop along this road. *What about that new place just opened, Harry, the Kings at Duramana?* Mother suggested, and Papa said, *Shush, Mother, do you always have to be so nice them?* Referring to Gret and me. We giggled like the schoolgirls we were, anticipating that we would soon be sipping lemonades. But the teashop had the closed sign up when we arrived. Papa went inside to see if anyone was about and beg a special travellers' favour, and when he came back out his smile had vanished into a grim blunt line. Mr King had just lost his final appeal case against the Crown a day or so before, over his diggings. The reef that had made his small fortune a few decades earlier had somehow become out of bounds; some sort of surveying error. And Papa was furious because he knew that a syndicate had already made an application for that same prospect. Furious at the forces of prejudice and avarice combined. They have clearly worn poor King Wong Lee down today.

'One man's penny should be as good as another's, that's what Papa said,' Gret says up into the trees. 'But it's never that way, is it?'

'No,' I reply. 'It's not the way of the law. Nothing just about it, as far as I can understand.' A Chinaman is not meant to have land or licences to it any more than a woman is. Although the law makes provisions that one might, too many other laws can prevent it; because it's against the natural order of things – a racial point upon which all politicians agree. Perhaps the only point. A fistful of slander and lies. A Chinaman is a slippery fellow who goes panning down on the river, tries his luck, eats a few white babies and disappears. Wash your hands after you've touched any money that's gone through his. That was about as much as we ever knew about that share of our own race, too. Not even Mother ever directly admitted to it – she would never say that dirty word: *Chinese*. Grandmother Pemberton, we knew, had been born in Hong Kong; her father, Louie Wing Tock, had come out in the first gold rush, when Grandmother was ten, first to Bendigo in Victoria and then north, following the finds, following prosperity. He was a bedtime story, a mystery with too few clues, a greengrocer whose bones were sent 'home' when he died, a traditional gentleman, a respectable businessman, and there was never a mention that we are Chinese too, where precisely 'home' might be, or what circumstance caused him to bring his small daughter alone to this place in 1853 – disguised as a boy. Along this very road: they would have travelled it too, at some time. I want to claim this road as mine. Ours.

'We didn't come this way going to the Hill, though, did we – it was on the way back,' Gret says now, memories drifting into dreams. 'Wasn't it a lovely time, Ryl?'

'It was. The loveliest.' Dream: our last precious time with Mother and Papa. We rock inside their love, along our last road here, with them. Real: it was the third of December, 1895, a Tuesday, when they met us in Sydney, at school, at St Cat's. I'd received the Junior Mathematics prize, and Mother and Papa had arrived especially in time for the end-of-year awards ceremony. Papa was so happy he was springing from foot to foot in the courtyard, grin chewing down on his pipe, as keen to be away from the school and off on our holiday as to see me applauded, while Greta was working very hard at pretending not to care that I had won anything at all. Mother was a little bit sad around the edges of her smile: it was the first time we'd seen her since the news that Grandpa Pemberton had passed away, snuggled up in his sleep, earlier in the term, and we were going straight out to the grave at Gulgong first: snuggled up now as he was with Grandmother who had gone the year before. We'd stayed a few days there, at Mother's family home, to see to Libby's roses, neglected through Grandpa's final bout of pneumonia and then her sudden honeymoon. The garden was overrun with them, Aunt Libby's scarlet tea roses devouring the front steps of the house, and the dahlias around the verandah beds were overgrown with ryegrass, which we all set to pulling out. I got terribly sunburned along my arms doing it; *Black as an old coolie,* Mother scolded, placing roses in the vase of her parents' headstone. Then we came down through Mudgee to the Hill, to that sweetest time of fizzy ginger beer and mermaid calliope tunes, so very happy all of us, stomach aching from too much laughter, and too many apricots. Fairy floss sticking to my teeth at a bustling, dusty fair somewhere there; chocolate ice cream dripping all down Greta's new gloves. Papa had some business at Tambaroora then and when he came back he hired a well-sprung phaeton to bring us from the Hill to Bathurst, along this Bridle Track.

Here is the fork, the signpost to it now:

HILL END 34 MILES
TAMBAROORA 36 MILES
HARGRAVES 57 MILES
MUDGEE 90 MILES

And Greta pointing out beyond it: 'Oh look, a fire's been through.' She sighs across the blackened trunks that lie along both sides of the road here as it winds away through the thickening forest. Fresh scars; I can smell the charcoal. She says: 'I love the way the new leaves sprout straight out of the scorched bark after a fire – see?' I do see it: bright green fuzzing around the sides of the black. 'Life defying death and it happens so quickly. The leaves laugh at the fire, don't you think, Ryl?'

'Hm. Yes,' I reply but I am still inside my dream road, the streaks of burnt bark blackening and caging my mind as I remember further and further behind us: Aunt Libby waiting for us outside the town hall, standing at the corner waving, with Mr Alec Howell, her new husband, by her side. I always imagine Mother didn't like him, sensed some corruption in him even then. I imagine her pressing her lips together disdainfully as we were introduced. But I can't be sure she ever did any such thing. She was so pleased that Libby had finally married, and married well, after nursing Grandpa for so long. Married a surgeon no less, a successful and handsome man. I suppose Mother was relieved, more than anything, that Libby wouldn't be alone. She was almost thirty-two years old; Mother was thirty-seven and so long and contentedly wed. More than anything, I remember Mother sighing as she kissed me goodbye that evening. She didn't want to leave us. But she had to. She and Papa had to go straight back to the mountains then, to Katoomba, by the train, to see to some business with the partners at Hartley Shale. A party to host, at Echo Point … They were to come back to Bathurst for a proper long holiday, for Christmas. *Only a few days*, she sighed. We never saw them again.

Phantoms, they seem, lost in the bush. Here and then gone. The engine brakes scream. The carriage falls from rails and into the gorge. Bush smoke.

'But you know, you won't make Mr Wilberry go away by refusing to look at him,' Greta says now, snapping me back into the present.

'What?' I look at her, unsure what she's referring to but reflexively defensive anyway. 'I wasn't looking anywhere.'

'I know,' she says. 'I don't mean just now. I mean you keep looking away from him whenever we are near. It's not very polite.'

She looks up the road to the riders ahead, Mr Wilberry and Mr Thompson, quite a distance from us now and disappearing around another sharp bend, and I am sharp with it, too: 'I don't know what you're talking about.'

'Yes you do, Ryl.' She bumps her shoulder into mine, and her eyes are laughing at me. 'It won't do to be rude to him – he'll see through you eventually.'

'Gret – stop it. Please.'

'It's got nothing to do with me.' Her smile curls with some secret laughter; she looks ahead again. We can't see them any more at all, only the traces of their dust as the road begins to rise around a hillside.

And Greta shouts, 'Oh!' with the first of the bumps in the rougher road, a jounce that almost sends me flying out of the buggy. 'Oh what fun!' She laughs and laughs as we're flung this way and that over ruts carved into the clay beneath us. The Track is a floodwater torrent set in stone.

'Oh God.' I hang on to the side rail for my life.

While Gret is instantaneously returned to the girl I have longed to see, the one who was always daring me, *Come along, Ryldy.* She's now shrieking at me as we hit another wave of solid clay: 'Isn't this terrific!'

No, not at all. Please let it not be like this the whole way up.

'Yay! Ho!' Gret squeals and my elbow almost breaks through the side timbers of the buggy with the force of the next jolt.

'Oh God!' God, why did I choose this way to come and not the way through Turondale, the way that has an actual road included in the journey? Because Greta is having such a wonderful time defying death and laughing at me along the scenic route, isn't she.

'Yous all right back there?' Buckley turns in his seat, chuckling. 'The higher road'll be easier,' he says to me and winks at Greta, enjoying her excitement. 'Soon as we see the river again, she'll even out,' he assures. 'Couple of miles.'

Couple of miles? He's right enough, though. Within another hour, just before my bum is flattened and smashed to the bone, the Track climbs a little more and the Macquarie appears again, to our left.

'Oh!' And Greta's deeper thrill now seems worth every juddering moment; this is why we have come here, along this old byway. 'So very … Oh … is it really? Can it be?' This vision of willows trailing limbs along the water's edge, slender gums reaching high into the sky above; she says: 'A sanctuary for every green that ever was. This is where they gather.'

She is painting it all in her heart right now, onto her very heart, and at last I feel my nerves begin to relax, too. The sun is warm across my shoulders and I follow its light through my sister's hair, picking out threads of chestnut amidst the black plaits coiled beneath her hat as she leans out towards the river, and then she is turning to me again, reaching for my hand again: 'Thank you, Ryldy.'

I smile into hers, with the promise: soon, very soon, you will have this one small freedom – this right of being – to find beauty wherever and whenever you want. There will be no one to keep you from this simple love.

'And here they are …' She is pointing up along a cutting that ranges above us now. 'Oh my goodness, look at them – our poppies.' Poppies. Yes, here they are. Sprung out of the rock face – two of them – burgundy purple petals fanned wide open against the rust-coloured rocks, black centres drinking in the sun. 'It's Mother and Papa, don't you think, telling us they are here?'

'Telling me you are a terrible romantic,' I tease her, even as I am squeezing her hand with that same yearning: yes, they are Mother and Papa, they are here, if only within us. They remain.

And there's a whole riverbank strewn with them now as we look towards the water again. Poppies everywhere. My whole face is a smile. It feels like the first time I have smiled so fully and so freely since leaving Flo in Sydney. Because I'm sure it is.

'Whoa!' And Buckley is pulling Sally up and through a dappled glade where the poppies lie thickest, right on the river. Poppies trampled under hoof and wheel now, and Buckley deciding, 'Good spot for smoko, you reckon?' But I can barely reply because I am laughing out loud without knowing exactly what I am laughing at, and Greta is already scrambling out of the buggy, sketchbook in one hand and my hand still in the other. We skitter over each other onto the grass; silly, hilarious girls. A glimpse of a wonder if this is all that freedom truly is: these glancing moments of unchained, unhooked joy. Tripping amongst poppies, burst from fields to wander wild. Between everything else, every dark and confining compromise we are otherwise forced to make.

It is inside this thought that I see Mr Wilberry here; again. And I don't look away. I can't. He is walking up the pebbled strand, intent upon something; searching the reeds. Tucking his too-long sun-soaked mane behind his ears, seemingly ignorant of the fact that he is near ankle deep in the water. Mr Thompson lies further up the bank: a pair of legs crossed above the long grass beneath a tree; a puff of pipe smoke on the breeze. Jack and Rebel are resting a few yards further on, muscles quivering with the sweetness of this grass. Except for the summer songs of beetles and birds, we might be the only living beings in the world.

'I'll get a billy on, miss?' Buckley is asking me if we'd like a cup tea, and Greta calls up from the bank where she's already settling herself and her sketchbook: 'I'd love one, please!' And goading me once more: 'Do you think Mr Wilberry and Mr Thompson might like one too, Ryl?'

But I don't need goading, not this time. I don't care if Mr Wilberry wishes for tea or half a cup of river mud; I am compelled towards him. I have been unpleasant, Greta is right, and I would like to show him that I am not that unpleasant person. He and Mr Thompson have done us an enormous favour by being here with us; I can't be rude to him, any more than I might entertain any other thought of him, or he me. And yet I am somehow as easily entranced by him as I draw near to him, watching him. An ibis watches him, too, from the shade of the bank opposite. What is Mr Wilberry searching for? Bent over the reeds now, poised, stalking up towards the bank now like the white shadow of some primordial hunter. In fact, as I come closer again, I see he's holding a knife. A small pocket knife.

He reaches into the reeds, to the back of the strand where the bank is steeply cut. Pulls out a reedy sort of thing, topped with a cluster of violet flowers, though I know they are not violets, I know that much about flowers. These are small, droopy and somewhat untidy star-shaped things, crumpled around their edges. He is turning the stem around in his hand, utterly unaware of my approach along the top of the bank.

I ask him: 'What have you got there?'

'Oh?' He startles, surprised as he looks up to find me looking down at him, but there is some triumph in his smile as he holds the flower out to show me: 'Pudding lily. At least, that's what they're known as where I come from. *Arthropodium strictum*, they are properly called.'

'Yes?' Not particularly fascinating to me. The blooms look like crushed voile; doubtless a native. Yet I see something of its delicacy now, held as it is in such large hands ... It seems impossible that these great, broad farmer's hands should hold such a fine stem.

'Yes,' he says; somehow unchained, unhooked himself here in what is obviously his preferred world. 'The scent of it – smells like vanilla custard. Do you think so?' He holds it up to me; somehow a different man, as if he's slaked off a burden, forgotten to be nervous.

The flower smells like something sugary rolled in dirt to me, and I'm sure the face I make says precisely that.

And his chuckle is the warmest sound I've ever heard. 'It's quite edible, too, the tubers at least.' His eyes are blue flecked through with brown, not unlike mine. 'Though I wouldn't recommend it. Pretty bitter really.'

'Well, we shan't have any for luncheon, then, shall we?' I do like this man; a sadness drags, willow-like, through me.

'No, I should think not.' He smiles again, our smiles meeting, just for a moment, before he steps effortlessly up the high bank, unbuckles

185

his haversack lying there and pulls out a little press, unbuckling that too. So deftly he cuts and places the flower stem in the press and snaps it shut, an action he's performed a thousand times.

'Why do you press that one?' I ask him as he buckles it up again. 'How is it of interest to you?'

'Oh?' Now he is surprised by my interest; how sweet he looks in that surprise. 'The pollen is very deep in colour,' he explains, 'unusually dark yellow, almost cinnamon, I suppose – ha? I must make a note of it – unlikely the colour will preserve well, you know, it'll leach out by the time it eventually finds its way back to Melbourne ...'

No, I don't know. I've never pressed a flower in my life; never likely to.

He takes a notebook out of the front pocket of his haversack. 'I could store it in my sand jar, attempt to keep the colour fast, but I'd rather save that in case something of greater interest ...' he trails off, absorbed in his note.

I continue to watch him, quick sharp scratches on the page, and although I cannot know what these next few days will bring, success or failure, freedom or worse entrapment, I know I shall never forget this man. I hear myself ask him absently: 'Would you like a cup of tea?' Somewhere off up the river.

'Tea? Oh, all right, why not,' he says, looking up from his notebook, before appearing to wince, perhaps at some self-admonishment, suddenly uncomfortable with himself again: 'Ah, I mean to say. Thank you ... yes?'

Yes? No? I don't know. For this moment time has stopped in the blush of his abashment, the sunburst of his lashes, looking down upon me and yet not. This warmth all over my skin. One lovely and impossible moment before I say: 'Right. Good. But we can't stop here long.' And I am rude once more, each word serrated. 'We must keep tight to our schedule if we're to make it to Hill End before sunset.'

As if I travel this road regularly. As if Mr Wilberry has done anything to earn my rebuke.

But he only nods now, and smiles that gentle, questing smile as if in fact he does seek to see through me and my strangeness.

He picks up his haversack and walks away towards his friend, and I watch him. He turns back to me after a few steps and he says: 'The poppies are beautiful, by the way.' Trailing sunlight over his shoulder: 'Exotics, though. You know. My interest is in the indigenous …' He leaves the thought trailing, too, and my interest remains in the loping strides: the world is his, surely. Any world. He taps his friend on the end of his boot to rouse him. The boot kicks out playfully, and Mr Wilberry grasps the toe, pretending to wrestle it. Then he walks on to the stallions, stroking Jack along the jaw, before hanging his haversack back on the saddle.

Such a good man. A man of quiet passion. I see my hand upon his arm at dawn this morning, my fists against the broad back of his dinner jacket last night, and I could touch him again now too. But I shan't. I won't. I do not know what that touch might do.

BEN

'Aw, it'll take as long as it takes, Miss Berylda,' Buckley is telling her over our tea, how long it might be before we break again for lunch. 'The road can get a bit tricky from here.' He glances at me to remind me of that, too, of my primary purpose here: to ride ahead.

'Oh?' She laughs, but it's a thin sound; nervous. 'Hasn't it been tricky enough so far?'

Ah – she doesn't like the travelling. I could say something about that – I could reassure her, couldn't I? I look into the tea leaves in the bottom of my cup for the words, but my entire mind falls around the sound *umm*.

And she has turned away again; only slightly, but definitely away. She seems to have spent this whole cup of tea at this slight turning away, so that we have edged around one hundred and eighty degrees from fireside to river.

Have I said something wrong? Did I talk too much about plants earlier? How might I know? I thought I was conversing quite well for a second there but ... I spoke only of plants, didn't I. Pudding lilies. Bloody hell, I don't know how to do this. I should give up.

Don't you dare, Mama warns.

I look behind me to Cos, as though that will help me; he's still lying there where I left him, wrecked and semiconscious, in the shade.

'Mr Wilberry?'

Yes, at last. She speaks to me. I turn back to the river. But it's the sister, Greta, stepping up towards the fire here from where she has been drawing in her book down by the water, waving at me.

'Mr Wilberry,' the sisters say it now at once: Berylda taking my cup from me and stepping away as Greta nears, holding out her book. 'Tell me, please, what do you think of my tree?'

'Tree?' What do I know about trees? Just don't go on too much about them, Mr Wilberry. I take the book from her and find good reason to be speechless anyway. God, she's good. I don't know enough about art to say exactly what it is – a movement, an emotion perhaps, in what she has sketched out across the page. It's a willow tree, but it's not merely a tree; it's two women: wood sprites, one wrapped around the trunk, twisted through the deep-fissured bark, tormented somehow as though caught by the tree, or inside it; while the other looks down at her from the branches above, reaching for her, trying to gain her attention, perhaps to pull her up. And then, in what appears to be the reflection of the tree in the river, I see yet another sprite: looking up from under the water, as though begging the one in the trunk to go. It's a haunting image.

'That's quite extraordinary, Miss Jones,' I finally manage to say, still looking into it. 'Extraordinarily good.'

'Greta, please. Just Greta for friends,' she corrects me, taking her book back, quickly, closing it, hiding it behind her back. 'Do you really think it's good?'

'Er ... yes. I very much do. You are –'

'We must get cracking, I'm afraid,' Berylda calls up from the river's edge, shaking out the cups she has washed there; and now she is walking away altogether, returning to the buggy.

'Oh Ryldy, there's no great hurry, is there?' Greta calls back.

'You won't be saying that if we get caught out here in the dark later on,' Berylda replies to the air, charging on.

'I might.' Greta laughs. 'Scaredy-cat!'

She shakes her head, and then smiles up at me in some sort of affectionate apology: 'My sister.' Before following her. I watch them both, dainty boots marching through the clover there, skirts brushing across the poppies.

'Kick out the fire and we'll get off then, aye?' the old man Buckley says beside me now.

And I say: 'Yep.'

We stamp out the fire and I get the feeling that he's enjoying a laugh at me, under his hat. I'm sure he thinks I'm all tangled up over a couple of pretty girls. And that's true. But there is much more going on here: some kind of maze of distraction. I'm looking down at the pit of smouldering, half-burnt bits of branches and the image of the willow sprites swims through me, more a feeling than a picture. Really, extraordinary. What a talent. One I don't have. I can't draw a convincing stick man.

But I had better rouse Cos.

'What!' He rattles awake when I kick the toe of his boot, and his little book of *Zarathustra*, open on his face, flies off onto the grass, pages rustling.

'Giddy up,' I say. 'Time to get back on the donkey.'

'No,' he protests, and then remembers he has no choice; holding out a hand for me to help him up. 'I have to piss.'

'Of course you do.' Because you're not my best friend, you're my infant. I glance over to Berylda, sitting in the buggy with her sister, golden everlasting heads bowed over something again; perhaps the drawing book. Waiting to be off. Waiting for me and Cos.

'Well, hurry up then,' I tell him, nodding across the trail. 'Go.'

And he looks across the trail too, into the bush. Helplessly. 'Where?'

'You are joking.' But he's not. Ever the devil-may-care radical, aren't you, until we stray too far from the cricket green. What was I thinking, asking him to leave Brisbane with me in the first place? I wasn't thinking at all. I was mad; I am not now. 'Just bloody *go* – anywhere.'

He rubs his beard, as near to embarrassed as he ever gets, as well he should be: he even has a lavatory in the main house at the Swamp, first thing he did when he inherited the place as a token of his grandfather's pity, and an eternal font of amusement for Susan: it's the only palatial part of the old relic. He says: 'But there might be snakes.'

There might. Undoubtedly there are. I saw a beautiful diamond python sunning itself further up the bank when we got here. There is also a nasty load of spitfire caterpillars in the gum leaves above him right now. But I won't argue with him further by pointing out that there is more chance of one of them falling down the back of his collar, or a bull ant crawling up his trousers, than a snake showing any interest in him, or that it is in the very nature of snakes to make every endeavour to avoid him absolutely. He's still terrified of them, obviously – barely ever set foot in a cane field at least partially, if not entirely, because of this phobia. I give in quickly: 'All right, I'll come with you.'

I signal to the old man that we're going for a walk in the woods, and we soon find a suitably dense boronia for Cos to go behind. I crush a handful of its leaves as I wait for him, breathe in the scent – of camphor, *ledifolia* then – and with it comes that note of rosemary and something … Everything is redolent with her scent, it seems. All the forest breathes out her scent, and I am as impatient as she is to be away now too – deeper into this forest, beyond willows and poppies, where the flora will be pristinely rugged, clinging to the walls of the gorge, to the mean soil. I take in another breath full of the earthy perfume, and with it comes renewed determination: when we stop for lunch, I'm going to have another go, I'm going to convince her to go for a walk with me. If I'm alone with her, I'll be forced to –

'What the flaming deuces is that?' Cos bowls backs into me, midstream, pointing uphill a way to what appears to be an outcrop of granite. But it's not a rock; it's a cairn of stones, with a cross set in the top of it. A gravesite.

'Poor bugger,' I say to this lonely soul. A miner, perhaps, out of luck and out of time; I've seen these kinds of graves before: along the Kuranda railway, in the rainforest of the far north; and one as far again south, in the wind-torn mallee scrub outside Castlemaine, by a decaying bark hut. Sad little memorials to the gold rushes, there'd be hundreds of them across the country; thousands possibly. I tell Cos: 'It's just someone's grave.'

'I'll probably die on this road too, Wilber.' Cos is in a hurry to button up. 'And you'll bloody well carry me down off it. You'll bloody well carry me all the way home.'

'I will, Cos. I promise you.' And I'll share a toast with your mother, too, for all the suffering that ended here.

I'm already halfway back to the horses; the buggy is coming onto the Track and Berylda glances over the carriage rail, the briefest hurry-up of a glance; Buckley lifting his hat to me: 'We'll find yous at the river crossing.'

I nod in reply, but I'm still looking at Berylda, at the back of her hat; wanting her to glance at me again, even as I'm taking the reins back over Jack's head.

'Ben – whoa.' Cos is shuffling up behind me, still tucking in his shirt. 'Steady on, old matey.'

'Steady on?' I reach for Rebel's reins now too, the quicker to be going; left to Cos, we'd be here half an hour. I tell him: 'Get back in the saddle – now. Or you can stay here with old matey over there.' I nod back at the grave.

He heaves himself up, and then he says: 'I mean steady on with that girl. Don't be so quick to jump to for her.'

'Why not?' I don't hide my annoyance with him at this. 'Have you decided you don't like her either?'

'It's not a matter of like,' he says. 'I don't know that she's the chasing kind. Hold your horses on her, that's all. She's a strange one, not normal, and you're –'

'Not normal? Unlike you?' I have a vague recollection of him having said something similar as we stumbled back to the pub last night; what did he call her? I can't remember at this minute. I tell him now: 'You think she's not *normal* because she's not shown the slightest bit of interest in you.'

'Aw.' He smacks his hand to his heart as though I've shot him, then he warns me again: 'I only say you should be careful, Ben. Don't go too off your kadoova on her. She's just a girl.'

'Just a girl?' As if I chase skirt the way he does; as though I ever would. He's cranked me up properly now; I say: 'Just a girl – like Susan?'

I kick my horse off towards the trail, not waiting for a reply, and I'm so cranked at that, as I pass the buggy, I forget to look at her at all. What does Cos know about women, really? What do I know? Nothing.

His horse follows mine and after a minute or two he's in my ear again, still thudding around in the saddle, as he says: 'I love Susan.' His breath catching on every word.

I look over at him: sweating, hopeless mess, as blithered as I am when all is said and done, and I say: 'I know you do.'

'Poor Susie.' He laughs. But he means it. He couldn't tell you why he is unfaithful to her, any more than he could tell you why he drinks, or paints, or generally confides more in Kevin the taxidermied curator than anyone else on earth. I don't know why I do anything I do either. You can only blame your father and your family so much, can't you.

Our horses settle into stride together, and Cos settles back into amiable whingeing: 'Moses in a roasting pan, it's getting hot, isn't it.'

And I have to agree: it is suddenly hot now. As the sun climbs so does this heat: exponentially, it seems. I fish around in my satchel for my hat. The cicadas are going for it as the road begins to climb too, winding round the side of yet another hill. I look down to the Macquarie below, a blue ribbon now, almost as blue as the sky. From this distance, perhaps three hundred feet up, the fine new-growth needles of the river oaks appear as a copper haze along both sides. And when I look up again we are surrounded by hills, precipitous now and closely set. Endless hills, and they are climbing ever higher too. Climbing into the sky. Two wedge-tail eagles gyre halfway to heaven above us, hunting together, as the male and the female often do – enjoying the view. This is breathtaking country. So magnificent, I could almost forget why I'm here altogether.

Bloody sheila.

Thanks for that intrusion, Pater.

Don't listen to him, Ben.

No, Mama, I don't. But I wonder what the bastard's doing now. Does he miss her? At all? Or is he too preoccupied with his embarrassment that I'm not abroad with the QMI, chasing Dutch farmers through the African bush? What for? Diamonds and gold for Empire? Glory? Honour? Queensland beef prices will be at the bottom of it, whatever his motivations are.

Coward, he called me like a shot in the back as I walked away from him. What would he know about courage?

'Not exactly a popular route, is it?' Cos adds beside me, mindlessly bored already.

And I laugh; God, but he can make me laugh, make me glad he is my friend. I ask him: 'Aren't you at all inspired by the scenery?'

'Not really, no.' A stupid question, of course. The only river he paints is the Brisbane, as fat and lazy as him, and his landscapes are most often of human geographies: of pin-headed bush cockies tipping cyanide tins into waterholes; black trackers leashed to constables pursuing Kanakas through the cane; the never-ending undulations of Susan's breasts. His hanging offences, as he calls them; his commentary on the sins of all our fathers – as disreputable and out of rhythm as everything else about him. And as concealed: none of them ever leave the studio.

But he offers now: 'I'll make some drawings of the girl for you, though. She is very pretty, I'll give her that.'

'Will you just?' I smile. This is an apology, of sorts, I suppose, and I accept it: a sketch of her from him would be good, too. 'I'll be sure to snatch it from you before you give her a curly moustache, then.'

He ignores that; too much whingeing yet to do: 'How far do you reckon now?' he asks me, looking painfully into nowhere – and blindly. Across the ravine a landslide gashes the side of a slope like a fresh wound cut into ochre flesh. Ahead, a bridge made of rubble straddles one point of nowhere to the next: who would not wonder at the nerve of the men who built it there? *That's* courage.

I look down at the edge of the road here, the sandstone inexorably crumbling towards the Macquarie below, and I can't resist: 'Oh, about a four hundred foot drop.'

He sees something now, staring into the abyss: 'Jesus!'

I gee up Jack to let him go for it, stretch him out, and he brings Rebel with him. The quicker to get to the river crossing too, to her – to try to talk to her again. *Courage.* That's all that's needed here, and I have it.

'Ben! You mad arse! *BEN!*'

I crack Jack on some more and yahoo like Wild Bill, higher and further into the hills, and I'm flying over that bridge: 'Yee-ha!'

BERYLDA

'Hello! Hellooo, Greta Jones!'

My sister was made to lean out of the side of moving vehicles, shouting her name into soulless, stone-faced valleys – as much as I was made to close my eyes for fear of falling headlong into them.

'Just about there,' Buckley turns and chuckles – at me – enjoying himself almost as much as Greta is.

I stare hard into the floor of the buggy to try to still this vertigo, reach for Gret's sketchbook there between our boots, to find a focus. But Gret smacks my hand away: 'I said don't peek!'

She's making me a surprise of the picture she began at the willows and doesn't want me to see it until she's finished. I could say don't worry, I'm sure I won't see a thing, really, but I can't speak. I am too fixed once more with listening to the slip of every stone that falls from the edge of the Track into this bottomless valley in our wake.

'You can look now, scaredy Ryl – we're going downhill. See?'

I'd rather not, but I glance up again, right into her beaming face, her happiness, telling me: 'I wish I could be in this shiny, *shiny* air every day.'

I wish I could tell her, *Soon you will, whenever you like.* I reach into my pocket for my watch yet again, as if its tiny hands will tell me precisely when. They only tell me it's not quite twelve o'clock. Lunchtime. My empty stomach groans around the hour.

'Here we are, misses,' Buckley says, and I look out at the bush. We are indeed inside it again, rather than above it, and I feel my shoulders relax a little in gratitude. I don't know how Buckley knows that we could be anywhere, though, through all the sameness of the trees, the forest as thick as thatch, but my stomach groans again, in its own gratitude: I'm so very hungry now I could eat that whole tin of jam – and its label. Sally picks up her step, head high at a jaunty trot; she's hungry too.

But, 'Oh!' the sound leaps from me now as the Turon comes into view and I am on the edge of my seat again as memory floods me. This place, this scene – it's as if we were here only one summer ago, not five. 'Gret – look.' I grasp her arm and point ahead across the river to one tree that stands apart and taller than all the others. 'That tree over there – do you remember it?'

It's a huge gum tree, perhaps taller and broader than any I have ever seen, and certainly more striking: a tangle of white limbs streaked with umber, the colour of dried blood. I remember this tree so well, standing guard over the crossing. It must have been here for a hundred years or more: what journeys it must have seen. How wonderful, how substantial it is, as if it somehow marks this way with proof that we were really here.

'Yes!' Gret remembers too. 'That's where we came down from that very steep part of the Track, so fast, we thought we'd hit it – remember the splash we made when the wheels hit the water?'

I do, suddenly. Yes, I do. Our blouses gaily bespattered. I could almost cry for the fun we had. My skin shivers with that warm, prickling sensation, filling me now from some depth I never knew was there. The oddest sensation yet passes over me. I never cry, for anything, and yet now what is this? This tingling ... everywhere. More an aberration of my hunger than anything else, I'm sure. I'm a little dizzy from it. And tired from my sleepless night. So tired.

Sal pulls up suddenly, snorting and stamping, jolting it away, jolting me back into myself. That's it for her, she's had enough, too. She's more than earned her rest. 'Whoaaa, my girl, that's the way,' Buckley coaxes her further along on to the bank, though, into the shade of a stand of those straggly, shaggy trees I don't know the name of: they look like some sort of dying pine undecided as to whether they might keel over into the water or shimmer away completely in the heat. That sort of tree, like so many trees – the wattle, the waratah, the whatever bush in general – that cause me to wonder, if there is a grand design to this world, why did its maker save the weariest looking ones for this corner of the earth?

Apart from that great umber-streaked gum over there. It's a wild and gargantuan apparition of a thing. Papa told us a story about it as we picnicked that day, one of his fabulous, spellbinding stories, right here. I can see him twiddling the ends of his moustache comically, rocking on his riding heels. *Well, let me tell you a little something for nothing, my lovely ladies …* that was the way he always began such tales. Greta had asked what sort of tree it was, why it looked so different from all the other trees, and he'd said it was because it wasn't a tree at all, but the bewitched spirit of a murdered trooper – someone he'd once known personally, of course, as Papa knew everyone from Newcastle to Narraburra – and whenever gold thieves passed this way, the limbs of the tree would reach out across the water to pluck them up and cast their spoils into the river, back into the water, from whence the treasure came. God, oh God, but I loved my father so. I think perhaps love might have stopped for me that day; that last day in his arms, in this place, looking across the river at this very tree: *Don't you believe me, Ryldy Ryl? Funny little mathemasceptician you are.*

'Hm. Where are our faithful and handsome chaperones?' Gret is looking about as she hops from the buggy, the contents of her paintbox clattering as her feet meet the ground, and her tone changing as quickly to worry. 'I can't see Jack or Rebel, either. They should be here, shouldn't they? There's no other way for them to have gone. Where could they be?' The sudden panic on my sister's face is the sum of all her loss, our loss, the crime of it: that she should be brought to fear so automatically at a meeting delayed.

As I am, too. Of course our visitors have plunged from a rocky height and disappeared forever into this endless ocean of trees. Even as I say: 'I'm sure they're not far, Gret …'

'Not far at all,' Buckley's brick-dust rasp is sure behind us. 'They've gone for a swim, misses, downriver a bit, caught sight of 'em from the road. They'll have heard us comin'.'

A canter of hooves over pebbles informs us that in fact they have and they did, and that Buckley can apparently see straight through walls of forest.

'Hey there!' Mr Wilberry waves from the saddle, from the lead, his hair damp and his shirt buttons half-undone. Walter Scott could not have imagined him at all. One would have to be completely blind to avoid seeing him. I cannot force my eyes away, not this time. My God, the manliness of him. Impressive. Excessively. As he pulls up before us, Jack's shoulders ripple with a pleasure all his own too. I imagine he knows he has a man astride him, for once.

'I must apologise.' Mr Wilberry is in this instance superbly unapologetic. 'The water was too much to resist and we stayed far too long in it. Was your journey good?' he is asking me.

Me.

'Yes,' I reply, the journey already forgotten. I am too swept away by wonder, by curiosity, and too suddenly. Even from this height he does not look down upon me; he invites me up to him. How is this possible?

'Beautiful country.' He radiates with some beauty deeper than I know; that something I so dearly want: to be, in the world, as he is, with such gentle, rightful liberty. 'I must thank you for inviting us.' He is humble once more; hesitant. 'It's … hm – invigorating. To be out. And about.'

'Hm.' He is a fine human being, uncrumpling a battered hat from his haversack, a Huckleberry slouch of coarse straw. 'And you must be hungry too,' I suppose.

'I'll try not to choke to death this time, shall I?' A bass note that seems to prickle up through the soles of my feet. He is the sun under battered Huckleberry straw. He is buttoning up those last two buttons of his shirt, tiny buttons, such a large hand; my heart demands: *Don't do that.* And I suspect I am now hungry in ways I have never known before. This is not an invention of my exhaustion, is it? No.

Greta sniggles surreptitiously behind me, behind her hand, a *ha-ha* dare, before she assures him: '*I'll* cut the tomatoes this time, Mr Wilberry, don't you worry. I won't let my sister near them.'

My face flashes with a dreadful heat as I find my will and reason to turn away now, to fetch the picnic from the buggy, and as I do I see Mr Thompson, waterlogged and weary as the bush, his Panama sat on his head like a wilted lettuce leaf. He is not the effusively obnoxious bon vivant of last night; without his dinner attire and a steady stream of wine, he is thoughtful, and quiet, and he is watching me. Watching over his friend. Measuring me with a cold and sober stare. As well he should.

I do not raise my eyes from the task of setting out the picnic: blanket, crockery, basket …

'Let me help you with that,' Mr Wilberry offers, stepping near.

'No need, thank you. Our guest.' I wave him off, and I sound like some sort of strangulated harpy.

Buckley has the fire going and Greta sets to slicing the tomatoes, while I attack the bread and the cheese with all of my attention. She is chatting merrily, and I am sure she is enjoying my discomfort now more than anything, asking Mr Wilberry lightly: 'So, have you always been a vegetarian?'

'No,' he replies, and I see his knees across the blanket by hers, as I feel his voice travelling through my own. 'There was a drought, through '85 and '86. It was a pretty awful time, the cattle began to starve at our station and I began to wonder. You know, that they would endure such pain only to be served at our tables.'

'And unceremoniously massacred at school,' Mr Thompson adds as he lounges by him, legs stretched out towards me, boots almost at my skirt, I am sure symbolically: Keep your distance, woman. As if he sees how I might use his friend. 'Remember that steak and kidney pie we got on Monday nights? That was enough to put anyone off – I almost might have gone the same way as our Wilb.'

'Where did you go to school?' Greta asks them both, passing Mr Thompson the bottle of wine to open. I glance up at him, and he is more than happily at that task.

'King's School,' Mr Wilberry answers and I look up at him now across the cutting board; I can't stop myself. 'You?' he asks, and he is addressing me.

'St Cat's,' I say, by rote. Meaningless.

'Ha. We are of the same tribe then.' He laughs softly. It takes me a moment to find my way back to the conversation to understand what he's referring to. Same tribe. Ah yes: King's, St Cat's, we are the daughters and sons of privilege, sent to Sydney for school. He keeps smiling, into some memory of his own, plucking a grape. 'On one of our few civilising excursions we went to a so-called *dance* instruction afternoon with the ladies of St Cat's – and I'm pretty sure I'd never seen a girl before. The poor young lady I had to stand hopelessly with – Miss Pentridge was her name – told me I stank.'

'Oh dear!' Greta exclaims. 'What a nasty girl.'

'Not entirely,' says Mr Thompson with a plunking of the cork. 'He did smell pretty bad, as I recall it.'

Greta laughs so much at that she keels over onto her elbow, waving the knife in the air. She makes a little sobbing sound of delighted hysteria, and it makes me laugh too. I simply can't stop myself. But as I join in the laughter my hand slips into my pocket for my wishbone half, right down to the bottom of my pocket, and I grasp it tight: *Please*, as I beg that this laughter might come from my sister every day from this day forward, I beg too that whatever might be occurring here with Mr Wilberry will not distract me from all that I must do to see my sister safe. Safe from the monster who hurts and perverts her. To see myself safe from him too, the pinch of his fingers, the wrenching of my arm: *You will stop this resistance, Berylda – you ungrateful little slut.* I am somewhat and bizarrely calmed by this more urgent, more desperate need; calm enough to assemble the logic here, at least: I am clearly attracted to Mr Wilberry; I have never been attracted to a man before; it was going to happen one day, doubtless, and Mr Wilberry is an attractive man. Attractive to me specifically. There is nothing wrong with that. It's merely inappropriate. Ill-timed. And all very amusing for my sister. Breathe.

I do, and the air is sweet. We eat, and we talk about how nicely sharp this Dunkeld cheddar is, how crisp the Mount Olivet Chablis, and how well aged the jam; I watch the ducks playing on the water and Buckley watches us all from under a tree, further up the bank. He rolls a cigarette as Greta decides: 'I'd like to get on with colouring my picture now, please. Forgive me then for abandoning you all for a time, won't you?'

'Now that's an idea,' Mr Thompson says. 'I think I'd like to sketch you, painting your picture, then. What about it?'

'Oh!' Greta couldn't be more pleased at the suggestion. 'No one has ever made a sketch of me, Mr Thompson, I'd love that. Thank you.' And she grins at me, with a dismissive princess wave: 'You and Mr Wilberry will just have to do without us – I want to get as much done as I can in this magical light.'

'Of course you do.' I squint at her in pretend reproach; let her have her game with me. Her fun. It is magical enough for me to feel that I am claiming her back; moment by moment, here, my sister returns. Her strengths returns; perhaps, I dare to hope, there is no child in her at all. Only my fear.

I am not so thrilled at the idea of Mr Thompson sidling up too close to her, though. Don't trust him any more than I suppose he trusts me. And he's had his wine, swilled down a full tumbler of Dubbo's finest, now reaching for another ...

'Yes. Ah.' Mr Wilberry clears his throat. 'I'd like to walk back down along the river, Miss Jones.' Mr Wilberry is addressing me again: 'There's a marshy patch I saw earlier and I'd like to – I mean, what an invitation that must sound. But would you care to –?'

Leave my sister completely alone with Mr Thompson? No, I would not. But then she will not be alone, will she. I look to Buckley: he is watching still, sipping his mug of tea. He will let no bad thing happen to her; not that he could ever help. I look to Mr Wilberry and he nods as if he hears my worry too: 'We won't go far; we won't stray from sight.'

'Yes, Ryldy, please go away,' Greta pushes again. 'I don't want you hovering.'

'All right,' I bend, but I should not go anywhere with Mr Wilberry at all. I must not encourage him.

And yet, I do. The sip of wine I took with lunch has gone straight up to my head.

'Your servant has moved down the bank a way, I see,' Mr Wilberry notes with that rich, soft laugh in his voice as we begin to walk, and I am distracted, not only by my company but by the searing blast of heat as we step into the sun – real heat. It must be well over one hundred degrees now, beating through my blouse, across my back.

'Servant?' I reply, annoyed with myself: I left my stupid parasol back in the buggy.

'Your man Buckley – he's keeping a watchful eye.'

'Yes.' I glance back at him. 'He will. He is more than a servant.'

'Oh?'

'He's very loyal, to my sister and I.' I glance at Mr Thompson now too, a warning: if you are not who you seem, don't you try anything untoward: our man Buckley will kill you. There is a pistol concealed beneath the tent roll in the buggy, for our safety. He will not hesitate.

'Clearly,' Mr Wilberry replies and I feel the gentling smile in it, not that it stops me from glancing up this same warning at him too, prompting him to say: 'I didn't mean to cause offence. He seems an interesting man, Buckley, the sort who's seen his share of life.'

'Yes.' I soften, or attempt to: Mr Wilberry is only trying to make conversation. If it weren't for him, my sister and I would not have got away from Bellevue this morning at all. 'Yes, he's a good man. And I'm sure he's seen a share of life, little that I know of his. He came to us through one of our father's business partners, after –'

After the accident, after the black curtain fell. Memory sears: Buckley simply appeared one day, just as the grounds at Bellevue were completed, just as Uncle Alec decided he would need a man for the garden and the stables. A letter of recommendation came with him, from old Mr Gabriel, of Hartley Shale. Uncle Alec made a deal of taking him on as a favour, since he and Mr Gabriel, it seemed, were to be partners now themselves, since Uncle Alec would have to represent Aunt Libby in all such business and financial matters. *Never mind, darling Libby – don't worry about a thing.* I remember Alec Howell smiling. It was as if he couldn't see Libby's tears. Her distress meant nothing to him. Not one word of consolation to Greta or me, either. Not one word to acknowledge our devastation.

'After what?' Mr Wilberry asks.

I can't answer; I can't speak of it. Talk over it with something else now – what were we speaking of? Buckley. That's right. 'I think he might have been a convict,' I blabber like some empty-headed gossip. 'He spent twenty years in West Australia, I know that much, building the road from Albany to Perth, and when he's grumpy he always complains, "All for a pound of butter and a sack of beans." Somehow he ended up on the goldfields somewhere around here, one of the mines at Tambaroora, I think, and then working on the shale in the mountains. I don't know, precisely.'

'Ah, mines,' Mr Wilberry replies, chuckling uncertainly, nervously. 'They provide hiding holes for many a villain to disappear into, don't they?'

'Buckley is not a villain.' I bristle instantly again, for him and for all my family who've made their lives in this quartz country, from gold, from coal, from shale. I snap: 'Australia might well be a place where villains come to disappear, but Buckley is not one of them.'

'I do apologise.' Mr Wilberry is quick to it and embarrassed once more. 'That was clumsily said. I'm good at managing to be clumsy …'

'Yes, you are. And I am good at bristling.' I force a smile, and I'm sure it appears as such. Must I always be so quick to snap, to judge, to think the worst? 'This heat is …'

'Fairly hot. Here –' He bends at the water's edge and soaks a handkerchief; rings it out and passes it to me. 'It's clean …'

I don't care much if it isn't: I sling it round my neck. 'Thank you.'

As I do, he says, looking at my right hand on my shoulder: 'That's a beauty of a bruise you've got there.'

'What?' I am disoriented again and scramble to talk over it as well, looking at the ugly, darkening thing. 'Oh this? Bashed it into a door, silly accident – the door between my bedroom and my sister's – she was opening it as I was reaching for the handle and –'

'Ouch.' He finishes my lie with a sympathetic flinch.

'Yes. Ouch.' My smile is genuine now, and I am relieved as sincerely, not only at his easy sympathy, but for the small square of bliss that is his handkerchief, dripping down the back of my blouse now – while he persists with his wretched conversation: 'Your uncle seems a … an interesting man too. How did he come to New South Wales? He's not a native, is he? His accent is –'

'No, not a native, and I don't know how he came to be here.' This more than bristles: for all that I wish I were able to tell Mr Wilberry the truth, tell the whole world the truth, on first reflex I resent his prying into it. A thousand pricks of the scalpel up my spine. But he is not prying, is he. Merely making conversation, and more than that: there is something in Mr Wilberry's expression, some depth to the question. He really wants to know; he is waiting to know, and so I dare to reveal a bush-smoke trace of our circumstances, if not the flame itself. 'I barely know a thing about Alec Howell,' I say; let Mr Wilberry know by my tone that I am not fond of my so-called uncle. 'Son of a clergyman, native of Devon, but we've never met any of his family. They live in Barnstaple, and I don't even know exactly where that is, nor do I care to know.'

Bile churns through the bread in my stomach with terror coming after it. It only now comes to me, here on this riverbank, after all these years, that I know of no one who might vouch for Alec Howell's bona fides. No old acquaintance from the Home country who might really know him. Reverend Liversidge, Dr Weston, Mr Gabriel – do any of these men know him? Are they his friends? Somehow I don't think so. They are all recent acquaintances, professional and political connections, made since he moved to Bathurst, not very long before we were forced to remain there ourselves. Where are his acquaintances from Mudgee, where he was the resident surgeon when he and Aunt Libby first met? No one knows who he really is, do they? Just as no one knows what he really does.

'Where did he study?' Mr Wilberry asks now, a simple and mundane question of who's who, but still with that look of concern on his face, his open face, forehead creased with it.

I don't conceal my contempt as I answer: 'Bristol, he boasts about it often enough – such a big fish he was, in such a small pond. He says such things to deflect from his shame at not being Oxford or Cambridge educated. But I've never seen a certificate from any institution at all – he's far too modest to display his credentials, of course. His degree might be in engineering, for all I know.'

That's as close as I have ever come to accusing Alec Howell of anything and my heart is beating so fast, my knees begin to tremble again. I fix my sight on Mr Wilberry's face. This man. This good man. Breathe.

Breathe.

This man will not hurt me.

'Yes. No. Well.' He winces over the longest pause, before responding, carefully: 'People disappear into this land for many reasons, don't they? Then fashion themselves into all sorts of things. My own father has made quite an art of it himself.' Mr Wilberry smiles as carefully, but I can only breathe; earth myself by the crunch of leather on twig and stone, and nod for him to continue. 'Yes,' he does, 'as a young man my father was sent away in some disgrace from the family business, in Sheffield, under voluntary transportation to avoid the possibility of a prison sentence. Umbrella factory, it was – still is – left in charge at the age of twenty-one. When his father was away on business, he beat the bookkeeper to within an inch of his life for making an error with the price of the turned handles, and look at him now? No one would ever suspect he wasn't born an outback cattleman, one that holds the parliament of Queensland under his fist – or would if it weren't for all you thieving southern Federationists wrecking his plans for world domination. Thing about him, though, is he's proud of it all – unashamedly proud of this consistency of character. Makes no attempt whatsoever to hide it.'

The blue of Mr Wilberry's eyes is bright with this suite of irony, and I might laugh at his self-deprecating revelation, I might even appreciate this exchange of intimacies, except for what it means to me: Alec Howell came here to disappear, didn't he? A criminal who came to fashion himself into another form. Terror or instinct, I cannot know how this comes to me but that it comes with a blistering clarity: what he has done to me, to Gret, he has somehow done before. Of course he has. This is hardly a revelation. It is some creeping knowledge. Knowledge of a particular animal. I want to speak of it with Mr Wilberry. I wish I could, I wish it would all pour from me and away. But there remains nothing I can speak of here. Nothing I can say without betraying myself; betraying my sister.

'How did you come to live with him?' Mr Wilberry wants to know. 'Your uncle, I mean.'

And I want to tell him; how I do. I begin: 'He married my aunt, just before our parents ... and ... then ...' I can't say any more.

'I'm so sorry, Miss Jones. I don't mean to press you – I ...' He can see my loss plainly enough.

I try again; force it out staccato: 'He married my aunt, whirlwind romance as they say. Swept her off her feet in the ballroom at the Star Hotel in Gulgong; fundraising dinner, for the little hospital there – he was visiting from Mudgee, where he worked at the time. My aunt told us every detail of that night, *that* whirlwind dance, but she is no longer here for me to ask her any more about it. Him. Not long after our parents were gone, she left us too. Typhoid.'

'Harsh,' he says to the twigs and the stones, that one word so full of concern it does somehow cool off the top of the pain. He asks me now: 'Is this why you have chosen Medicine? A need to heal, perhaps?' A funny grimace scrunches his face, as if I might snap at him again or whack him with a stick.

It forces a laugh from me, or this strange familiarity we seem to have with each other does; it's a barely-there wisp of a laugh but a laugh nevertheless, as I say to him: 'I don't know that either.' But I wonder at it aloud: 'I choose Medicine, I suppose, because I am good at hard facts, hard work, and I must have some career, one that might provide an income to keep my sister and me, independently. There's Medicine or utter penury as a school teacher, and that's about it for the professions, and neither of them easy on a girl. My best friend at Women's College is doing Law, and although her family is stacked with esteemed wigs, there's no guarantee that she will be able to practise – who would go to a lady lawyer anyway?'

The law that allows Alec Howell's theft of our parents' estate slices into me, again and again; this law that says he's the one who collects the rent on our homes, in Gulgong, in Katoomba, the places of the love that made us. Hatred and heat and loss drive a fever in me, all prickling warmth of attraction smashed away by a stinging skinlessness, and I am certain I will never heal. As I could not

206

make Libby heal by wishing it. Oh how she suffered as she left us, Libby. I dived into the few general medical texts in the study, I kept looking for the telltale rose spots of the infection on her lovely skin, hoping that their absence meant the diagnosis was wrong. It wasn't of course: any fool could see. The bacteria clawing its way through her so fast it didn't bother with the rash. Yet I was so desperate for her to heal that – that Mr Wilberry is quite possibly right. I say: 'But perhaps yes, perhaps I make my choice to heal, as futile as that may too often be.'

'Not futile, Miss Jones,' he says, and I wish I had a fraction of the compassion that this man can transmit by merely glancing at me. 'You are admirable in every way,' he adds.

I wish he hadn't.

He says: 'I have brought you down.'

'No. You haven't,' I assure him. 'Stop apologising, please – it's irritating.' I suck in my cheeks facetiously, at my own brittleness. 'It's a touchy subject – you must know, there is no guarantee that I will ever be able to practise medicine, either, in any meaningful or profitable way – no great stampede beating a path to any lady doctor's door, whether I get my degree or not. I'll probably be relegated to weighing babies and treating dizzy spells and other such earth-shattering feminine issues – in Duramana – for two bob and an old tin of jam per week.'

'Ha! Too funny – awful.' He jollies along with me, but he continues to regard me quizzically, wanting to know yet more. 'You are a hard one to read, Miss Jones. Not that I'm at all adept at reading girls – women. Er. Clumsy – I …' Grimace.

He reads me well enough, and he is close enough; I send him back a deterrent: 'You can be forgiven – I'm sure it's because of the Chinese in me.' I'm sure he won't be as taken with me now. 'I am a tricky and inscrutable Oriental when it comes down to it. Grandmother's name was Millie Wing Tock, daughter of a Hong Kong greengrocer. Can't you see her in me now I've said so?'

'Ah, that's the shape …' he replies, and it has an *of course* in it, now he's found in it my features. But he surprises me once more with what appears to be delight: 'Indeed there is no such thing as a White Australia, is there?'

'Precisely. Apart from you.' I send it back again.

And he laughs, with a warmth gentler than any sun could ever be. 'Apart from me,' he agrees, looking at the blond hair along his forearms. 'I don't think you get much fairer than me before you reach albinism.'

He's not that fair; I bask in his burnished warmth. I drink it in and it quenches and stokes at once.

'Cos, though,' he smiles deeper, a crooked grin for his friend, 'he's in rather another category. I shouldn't tell tales, I suppose, but you look like you can keep a straight enough face – he's in common law marriage with a half-caste black woman, his *domestic*, shall we say for the neighbours. Susan, her name is, she's a lovely sort, and they have twins, a boy and a girl, two little brown babies toddling about. Only in Queensland. But he's one of a kind, our Cos. Doing his best to be subversive, in all ways, always. I don't know how Susan tolerates him.'

'Really?' I begin to laugh again, too, and properly, recalling Mr Thompson's cries of *SHOOT THE BLACKS* last night. How wonderfully, deliciously shocking. 'What about you?' I ask Mr Wilberry. 'Any illegitimate children of dubious racial origin?'

'None. I'm rather ordinary, I'm afraid.'

I'm afraid too. You're rather excellent. I jest away from him again: 'You can't be too ordinary if you survived the King's School with so much of your personality intact. How did you manage it?' In such a place notorious for its brutality, beating young men into the rough shapes of their fathers, and sending them off to the Transvaal, like Clive, who seems such a boy compared to this man.

He sends it back in perfect time: 'I rowed, in summer at least. Single sculls.' That funny grimace again: 'I rowed a lot, on the Parramatta – I might have rowed right up to the harbour and out to sea, if I could ever have managed to steal enough decent food.'

His laugh is gentler and deeper still. It is a river, this river.

'Came out to Bathurst with rugby once, but that was ten years ago – more actually. Rugby was compulsory – except for Cos. He'd cop a thrashing from the sportsmaster instead and go and sit under a tree and wait for cricket season. I wasn't much good at rugby but it was some sort of fun.'

Rugby? Whatever. I want his arms around me here, by this river. I want to lie with him and look up into the arms of the great tree there and wonder at … At how unfair this is, this next turning of my curse. This is too cruel.

'Oh. Look at that – mint bush.' He points out some thing or other at the edge of the glade ahead. He leans down to pick a sprig of it as we step into the shade and I see the plant, a small mound of lilac cloud; quite pretty. 'Medicinal shrub, apparently,' he explains to me. 'Blacks use it for … I don't know, something. A disinfectant, I think.'

'Do they? I prefer soap and water myself.' It's pretty, though, this bush mint – tiny lilac trumpets of prettiness – and I would like to catch its scent, take a guess at its antiseptic constituent – oil or astringent? – but he is walking away from me now …

Further along the edge of the glade, somehow poised, just as he was along the strand when we stopped earlier this morning. Benjamin Wilberry – Flower Hunter. I smile to myself at that, and this blessed shade, however thin it is. I follow him – straight through a deep puddle. And I don't care that my boots and the bottom of my skirt and petticoat are wet. The water seeps up my stockings: heavenly cool.

'What?' Mr Wilberry asks himself, transfixed upon some other thing. Pocket knife raised, half-crouching to it now. 'Strike me – what is this? No. It couldn't be. I don't believe it.'

BEN

*B*elieve *what you see, Ben.*

Not here, now – surely? The rows of fine, long outer raylets, the satin sheen of the bracts beneath, huge blooms, two inches across altogether from tip to tip, set upon dark grey stipes, slender, tough, the foliage confined to the base ... the flowerheads raised circlets at the centre, fat, full, open, like tiny crowns, and positioned perfectly to take in whole mornings of the sun here ... *Helichrysum macranthum*? But this species is from the west, from about as far west as you might get – along the Margaret River, on the continent's most southwesterly boot heel. I look behind me as though the old man Buckley might have walked them here under his own boot heels. These are ...

Not macranthums, son ... look at again. Take it into the light and look again.

I cut one of the stipes, from a plant of three singular blooms, and I know already that this is not *macranthum* – generally there might be a hand of four or five blooms to a stipe with that species; ten or even twenty blooms at once on a plant. I spent a fair amount of time looking, never expecting I'd visit the Margaret River again anytime soon. When was that? Three years ago now – four? Perhaps my memory does fail me after all.

Give up on doubting yourself, Ben – look at the bloom again, Mama insists: *You've been blinded by the shade. Look again.*

I step back into the sunshine and yes, there I see it: the colour of the raylets. They are not white as *macranthum* are. They're ... I'm not sure what colour it is. Not a rose shade, not apricot. Some colour in between – smoky. And the central disc is bronze: a bronze crown, the pollen almost iridescent in the light. Outstanding.

I have never seen this daisy before, in the field, or in a study, and I have lately studied this whole damn genus as it appears in New South Wales.

It is its own. It must be. And I've found it.

I've never found a new species before. Stick this in your pipe, Dubois. With any luck. Here is one fairly incredible daisy.

'What is it?' Berylda Jones is at my side, staring up at it too.

And I can only tell her: 'I don't know.'

BERYLDA

I've never seen someone so excited to not know something.

'I have not the slightest notion.' He fills the gorge with it. 'Oh this is great. Spectacular. I've never seen anything like it.'

'It's one of your native daisies?' I offer, though I'd never know: it doesn't look like the bedraggled wet-feather ones from Bellevue, or those dried, ever-tired yellow things you might see on railway-cafeteria table arrangements that look like they're made from balls of raffia. This one looks like a daisy, on an elegant leafless stem, a seaweed pink daisy, the same colour as my silk camellia, the one Greta wore last night, not quite real, and the centre of it is like rusted velvet ... I've never seen anything like it either.

'*Helichrysum* most definitely is the genus, but what species?' he asks the hills. This face, this pleasant, manly face is transformed: both inspired and maniacal. Turning now back to me, promising: 'If it's new, and I suspect it is, I'm going to name it after you.'

Oh no, don't. No. This is too far. Please. 'It's a handsome flower, lovely, but –'

'*Helichrysum beryldii*, that's what it shall be.'

And he strides off, calling out: 'Cos! Cos, old matey – stop whatever it is you're doing.'

I follow him back to our picnic spot, almost running to keep up, and he's ordering his friend about, shoving the base of the flower under his nose. 'Catch this particularly, Cos, this involucre–' some word, some thing I don't know. A language I don't know and

212

one I find myself now scrambling after, too. *Helichrysum*, I search my scanty Greek. What does that mean? *Helio* – sun. *Chryssos* – Christ? No – *gold*. Treasure. Sun-treasure. Sun-flowers, of course that's what it means.

'But I doubt these colours will stay fast in drying – they are so subtle.' He is all action, all-consumed.

And Greta is like a magnet to the excitement, dropping her own work, offering: 'Let me see if I might mix the colour for you. May I try?'

'Yes, please – would you?' He appears elated that she has even asked, and there he is putting his head together with my sister's, discussing colour, listening intensely to her opinion on the best way forward with this most particular and intriguing shade of pink. He is quite possibly the most excellent man ever to exist.

Dashing back now to the plant again, stooping over it, examining it under a glass, from the nest of leaves near the ground, to the blooms on top of those fine, long stems, and I cannot help but trail him like a lost student. 'Ah, yes.' He is thrilled again at finding what looks to be a half-dead one, taking a small wallet from his trouser pocket and opening it. It contains tiny brushes, a tiny scalpel, tweezers, and the tiniest envelopes ever made. 'Seeds. Ripe seeds,' he says to himself, or at least to some other presence of the forest crouching with him by the plant. 'I can't believe this luck.' Tweezers and envelopes Lilliputian in his hands, he looks at me now and with enraptured astonishment: 'I've captured some seeds.'

'Such excitement, for one plant, one flower?' I am hardly less astonished in return.

'Oh no,' he replies. 'There's at least seven plants here.'

I'm sure that's tremendous. It is to him. He takes another cutting of a full bloom and explains: 'One for the herbarium – my collection – in Melbourne. I hope this colour lasts, at least a bit.' And I trail him back to the picnic, back to his haversack, from which he takes a long square jar and a packet of sugar – no, sand. He fills the jar about a third of the way, on an angle, and eases the flower into it, and then gently, gently, gently he fills the jar up to the top. He fills it with such tenderness my feet might strike root and never move from this spot again.

'What you got there?' Buckley has come down from under his tree to see what all the fuss is about, and Mr Wilberry points over at the cutting his friend is sketching in all its parts: 'This daisy – I've never seen one like it before.'

'You haven't?' Buckley scratches his head under his hat. 'I reckon you might find a few of them coming round Sofala way – up over the other side, round Monkey Hill, you see them.'

'Dinkum?' I see the boy in Mr Wilberry, the euphoria of the hitherto impossible made real and true. 'How far is that?'

'Too far today, Mr Wilberry, 'fraid to say.' Buckley can only disappoint him. 'Another day's travel again from here.'

'Oh. Right. Well. For another day, then.' Mr Wilberry clears his throat, tucks that too-long hair behind his ears, coming back into himself as if he were shaking off a dream. 'Great. Good.' He looks to me, apologetic once more: 'That was all a little unexpected, wasn't it?'

Perhaps. I want to say this is how life is meant to be. Should be. Mystifying journeys punctuated by such serendipity. A puzzle constructed and solved by hope. By love. But all I can say is: 'Yes.'

And I turn from him, the skinlessness shivering up from my boots to consume me once more. Burning. I can't tolerate this nearness to him any longer. We cannot be friends, no matter how I am drawn to him, no matter how reasonable the attraction might be. I do not have men friends. I cannot and never shall, no matter how noble, how excellent this one appears to be. They are wolves, in one way or another, all of them. I force the steel back into my spine, into my will, and remind myself: I am here to erase the one that slaves my sister and me. I am not here to play games of sweet nothing. Of hearts and flowers and fantasies. I catch a taunting glimpse of it, a wedding veil, a tossed bouquet, an escape – the most ideal of escapes there could ever be – before Alec Howell grasps my wrist: he would never allow me to marry Mr Wilberry. Should Mr Wilberry even want to marry me. In the next two days. And why would he? Beneath this sunshine, my soul is black with hate and fear and pain. Step away from him, Berylda. Step away.

I do, and I return to Gret, kneel on the blanket next to her, my shoulder aching as if the devil has in fact just wrenched my arm again.

'Can I see your painting now, Gret?' I pick up the sketchbook discarded behind her. I can barely hear my own voice above this clashing mayhem in my head.

But I hear Greta: 'Ryl! No. Don't look yet. It's still not finished. It's supposed to be a present for you.' Snatching the book away.

Too late for me to fail to see what picture she is making: beyond a poppy-strewn bank, amidst the whirl of half-coloured lines it is she and I, in the willow, and Libby –

Oh dear God.

Libby's face looking up at us from the river. In the river.

I am washed through with heartbreak. And then as suddenly numb to it, somehow across the other side of it. I am barely here at all.

I hear myself say to my sister: 'It's finished enough for me to say it's lovely.' The sound of elsewhere, far, far away.

'Well, you would say that.' Greta remains annoyed; and I am so sorry that she is. 'But Mr Thompson peeked, too,' she says, 'and he said I should make drawings for children's stories. He might know someone that –'

'Really? That's nice.' I stare and stare into the fringed edge of the picnic blanket, the fibres of the wool scribbling into tiny spikes of mean grass. Struggling to bring myself back to the earth. Here.

'Nice,' Mr Thompson's drawl is sneering, at me. 'Really *nice*. Lovely.'

Mr Wilberry clears his throat again. 'I think I'll just take a wander further downstream for a bit.' I can't see him, but I watch him walk away, alone along the bank.

BEN

Damn that. She turns her back, she turns away. What must she think of me? What in idiocy's name has got hold of me? Carrying on all round the place. All my blundering questions to her, pressing her about the uncle, pressing for answers I have no business knowing, and then – save me – *Helichrysum beryldii*? Did I really press that on her, too? Yes, I did. I've known the girl less than twenty-four hours and I've gone pretty well straight from dumbstruck imbecile to how about I name a new species after you?

Even Mama has nothing to say about that. How could I be so presumptuous? So inept. Such a bloody – *Seeds! I've captured some seeds!*

Because it's just me, isn't it. Can't help myself. And I'm doing it again right now. I've just spotted a *Hakea saligna*, a good-looking eastern needlewood, and my head is turned: fine spread of the branch ribs, good length to the leaf, it must be happy here. Past flowering, though. Pity. All we have today is the flat-headed warts of the fruit.

Little wonder she turns her back.

I have spent too long alone with my obsessions – *making daisy fucking chains*.

A copper-wing butterfly suns itself on a leaf, a flash of turquoise before it flies away, too.

Leaving the frown. The frown devours me.

216

BERYLDA

'He's been gone a long time,' I say to the hands of my watch. Almost two hours, he's been gone. It's half-past three. We must leave soon; we must get up the last of the Track before we lose the light: the sun sets early on the Hill, rendering it infamously treacherous. It already seems to be darkening, shadows seeping from the gorge, the air cooling now. It can't be, though, can it?

'Probably only lost his sense of time – he holds a PhD in advanced rambling, don't you know?' Mr Thompson shrugs, unconcerned, gnawing on his pipe, flicking me a look of cool abhorrence. I flick him one back. This Mr Thompson is so habitually inconsiderate he might remain unconcerned if his friend were being eaten by a lion. There aren't any lions here, though, are there, I hardly need to remind myself. I look across the river at the great tree, its wild forbidding arms affirming that there is no need for lions in this place: there are snakes and river snags aplenty, the hungry arms of the bush itself. Something unseen slithers and ripples through the water now.

What if he's gone for another swim and – what if he's fallen from the edge of a rock, or –

'Please, Buckley, go and find Mr Wilberry,' Gret asks, a nervous urgency in her request, screwing tops quickly back onto paint tubes, packing away her things: *He's been gone too long.*

And I agree: 'Please, Buckley, do look for him now. We must get away.'

'Don't worry, misses, he won't be far, I don't reckon. I'll find him, you can be sure of that.' Buckley gives us a confident nod, and he sets off along the riverbank calling: 'Cooee!'

'*Cooee!*' The call soars like that of a sad and ancient bird. Lost. The air cools and cools. Can the temperature be dropping so rapidly?

'Gret – you've left your palette on the grass, behind you,' I snap at my sister roughly. 'There – and a brush, two of them.' As if it's her fault Mr Wilberry has gone off. Perplexed by my horridness. Come to misfortune by my –

Nothing has happened to Mr Wilberry.

But the weather is changing. The bright tops of fat silver clouds are rising above the hills behind us, coming up from the south, promising a squall. Oh jolly good, it's going to rain, and we'll have a river for a track and bogs to contend with, too.

Hurry up, Mr Wilberry.

But Buckley's call goes on: '*Cooee!*'

'Honestly,' Mr Thompson sidles up to me, with his stale tobacco breath and crumbs in his beard, staring down his long nose at me, so convinced of himself. 'He'll only have forgotten all about us. He does that – loses himself in the bush. He's quite at home here, Miss Jones. Quite secure in the *natural* world.' The sarcasm of this man makes me want to slap his face, to leave him in no doubt as to how handsome I find it. 'You're not worried about Wilber, are you?' he asks, large, round eyes blinking grey crystal scorn.

'Worried? Why should I be worried?' The scritch in my voice is high and hard enough to shred stone, and turn from him to attend to the mess of our picnic remains. 'We must get away, that's all I'm worried about.' I shake the last drops in the wine bottle onto the grass: Mr Thompson drank it all bar the sip each the rest of us had. Needed it to wash down those three pieces of cake, didn't you, Fatso.

But he's not drunk. He's turned from me, too, and is packing Mr Wilberry's botanical paraphernalia into his haversack, muttering as he does: 'And for a moment there, dear, I thought you cared.'

'What did you say?' I snap and challenge.

'Merely talking to myself, Miss Jones. Talking to myself.' He shrugs again, folding his own sketchbook away.

I glare at him, to let him be sure I heard exactly what he said. How dare you presume that I don't care. I *never* don't care. But he doesn't look up from his buckling of straps. He stuffs another pipe when he's done, and stares down the river.

'*Cooee!*'

Instead of thumping Mr Thompson on the shoulder as I'd like to, I snap at my sister once more, as we begin folding the picnic blanket: 'No – take the corners this way.' I shake it at her, hurting my own sore shoulder as I do, and just as the breeze whips into gusts and tears one side of the blanket from her hand. 'Oh, come on, Gret.' I scowl as the light falls and falls and the bush closes in. The hills range higher, tighter, around us, and the rising clouds above them are bright bruises filling the sky; a rumble of thunder and a burst of low sun flashes over us all, picking out each leaf lurid against the bruises, picking out the blood of the great tree and making it run.

'Ahoy!' Mr Thompson shouts now, and when I look back at him I see he is jogging into the wind. To Mr Wilberry.

'Mr Wilberry!' Greta might run, too, if I didn't have her by the blanket corners.

Of course, there he is, looking just as he did when he left, just as he did throughout my thoughts: a man walking along a riverbank. Conversing with Buckley about something, pointing back to the west, now turning, to see his friend jogging towards him. Mr Thompson is not a man used to such physical exertion: he half-stumbles as he runs. He was worried about Mr Wilberry, too, then.

Irritation scrapes at me. How dare Mr Wilberry make me care so much. I call into it: 'Hurry up – hurry up, it's going to rain!'

The three men stare at me for a moment – is she insane? – before Buckley waves and breaks off from them to attend to Sal. My face is scalding me with – what is this strange rage? This strange palpitating of my heart?

It is the storm. Only the storm. How I hate storms. Thunderstorms: there it goes again, rolling up through my bones.

'Ouch – Ryl, what's the matter with you!'

I have trod on Greta's toe, pushing over her to heave the basket back up into the buggy.

'I'm sorry,' I say, and I am sorry in every way, but the thunder comes yet again, and I am wild: 'Get in, Gret – now. The storm.'

Mr Wilberry calls out something to Buckley but it is lost to me on the wind – the force of which I am fighting as I try to raise the canopy of the buggy against it. 'Help me, Gret!'

'Don't fret, Miss Berylda, we'll make it,' Buckley assures me, chuckling rumble under his brim, winking at Gret. 'There's only about three and half drops of rain to them clouds, I reckon. We won't be washed away today.'

No, of course we won't. I know this. We have been here before. But even so I hold my breath as we watch our visitors take the crossing, the hooves of the stallions ringing on the pebbles, and then they're quickly up to their knees in the river, and I don't let this breath out until I see they are well past the middle, and making their way up the other side. Just as Sal takes it and us with her and Greta knocks against me: 'Oh but I love the sound of wheels through water.'

She loves all of it: lightning, thunder, this gale steadily unpinning the coil of her plaits, strands of hair whipping against her happy face. Her arms are held wide around the rails, as mine are held fast to edge of the seat, my knuckles white.

As thunder shakes the air again, a rumble that goes on and on. I look up the steep incline ahead, one which will go on and on, these last few miles, all the way to Hill End. Mr Wilberry and Mr Thompson are already out of sight around the bend. *Hurry up, Sal*, I dare to take one hand from the seat to grasp the losing-half wishbone in my pocket, but I know our little mare can't go any faster. She snorts hard to say she'd like to but Buckley won't let her. 'Whoa, Sally, whoa,' he warns her and warns her.

And the thunder continues to rumble and crack, rainless, so that I'm waiting for lightning to split a tree and start a rampaging fire next. I am held and surprised by how much I hate this. This endless bashing through the bush. Did I hate it as a girl with Papa at the reins? I don't remember it being so, but I can't be sure. I glance back out of the small round window in the canopy for the great tree, but it is gone, as the river is gone too. All is the bush: even the trees close in together here.

'Whoa, girl!' Buckley pulls Sal up suddenly, veering right with a sickening crunch of branches through spokes. 'Whoa!'

The thunder is growing louder. 'What?' I almost scream it. The thunder is bearing down on us. 'What?' Can it be?

'Steady girl,' Buckley is warning Sal again more urgently, a note of fear in his voice too, I'm sure of it.

Because it's not thunder but another party, careering down upon us.

There is no room here for another vehicle to pass. To pass us it must crash through forest or rock or take to the air.

Why, oh why did I choose the Bridle Track? Picnic? Greta and I shall find our freedom in annihilation any moment.

'Oh Ryldy.' Her arms are tight around me now.

And I hold her as tight to me.

As we wait for the collision.

We hold each other as we watch the hooves smashing down through the dust towards us, and I am too stuck in terror to look away. It is a hundred-hooved demon of dust.

But there is no vehicle behind it.

The riders pass us in a single file, without breaking their gallop, without acknowledgement of any kind, only a savage urging of their horses.

'Yar! Yar!'

'C'mon!'

'Gorn! Yar gorn!'

Three or four of them, I could not tell.

Buckley turning to us: 'It's all right, misses, yous are all right.' He brushes a hand through the air, a signal to us to keep where we are and keep steady, and he's warning Sal once more and firmly: 'Wait, girl, wait.'

What are we waiting for?

Two mounted policemen in pursuit. Naturally. This is Hill End. The journey would not be complete without encountering a gang of bushrangers and a couple of troopers flying down the Turon Gorge after them, would it? One of the policemen touches his cap as he passes as if to say good afternoon.

And my afternoon wouldn't be complete without Mr Wilberry galloping down behind them, pulling up as he finds us, Jack rearing and tossing his mane; man and beast as one with the question: 'Is everyone all right? Are you safe?'

In a more incredible world where great trees do truly pluck miscreants up from river crossings, I might be.

'Yes,' says Buckley. 'We're right. Other feller good, your Mr Thompson?'

'Oh, he'll live.' Mr Wilberry replies and begins to ask Buckley, 'But what in the —' His nostrils flaring as Jack's, he's ready to gallop on in pursuit at a word.

Buckley shrugs: 'Dunno. Only young fellers – thieving maybe, or most likely fighting. Must've got up someone's nose properly to have the coppers after them, anyway, aye.' Our Buckley, so steady himself, you'd think he stared down sudden death every day.

'Well, as long as there's no harm done here, I suppose ...' Mr Wilberry looks at me; smiling, tentatively, searchingly. Looking to see that we are still friends.

'No harm whatever,' says Gret beside me, squeezing me around the waist quickly and with mischief before drawing her arms away. 'I'm sure that by the time we're at dinner we'll all find that was a great load of terrific, won't we?' She is exhilarated by the whole thing, of course.

'Ha!' Mr Wilberry smiles at her – briefly.

Before returning his smile to me. An open smile. A forgiving and insistent one that is asking me directly: 'Yes?'

I don't know what to do with my own face any more than I know how to answer his hopeful question; but I barely have the chance to consider either before Mr Wilberry's attention suddenly shifts elsewhere, somewhere into the bush behind me.

He dismounts and hands his reins to Buckley. 'Would you mind? I'll just be a – excuse me. *Callistemon* – ah, won't be a moment.'

As he leaves us to stalk his floral prey just beyond these roadside trees, Buckley chuckles again to himself: 'Funny feller.' I can't reply to that either, predominantly because I have just become aware how close we are to the edge of a chasm here, and that Mr Wilberry has grasped a too-spindly trunk to lean out over it from a rocky ledge for … Is that a banksia he's plucking from that raggedy scrub? The man would risk his life for a common ratty scrap of banksia bush?

'Oh Ryldy, look – look, it's a bottlebrush. A golden bottlebrush. Painted on the sky. How lovely is that!' Greta cries as he holds his prize up to show us. 'Look at that colour,' my sister shouts, soprano soaring around the walls of the gorge. 'I've never seen a golden bottlebrush before.'

'Hm,' is the best response I can utter, and I don't see the delicate gilt quills of the bottlebrush, don't see them at all, or the very lovely way he is smiling at my sister now as he gives her one of the flowers she is reaching across me for, explaining: 'It's an alpine species. I was hoping to see one in the field, and here we have it. What a day this is.' I don't smell the salt of his sweat drifting to me from soft, crumpled calico sleeve, or see his effortless lope back into the saddle, either. The sinking sun has parted the clouds now and blinds me.

It stays in our eyes for most of the rest of the way up, and I am glad of the sting of the empty tears it forces. I never want to see this most excellent man again.

'You're not feeling unwell again, are you, Ryl?'

'No, darling – just a bit weary.'

So very weary. This cruelty is too much, a labyrinthine trap that lengthens and shifts by the moment. Transform me then, too, so that I might be as cruel, to find our way through. I am not in this place to love. I am in this place to find the means to kill. I look into the hills, into the mine entrances peppered all around their blank-faced slopes now, the timber lintels of all our many portals into hell.

THE HILL

Untroubled, scornful, outrageous— that is how wisdom wants us to be: she is a woman and never loves anyone but a warrior.

Thus Spake Zarathustra

BEN

'What a sad little shitter is this End of the Earth,' Cos says as we sight what I take for the main street.

And continue to ignore him. The light is dimming, the sun well behind the ridge that sits over the town, but it dims nothing of the place: a dogleg of pubs and faded shop awnings advertising their wares along with their inventive approaches to architecture. There would not be a square in any joint here but by accident, I'll bet. The whole town is an accident, of the rushes, now half-forgotten, and more than half the shops appear permanently closed, boarded up, just as several huts on the rather less colourful dogleg in looked abandoned and half-scavenged of their tin and timbers, bark roofs long gone. The yard we are passing now is bounded by wire-strung pickets lurching drunkenly in want of a nail, and all that stands in the yard is a brick chimney – all that's left of whoever once dwelt there. Extraordinary to think that, not so long ago, no further back in human history than the year I was born, this would have been one of the richest places on earth, teeming with optimism, but there's not a street lamp to be seen as testament to it today.

'You just let me know when I'm supposed to be glad I almost died for the privilege of being here, won't you.' Cos is sniffing the air, discerning that the stale manure pervading beneath the wood smoke is both equine and otherwise. Not too much indoor plumbing around this place, by the strength of it.

I laugh, and finally respond: 'You did not nearly die. Though I'm sure in a town like this arrangements could be made ...'

Cos stares at me, and he does look half-dead. I should congratulate him for making it to our destination, but he's not dead enough yet to stop whingeing: 'And I suppose you're happy to be here, are you?'

'Yes, as a matter of fact, I am.' Apart from wanting to explore what I can of the terrain tomorrow, there's something about the impermanence of these sorts of mining towns that cheers me: nothing Man could ever do can last forever. We're as ephemeral as gold strikes themselves; the bald and slaggy hilltops all around us will recover one day, too.

'Must you be so vomitously happy about it, though? You did almost kill me, you know. In fact, this is the worst thing you've ever done to me. You do know that, don't you.'

'*I've* done this to you?' For the hundredth time I remind him: 'You didn't have to come.'

'Oh, yes I did,' he mutters.

And I return to ignoring him, leave him to grumble around all his weird anxieties. He was never in any danger; our horses are too well trained and dauntless – they were never going to startle in the gorge or bolt when those tearaways came down on us. But I am probably a bit annoyingly cheerful, it's true, and weirdly so. Or perhaps settled is the better word. Saner than I have felt for some time, perhaps; possibly ever. Berylda Jones might despise me, or she might think nothing of me – that would represent little deviation from my general experience with women – but I came to realise on my solitary walk along the Turon that it's quite beside the point what she thinks of me.

In the first instance, I have discovered what I am fairly certain is a new species of native daisy, and that is something to be very cheerful about, no matter what she or Cos or anyone else might think of it, or what name I give to it. Whatever it is, it will entirely justify my absence from the university this time, too. Professor Jepson will be nicely pleased when he is informed of both the discovery and my intention to return to Melbourne directly after my explorations at Manildra – I'll be back within the month – the sooner to get a paper out on the find and then get back to the work that the whole faculty would much prefer I apply myself to: collaborating with the Board of Agriculture on the development of that science as a university degree course. While maintaining whatever influence I might exert on the classification of so-called 'native weeds', and all in good time before lectures resume. So Dubois can despise me all he likes, and to no effect.

In the second instance, and of more serious consideration than anything else, Berylda Jones is in some jeopardy. I don't know what it is, but on my walk I listened and relistened to our conversation, and there is something there. Something wrong. As much as she made her lack of affection for her uncle clear, I am sure she withheld as much as she revealed about him. About this conflict between them, the conflict in her. She is determined that she and her sister will be independent of her uncle; why? Odious as he is, why eschew the comforts and connections that man might afford her? Then there is the sister's painting, of the river sprite tethered into the tree, it comes back and back to me, haunting indeed, as does the image of the bruise blooming across the back of Berylda's hand. There is a picture to be made of these pieces, a picture yet obscured. A most unhappy one, I am sure.

And in the third and simplest instance, Berylda Jones has suffered a terrible amount of misfortune and grief in her young life. Little wonder she frowns. It is arrogance to imagine she frowns specifically at me. She does not know it yet, but she is alone no longer: I will help her in any way I can. I will be her friend.

'Whoa, ahead,' Buckley calls from behind us, catching up as we have slowed, and I see the awning of our final resting place: *WHEELER'S FAMILY HOTEL* emblazoned in carnival lettering propped along the length of the rusting tin roof that's nevertheless bordered with a wooden frieze of blue ocean waves. The building itself is painted yellow – an eye-watering yellow even in this light. This is an establishment one could not fail to notice, or wonder at its displacement from the seaside amusement pier it surely belongs to. What a fantastic wreck of a thing it is.

'Well, blow me down,' says Cos, livening a fraction. 'It's the tart shop at the End of the Earth.'

'And you'd know, wouldn't you.' I laugh as the buggy overtakes us, and the sister, Greta, wonders almost in my ear: 'Where have all the people gone?'

I don't hear Buckley's reply to her, but I look up this crooked street again: little sign of life but for the puffing chimneys and a bored dog wandering from side to side, sniffing the dirt – no, actually, that's a goat. Eerie, as though the Wild West Rodeo has just left town, taking every cowboy with it. But then, it is New Year's Day, isn't it – perhaps the miners who live here are sleeping off last night and couldn't be bothered with Federation either. More than past it now myself. I yawn, and as I do I hear the creak of boards outside the pub. I look around, back to the verandah, and find myself looking right into the round, ruddy face of a man stepping up on a ladder, to light the lamp under the awning.

'Good evening, travellers!' He smiles from ear to ear at me and Cos. 'What can I do for you, gentlemen?' he asks with a hearty bark that's barely left the Cornish coast, and I do believe this might well be a tart shop.

Before I can answer and Cos can stop coughing with misfired laughter, the man peers up the verandah, at Buckley hopping out of the buggy, and his grin widens with recognition. 'Roo? Is that you? Roo! Well, if it isn't Roo Buckley!' he bellows. 'And what can I do for you, my fine friend, my cobber, my old boot?' He's wiping his hands on a short apron and extending one to him.

'Did I hear you say Roo Buckley?' A woman appears at the double doors to the saloon with a broomstick, round like the man, she could be his sister but that she has a thick European accent of some kind.

'Olga!' Buckley calls her, grinning too. 'Mick,' he calls the man, and he clasps him round the shoulder as he shakes his hand. 'Still here!'

'Yup,' the man replies with a wink. 'Still here. Wouldn't get rid of us with a packet of Pitt's.' Rat poison, I presume.

The proprietress gives Cos and I a big smile and a nod each, before peering at the buggy and seeing the ladies there. 'Oh! Look! Who is this?' She grabs Buckley by the arm. 'Is this the Jones girls? No!'

'Aye,' Buckley says. 'We come up for a little drive. Yous got room for us for the night? Two'd be good – one for the fellers here as well. I'll sleep out back of the kitchen, if that's all right.'

An uncertain glance is exchanged between the Mr and Mrs, before the man says: 'Yup – well, sure! Make yourselves at home!'

A flash of what appears to be dismay in the woman's eyes, before she lunges at the sisters now alighting onto the verandah too, at the same time screeching instructions through a window: 'Katie, get the water on!' and over the roof, 'Come, Tommy, for the horses!' and back to the sisters, 'Come in, come in, oh, if it isn't the Misses Joneses, goodness to me, well haven't you two grown – ooooh so very beautiful, beautiful! So long it has been but I would know you anywhere, your poor beautiful girls.' She presses her hands around their faces as though they are small children arrived for her maternal pleasure – which is now pouring forth in an unstoppable stream: 'Beautiful! Come in, come in! What a beautiful surprise!'

Berylda laughs as she's swept along, but the frown is bemused, surprised herself by the reception perhaps, and I wonder if she doesn't quite recognise this woman making a fuss of her. Arm in arm with her sister, or more probably holding each other up at the end of this long day, Greta sighs: 'Oh Ryl, but I don't know that it's possible to be as worn out as I am. So suddenly – *whoosh* – I've had it now we're here.'

'Your horses? Misters?' A boy has appeared for Jack and Rebel, a sleepy-looking kid with his shirt hanging out, and when my feet hit the dirt they don't feel altogether there: whoa, that was a long ride indeed. When Cos steps up to the verandah ahead of me, I'm not sure that it's the boards that creak or his knees.

'Who?' I am being introduced by Buckley to Mrs Wheeler, and Mrs Wheeler is hard of hearing: 'Oh? Mr Wilbarrow and Mr What? Come in, come in.'

We all stamp in through the saloon doors, down a hall, and inside the place is empty; seeming emptier as the lamps are lit. A typical country inn, this is, more accommodation house than pub: one big dining room in the centre, with couches ranged around, and a bar, four or five rooms all leading off it, and a fireplace either end to make sure it's an oven no matter the season. It is sad that it should be so deserted; my sympathies as contradictory, for those who live here and the forest that waits for them to leave, as the bright checked tablecloths in this empty room. Still, for all this emptiness, it does feel like we've interrupted something.

'Here, here, gentlemen, you can be in this room here.' Mrs Wheeler is just about shoving us through a door just round from the entrance hall, at the front of the place. 'It is good, yes? To your liking, sirs?'

'Yes. Marvellous,' I reply before looking at it, and when I see it, it is rather marvellous: a small room but quite lavishly furnished, two iron bedsteads with a night stand in between, all grandmotherly frills and flounces and flocked and heavily florid wallpaper – impeccably kept Continental tart shop? With a bed length I'm accustomed to: at least eighteen inches short of comfort.

'Yeah bonzer.' Cos collapses on the nearest bed, but Mrs Wheeler doesn't notice; she has gone back to her hurried cooing and clucking: 'Oooh, Misses Joneses – come, come with me, over here, here ...' Closing the door behind us.

I hear one of the girls outside, crossing the dining room: 'Oh Ryl, oh dear.' Greta. 'I think I'm going to need to lie down for a little while and wait for my head to stop travelling ...'

That's a good way of putting it. Cos has his own: he writhes and groans on the bed, stretching and moaning. 'I think my back is broken. Drink, Wilb, get me a drink. Don't care what it is, just plenty of it. Or I'll never speak to you again.'

I don't ask him to promise. I'm sure he is actually in a good deal of pain. My own arse isn't altogether pleased with me either, and I leave to find us both a bit of something soothing. Across the dining room, Mrs Wheeler is bustling along, opening and slamming doors, and issuing a muffled squawk into one marked PRIVATE, on the far side of the hearth, diagonally opposite, and slamming that, too. I stare at that door blankly for a moment, before I remember why I am standing in this dining room: that's right – drink.

The little countertop of the bar is just to my left, practically in front of me, and Buckley is already there, in discussion with the publican, over the taps.

'Couple of them McEgan boys, it were, and one of the Schwartzes,' Wheeler is saying, filling a glass. 'They've been causing trouble with union talk for a while now. If the unions get a hold in here, this place is gone – the companies'll just up sticks.'

Buckley shrugs. 'Man's got to eat, hasn't he? Couldn't feed himself on them wages let alone a family. Someone's got to stand up.'

'Rock and hard one, ain't it, Roo. What do you do? Government fellers come up every so often, have a look, promise things'll get better, then buzz off again. It's a crying shame. And it's tearing the place apart. Fellers flogging the snot out of each other fighting for shifts, and young'uns leaving faster than them McEgans did this arvo.'

That makes my feet move towards the bar, and I can't help interrupting: 'You discussing what happened on the Track this afternoon? That chase?'

The publican looks to Buckley, who gives a nod of assent before I'm told: 'Yup. Some lads here had a bit much fun last night, had a go at blowing up the shed at Carney's battery – one of the company crushers, up on Bald Hill. Just a bit of a laugh gone wrong, it were.'

'Oh, right.' Don't let on about the dispute behind it then, and fair enough. These chaps don't know who I am, and wouldn't care a fig if they did know, but they know I'm not one of them. It's the same dispute everywhere anyway, in every mine, stock run and crop field: How exactly can you make money without indentured slavery these days? I ask: 'Did they do any damage?'

'Nah, not much,' says Wheeler. 'Blew the roof clear off the dunny by it, though – blew it to billy-o!'

'Did they?' Buckley snorts and raises his glass. 'Good on 'em.'

'Did you used to live here too?' I ask him, and immediately regret doing so as the stonewall stare comes at me for overstepping my place in the scheme. But I am curious – curious about him – have been since he came looking for me along the riverbank this afternoon: he seemed to know the Turon so well.

It's a long stare before Buckley decides it's all right to tell me: 'I've lived in a lot of places.'

There's another look passed between the men, another nod, and Wheeler says: 'Small towns breed small minds – last one in gets the blame for whatever happened Tuesdee a fortnight gone at three o'clock and it's time to move on. But, let me tell you, fine traveller, as I'd tell anyone, you'll never meet a better feller than our Buckley here.'

I nod. He left on bad terms and the details are none of anyone's business. And I don't have to wonder if it is all that much harder for an ex-convict to shake off the sentence of the past. It must be. It must follow you like a bloodhound, follow you right across this continent, across half the globe from the Old Bailey. It is very much none of my business, but I can't stop my questions before they come. 'Were you a miner?' I ask him.

'I was,' he says, shaking his head as his old grim face cracks into a smile, one of forbearance, around teeth as grey and rough hewn as fence posts. He says, 'Road building, mining. Beast of burden for all trades. Too old nowadays for any of that.'

'We had some good old days, though, didn't we, Roo?' Wheeler says, placing a beer on the counter for me: I've played some card right here to get a drink without asking. He says: 'Boom time!' and starts laughing, a great big wheeze of a belly laugh for his old friend, sharing some old laugh with him.

'Aye – *boom* time, it was, all right.' Buckley rolls his eyes.

'Boom time?' I ask them.

'Back in '93, it was,' Buckley explains: two old men reminiscing. 'Hill End was taking off again, so we thought. I was doing some ale carting up from Lithgow at the time, that's how me and Mick got to be cobbers, and I thought I'd go back in mining when the word went round that all these new companies were setting up. Wages can get good when the price gets high. Didn't happen but and work didn't last long either – what, couple of years, Mick?'

'Yup, no more'n that. And me and the wife had waited twenty years for it too! You should have seen this place when we first got here in '73.' Wheeler is still there in his great wide grin, gold tooth winking at those better days. 'It were town then, all right – the things that went on in this place. I couldn't tell you.'

'Sit here long enough, he will,' says Buckley, dry again. 'Wild Wheeler's we used to say. Fun times. Game of Heading 'Em every night, music going, dancing all round the coin toss.'

'Ten thousand we had here in this town – not including Tambaroora neither.'

'Ten thousand? No! Twelve.' Buckley ups the stakes, playing along with some old game between them. 'We had half a million and seventeen at Tambaroora, don't tell *me* about a town.'

'We had the whole *world* here, and you know it!' And then Wheeler sighs, to no one in particular: 'Till they rolled up their tents and went home. Now there's about eight hundred stayers – maybe a thousand when the work on is good.' He tells Buckley, not hiding the strain of it: 'I tell you, Carney's has turned out not more than ten or twenty ounces a hundred ton for months, nearly a year now. It is hard.'

I can't imagine how hard. To exist ever at the mercy of –

A door creaks open and I know it is her by the beat of that swift and heavy footfall. Berylda, there she is, emerging from the other side of the room: 'Gentlemen.'

She has removed her hat. I haven't seen her whole face unshaded by her hat since last night. I can't move my eyes from her face as she steps towards us, but she doesn't look at me. She hasn't met my eyes since my carry-on over the new *Helichrysum* by the river; I'll change that, eventually, when I get a chance to talk to her alone again.

She seems preoccupied at the moment, though, looking about the room, frowning into every corner, something fretful about her, the tight clasp of her hands, and now she is asking: 'Mr Wheeler?' turning about on her heel. 'Mr Wheeler, is my memory playing tricks, or did you once have a calliope here?'

BERYLDA

'You mean the old Victory, Miss Jones?' Mr Wheeler's eyes light up.

'Yes,' I say. 'The steam organ – where is it?'

'By gee …' His eyes dull again, with regret. 'We haven't cranked her up for a while.'

'Where is she?' She? 'It.' Please don't say she is gone. I want the calliope to be here; Greta wants to listen to a tune, to enliven her from the fatigue that's overrun her. She is sore again now, too, and not only from all our rough travel today, I don't think; she is sore within, as sore as she was last night – from him – curling around the tenderness, and her discomfort enlivens me. 'Please. She's not in this room?'

'She's out the back, where she always were,' Mr Wheeler says cautiously, as one might respond to a question from one who is demented. 'She were never in here, Miss Jones.'

'Is that true?' Memory has played a trick then – I was sure the calliope was here, in this room, like a window in a wall, the mermaids either side of the pipes sitting atop a treasure chest.

'True.' He smiles, a kind smile around a gruff pirate voice. 'She'd blow us out the chimneys if she were ever in here. Never get her in the doors anyway. Come on out back, I'll show you to her.'

I follow him outside, to the back verandah, where the dusk has gone quickly black, but the shapes of the hilltops all around are visible yet, as velvet on crepe; the tower of a mine poppet head blacker still above the stables.

'Here y'are, Miss Jones.' Mr Wheeler lights the way around the side of the hotel, hefting his battered old hurricane lamp up onto a hook for me to see. There, through the swinging shadows, it is, under a lean-to – on carriage wheels. Of course. Not a window but an ornately carved cabinet, all royal blue lacquer and marzipan scrolls, set up on a cart. It's just like any other calliope one would see at a fair.

'But it was only five years ago – can my memory be such a muddle?' I wonder out loud. I am incredulous that I could have misremembered such an obvious thing. 'I was so sure we were inside, Mother popping the cork on another bottle of ginger beer, and this hurdy-gurdy going ...'

'The way we want to remember happy things is probably the right way to remember them.' Mr Wilberry's deep and gentle baritone rolls out of the dark behind me. Go away, I want to shrug him off: I do not want your warmth any more than your platitude. You do not know me, and you are not going to know me. You won't want to once this excursion is ended, believe me.

I ask Mr Wheeler: 'Open the doors, please, could you?'

'Sure, Miss Jones.' He's jangling about his keys on their chain, telling me, 'We did have the music going – most nights, we did, once. Not surprising you remember the music – she does blast it out, so you can hear her all the way to Bathurst, no exaggeration. But she's always been out here – run off the boiler, you see.' He points to the rusted hulk of a boiler at the back of the chimney breast beyond the lean-to here, then scratches his head, thinking, before he says: 'Now, that's right, when yous were here that time, we had a Christmas fete on out in the yard and she was playing the whole time – egg and spoon races, ice-cream stand, talent competition and all that. I remember your father were very proud of you for something – you'd won a prize? At school? He shouted the bar. I remember that!'

'He did?' That catches me round the heart. Oh Papa, did you really?

The cabinet doors fall open and I am caught again. Here are our mermaids: chipped and lustreless. The one on the right is missing her thumb. Their tresses lank, their scales dead. The treasure chest I imagined overflowing with coins and pearls is shut. Like this whole town; I suppose Gulgong would be going the same way. Dying, dulling. Oh, it's sad.

'You want me to get the steam up to her for you?' Mr Wheeler is already stepping behind the cart to do so.

'No. No, thank you.' I almost shout it. No. I don't want Greta to hear this now, nor see it. This ruin. Not tonight. Not ever at all.

'Don't you dare start that thing up. No!' Mrs Wheeler bursts from the kitchen door onto the verandah to put an end to the question, shaking her finger at her husband and shrieking at him: 'Don't you touch that thing, Michael!' She slams the doors of the calliope closed again.

Mr Wheeler opens his mouth: 'We were only look –'

'No,' she cuts him off, chopping the air with her hand and taking me by the arm. 'That *thing*, it has bad spirits in it. I hate it. *Waaa waaaa waaaaa*, it moans. It has nearly caused many divorces between us. Ever since he brought her up the Track. You know how many times I wish she had gone over the edge? *Waaaa waaaaa waaaaa* for every song. What's wrong with a piano and a normal person singing a normal song?' Mrs Wheeler is not normal: she can talk underwater, and hold seventeen conversations at once, turning back to her husband again now before she pulls me along, warning him: 'Michael, you start that thing, I go back to Vilna.'

I go back to Vilna … The words send me my mother's laughter, hurdy-gurdy heady under this very verandah, her arm in mine. Where is Vilna? I had asked her, on that summer night five years ago. *Lithuania, darling, I think – Harry, Harry? Where's Vilna?* she called to Papa. *Lithuania or is it Russia?* she asked him. Lithuania, it is, but my memory stops there at Papa's smile as he turned to us: *What did you ask me, my dear chickadee?* The jolly sound of Mother's wedding rings clanking on a door handle with his sweet silly name for her: *chickadee*. Her name was Rosemary. Harry and Rosemary Jones, my perfect parents, stepping through some other, perfect dream. Too perfect.

Lost again amidst Mrs Wheeler's shrill cawing now, at the door that leads back to the saloon: 'I wish those Frenchman would have shot it to bitses long ago.'

'Frenchmen?' I have quite lost the conversation altogether. 'Shot what?'

'The calliope, Miss Berylda.' She squeezes the inside of my arm. 'The night after Mr Wheeler had this awful thing dragged up the Track there was a big fight in the yard. Frenchman and the German miners that were staying here – they started fighting. Bang, bang, bang. They wanted to kill each other over Alsace. They bring all of Europa into my house. *Three* of my chairs were broken. But the calliope kept on going *waaaa waaaa waaaa* all the whole time – it has the devil on its side. It must.'

'Oh?' That does sound like a funny tale, a Wild Wheeler's legend no doubt, but I have no sense of humour left to me even to smile at it. I am so tired, so overrun myself, I am little more enlivened than a corpse. I doubt I can even blink my eyes.

'Yes. Terrible business,' Mrs Wheeler continues with a click of her tongue, pulling me through to her small rear parlour, patting my hand, in this overly fond and familiar way of hers. 'But enough of that. I was wanting to look for you – what would you and your sister like to be eating? I have roast beef from only yesterday and potatoes and chicken soup and –'

I force my mouth to move, to respond: 'Soup and bread will be fine. We're very tired. Might we have it served in the room?'

'In the room? You want to eat in the *room?*' Poor Mrs Wheeler, waited an age for guests and they don't want to eat in her saloon.

But my patience slides off the mantelpiece and shatters on the hearth stone right here: 'Yes. Please.'

'Oh. If you are sure. All right then. I have Katie bring supper on a tray, yes?' Mrs Wheeler acquiesces, and within half a breath she begins prattling again: 'You are not unwell, are you? It is a very long way, if you are not used to it. I thought your sister looked a little bit pale. She's not sickening, is she?'

The black night swoops through the window and envelopes me. 'Sickening? No, I hope not. Only tired.' My sister is only tired. Only pregnant. Only ruined.

My nerves are ruined too; thoroughly. I prattle back at her: 'Mr Wilberry is a vegetarian, I must tell you, please make good provision for him in that regard. And. Hm.' Petty spite adds: 'He and Mr Thompson must have the best of whatever is in your pantry and your best wine too – my uncle, Mr Howell, will pay the account by telegraph when we return to Bathurst, if that is all right with you?'

'Yes, of course,' Mrs Wheeler beams, eyes disappearing into plump cheeks, and off she goes again – about how wonderful Mr Howell is, et cetera, et cetera. She's a Free Trade party fan through and through: who else will save us from miners wrecking the whole country with their unions and their punch-ups? Astonishing. This would almost be hilarious on any other night.

On this one, I shudder now where I stand: Alec Howell won't be alive for long enough to arrange payment of the bill if I can help it. I shall be paying it. With my money. Our money. Speaking to the accountant. Oh please, yes – I shiver with dread and yearning both.

While Mrs Wheeler has moved on again, pointing out the bookshelves and the magazines here in the little parlour room that we must help ourselves to, pointing out again that the ladies' bath and convenience is outside at the far end of the verandah, but not really outside because it's under the awning all the way, call for Katie at any time for hot water, nothing will be too much trouble for us, babble, babble, babble, and then asking me a question about something else I fail to listen to.

'I beg your pardon, Mrs Wheeler?'

'I asked you, what are your plans for tomorrow? What are you going to do on your visit? Tell me all about your plans.'

No. Enough. Be quiet. I want to return to my sister; I must. And before I fall over. I am swaying in my boots. But I have just enough wit left to me to see an opportunity here, to set tomorrow's plans in train, to find out exactly where Dr Ah Ling's thatched hut might be, how far away. I say: 'This visit is partly for study, Mrs Wheeler. I shall commence my degree in Medicine at the Sydney University in a few weeks' time and –'

'You are saying what to me – oh?' Mrs Wheeler holds the back of the chair near her to steady herself. 'Miss Berylda Jones! You are a wonder. Oh not only beautiful! You look at my words – I said to Mr Wheeler all that time ago, I said that girl is so intelligent. I said she is a clever one to watch –'

'Yes,' I interrupt her before she can set off around the world again. 'Yes, and so I am hoping I might make a visit to the famous Dr Ah Ling tomorrow – to ask him about that case, where he cured the miner, the one with the cancer in his arm. I am sure you would know of it. The story was in the papers, in Sydney. My uncle is most interested in the case too – he'd heard about it when he was last here, a few weeks ago, but didn't have time to quiz the man himself. Does the doctor live in town, or far from …?'

Mrs Wheeler pulls her chin into her neck, grimacing as one might at an open drain. 'You want to visit that ching chong witch doctor?'

'Yes, I –'

Must listen to a diatribe on Celestial slipperiness first. 'But you don't want to visit him, Miss Berylda. You cannot trust a Chinaman. I know more about medical business than him – I can tell you! You cannot trust anything a Chinaman says or does. Oh but the way they come and go; only to make their money, not their home. They take from the mouths of our little children, and then they go back home and fatten their own. All thieves. All the ching chong coolies that were here when we first came to the Hill – I thought we came to China! They are nearly all gone now.' She nods as if she might be personally responsible for that achievement. 'And they took all of the gold with them!'

'Yes,' there is never any room in that open drain for argument, is there, 'but Dr Ah Ling is a doctor, a herbalist, reportedly a successful one, and I would like to ask him how he cured the tumour.' And that's entirely truthful. I do want to know about it, even now; tell Flo all about it, too, this Chinese medical miracle, even though the picture of her scrunching the newspaper at me over her cocoa seems so long ago. Has it really been only a fortnight since I left Sydney? So long ago since yesterday, since Greta was ruined and I was betrothed – to the devil real and plain. And I must know: 'Where does Dr Ah Ling live?'

'Ah Ling, you talking about in here?' Mr Wheeler appears at the door from the saloon.

'Yes,' I reply and exhaustion begs, *please*: 'Where does he live?'

'He's out at Tiger Sam's, Miss Jones, past Tambaroora towards Hargraves. Tobacco farm, but it's off the road a bit. What you wanting to know –?'

'I don't know that we'll want to be going out there, Miss Berylda,' Buckley's voice follows in from the gloom; I can just glimpse him by the hearth, throwing the remains of his cigarette into the coals. 'I'll go out there for you, whatever you might need from him.'

No. You will not forbid me, Buckley.

'If you're going out there, Roo, pick us up a sack, will you?' Mr Wheeler says over his shoulder.

'A sack?' Buckley replies, sharp, surprised.

'Man's got to eat.' Mr Wheeler laughs; a wheeze like a broken accordion. 'How else do you reckon we're making ends meet then? You have to do what you can, don't you. You have to go round through Golden Gully way, though, too, for Tambaroora, if you're going – Mudgee Road's got a tree come down on it, waiting on a bullocky to move it.'

I could scream it out of my way: you will not forbid me. Rage scalds through me so that I cannot grasp at any response. I place my hand on the side table by me, grasping only the edge of the crocheted doily upon it.

'I will accompany Miss Jones to wherever she needs to go.' Mr Wilberry has come in from the verandah now too. The long slow strides spin the parlour around me as he steps towards the door. I must fix my mind to the threads under my palm. Be still. Be calm. Breathe in. Breathe out.

'It's a sly tobacco place,' Buckley explains to him. 'That Tiger Sam is not a licensed grower – and they have the ope going out of there too. It's not place for a lady to be, in any company.'

I am no lady. I am wretched and desperate. I am condemned to be Alec Howell's wife if I do not succeed in this. My sister is condemned to submit to God knows what new hell – and the devil's child into the bargain if I do not see to it first. If I return to Bellevue with nothing, we return to a life sentence of misery. Or I might just find the strength to plunge a knife into his back and take my last dance at the end of a rope to get away.

I say to these men who presume to decide my path, as I drive the words into the doily under my hand: 'In the morning, we will visit Dr Ah Ling. It is important that I speak with him myself, to discuss a matter of medicine – unless, of course, anyone else here has a particular interest in cancer, its causes and cures.' And you will not deny me this. I look up at Mrs Wheeler beside me, and only Mrs Wheeler: 'Now. What were we talking about? Supper. May we have ginger beer with the meal, too, please? I remember having a lovely ginger beer when we were here –'

'Yes, Miss Berylda – the ginger beer.' Mrs Wheeler is already bustling me past her husband for it. 'My ginger beer. We are in luck! I made some only on Tuesday – I must have seen you were coming. It will be beautiful tonight!'

She takes me with her back through the saloon and I fix my gaze on hers. 'I recall it as having been delightfully fizzy, Mrs Wheeler. The best.'

'Oh! My ginger beer – yes, it's very, *very* fizzy.' She boasts and explains to me how much yeast to lemon is necessary and whatever other things are in it, on and on until I'm closing the bedroom door on her: 'Thank you, Mrs Wheeler. Thank you so much, you're too kind.'

Once inside I slide the latch behind me, finding Gret just as I left her, curled around herself and looking up at me: 'Are they going to play the calliope?'

Some wave of pain closes her eyes and I say: 'No. Mrs Wheeler put the mockers on that idea, I'm afraid. You don't look like you're about to liven up for anything, though. Is it very bad? The pain?'

'Ooh. Not too bad. Just sore.' She presses her hands into her stomach. 'And I feel a little bit queasy again. Whoosh, whoosh it goes inside my head and in my belly, all whooshing out of time.'

And that makes no other sense to me but that this must be pregnancy. A scrambling together of all the knowledge I've magpied of female anatomy and function, in this text and that. Something about the settling of the seed, setting off a mystery train of chemical changes, that makes a woman weak and more feeble than usual. And burns a hole in me.

243

I ask Gret: 'Please, will you let me feel where it hurts? Let me see?'

In case I am wrong. And it's something else: an infection, a growth. What else is there to make one ill? I don't know enough about anything.

'All right. You can see,' Gret accedes, moving onto her back, but looking away from me into the wallpaper, looking away from her own shame and humiliation.

I don't know what I am looking for as I lift her skirt and petticoat back and then her drawers, just enough to find her belly. But I find the marks of his fingers impressed into the side of her hip, like a brand. I don't have to be a doctor to know that this is where he has seized her. If he were here now, I would stab him in the face.

But I can see or feel nothing else unusual. She does not tense at my touch; there is no redness, no firmness where none should be. There is no blood. She is well in every other way, for all that I might guess. My darling sister. My poor Gret. Her fingernails still streaked seaweed pink from her joyful painting day, still holding that golden bottlebrush from the gorge.

She curls away from me, and I curl behind her now. I pray to every god there is, please let tomorrow bring the solution, and make steel of my resolution, for this act that no god might ever help me with.

For if the One and Almighty God were truly good, or true at all, he would have pushed the seed from her. He would have shaken it from her along the rough track today.

Perhaps He has.

Please.

Please take this need to kill from me.

Show me a way. If I cannot make Alec Howell gone, then show me how Gret and I might go ourselves. Show me how we might disappear ... into these hills ...

Show me our life.

Free ...

Free of all men. Free of God, too, if that is how it must be for me.

BEN

I want to knock on the door and tell her, yes, as a matter of fact, I do have an interest in cancer, its causes and its cures. I want to tell her about Mama. I want to tell her everything that I might say but –

She shuts the door. It seems to be her way: she'll open it just enough to dazzle me – with a smile, a word, a shower of laughing stars – and then she slams it shut again. She is a closed door.

'She has her own mind about things, Miss Berylda does,' the old man Buckley says quietly, staring at the door with me. 'She's not much of one to say no to.'

'No, I'm gathering that.' She is determined to see this Ah Ling. Who is he? A famous cancer doctor? I've never heard of him, and I made a fair few enquires after Mama's diagnosis, wrote to every advertised medical 'expert' up and down the eastern seaboard; investigated all sorts of snake oil garbage, too, as Howell termed it himself. I even contemplated the services of a clairvoyant in St Kilda before accepting that there was nothing to be done. But what is behind Berylda's urgency now, her rush to see this Ah Ling? What is it that drives this constant charging, charging, charging? I want to grasp her by the hand. Stop her. Ask her. *Berylda, please.* Open the door.

The word *PRIVATE* on the next door along stares back at me.

'If she's so set on it, we'll take her out there in the morning,' Buckley says. 'And don't worry too much about it, Mr Wilberry. I've got a pistol in the buggy. Always carry it.'

Strike me, don't worry? 'What? Would you expect that kind of trouble?'

'Not from Ah Ling, no,' the old man says. 'He's a decent sort by all accounts, and he did fix that feller, too. George Conroy is his name, lives right here at Kitty's Flat, just down the road, at least I think he still does, last I heard. The doc in town was going to saw the arm off, but he's a new feller and not got too good a track record, so George thought he'd try his luck with the Chinaman. And that Ah Ling worked a bit of a miracle on it, so they reckon. It's that Tiger Sam, his brother, who's the doubtful character – gibbering bag of loose change, if ever there was one. Sick in the head from all his ope smoking, liable to turn on you with a meat axe and chase you up the road, that one is.'

'Oh?' I have to ask: 'Is there some reason the local constabulary don't go after him instead of chasing larrikin miners round the hills?'

'Heh.' Buckley enlightens me: 'Coppers like their cheap tobacco too, don't they. The costs of them growers' licences pushed the price of smokes right up.'

'Of course.' Everyone's a criminal and we need to get our priorities right. I smile at the double standard, sharing it with Buckley, the gulf between us pinched down to little more than the lines at the corners of his eyes.

He stops smiling and stares at the door again. He says: 'She's a very good and hardworking young woman, Miss Berylda is. She doesn't mean to be impolite. She's had her troubles.'

'I'm gathering that too.'

'Their mum and dad killed in a railway crash, poor mites.' Buckley glances back towards the hearth to see there's no one here but ghosts and an old upright piano, before he tells me through lips that barely move: 'And the uncle – he's no good. I don't know what he gets up to. But it's something no good.'

'Hm.' I share this wonder at the uncle with the old man too, and the sympathy: A railway accident? Awful. Devastating. I can't begin to imagine. But I will discover what this uncle does; I will help the Jones sisters be independent of him. I will do all I can.

For Berylda. I want to ease all that troubles her. Perhaps if I wait at her door long enough, one day I will.

BERYLDA

The mermaids drag me deeper, deeper still; the slimy reeds slip through my hands as I grasp for them, desperate for air.

Hurry, Berylda, hurry, your mother and father are waiting at the station.

No, they're not. They're not waiting anywhere. They are dead. Cold and dead as the river pebbles pummelling against my shins, my elbows. My face.

Let me go!

Turn around – look, Berylda. They are here, behind you.

No. I shall drown.

Come down to the caves, Berylda, it isn't far. Libby is waiting too. She is calling out for you. Listen, listen. Don't resist. Be a good girl and come with us …

I let go. I am so very, very tired, I can only let go.

I let them drag me over the ruts of the riverbed and down, down, down, over a gravel of shattered bones, down and down.

Drag me and drag me until it doesn't hurt any more. Drag me until I drown. Until gravel becomes silk. Velvet. Gold velvet.

And Libby is here, she truly is, brushing the rich fabric against my cheeks, either side, so happy to see me. *Oh, this is the one, Ryl, this gold is perfect for the drawing room, don't you think?*

It is the same bright yellow gold of grandmother's fan bracelet. The catch chain glints against the silk, gold on gold.

Where is Mother now? Where is Papa?

Who?

I look up and Libby is gone. I turn around and no one is here. It is dark. I run out into the rear parlour, here at Bellevue, to the windows that look out across the hills, and they are walled up with bricks.

There is no air. I cannot breathe.

Of course, I cannot breathe. For I am drowned.

Let go. Drift. Free.

Is this death? Is *this* freedom?

'Ryldy?' Greta's arms are around my waist. 'Ryl? Wake up.'

I am breathing? Yes. And I am rousing. I open my eyes and turn in her arms. 'What is it?' I ask her through the darkness.

'You were having a dream, a bad dream, yelping like a puppy.'

'I know.' Just a dream. The dream of our life. A gold tassel swishing through the black like a fistful of silken keys.

My sister's arms tight around me. We are still here.

'That noise – listen,' she whispers. 'What is it?'

I listen. A distant thudding has begun: *bang-bang-bang-bang-bang-bang* … a metronome set to prestissimo. Where are we precisely? The Hill, yes? Wheeler's Hotel. I can just make out the shape of the ginger beer bottle on the night stand, from our meal. Two sips and we were both blessedly cataleptic – that brew is medicinal strength. Mr Wilberry's golden bottlebrush remains there too, by our glasses. A board creaks; someone coughs softly in the next room: a woman. Some woman. And I am no longer dreaming. I sit up and open the curtain. Not bricks but sky: the grey before the dawn, the painting out of the stars. I blink up into it, as another metronome begins – *bang-bang-bang-bang-bang-bang* – syncopated against the first, and closer.

'Some sort of mine workings?' I suppose.

'The birds don't like it; they've stopped singing.' Gret pulls me back under the covers. 'Whatever it is, that noise frightens the birds away.'

'I'm sure it does.'

We listen to the birdless banging as the dawn creeps up the pane, and my sister begins to weep, silently. She shakes in silence as she weeps. Our dreams as one. She is trapped in the house that has never been our home and he is growing more and more savage the more she weeps, the more she yelps for him to stop.

She whispers: 'I know it's a terrible sin, but sometimes I don't like waking up. Remembering.'

'I know.' I hold her now. 'Sometimes I can't believe I'm awake at all.' She flinches in my arms; I feel her clench down the urge to wail. I ask her: 'Is the pain still bad?' The pain in her belly, I mean.

'Not too bad, no,' she whispers. 'It's much better now.'

She clenches again: she is lying. She doesn't want to ruin our little trip away. She couldn't ruin anything if she tried. But I know that she has guessed there is something wrong with her inside, even if she doesn't know what it might be.

I hold her tight to me and promise her: 'I'm going to get you something, for this pain. I want you to rest here while I'm gone today. Paint me a postcard of a tumbledown dungaree town from this window and finish that ginger beer, will you? I expect you to be in a ginger beer coma until I return. In fact, I insist.'

She breathes out a laugh that's barely there: 'You're lovely, Ryldy, honestly you are. What would I do without you?'

That question is too terrible. But I am lovely, yes, if loveliness includes the worst of humanity. I will be the devil's for all time, once I have done what I must do. No better path has come to me in the night, nor will it this new day. There is no other escape for us, just as there is no one who might answer any prayer. God is deaf to justice. Deaf to me. I have no choice but to seek to kill Alec Howell. Say it into my soul, should I even possess one: murder. I shall murder him, as I shall murder his child.

BEN

'No, I am not getting up.' Cos declines my offer of a stretch and stroll before breakfast. 'I can't – because I am paralysed.'

'Come on,' I say. 'It'll do you good – it'll only get worse if you lie there. Better to get moving.'

'I would if I could.' He reaches for his pipe, looking at me as if I am the one who might be a bit detestable.

Look at him, here in his most natural state: lying down. I'm sure he really is suffering from yesterday's ride; so am I. But he hasn't moved since we arrived just before six p.m. last night. A gut-scrubbing two and a third bottles of Californian angelico went into him, because he'd decided he craved only dessert from the extensive cellar of the world's worst wines on offer here, and a whole piss pot's worth has come out of him, the full-bodied aroma of which fills this room from where it sits beside his bed, on the floor between us. While *Zarathustra* has not moved from where it lies either – open on his chest – and from which he sermonised me into oblivion at some time during the night on the evils of sentimentality and the inherently manipulative nature of love. Thanks for that.

I say: 'Righteo.' And turn to leave him to it.

But he says, lighting up: 'As much as it pains me to miss out on watching you follow that girl around like some starving stray begging scraps from her high table. You can have that pleasure all to yourself today.'

'That *girl*? Just who *are* you to judge her? There's more to her story, you know –'

'I have no doubt,' he cuts me off. 'And whatever it is, you'd be well advised to remain in ignorance of it, Wilb. Trust me.'

The dashed-off scribble of a portrait he sketched of her yesterday by the river lies between us, too, propped against the empty bottles on the night stand: her face stark, all her fine features made almost invisible by the ferocity of the eyes that stare out of the page. That is not her. That is not what I see. *What's she looking at?* he slobbered at me last night in the midst of his lecture on the perils of affection. *Not you, old matey. Not you or me. Something wicked in the hills …*

Go to bloody sleep, for Christ's sake, I said to him then; I say to him now: 'Why would I ever trust you with advice on women?' I am past fed up with him today already, and I let him have it: 'All you know about is faithless, indiscriminate rogering – you're a joke. And Susan knows it, too.'

He stares at me for a moment. Eyes hooded with some threat, before he picks up his book and waves me away: 'Don't listen to me then. I don't know anything about women. I don't know anything about life. There is no more to *my* story, is there. I don't know what it is to have a difficult time of it loving someone I'm not supposed to have – one that I can't even step out with into the street, for if I did my family would have me cut off, and unlike you, I would have no recourse. I would be on the street. And so would Susan and the children. Do you know what it's like to pretend that your children are not your own? I don't know what it is to suffer at all. I don't know what it's like to work at ideas and at art that no one – not one single arsehole in this entire continent of a shitter – is interested in. So run along, Wilby Wilber. Run along and have a wonderful frolic of a day with your freakish little kitty cat sweetheart. I'll be here when you return. I always am. So off you go.'

And so I bloody well shall. Get into the day, and get away from him. If only he could hear his own hypocrisy and idiocy, his head would explode off his shoulders. But he won't; can't: why would you when you can spend the day in bed, indulging yourself with the fictional ramblings of a mad, dead German, imagining that you might be Nietzsche's own Super Man – an elaborate excuse for all that is indolent and selfish feathered up today as twentieth century enlightenment, as though I'd know anything more about it than the scathing review in the *Age*. But I *do* know that you can't possibly know anything about anything without living it, *being* in it. Not truly. Nietzsche probably observed that too – from an apartment window. If Cos loved Susan truly, he'd bloody well take her to Berlin, wouldn't he? Take her to Rio de Janeiro. Take her as well as himself and the twins from this shitter. He'd find a way. He'd do something about it. Get a job – make some actual attempt to sell a painting to someone who might be interested. Let's be frank, he hasn't mentioned his children by name the entire time we've been away: because Tildy and Ted are little more than inconveniences to him. They get in the way of Susan's undivided attention. They are possibly at least part of the reason he's here with me now, if we're going to be especially frank.

'Work at ideas?' I mutter at him. 'Art? Suffering? You're just lazy.'

'Arsehole,' he mutters back.

And despite the note of genuine disappointment and hurt in his voice, I retort: 'Super arsehole.'

'Mirror.' He raises his palm to me. He snorts and I leave.

BERYLDA

'Miss Jones? Good morning?' I hear him across the saloon, closing his door behind him, precisely as I do mine. *Click.* Unavoidable, as I am sure he will be all day, unless I miraculously find the courage to throw myself across Jack's saddle and make my way to Ah Ling's farm alone, wherever it is along the road from here to Tambaroora. Could I do that? Go alone? No. I hardly possess the courage to return Mr Wilberry's good morning.

But I must. Consider this a test of will, of nerve. Turn around. *Look at him.*

I look at his stockinged feet, finding his boots outside the bedroom door, and my heart both sinks and flies at the sweep of sunlight that is his hair falling across his face as he bends to pick them up by their laces. He hasn't made himself somehow less attractive during the night. Bright, expectant eyes looking up at me across this room, asking as if he's just found the words with fresh uncertainty: 'Early bird?'

'Hm? What? Yes,' is the greeting I give him, as incoherent as it is graceless. 'Morning. It is.'

'Hm. Yes, apparently. Well …' he replies, and I am caught up in the warmth of his early bird embarrassed smile, the warmth of that voice, saying: 'I was just about to take a wander, a stroll, before breakfast – you wouldn't care to join?'

'No.' I hurl this word at the boots in his hand. 'Thank you. I am not yet prepared for the day, I'm afraid. I am on my way to the kitchen, for warm water, for my sister. She is unwell.'

My mouth is dry with a strange fear, that truths will slip from me if I allow too many words to pass from my lips, that all will be undone. How am I ever going to find the face, the words, the firmness to do what I must do? Today. Tomorrow. To be this murderess I must be.

'Oh. No. Unwell?' he asks me, his concern so very quick, so real. This man is no wolf; he is like no other man. I know this; he is just what Greta says he is: a prince. 'I hope it's nothing serious,' he says.

'Nothing serious? No. I hope not, too,' I reply and I wish that he could be my friend, a friend like no other, so that I might tell him everything. How I hate that time has set the rhythms of our lives one against the other, like the rock crushers that pound out over this town, dissonant, incongruous – impossible for us to be in any way together. But the sadness of this thought is a shroud thrown across my fear, at least, and I regain a firmer grasp on my senses. I find a steadier rhythm for my heart as I allow myself to look into his gentleness, and I say to him: 'Greta will be unable to join us today, however. Forgive me my preoccupation, please –'

'Not at all,' he says. 'Is there anything I can do to help?'

'No.' How I wish and wish and wish there were; how I wish his very gentleness would cause all wolves to disappear. Vanish. All turned to rock and crushed to dust by the fact of his existence. But in this I suddenly see there is something he can help me with, and immediately: I am safe to test myself with this man and his kindness. I might try my face, my words on him. Practice deception. Now. Find a lie. *What* lie? I'm quite good at lying when I need to be, but this is hardly pinching books I shouldn't have, is it. Why should it be any different, though?

'Oh dear,' I say pinching my forehead, snatching at the first thing that comes. 'I've just now realised I have done something very silly, Mr Wilberry, and left Bathurst with my purse full of nothing but handkerchief, and I need to obtain some headache powder, for my sister.' I have loose change enough in my purse for that, and more than enough ability to obtain credit, I'm sure, anywhere in this district for anything, just as I am sure Mrs Wheeler has half a cupboard of headache powder somewhere in this house, but I ask him, 'I couldn't possibly borrow a few coins from you, could I?'

'Borrow?' He is appalled at the idea; already has his hand in his pocket, stepping across the room towards me in his stockinged feet. This manipulation is so easy, too easy, it shames me so that I don't think I can keep my nerve a moment longer. 'For your sister? Oh no, please don't consider it a loan. It's the very least I –' He holds out his hand to me: a crumpled pound note and several coins.

I will fail this test; I will fail every test: I can't deceive this man. I can't deceive anyone. And yet I have to. I *must* try. I must succeed.

'How awful of me to ask.' I pluck two coins from his hand, whatever they are I don't know, and shards of truth rattle out of my lies as I do: 'I shall repay you. Thank you. Or at least my uncle shall have to repay you, when we return to Bellevue. I don't have any money anyway, I must admit, only allowed five pounds per month and resentment causes me to spend it all on fripperies –' *Ha ha ha ha ha ha ha*, fake gaiety hammers out of me, flinty and crude as shale. 'Starve myself for silk flowers and perfume. Just as well my roommate at Women's is a vegetarian – like you, although she doesn't eat eggs or dairy. Isn't that funny? I mean that she's a vegetarian, too? I told you about her yesterday – the one studying Law? We live on shredded air, the pair of us, and I'm still always short two bob.' What stream of nonsense did I just blabber at him?

'You don't need to repay me, Miss Jones, please,' he says to me, holding out the pound note for me to take as well, his voice deep with affection, reaching deep into me. There is a small crack in his bottom lip; I should like to salve it with some glycerine. 'Five pounds a month doesn't amount to many fripperies, or too much of an overabundance of vegetables, I'm sure. At least not in Sydney, I don't imagine.'

No, it doesn't. That is certainly true. I look at the pound note in his hand, its edge trembling at me; its Royal Bank red ink drawn on the Queensland sun. I might have three or four shillings in my purse, in total, I suppose, a farthing or two somewhere in the bottom of my carryall. This pound is something I might need between now and tomorrow. Who knows what for? Take it. Take every opportunity as you must. *Take it*, I demand of myself.

And I take it. I grab the note and I cannot look at him again: 'Thank you.'

I scuttle from him like the vermin I am. If I can't keep my resolve with even this small deception, how am I going to achieve what I must do today? How will I speak as I must to Ah Ling? How will I convince Alec Howell to drink from my cup tomorrow?

Where is my courage?

I arrive at the kitchen to find Mrs Wheeler and her maid already busy about their day. Bread baking. Pots steaming. Ordinary life bubbling and clanking away in here.

'Miss Berylda – oh, but what is the matter?' Mrs Wheeler looks up at me over a cup full of oats, perceiving so clearly and so instantly that I am lost.

I must not be lost. I snap my orders to Mrs Wheeler, snapping at myself: 'My sister is unwell today, after all. It's the time of the month,' I grab at another lie. 'She takes it badly, and the timing is bad. May I have a bowl of warm water for her, please, to wash, and a headache powder, if you've any?'

'Ah, but I knew she was pale, didn't I.' Mrs Wheeler appears as delighted at her correct guess as she is diligent about fulfilling my requests, bowl and powder produced in a single heave of her bosom. 'Wasn't I saying this to you last night? Yes I was, remember. I know these things – I *know*.'

You don't know anything, Mrs Wheeler, I say to myself. She can't know anything, not of the devil in her calliope nor of the devil in me. Lithuanian gypsy she might be, but she cannot see what runs through my mind. No one can. I say to her: 'Thank you so much. See to it that my sister is disturbed by no one but you today.'

'But Miss Berylda, of course!' Mrs Wheeler assures me; she will bar all the windows and the doors with her own good name. 'I will care for your sister in all ways.' Good.

I return to Gret with the powder and the bowl, my mind ragged already as I set about dampening a flannel for her and pouring a fresh cup of water from the night-stand jug. I am so distracted I don't even glance at her as I hand her the flannel.

'Ryldy?' I hear her, though, through the crashing and rushing of my thoughts. 'Ryl, are you angry? Please don't be angry. There's no point; it's a waste to be angry.'

'Angry?' If I were any more angry I'd burn this hotel down to the ground with the heat of this emotion alone. I could scream at her: *And what do you propose I do instead of being angry? Pretend this isn't occurring? Pretend that you are not in the condition you are so very obviously in? Ignore it and it will all go away?* But I will not so much as whisper any such thing to her. By tonight, there will be no condition to worry about; tomorrow, there will be no monster, either. I have refound my courage here. My sister is my courage; her innocence is my courage, as is her quiet and enduring fortitude. I say to her: 'Yes, I am angry, darling; you know me too well, don't you. But I'm not going to be angry in a moment, because I'm going to take myself out into the air right now and let it go from me. All right?'

She nods. 'Yes, good. I don't want you to be angry and always burdened by concern for me. I want you to be happy, Ryl – please. I feel bad enough. Enjoy the day. For me.'

'I'll try,' I lie to her, too. I will never be happy; I will never enjoy a day again. But such is our life. I will be courageous instead.

I find something of a smile for my sister as I step out onto the verandah from our room – to startle another woman making her way to the ladies' conveniences from the room next to ours. Another guest? I didn't notice any others here yesterday, but then I'm not sure I'd notice a great gnashing Jabberwock in my path unless it were specifically addressing me. The woman makes some sound of acknowledgement, clutching her toilet bag to her breast, and I suppose I make some similar sound in reply as I step past her.

Step out into this town of filthy rock-crushing metronomes thumping out the rhythm of my purpose. Listen: let that sound *be* my purpose: *bang-bang-bang-bang-bang-bang-bang.*

Past the ramshackle fence by the Wheelers' tank stand the road bends away through the centre of the town, and I keep walking down it. One step after the other, my actions must be thus from now: small, alert, deliberate. Intent. A yard of knotted grapevines, gone wild with neglect, is strangling an apple tree as I continue into the town, and I ask this air: make me as wild and uncaring of what I will destroy. For who will suffer when I erase Alec Howell from this world? Who, truly? No one. Another surgeon will be found for the hospital; another candidate found for the Liberal League Free Traders; Mary will cry her fantasies to sleep in the kitchen. He is no saver of lives for any reason of compassion; a doctor only for the control over life it affords him; a politician craving power for the same reason. Life will go on once his is ended. The natural order of all other things will remain, such that it is. Bread will be baked; pots will steam. This town will go on, grinding itself into nowhere for the dividends of distant investors. The children playing hopscotch in this street between the draper's and the next public house will still be runny-nosed and poor. Their mothers will remain trapped here, never having left the goldfields since they got here, or were born, and the window of the draper's will continue to advertise Grand Prix P.D. Corsetry.

I reach into my pocket for the wishbone, and I feel the crumple of Mr Wilberry's pound note around it. I push the rough edge of the snap through the soft paper, and I stab it into my palm.

We will be free.

Tomorrow: we will be free.

I am ready to succeed in this. Ready as I will ever be. I simply have to be. I turn around, and head back to the hotel – I want to be on the road as soon as possible. The time for thought is past. The time to act is here.

'Morning, Miss Berylda.' And Buckley is at the stable gate to meet me. Good. Excellent.

'Morning,' I reply before snapping out an order at him, too: 'Have Sal ready within the hour. Please.' As if we might crack out to wherever this Ah Ling is and back in time to return to Bathurst today. Impossible.

And Buckley underlines it for me: 'I'm resting Sal today, miss. She had the longest day of all yesterday.' There is rebuke in that, and I deserve it. Yes. Poor Sal. He says: 'We'll be taking the Wheelers' mare out and when she's ready.'

There is more than rebuke in that, and well beyond a servant's place, but before I can make my rankling felt and understood, he says: 'And you'd do well to take moment too – think about what you're doing.'

'I do beg your pardon?' You don't challenge me.

258

Yes, he does; he holds my stare for the longest time, sticking me to the gravel with his old black eyes. Then he says: 'It's not all up to you, Miss Berylda, whatever might be going on with all your rushing about, getting here, going there. I'm not too fussed if you want my word on it or not, but I'll tell you anyway: you might miss what's right in front of you if you don't take a moment to see.'

'See what?' I blink into his impertinence, astonished.

'What's looking right at you,' he says, remaining not too fussed at all, and he nods up the road, behind me.

I look over my shoulder and there is Mr Wilberry coming down the other way, returning from his walk, a slow loping streak of unbleached canvas and Huckleberry straw against the hazy grey hilltop behind him. He doesn't see us; he has stopped to look at some sort of plant poking through another derelict fence there, a half-dead bracken frond by the look of it.

Buckley's brick dust scours into me: 'You'd do worse to look at one such as that feller.'

'What?' What is Buckley suggesting? I remain too astonished to ask.

'You know what he was doing when he wandered off from us yesterday?' Buckley is as unperturbed, informing me: 'Following a platypus, he was. Lost track of the hour following a platypus up the riverbank. That's the sort of feller he is.'

I know. He is wonderful for the wonder he takes at the life he finds around him. And Buckley has no business pointing that out to me. And at what suggestion? I turn to Buckley: 'Mr Wilberry can do as he pleases.'

And I cannot. I cannot believe what have I just heard, either. Is the gardener playing fantasy matchmaker for me, in league with my addled sister, or is my mind beginning to unravel? Mr Wilberry is no solution to my *rushing about*; he is no timely and convenient rescuer. His loveliness can do nothing for me other than taunt from outside the bars of the cage. For Alec Howell is keeper of my keys, my guardian, and he will certainly do as he pleases: he will drag me by my hair to the altar before Mr Wilberry could so much as think the word *wife*. But Buckley doesn't know any of that; couldn't do. Just as he couldn't possibly have been proffering marriage advice to me just now. Strange old man, merely being strange, telling me to take a moment to smell the half-dead bracken fronds. Being kind in his gravel-gruff way; catching me from a fall; being my friend. He shrugs into my wonder now and walks away, back inside the gate, and down towards the stables.

And I turn back to Mr Wilberry. I watch his powerful form, twisting off a sprig of whatever it is that's caught his eye there. His hands, his back, the crouch of his knees: all powerful. And I have a power over him. Yes, I do, and I have known this from the first moment, too.

I could, if I must, make him do anything.

Whatever I must do, I shall. And courage, you will not fail me again.

POISON

I am a forest, and a night of dark trees: but he who is not afraid of my darkness will find banks full of roses under my cypresses.

Thus Spake Zarathustra

BEN

'How is your sister now?' I ask Berylda as she approaches the stables from the rear verandah of the hotel, her hand raised to shield her eyes from the sun rising over the hayloft. As she strides straight past me. She has been busy for the past hour or so, that swift and heavy footfall charging back and forth from the kitchen to the room she shares with her sister, and now from the kitchen again with a basket of food for today over her other arm. Busy, busy, busy, she is. And possibly worried; no pretence in my concern, either: sylphlike as the sisters are, I wonder if there is not something more delicate about Greta. Perhaps Berylda didn't hear my question?

I am about to ask again when she replies, to the mare at the head of the buggy: 'My sister is comfortable enough, thank you for asking.' She glances behind her, in my direction, as though she has only just become aware of my presence, or perhaps she is still embarrassed about having to ask for that bit of cash; terrible thing, being forced to beg and justify the smallest amount, as Mama always had to, as though she might have spent a ha'penny too much on a packet of pins or a length of ribbon for her table arrangements.

'The headache powder?' I ask Berylda. 'You got some all right, then?' I presume so, as she hurried in and out of the hotel earlier.

She doesn't reply for a moment, though, settling the basket under the seat of the buggy, before glancing behind her again: 'Oh yes.' And I sense she is indeed embarrassed, so shut up about it, Wilberry.

263

'Buckley,' she asks the old man, who's busy at the coupling straps of the harness, 'what is the name of this horse? She's a pretty thing.'

'Whiskey,' he says, not looking up from his work, a careful man checking over every aspect of the vehicle twice.

'Suits her,' Berylda says.

'It does,' I say, as the name might suit any sorrel chestnut. 'She's a very pretty animal,' I add, as pointlessly, because Berylda still doesn't look at me. But I will have her look at me. She will not shut the door in my face again, not so soon. So I attempt another line: 'Cosmo won't be joining us. He's taken ill himself, in a manner of speaking – not interested in getting out of bed is the truth. Couldn't be bothered sending his apologies.'

'Ha.' Berylda turns to me now, slowly, at last, and with something of a sardonic smirk under her hat. 'Ill? I should say your friend is by far the one in need of headache powder, no?' She raises her face a little more and her eyes seem to be smirking too. Strike me but the wit amidst her beauty is a song; perhaps one only I can hear, but it is everywhere and real enough, to me. She's asking me something; what? She asks me again: 'I said, did he drink all that angelico himself or did you help him?'

'Ah. Yes. Solo effort, that one was.' I smile back, and cringe: how anyone can drink that sort of fortified cough syrup at all I don't know.

She doesn't either; she twitches her nose and our smiles are one inside the other as she says: 'I saw the evidence of the empty bottles in the kitchen – you know that wine contains over twenty percent alcohol? It's amazing that Mr Thompson is still with us. Mrs Wheeler and her maid are most impressed at the effort – and they thought you had *shared* it.'

'He's a problem.' I nod.

'One best left behind by the sound of it.' She nods back, sharing the joke with me, a little twist to the smirk again; and she's pleased he's not joining us? Well, that's good too, then, isn't it.

And as much as my guts are twisting into idiot knots right now, I am struck and struck again with some kind of joyfulness: I am about to spend all of this morning and perhaps even some of the afternoon almost entirely alone with this girl. Berylda Jones. What sort of fortune do you call this? Of all the random occurrences in the world, I meet her now. Of all the drifting I have done, I drift here. At a time when I perhaps have never been more ready to believe –

'Now, listen to me before we get anywhere,' Buckley says as he steps up into the driving seat, warning above the creak of carriage springs: 'I'll say it again so you are in no doubt that I mean it – if I don't like the look of things out at Tiger Sam's, we will turn around, no arguments about it.' This is for Miss Jones, but Buckley adds a nod to me: the pistol lies in his utility box, which sits under the swag roll at his feet there at the head of the buggy, should either of us need use of it.

'Oh Buckley, I'm sure I'll see worse than sly tobacco plantations in my time.' She ignores my offer of a hand up into the vehicle too, grasping the side rail and taking the distance at a leap. 'I intend to be a doctor, remember.'

'There's worse than sly tobacco out there – it's an ope house too.' Buckley is adamant. 'You don't know what goes on.'

'As no one knows what goes on in any house,' she mutters as she bends to sit, but I hear it clearly, and I want to know: what goes on in her house? What goes on at Bellevue? What sorts of worse has she seen already? But of more immediate concern: where should I sit? Beside her or with Buckley? Indecision grips me for a moment. Beside her is too near, isn't it? The seat is so narrow. To be so close, for this journey of what will be at least an hour outwards, or even two, depending on the state of the road? But then, I *should* sit beside her, shouldn't I, in case –

'You getting in, cob?' Buckley grunts like a cabman, a chuckle at me in it, one which is becoming a little too customary, and forces my choice as he kicks off the brake lever: 'Git up, Whiskey.' It's beside her or nowhere at all.

I'm still half-standing on the footboard as we move off, calculating how I might avoid sitting on her. 'Er, excuse –' She shifts across with the slightest of glances, and as Buckley pulls out of the gate and heads slowly up a lane off the main dogleg, she remains turned away from me, looking out across the scarred hills to the west, over the tops of make-do cottages that might have been scattered here by the wind. An elderly woman looks up from her vegetable patch, harvesting marrows, and she waves a good morning to us; I wave back, but Berylda doesn't seem to notice her at all.

'Yes,' she says, as though to herself as we pass a signpost at a fork, 'this is Germantown – I remember. Germantown and Irishtown, funny names in this place … and that shaft well over there, ahead, I remember that, too.'

I cannot think of a single word of conversation to pull her back to me. What interesting facts do I know about mining shafts, wells, bald hills, signposts, marrows … I could possibly write a substantial paper on the perfection of her profile, her hands clasped one over the other in her lap, each ovate fingernail so flawless, a petal, a proof of nature outdoing itself. In every aspect of her. She is so small beside me, impossibly small, but she is the most magnificent being I have ever met. She is the sky. God, I think I love her. I'm sure I do. She moves her hands and the bruise on the back of the right one stares up at me from her lap. It aches; it throbs in me. I'm not sure why I don't believe she had an accident with a door, as she said; perhaps because it looks more like she's been kicked by a horse, rounded edge to it like the top of a shoe. Or more probably, simply because it causes me pain to look at it.

'What's the name of that shaft well? It was something funny, too.' She leans forward now to ask Buckley as we pass an old mine works, stripped of half its timber and its winders idle but for rusting.

He says: 'Just In Time, it's called. Dunno why. Someone was thirsty when they got here, I s'pose.'

'Hm.' She smiles faintly to herself and resumes her study of the western hills above another dogleg of cottages, another signpost for the Mudgee Road, this one rotted and listing. What is she looking at? What is she thinking? Come on, Wilberry, think of something to say. Don't the batteries pound it out around here? Echoing through the valley – *chuck chuck chuck chuck chuck chuck*. Imagine living amidst these crushers every day? Fascinating. Come on, man. What else is there to remark upon? Oh look, we're heading into yellow box wood again now, both sides of the road, as we leave civilisation, such as it is, behind. What can I say about yellow box? These ones are not particularly interesting even to me: uniform and average in height and density. I'm not sure she's much interested in trees of any sort anyway. There's a spectacular avenue of exotics directly to the north of the township, which I saw on my stroll, some remnant of lost grandeur, but they are trees, too. Don't talk about trees. A stand of long-abandoned plums now appears out of the bush, massed with fruit. Bloody trees.

I look into the spiralling weave of the top of her boater instead and see only hemp straw. You can smoke the leaves like tobacco, there's some medical botany for you. Turns you into a proper imbecile, too, as Cos demonstrated to me the Christmas before last, at the Swamp, rolling round the floor with Susan, feeding her slivers of mango, imagining he's Gauguin. I tried it too, at his insistence: thought the top of my head would lift off from coughing before I became distracted by my own imaginary conversation with taxidermied Kevin, which wasn't very interesting either.

No, it appears the best I'm able to do at this time is belt my thigh into Miss Jones's knee as we turn onto a rougher track and stutter something unintelligible at it, followed by something that I hope sounds like: 'Nice track for a creek bed.'

She says nothing, and still she doesn't turn to me. But is there a smile again on her lips? I don't want to lean around too obviously to see. Instead, I stare far too long and closely at the arc of her cheek, this curve of the world I want to know, as she watches the hills disappear behind the steep side of the valley we enter now.

'Here y'are, this is where it all took off, the rush of the seventies,' Buckley splits the silence. 'Golden Gully, called me right cross the country, the finds what they got here. You been this way before, Miss Berylda?'

'No,' she murmurs, a long, soft sound, and I follow her gaze up to the top of the high ochre wall that now rises above us, first this side of the road and then the other, rock sheared away by water, flood after flood, over millennia, forging through this narrow cleft in the earth – and hollowing out a great arch in it ahead. 'Oh?' she seems to ask some question of it as we pass under its impossibly fine span; perhaps the same one I am asking: How is it that this overbridge stands at all, comprised as it is of grains of sand held together by a few tufts of millet grass and a lone hickory wattle leaning worriedly out over the abyss?

Yes, if you were to look for treasure, you might begin here, along this channel of cool summer air, swallows darting from wall to wall, the sounds of water trickling somewhere unseen to emerge as blue pools marking our way.

One of the wheels finds one of the creek pools, and the buggy tips to the left, then to the right over a mound of gravelly silt, almost tipping me out, and I have to laugh at the ride. My laughter bounces round these ochre walls, but still Berylda doesn't turn; she doesn't move – she is grasping the rail on her side so tightly, her back impossibly straight. And a terrible wave rushes through me. A terrible want of her gaze. I've only known her a day – a day and a half – but if she doesn't look at me again, and soon, I don't know what I might do to make her.

BERYLDA

'What are those tunnels?' I ask Buckley, staring into them. Giant rat holes, burrowed into the walls of this sheer-sided valley, round and spewing rubble at their mouths. My voice is flat, dull and clanking metal, not my own, above the ceaseless drumming of my heart.

'Chinamen's ones, them,' Buckley says. 'None of that lot mining here now but.'

Gone they might be from these diggings, but my desire flies into their black rat holes, gathering my courage from inside each one. What preposterous courage takes one across the world to dig a tunnel in the side of a mountain at a blind guess? That of my ancestors. And they did it with hatred clawing at their backs. Blind hatred. Let my hatred not be blind but clear and cold as steel. Finer than a scalpel blade. Free of anger. Free of passion. Let it be a lightning strike of justice, for me, for my sister, for all the bent backs lashed by cruelty.

'Not a stick of wood to prop 'em up inside,' Buckley explains. 'There's graves amongst 'em for the ones that weren't so clever at it.'

Then I must be more than clever. I must not leave the slightest trace of my intentions here except for a Chinaman's worthless word.

'It's a superior design, though, I would suppose,' Mr Wilberry adds. 'The cylinder – far stronger than any stanchioned tunnel might be in this silty rock. A squared structure is always going to be more vulnerable to ...'

Pressure. Of course it is, and I would suppose one can work a rat hole alone then. As I must act alone now.

I turn to Mr Wilberry, at last, and reply: 'Yes, a cylinder would be stronger.' And I wish I could tell him that I am sorry, that the way should be built differently for us, for dear lovely him, but I can only say, in this flat, clanking way: 'The circle is the strongest of shapes.'

'I'd bet you know your maths better than me.' He smiles, and his sun-like hopeful face, would break my heart if I had one in any state left to break. I wish I could touch his face, kiss the fine blond stubble along his jaw, somehow let him know all that I might promise him: my sorrow and my refusal to use him in any dreadful way. Make the only vow I may: that I not play him, of all people, in this devil's game.

He says: 'But I do know the sphere, the orb, is king of structures – eh? Such as an unopened bud – there's nothing much tougher in this life than that.'

As he says this, his leg touches mine again with the swaying of the buggy and lightning of a different kind flashes through me: this now familiar sweep of prickling warmth across my skin, up my neck and down along the tops of my thighs, a tingling that seems to emanate from somewhere in the centre of me, just below the solar plexus. I have never loved before, I have never been touched by a man in this way nor ever wanted to be – Marvell's 'Coy Mistress' had me running for the med library to try to work out what all the whispering and snickering was about – and yet I know what this sensation is now as if I've known it since the day I was born: my desire for Mr Wilberry. *Then let us tear our pleasures with rough strife thorough the iron gates of life* ... It makes sense now: perfect, and terrible. And it must be overcome. It will be. It's only a feeling, isn't it? Like any other. It's just an emotion, just another longing to be put aside.

It would be more useful by far if my fear was as easy to rationalise; control. As the gully opens out again now into forest and we return to what looks more like a road, I stare into the hellish confusion of trunks and limbs either side of us and see only monsters: armies of them, gathering, waiting to move on me. Devour me: perhaps they have already.

'Oh that's a good one,' Mr Wilberry says beside me, and I follow the gesture of his hand to the right: a cottage almost entirely collapsed to the ground but for a branch that's grown through one corner of the roof. I can't reply; the only thought I have is that I am that house exactly. Consumed but somehow remaining. And almost calm at seeing it: that I am becoming something else.

Until I see a lonely kerosene-drum letterbox a little way further along and I sense that we are at our destination. My chest screams with redoubled alarm for what I must do here. What I must ask, and how I must ask it; I have rehearsed a thousand ways in my mind, but I can hold no firm decision; no clear plan.

'Whoa, Whiskey.' Buckley slows us to a cautious walk, turning into what appears to be utterly trackless bush. Within a few yards we are inside it, and it is one monster. We are travelling through the spines along its back: trackless bush in every direction, distant and near, a million square miles of it. A dog howls and I might well be instantly petrified where I sit.

'Well, I hope we don't need to make too quick a getaway.' Mr Wilberry inclines his head towards mine and his breath brushes my cheek. 'I've just spotted a crimson grevillea,' he says, his self-deprecation deliberately jolly, 'and I should like to have a bit of a look at it on our way back, if that's all right with you, Miss Jones.'

'Hm, all right.' My voice is duller still, my mouth so parched I don't know how I shall speak to Dr Ah Ling at all.

The cicada hum rises to a roar here in the high sun. A million square miles of piercing threat: *Go away from this place, go away, go away.* Every instinct warns me to run.

'It will be all right, Miss Jones,' Mr Wilberry's gentle baritone assures. 'I won't let anything bad happen to you, here or anywhere.'

And all my senses jolt at his words. Only bad things will happen now. As they must. I see Greta as I left her with the hand basin beside her on the bed, *just in case*, her stomach upset again. *Don't worry about me, I'm sure it's nothing, Ryl.* Nothing mentionable; just a *whooshing* in her head. For that alone, Alec Howell must die.

The trees thin now and the tobacco field appears, or what I assume is the tobacco field – I've never seen a crop growing before. Plants as tall as a man, with fat leaves of bright green and gold, harvested bunches of them hanging like sheaves of brown paper bags from a thatch-roofed colonnade along the edge of the field. And, just beyond it now, a line of tin huts.

And a man jumping out of the nearest one to halt our further progress. He is bow-legged and pig-tailed and screaming above the barking dingo at his side: 'What you want?'

He has a large knife in his belt, it must be a foot long. It is a machete.

'G'day, Sam,' Buckley says more steadily than seems humanly possible. 'I've got a Miss Jones here to see your brother, Ah Ling, about a medical matter.'

'Who you?' The man steps closer, squinting myopically; denim trousers filthy with who knows what muck, face wizened and hollowed by some other, internal purulence.

'Buckley – Roo Buckley. Old cobber of Wheeler's.'

'Ah! Yeah, Mick Wheeler, he a good bloke. Yeah, you want Ling? You see him up there. My brother, Ling. Last door up there.' He waves towards the line of huts, the last one set a little way off from the others, towards the far corner of the tobacco field. But he doesn't step out of our path. He squints again and says to Buckley: 'You want smoke?' That doesn't sound like a question so much as a demand.

'Wheeler'll have a four-pound sack of stripped, thanks, chum,' says Buckley, as if he's asking for a sack of sugar, and I take in a long, deep breath, as if I might will some of his cool composure into me.

'Yeah, yeah, good. Ten bob for Mick.' The exchange is as quick as that, Tiger Sam throwing a hessian bag of the stuff at Buckley's feet, and then squinting yet again, at Mr Wilberry now: 'Who this man?' He might change his mind about us yet; his nostrils flare as if he's trying to discern some plot in Mr Wilberry's scent.

'He's me mate, Jack Smith,' Buckley replies, and no one might disbelieve him, the lie comes so easily, while Mr Wilberry doesn't blink, his expression remaining mild and pleasant as it ever is.

'Jack Smith.' The Chinaman laughs at who knows what. Yellow-toothed, utterly repulsive; if this is the devil come for Alec Howell, he could not be more appropriately designed: an evil

Oriental cartoon. 'Yeah, you go, you go.' He waves us away and he and his dingo disappear back into his hut with a jangle of tin as the wire screen whips shut behind them.

Buckley takes us slowly up the cartwheel ruts that run along the front of these crude dwellings. The second hut along is open-fronted, doorless, more like some sort of work shed than a hut for living in, if life is what people have here. As we pass it, inside I can just spy men playing cards, white men, smoking, one asleep on the dirt floor, testament, if one were needed, that opium should never be made available outside a hospital dispensary. The air is languorous, suffocating, the reek of manure from the field mingling with some other sweet, cloying smell. Even the flies are tired and listless here. Yet in between this hut and the next a child plays under a line of washing, a little girl playing peg dollies, as any child might. Her hair shines like black lacquer but she doesn't look up from her game for me to see her face, see if she is a mix, like me, and sorrow stills my fear now as nothing else might. Sorrow for that happy girl I was, with Gret, running through the misted daffodils at Echo Point, pegs clinking in our apron pockets.

'Stay there in the cart, Miss Jones,' Buckley says to me as we pull up at the final hut. 'I'll see this Ah Ling first, and see to it that you won't be alone with him.'

'No. Please. I must be alone with him,' I insist, with some sort of tortured whine. 'Along with the general discussion of his cures, I must ask about things I do not want you or any man to hear – things of a feminine nature, and of a personal nature. Please. Please don't make me explain myself further.'

'Oh. Righto, Miss.' Buckley scrunches the brim of his hat in some shame, and Mr Wilberry clears his throat in agreement. Men, I see, really are astonishingly easy to manipulate in this way, aren't they? Good men, anyway. May Ah Ling be as easy to plead with as these good men are, and as compassionate. *Please.*

Please, help me.

Buckley knocks on the timber frame of the wire screen of the hut and I send my plea into the blackness beyond, as Mr Wilberry bends to me again: 'Nothing you might need to say would ever shock or disturb me – are you sure you must be alone?'

'Yes, thank you.' I can't meet his eyes. If I did, what truth might rattle out of me? I look at the hut instead: contrary to the newspaper reports, it doesn't in fact have a thatched roof, but it is the sturdiest of the constructions here and the most home-like in appearance. It has a window by the door, and a garden bed of herbs at the front here; beside it a small patch of some other unfamiliar crop and then beside that – oh, I see the poppies. They are paler in colour than the poppies on the Track, their petals fading to mauve and falling in this blinding, blanching sun. One tilts its face to me over the raised edge of the herb garden: its centre is a black heart. A field of black-hearted poppies stretching up to the forest. A lone worker in amongst them, bending to them under his conical coolie hat, harvesting the bud sap, I suppose.

'When my mother was ill, in her last days, I was privy to much medical discussion that – well, you know, cattleman's son and all that, there's no mystery about the nature of things for me. I –'

'No. No, please, Mr Wilberry.' I just about scramble from the buggy in my haste to be away from him. He cannot be privy to this.

'You tell the lady to come, yes.' I hear Ah Ling before I see him, a spry, round-faced man as vivid with health as his brother is sick with living death. He wears a black silk cap and long, frogged shirt: as traditional as his brother is … whatever he has become.

'Dr Ah Ling?' I hold out my hand to him and my calmness surprises me, now that I am finally here, now that this chance is mine to take, my voice is crisp and bold.

'I am Ling.' He holds the wire screen open, avoiding my hand. 'You come in, come in, tell me what happens, I help.'

'Thank you.' I nod, once more making my silent prayer to whomever or whatever might listen or care. 'I hope you can help.'

Inside the hut, it takes my eyes some moments to adjust to the dimness; I can barely see the chair Ling directs me to: 'You sit, sit, lady.'

'Thank you.' I feel my way, and shelves appear behind his white moon face. Jars and canisters of all kinds, his dispensary, I suppose. There is another screen door on the other side of the room, opposite the one I entered by, and a breeze of that sickly sweet smell pervades through it. What *is* that smell? The poppies? No, they have no scent, I don't think. Perhaps it's the opium.

'So, you tell me what happens.' Ling sits over the other side of the table, as any doctor might, clasping his hands, waiting to hear what ails.

'Well,' I begin, as far and as firmly as my rehearsal had taken me, 'as it happens, I am about to become a student of Medicine, at Sydney University.'

'Ah, good, good.' He smiles and nods, but not in any way that would suggest he is especially impressed by that one way or another, and somehow I find this encouraging.

'I am interested in the case you treated,' I continue. 'The man with the tumour in his arm. It's quite famous. I heard about it from the newspaper, and –'

'Yes, good, good,' Ling interrupts, smiling and nodding now as if urging me to get to the point, not moved in any way by my attempt to flatter him.

'I would like to discuss your treatment of the tumour.'

'Yes.' He nods, but he has ceased smiling. 'All medicine is different, one case to the next. No person is the same as the next one. What is it I will help you with?'

Right. I see. He is not going to discuss his methods with me. Too bad – it's hardly of great importance to me now. Let's get to the point. I place my hands on the table before him. I close my eyes: I am the blade. I open them and say to him: 'Yes, I am here on a personal matter. A very personal matter. My sister is pregnant to a man who raped her. I would like advice on aborting the foetus safely, what quantity of pennyroyal or tansy might be used, or perhaps you might have an altern –'

Ling holds up a hand and says: 'You go to a different place for this. Not here.'

What? 'No. Please.' I beg. 'Someone must help us.'

'Not here.' He nods, telling me he can't possibly help us: he is no abortionist, I must suppose, and he is possibly offended by the suggestion that I may have considered him as such.

Tears sting and they are as strange as they are hot, sliding down my face. Tears that I have not shed for so long. When did I last cry?

Homesick at school, knowing Gret would finish in the junior dorm at the end of the year and I would be a baby alone without her the next. Idle tears of a happy girl who longed for Christmas at Libby's with Mother and Papa. Then tracks along my cheeks I could barely feel in the churchyard, and another churchyard, for them. But these tears? These are for the end. For defeat. Because no one will help us. No one can. This was fantasy all along, base and pathetic. A Chinese doctor will help me solve all our problems in one shake of a mystical chicken bone or some other ludicrous thing? I am a fool, a desperate fool. I reach for the wishbone in my pocket and snap it in half again with my thumb, ripping through the pound note again, too. What do I do now? Purchase a bottle of oil of pennyroyal from the nearest chemist and risk killing my sister with a fatal quantity? No. I'll ask at a brothel; there must be a brothel madam in town who will know. Give me a packet of bitter-apple menstrual pills and tell me how many might be effective. But how will I find that madam? How will I ask … *who* will I ask? Mr Wilberry?

'Don't cry.' Ling taps the table between us with his index finger. 'Don't cry, lady. You tell me, who is the man who hurt your sister?'

'Who hurt my sister?' The truth lashes out of me: 'Our uncle, Alec Howell, the district surgeon, of Bathurst Hospital – a *real* doctor. He hurts my sister.'

Ling sits back in his chair and lets out a long breath. His eyes fix on mine, expressionless but regarding me with an intensity that stops the course of my tears. He asks: 'Howell, the surgeon?'

'Yes.'

'He hurt your sister in this way? He make her pregnant?'

'Yes.'

'He has hurt many in this way,' Ling says simply, with that same expressionless intensity.

Many? The word spears into me as the greatest truth yet: of course Alec Howell has hurt many. Of course he has. I know this. I feel his beard scrape along my neck: *Good girl.* My scalp screaming; burning. I hear Greta yelp: *Please!* I see him in some memory not my own waltzing round the ballroom of the Gulgong Star, reptilian senses hunting for her, the next one, and the next one, whoever she might be.

Ling clasps each of his hands into fists on the table before me. 'I will help you.'

'You will help us be rid of the child?'

'I will help you be rid of the one who hurt your sister.'

A force charges through me at this, a maelstrom of terror and relief. 'Thank you. Oh God, thank you. You mean …?'

Ling stands and searches the shelves behind him, selecting various items and placing them on the table: a beaker of translucent amber liquid, a jar of some sort of dried herb, then a gold satin box of something else, and three small red beans placed on a little green dish. The beans jiggle like red beetles on the dish, as he pours the merest amount of the liquid, about half an ounce, into a tiny blue bottle that's stopped with a syringe dropper; a medicine bottle, just like one that might carry any household serum for colds and bellyaches or such chemicals as tartaric acid for making jam. Do I dare to believe this can be occurring?

'What is that?' I ask.

'Dragon tears,' he says. 'Carry the bad spirits away.'

It looks like castor oil to me, in viscosity and colour, and it is not for me to know what it is. From a drawer at his side he takes a small square of fine paper and makes a funnel with it, placing it in the neck of the bottle. He adds the herbs, half a tiny pewter spoon of one that looks like dried lavender, powdery specks of some purple flower, perhaps a drachm of it; he says: 'This will go to the stomach.' He adds as much again of one that looks like thyme from the satin box: 'This will go to the mind.' Then he grinds the three tiny beans in a mortar with a pinch of what looks like lunar caustic from a snuff box and adds that to the bottle too: 'This will make the fever that will go to the heart.'

My own heart is racing once more, to have this done. 'Will it be quick?' I ask Ling. 'Will it look –?' Like murder.

'It will be one symptom coming after the next,' he explains as he stoppers the bottle and slowly swirls the mixture. 'First will come the stomach sickness, then the madness and the fever. It will look like typhoid. But quick, yes. Only half a day, maybe less. Howell is not a big man in size, yes? Maybe less than half a day.'

'Oh yes.' My smile is as irrepressible as my desire is murderous. 'Typhoid? That is excellent. That is more than excellent.' He will suffer as he dies. He will suffer as Libby did.

Ling places the bottle on the table. 'Be careful, lady. Do not get on your skin or the poison will get inside you too. Do not get the poison in your heart, this poison of vengeance, clean your heart of this, or you will follow after him. You understand what I say?'

Not really, but I nod. I will understand. I will not get it on my skin and I will not carry this in my heart: we *will* be free. 'Thank you. Thank you so much.'

'Be careful. You not sure, do not do this. Throw it away and do not do.'

'I will, I will be careful and I will be sure.' I promise him, a promise I can more than guarantee. 'What do I owe you?' I reach for the note in my pocket, torn as it is, it's still a pound's worth, and I reach for my precious watch in the other: he can have both if he wants them.

But Ling holds up his hand again: 'You don't come back. I don't know a lady, you don't know a Ling.'

'Of course.' This transaction never took place.

He smiles and pushes the tiny bottle of freedom towards me, but before I take it, I want to know, I must know: 'How many women has Howell hurt?'

'I do not know,' Dr Ah Ling says to the bottle, and his eyes slide away out the door to my right. I follow them, and as I do I find the source of the sickly sweet fume: incense, clouds of it, coming from yet another hut, a tiny temple, not ten yards away, between the tobacco and the poppies, bundles of joss sticks burning at either side of its open front. The rough-cut boards of the temple walls are painted red, with twin copper lions of verdigris jade incandescent against them. I gasp: How did I fail to see that before?

I look back at Ling. He continues to look away towards the temple. He does know something and deeply, I am sure: I can feel his vengeance is as close as mine, a sister, a niece, a daughter: someone he knows. Something that his honour and his religion will not allow him to divulge. Is this why Alec Howell didn't want me coming here? I am too close to the truth in more ways than I know?

A newspaper paragraph read on the train two weeks ago comes to me – two weeks ago when Alec Howell was last here – that glancing mention in the *Evening News* of the nameless girl gone missing at Hill End. Was she Chinese? Was she one of the girls?

'The girl who was reported lost –?' I begin to ask Ling.

But he raises his hand again for me to be quiet, and then he nods, still staring at the temple.

And I can't be quiet: 'Has she been found?'

He nods again.

Alec Howell's predilection for molesting little yeller gals is littered through these hills and he remains unpunished; somehow untouchable. Such is the limit of Ah Ling's reach and opportunity, the worthlessness of his word; such is the power of the district surgeon. And he is gathering in depravity the more his ambitions are realised. Whatever the precise details of his outrages committed quietly in this hidden backwater, it's too late for Alec Howell to stem the consequences of it now. My own knowledge is truth enough. Conviction enough. I will be his justice.

I clasp my fingers around the bottle and ask Dr Ah Ling one last question, one for my grandmother, for all the poppies cast across this Gold Country. 'May I ask what brought you here, Dr Ling, to this place in the world?' This elegant gentleman, with his joss sticks and his medicine and his utmost discretion, here in a tin hut on the wrong side of the Hill. Why?

He smiles, with the trace of a chuckle on his breath: 'My father sent me from Shanghai to get my brother to come home. This was twenty years ago. I can't help brother Sung, so I help you.'

'Well, I am very grateful you are here,' I tell him. 'More than I can say.'

'Yes.' He nods and he gives me a parting instruction: 'Three drops, no less, on sweet food and throw the rest away. Throw it away in the ground or in the fire, not in the river. This poison is strong. Good luck to you.'

'To you also.' I wrap the bottle in my handkerchief and wedge it deep in the pocket of my skirt as the doctor ushers me out with a sweep of silk sleeve, closing the wire screen behind me.

And outside, the sun is bright and hard and merciless.

279

BEN

'I don't know about you, Mr Wilberry, but I am famished,' she says as she steps out from the Chinaman's hut.

Her smile is glittering, casting diamonds all around and spinning me upside down with these changes in her mood. She is striding towards me and yet past me again for the buggy, smiling wide, up into the tops of the ribbon gums that tower behind me, drawing in the sky with her eyes.

'Famished?' I think I say, following the sway of her skirt as she nears.

'Yes,' she says. 'Let's have our lunch back in the gully, shall we, and fast?'

'The gully?' She stumps me again. She didn't seem all that comfortable back there; I thought she might have been a bit spooked, but what would I know? I'm nodding, and thinking I wouldn't mind taking a closer look at the alluvial grasses along the creek bed there – because I'm sure she'd find that terrifically interesting.

'What's your hurry now, Miss Jones?' Buckley steps out from the side of the hut, where he's been listening for any murmur of trouble through the joins in the tin sheeting there, while I remained here at the front, by the garden bed, in reach of the buggy and the pistol, it being far preferable in the eyes of the law that I shoot a man should one need to be shot. I try to catch Buckley's eye before Miss Jones turns to him, but all I catch is the grim set of his mouth.

'Hurry?' she replies with a cheerful toss of her head; captain of the ladies' tennis team: 'I'm hungry, and I hope that's not yet a crime, Buckley.'

'Nope,' he says bluntly, stamping after her, tight-shouldered. He seems annoyed; perhaps he heard something he shouldn't have. I don't blame him for listening, though; I would have, too, had it not been wiser for me to stay here.

'Well, isn't that a relief.' Miss Jones smirks – at me, sharing her teasing of Buckley with me.

She captivates me, thoroughly. And how light she now is; some weight appears lifted from her, perhaps some difficult question has indeed been answered by the Chinaman, perhaps something for her sister's health procured, not that I'll ask after anything like that again. I ask her instead: 'So, you were successful then – you got what you came for?'

'I did, in fact, yes,' she says and her smile drives into me, lifting me somewhere above the trees.

From habit, I hold my hand out to help her back into the vehicle, and this time she takes it. She presses her fingers into my palm and as I hand her up she looks down at me and my chest explodes in her diamonds.

I tumble up after her; she moves across the seat to make room, continuing to smile at me, her face haloed by the brim of her boater, and for the first time I am sensibly and logically speechless. Who would not be lost? In this hope that I shall by some divine stroke be allowed to always be beside her. I am so alive in her gaze, I am ... made something else altogether.

'Oh, but we must stop first for that plant you wanted to see, mustn't we?' she says as Buckley moves us off. 'The grevillea, was it? Crimson?'

Was it? I hardly care in this moment. Something has shifted here, today, in me, again and deeper, something that cannot be reversed, as a bud once opened can never again be closed.

BERYLDA

I can't stop myself. I want him too. Oh, how I do. Doesn't this wanting quiver between us? So strong it is the pulse that moves cicada wings. This screaming song. I know that I am high with excitement, with anticipation, and, yes, with what can only be called lust. I am so high, I must have him too: Ben Wilberry.

A real man. A good man. Just once, before I am ruined by worse sin. Before I make myself unworthy of love of any kind.

So I shall love him now. I am already sorry for what I do to him, but I shall do it anyway.

Grasp at this slim and tender reed of happiness. Before it dies for all time.

BEN

'Do you play tennis?' I ask her.

And she says: 'No. Why? Do you?'

I say: 'No – not me, far too clumsy.'

And we laugh, and laugh. At nothing.

She sits amidst a carpet of hill daisies on the low bank at the mouth of the gully, a colony of saffron lilies bobbing their heads in the breeze along the ridgetop at her back, the toes of her boots ochre dusted.

'Hm!' she says now, swallowing the last of her sandwich. 'Cheese and quince paste – I do believe Mrs Wheeler makes the best quince paste I've ever tasted. Unnaturally excellent, isn't it?'

'It is.' Even if I couldn't disagree with Berylda Jones to save this gully bursting into flames. Watching her eat the sandwich has been unnaturally excellent enough.

'What sort of daisy is this?' She picks one of the tiny blooms at her side now, darting from one observation to the next, and I am slow in answering, caught once more by the sprig of crimson *Grevillea lanigera* in her hatband, the cutting she insisted I make for her as we left the Chinamen's place. My own observations move dopily from her hatband to the daisy in her hand via the ivory ribbons threaded either side of the section of lacy embroidery set at the front of her blouse, and back along them to the hazel fire set inside the sky of her eyes. I look at her without reserve now, all of her, and she is asking me to with those eyes. She holds me with her eyes as I lie beside her on this carpet of flowers, as she asks me now: 'Is it even a daisy?'

'Yes, it is a daisy,' I tell her, as easily as I am looking at her. Incredible. Sensational. 'It's a hill daisy,' I tell her; suddenly suave about it, too, as though I had not been inept an hour ago, or indeed for the first twenty-seven years of my life. '*Brachyscome*. Common.'

'Not an everlasting sort, I don't suppose?' She grins. Unnaturally delightful. 'Is it even a native?' she asks. 'It looks like a *daisy* daisy, to me, you know – a real one – one a child might draw a smile inside.' She laughs. She holds me in the softest petals of her laughter.

'It is a real one, *and* it's a native,' I tell her; it is nothing short of magical. 'It's not an everlasting, though – these little ones only last a day or two.'

'Only a day or two? All that work to make a flower, just for a day or two …' She frowns into the daisy, studying it, and then she looks at me again. She studies me for what I hope will be eternity, before she says: 'Kiss me, Ben Wilberry. I want you to kiss me. Now. Here.'

I have not the slightest idea how I might kiss Berylda Jones, but something in me seems to know what to do. Somehow her rosemary scent guides me, my lips finding hers, and I kiss her on this carpet of hill daisies, with the saffron lilies looking down on us, and with the touch of her hand on my face. Her hand on my chest. She tastes of sweet quinces and black tea.

Her hand slips into mine as she moves her face away as suddenly, springing up to her feet. 'Show me all the flowers here, Ben. Show me all the flowers you can see – tell me what they are, each of them.'

'All right.' She pulls me up and along the ridge, and the weeping meadow grass is thick beneath our boots as I show her the red bush peas here, native bluebells and wild sorghum, tendrils of cobalt sarsaparilla cascading off a ledge. 'So small,' she says. 'One would never know there were so many, the flowers are all so small.' I would tell her the best things evidently are, I would tell her there were many much smaller, but that I find a rangy clump of endemic *Helichrysum apiculatum*, its hands of a dozen tiny golden pompoms each almost spent, and I have to bend to pluck a sprig of it for her, and tell her instead: 'This is a daisy too. The most common of the everlastings, actually.'

'Of course it's a daisy, actually.' She smirks at it, threading it through that lacy embroidery of her blouse, so that it sits above her left breast. 'It looks precisely like a wattle to me.'

It looks nothing like wattle, but I suppose it must to her.

'And look,' she says as we walk on, 'there are some more of my wattle daisies over there, only it's a shorter plant. I'm quite the expert now, aren't I. Or is that just a bunch of dandelions?' She eyes the plant she's pointing at with playful suspicion. How could I have read her so wrongly? There seems no trace in her now of that serious, charging girl I met at that weird house in Bathurst. Is she not that girl at all? What is happening here? Has she changed, or have I?

'Neither,' I hear myself reply to the dandelion wattle daisy at her feet. 'That plant is called button wrinklewort.'

'No. It is not.' She snorts; most unladylike: most lovely. 'That is not a real name.' She taps me on the arm with the tips of her fingers. 'Does it give you wrinkles? Does it carry a curse of an old crone?'

'I couldn't tell you that,' I say, and I put on a bit of a stupid lecture hall voice for her. 'But I can say that goats love the stuff. They're eating it to extinction up and down the eastern seaboard. I'm having a bit of a battle over it with my superior at Melbourne, at present, actually, this very plant, amongst several others. He's convinced it's a weed. He's convinced your wattle daisy is a weed too. He's French.'

'Oh!' But she jumps away from me, and I'm not sure that she heard a word of what I just said: she's waving madly at a bee that's followed the *apiculatum* onto her blouse, turning her back to it to try to get away. 'I hate blowflies. Dirty – fat –'

'It's only a bee.' I smile, cupping it away from her.

'A bee!' She jumps again. A beautiful girl jumping away from a bee.

'And it's a native, too,' I tell her. 'It won't hurt you at all, this one. It doesn't have a sting. Native bees don't.' Which is fortunate, as this one is determined to hang about her.

'No?' She looks at it now, studying it too, as it hovers again over the flowerheads on her blouse, and she then watches it, curious, as it finally flies away. 'Well, what do you know, a native insect that doesn't have a sting – who has ever heard of such a thing?'

I would tell her that there are native flowers that sting insects, too, but I can't say anything more for a moment, dumbstruck with my own incomprehension: Did I truly kiss her on the bank just now? Or was that just a dream?

'I'm sure it was only confused by your perfume,' I say, and I've forgotten what we were talking about altogether.

'My perfume?' She is studying me once more.

What am I talking about? Perfume. 'Yes, what it is? Your scent, it's …'

'Oh, just some silly overpriced thing I had to have in Sydney, because … I can't even remember why.' She waves it away. 'I thought it was pretty, but it's just some bunch of weeds I don't know anything about. It's called Jicky. It's French, too.' She laughs again, kicking her feet now through the grass ahead of me, following the bee. 'I wish I could take off my shoes and run barefoot.'

'I won't stop you,' I say, and I say her name, too, for the first time out loud: 'Berylda.'

'Hm.' She turns and studies me again, smiling. Sure. 'Some other time, perhaps,' she says, pressing the side of my hand with all of hers and my hand has never felt so small. 'But we should go now. I should return to my sister, to Gret.'

'Yes, I'm sure you should.' I return to the world, the one that has others in it apart from the pair of us, or at least I attempt to. 'We should get back.'

It must be some time after two, I imagine; we've stayed here so long. I look down at the old man Buckley in the shade of the gully wall opposite, flicking the last of his smoke into the billy coals before kicking dust over them, stamping them out.

Berylda turns again and darts back down the bank without me. As I follow, I smile into the shape left by her hand upon mine, and I am a small boy balancing along the top of a wall, risking all with every step and wilfully. Because I am alive. I am so alive with her.

BERYLDA

He points out koalas and gang-gang cockatoos high in the trees along the way back into Hill End and I see none of them, it's all grey against greyish green-grey to me, a flicker of tangerine head feathers just missed, and I laugh with the rough and lively shouting of the birds above us, the splashing of the cartwheels through puddles, and I allow myself to enjoy it, the sounds of this make-believe happiness, brief as it must be.

Before we sight the first cottages of the town, I reach for his hand again, and I pull him towards me again. I must, as if some magnetic influence drives me to. I cannot push this wanting away. I feel the crack in his bottom lip against mine and I caress it with my kiss, just for the barest moment, no more than our faces meeting with a sweet bump in the road, the tingling brush of his beard, soft, warm, that sort of beard which might be clipped short or might merely be the result of his neglect to shave, impossible to say. And then I look away from him again, with all my terrible thoughts. My desire for him, for this one fleeting chance to be free with him, overlays a need to test my nerve, my skill at deceit: Can I make Ben Wilberry love me? Tonight? This one night that might be ours. A whisper in the darkness that none but us will hear or know. As no one must ever know what I will do tomorrow at Bellevue. Our hands are held hidden under the folds of my skirt at our hips; his large, warm hand around my bruised one; the bottle of poison lies hidden there too. Can I dare love him? Just this once? Before ...

'Berylda,' he whispers to me now, his breath so gentle and warm against my ear. 'Berylda, does this mean ...?'

'Yes,' I breathe the word out and back to him; I send it up to the grey, invisible birds: let him believe what he wants to believe this means. Let him have his semblance of happiness this day, too. Just this one day.

One day, one night, of love, and I will ask for nothing from this life ever again.

I turn to him, place my finger across my lips, rolling my eyes towards Buckley's back, and then clear my throat theatrically: 'Ahem. So tell me, Mr Wilberry ...' I cast about for another subject and, finding the sprig of daisy-wattle things just about under my nose, I say: 'Tell me then, what is it that makes a daisy a daisy? So many kinds – but what is it that makes them all the same?'

'Well ...' He clears his throat too, smiling slowly at the game, and he speaks more slowly still, so that Buckley might hear every innocent word, 'that's not a very easy question to answer, Miss Jones. There are so many varieties of daisy – ninety-four genera on this continent alone and an inestimable number of species – it can be difficult to tell one from the other at times, and with others it can be difficult to find the daisy in them at all. I could bore you rigid with the details.' He strokes the back of my knuckles with his thumb so softly that the tingling it sends across my skin dives within me and swells outward again, for him. I wonder how we might fit together as man and woman; how does this puzzle of anatomy work, from diagram to living flesh? Is it even possible for us? He is so large a person in every other way; will we fit together at all? Oh, how I want to know this. How I want our flesh to touch however it must. 'But the simple answer,' he continues, 'lies in the flowers: the heads are all generally comprised of a complex of multiple central florets, and of both male and female parts.'

'Are they *really*?' I feign enthrallment and don't feign it at all: I could become quite stupefied from it.

Even before he adds: 'And they mostly all share a certain flocculence.'

'Flocculence?' Our eyes spark together with an energy that is our own. A true sense of fun that I have never before found in the company of a man. I begin to shake with the effort of holding off a collapse into hysteria. For the second time today, my eyes fill with tears, but marvellous ones. What an outrageously fleshy word. 'Do tell me, Mr Wilberry, what is flocculence?'

'Well, Miss Jones, flocculence is a kind of fluff, a woolly down, that exists on the foliage.' He touches the stem of the flower on my blouse, and as he does so his finger trails the side of my breast, just for the tiniest sliver of a second, before the buggy pitches a little again on the rough rills of this track, and then he touches my cheek as lightly: 'Tiny hairs.'

'Is that right?'

'Yes,' he says and my mind is the shape of his smile: tangerine-sliced; sun-shaped. 'Tomatoes have them on their leaves and stems to catch tiny insects.'

'Do they indeed?' I banter back. I have not had such fun, such joy, in … ever. 'You're not suggesting that tomatoes are killers, are you, Mr Wilberry?'

'Why yes, they are, Miss Jones,' he says. 'Dangerous things, tomatoes, aren't they? And the flocculence on certain native daisies render them quite deadly to cattle as well – the whole of the Board of Agriculture wants to rip them all up for weeds, never mind the French. But flocculence can be beautiful and more tiny still, too.' He touches my cheek again, more softly still. 'Like that on a peach skin,' he says. 'Hardly there at all, but there nevertheless. That's flocculence.'

'Is it?' I am breathless at his touch, lingering though he has now moved his hand back to his knee.

'Yes.' And his other hand continues to hold mine beneath my skirt; he holds my hand with his gentle power as he says, 'Most of the seeds of daisies are flocculent too. The seeds of the *beryldii*, for example, they are rather a hairy lot – so they can float well and far on the breeze.'

I cannot reply to this sweetness: that he will truly name his flower after me. I hear it anew. The seaweed pink daisy from the Turon will be *Helichrysum beryldii*. I am astonished by this compliment now, this honour. Ben Wilberry is the sun and he names his flower after me.

'Why do you study plants, Mr Wilberry?' I ask our hidden hands.

'Hm. I ...' He ponders the question for a moment before he says: 'I want to understand how beauty is made, its genius, in all its parts, from leaf to forest, I suppose. I seem to need to understand this, how it all works together, where and why. The ecology of life. A fairly new branch of ... beauty. I find answers often in the smallest ... Ah –' He bends to me again and whispers: 'I am in love with you, Berylda Jones.'

His sun reaches into my bones. Even as my blood rushes weeping through me for the tragedy that this is and can only ever be. This absolute impossibility. But still I reply: 'And I you, Ben.'

And I turn away again. For I know this is no lie. I believe that I love Ben Wilberry in return, such as I am capable of loving.

This one, brief day. This is all we have. Before I am destroyed forever.

I force my thoughts back to practicalities, the realities, as the first of the mine poppet heads of the town rises out of the bush with the distant banging of the crushers; douse my passion with the true facts of the matter. Amongst the many hard, cold ones I possess, I find a litany of intimate abuses: *You ungrateful little slut*, my hair screaming from my scalp, each creeping threat across these past five years, each demeaning criticism, each pinch of his grasp. The scrape of Alec Howell's thick-bristled beard on my neck. A bitch kicked, yelping on the floor. *Be a good girl now.* Predatory footsteps down the hall, coming for my sister. Coming now for me. *I want you visibly gravid by election day.* As my sister is gravid by him now, and it remains that I have failed to find a cure for this today, for Gret. What step next with this then? Perhaps I can do nothing about it today at all. Yes: perhaps it is even best to wait. Alec Howell will be dead at some time in the night tomorrow, and once he is dead, I will find a text amongst those he keeps in the locked cabinets at the hospital to tell me what purgative and what dosage I might use. Of course. That is what I will do. In my grief for my dear uncle, I will ask only for his books.

'What are you thinking of now?' Ben Wilberry says beside me.

'Think?' I return to him once more. 'I'm sure I don't have the foggiest clue.'

Because I have quite lost my mind, haven't I? I look ahead. Clouds are gathering grey-green bruises, just as they did yesterday afternoon. Bright white lightning forks between the cleft in the hills. It shatters the air, scattering the birds. It startles Whiskey in her harness, too.

'Whoa.' Buckley is pulling her back hard to keep control.

And yet, though I hate storms like nothing else, I am unmoved by this one. Delusion over delusion: Tomorrow, I will be free. Gret and I will be free, and that is all.

One desire over all: freedom.

Ben Wilberry's arm is around my shoulders, his body a shield absorbing any fear I might otherwise have had. 'Strike me,' he says as the rain begins to spatter, 'that one was a bit too close.'

BEN

The wind tears across the top of the pear tree in the yard, stripping leaves, as we run from the stables towards the back doors of the pub, Mrs Wheeler waving from the verandah: 'Inside! Oh my Saviour! Come inside!'

There is no rain now, little that there was, but the wind is cold and just about gale-force, carrying dust and twigs and possibly most of the mine tailings off Bald Hill and pelting it all into us.

'Oh!' Berylda shouts as I grab her up by the waist halfway across the yard, the quicker to get out of this weather, and inside. As I set her down upon the boards again, she leans back and our hands shut the door together. Shutting the cold wind out together, our faces side by side, so together, just for half a blink, before we turn back to the room. The rear parlour, we find ourselves in, not the saloon, and here is Cos, playing cards with the maid. He is evidently much improved in mood from this morning, having found a miracle cure for his paralysis.

'Well, well, now look what the cat dragged in – Wilby sweetheart, you've come back to me!' he bellows above the deck he's dealing, well into his cups, several empties on the mantel behind his head, into the stout and some other thing, and the toe of his boot under the card table is tapping against the shoe of the maid: that explains the change in his mood. What's her name? Katie? Would it matter? I shake my head and return the self-satisfied smile of my friend: insufferable bastard that he is.

I could not shake my own mood right now if I tried: I have never been so happy.

'Ryldy!' Greta rushes into the room to embrace her sister. 'You were ages – and you're a disaster. Look at you – you've got leaves all through your hair. Look at your hair.' Greta Jones appears much improved too, all rosy and full of fun, as if she might have been plied with some beverage as well, something to make her bounce right up out of her sickbed. 'We were just getting worried about you, weren't we, Mrs Wheeler?'

'Worried?' says Mrs Wheeler with that flustering dismay of hers, despite her having just witnessed our safe arrival. She peers hard at Greta and half-cringes, half-winks. 'Oh yes. Worried. We were. But Miss Greta, what are you doing out of bed?'

'Oh shush – it's all right! I'm all right!' Greta waves her away.

'Too much ginger beer?' Berylda is smiling with her sister, who is picking out the bits of leaves caught in her hair, most of which has come loose from under her hat. Long dark hair falling everywhere across her blouse. She is a disaster, an exquisite disaster, and she tells Greta: 'Good to see you have obeyed my prescription.' Her laughter chimes high and loud as Greta sways against her. 'How much ginger beer have you had?'

'Oh lots – lots of something.' Greta is quite well schnigged, I would say.

And Mrs Wheeler mutters: 'Sometimes is stronger than other times – sometimes too much sugar in the lemons. Oh God.' And some Baltic oath.

'And sometimes simply too much ginger beer?' Berylda offers, as Mrs Wheeler flusters away muttering something about getting cake and tea, and the curve of Berylda's smile for her sister makes me love her even more. How could Cos fail to catch that in her? That love, right there, in her face, her eyes, her soul. But he does not directly acknowledge her presence in this room at all.

He speaks only to Greta, asking her: 'Did you finish your picture, Miss Greta Jones?' Pretending to admonish her: 'I can't recommend you anywhere as an illustrator if you have no portfolio of works to show – you'll be dismissed as just another reprobate layabout dabbler.' Does he admonish me in that, too, for our argument this morning? I can't tell; he's looking down at his cards once more.

'Oh yes, Cosmo, but I've been working away most diligently. I've been very, very busy.' Greta grins at him, firm friends they seem now, and she fairly leaps out of the room: 'I'll go and get it, shall I? And so I shall!'

She is gone and returned with her sketchbook before I can blink the grit from my eyes, and she is showing us all the drawing she has done today, another fantastical scene. 'See?' It's a picture of the mermaids from the steam organ swimming up out of the chimneys of the hotel, swimming into the sky, somehow like music, somehow becoming a flock of birds towards the top of the page.

'Oh, Gret ...' Berylda sighs, covering her face with her hands, closing her eyes; she seems touched by whatever this picture means to her, or perhaps she is only taken over by amazement at her sister's talent, that emotion Greta is able to bring to what she sees, or dreams – bringing lines on a page to such life. I am amazed again too.

But Cos doesn't seem to see or hear the admiration and devotion in Berylda's sigh; he sees only her face in her hands, as if he is determined to misread her, and he says to the ceiling: 'Oh but it's the artist's lot, isn't it? Can't please everyone – or if you're very lucky, any bloody one.' He says to Greta: 'I will purchase that – go and do another.' He snaps his fingers.

Greta throws her head back in her drunken fun and waves at him dismissively: 'You are an awful, awful person, Cosmo Thompson. Hard taskmaster.' Her laughter rings around the room.

Berylda rubs her forehead; weary. She rubs her eyes; no doubt gritty too.

Cos shrugs, turns back to his cards; back to the maid: 'Katie – ahoy there!' She sits mute as a mermaid sculpted of paste as he smacks a card down on the table in front of her. 'Now, what were we talking about before we were so rudely interrupted? That's right, I was telling you the truth about storms – the Blacks know by the skedaddling of the insects when one is on the way. Pity you don't have any Blacks around here then, eh, isn't it? What did you do with them all?' He looks under the card table and grips this

Katie round the ankle to make her scream, and make Greta scream with laughter again too, as Mrs Wheeler returns carrying a tray and screaming, 'Cake!'

And I must make an exit, not least to wash this grit from my eyes.

'Mr Wilbarrow! Mr Wilbarrow! You don't want cake?' Mrs Wheeler squawks at my back. 'But you must be hungry!'

'Thank you, sorry, please, in a moment,' I make some vague apology, as I cross the saloon, to return to the bedroom, for my towel and the water jug.

Where, on the night stand, I see Cos has replaced his sketch of Berylda with his completed illustration of my discovery. I blink at the page. What does he mean by this? Apart from that, technically, he is very bloody good. If he could be bothered, I'd have him draw the entire world for me. So exact; unprettied, unlike so much botanical illustration. He has even captured something of the bronzed sheen of the involucral bracts underside the bloom. Such an acute perception; understanding of structure. Why can't he see Berylda? For *my* sake? Or has something here changed too? Between Cos and me. I pour out a basin of water and splash a face full into my eyes. Perhaps if he could see something a little deeper in a woman than the size and set of her breasts … but that's not true, either.

'So what do you reckon is happening here?' I ask aloud, into the mirror.

Ignore him, old bear – everyone else does, Mama doesn't hesitate to advise me, or add: *You could change your shirt, too, dear, you're a bit spicy.*

And just for a moment, I feel her at my back, her hands grasping me by the elbows, urging me. To do what? I don't know. My mother is dead. She is not really with me, except in my mind. Am I the one then who is confused, about Berylda, because my mother wanted above all else to see me settled, see me in love? Do I see things in Berylda that just aren't there? Things that aren't real?

A sound at the door interrupts my thoughts, not a knock but a creaking of boards, and I think it's Cos, come to have it out. But it's not. It's a note, slid under the door quiet as smoke. A torn corner of art paper, an untidy pencil scrawl:

Meet me in the stable loft – midnight
B
Shhhh

What's the time now? Perhaps half-past three? Make it four. Make it midnight – make it now. This is real.

BERYLDA

'Oh dear, I think my watch must be in the buggy, worked its way out of my pocket on the journey,' I say, rounding the door of the parlour. 'I should really get a new pin for the fob chain.' And really not, because it is safely pinned in my pocket as it is.

And no one is in the least bit interested, apart from Gret, suddenly sober: 'Your watch? No. Do you want me to help you look?' Worried that I should lose something so precious to me, to us. She clasps grandmother's fan bracelet to her wrist: we can't lose these tokens of our history; it's all we have left to us.

'No, no, no – you're in no fit state to be outdoors.' I try to sound playful; I must sound like a finger-wagging shrew. 'I'm sure I know where it must have fallen.' I scuttle away, back out across the yard, looking for the stableboy, to make sure he doesn't sleep up there in the loft. I'm sure he mustn't – there'd hardly be a shortage of dirt-cheap accommodation in this town – but I need to be absolutely sure, don't I. My heart drums out the lesson here: do not make such a careless mistake again. Writing that note before thinking out the implications and complications fully. Think like a criminal, if you must be one.

The wind remains high, swirling around, blasting away my breath as I reach the stable door, and find the boy brushing Whiskey down, whistling some tune to her.

'Excuse me, boy,' I say, 'where is Mr Buckley?'

'Mr Buckley, miss?' The boy almost jumps to the loft in fright.

'Yes, my driver – Buckley. Do you know where he is?'

'Yes, miss. He's gone across with Mr Wheeler to K-Kitty's Flat, for – f-for a game,' he stammers. And I know this. Mr Wheeler was waiting at the stables when we arrived, waiting for Buckley to take him out for a game of Heading 'Em; they haven't had a mindless flutter on the coin toss together for years, apparently, and, according to Mrs Wheeler just now in the parlour, will highly likely be mindless and penniless when they return, fortuitously for me. There will barely be a sober mind in the entire house. I glance over my shoulder, back at the hotel, at the corner room beside mine and Gret's, where I saw that woman this morning, that other guest; I'll have to find out if she's still here: that room is the only one with a direct view of this stable door.

I wheedle at the boy: 'You don't go along to the games of Heading 'Em, too?'

'No, miss.' He's alarmed at that thought, of course; he's all of about thirteen.

'I wasn't serious,' I assure him. 'You look like a good, hardworking boy to me.' And then I ask the question I need the answer to: 'So much so I suppose you sleep up here, do you?'

'N-no, miss.' He gives me a shy smile. 'Me mum's only up the road. I go 'ome when I'm done 'ere.'

'Good.' I smile too, and look up at the loft again. Neat and clean like the rest of this place, Ben Wilberry will love me on a blanket in a nest of hay here, amongst the rich earth smells of the horses, their leather and the sack of fresh tobacco. Our night. One precious night.

I return across the yard, head down against the wind, hands in my pockets, and I feel the bottle there as I do; the bottle of poison still wrapped in my handkerchief, and still *there*. Another oversight blasting away my breath now. Carrying the bottle around with me as if it's a scant ounce of Jicky? *Do not get on your skin*, said Ah Ling. How very stupid of me: if it leaked there, would it not kill me first? I scuttle back to my room, taking the door to it directly off the verandah, and I push our freedom deep into my carryall under the foot of my bed.

As I rise again, rehearsing my next line, *Oh heavens, how lucky, my watch was there in the buggy all the time,* the mirror on the night stand tells me again what a disaster I am. And I am exhausted. I must be, with the too few hours I have slept since New Year's Eve. I must be mad with exhaustion, as with everything else. I'm sure I am. Mad. But my face shows no sign.

The mirror mists slightly, as if from some breath inside the night stand, and I see now a bowl of warm water has been placed there for me; scented with some oil; how thoughtful. What is the scent? Orange blossom? No. Some rosy bergamot summery thing and Aunt Libby comes to me with it, a melody I can't quite hear, the fringe of her shawl disappearing around the door as she leaves the room.

Oh Libby, I ask the mirror, what is this flooding and falling and rushing and crashing of love and hate in me? Will it end when he is gone? Will it all stop? Will it simply be quiet?

Help me! Help me, please! No, Alec – help me! she wails and wails through the night. The sound of grasping, tearing desperation that will never, never leave me.

The crushers seem to have gone quiet, though. Ended for the day. Distant thunder rumbles under the wind, over the mountains. I wash my face and I change into my organdie evening blouse. I arrange its soft ivory mantle around my shoulders to show them a little and pin Ben Wilberry's wildflowers there, crimson and gold, in the gather between my breasts. My plaits, such that Greta remade them, are wind-blown and slipping again; I shake them out and twist my hair up into a tousled mess of tendrils. I am a gypsy tramp. A pirate princess. Oh Libby. I can barely recognise myself. I am mad, mad, mad. And still my face shows no sign.

BEN

Greta is playing the piano now, that Chopin thing of sweet melancholy, and here, in this mostly empty pub saloon, the notes move through the space like lengthening shadows, trailing off to some point towards infinity. How that uncle of theirs draws the conclusion that this woman is a waste of an education, I'll never understand; she plays without the sheet. I can't play 'Chopsticks'. God, but the piece is endless. The music drags through me; the evening drags. It's seven twenty-five. And we've already eaten.

Greta yawns over the keys; she'll be asleep before it's finished.

'Your other guest isn't lured out by the music, Mrs Wheeler?' Berylda asks beside me on this old but comfortable lounge, and she remains perfectly poised despite the sag in the middle threatening to throw us together right here.

'What?' Mrs Wheeler almost jumps out of her chair, woken with a fright from her own drift. 'What other guest?'

'Oh? I thought I saw another woman here, this morning,' Berylda says, 'coming out of the room next to Greta's and mine.'

'You are seeing ghosts.' Mrs Wheeler turns in her chair, to the room in question, the one marked *PRIVATE*. 'This is no bedroom, this is where I keep the stores for the house – the brooms and the bleach. I wish she would help me clean this house if she is here.'

'Funny.' Berylda frowns to herself, and she shrugs. 'Never mind.' And then she rises, just as Greta looks set to rest her brow on the music stand inside the lid. 'I think it's time for bed anyway, don't you, Gretty-poo?'

Greta turns in the piano seat and nods, so slowly, she is already asleep.

As Berylda glances back at me, down at me, where I'm half-sprawled on the lounge, and she whispers under Mrs Wheeler's flustering over Greta about hot milk and honey: 'Should have made it nine o'clock, shouldn't I?'

I can't respond to her in words; my body is overtaking all responses now.

She says, 'But midnight it is.' *That* smirk, teasing me.

And the women are gone, leaving me to contemplate the incredible for the next four hours and fifteen minutes. That there must be such a thing as destiny in love. Stars crossing, planets aligning, tea leaves spelling out our names and all that. How else is it that Berylda Jones would ask to be alone with me tonight? In a hay loft. Does she know what might happen? She must know something of it, mustn't she? She is a very well-educated young woman, one with more than a passing interest in the biological structure and function of humankind, I would think. She seemed to dress differently this evening, too: her hair pinned back somehow more loosely from her face, her shoulders bared, the corsage of grevillea and everlasting drawing my eyes across the dining table to her breasts. I wonder if she dresses this way at her college in Sydney every night. I wonder if she smokes cigarettes at poetry readings. She seems so confident; she knows what she does here with me, doesn't she? It's me who doesn't really know what might happen. Bloody hell. I haven't been anywhere near that side of things since Cos dragged me into a place on Wharf Street, in Brisbane, for my twenty-first birthday. Arseless. I have no idea. I live like a monk in Melbourne, in an old but comfortable three-room terraced cottage on Swanston Street, nondescript but for the quantity of plants and cuttings that spill from the kitchen out into the courtyard and the amount of soil embedded in carpets and between the boards, and I can't say it's ever bothered me all that much. Nothing a long walk or a few hundred laps of the baths couldn't address. Until now.

Cos snores from his place on the lounge by the hearth; I'd forgotten he was there. Not that I'm about to ask him for advice. He's been out cold since five o'clock, missed dinner entirely, too contentedly grogged and serviced, and I haven't missed his company. I stand up, stretch, stare into the embers glowing along the top of the fresh log on the fire, about to burst through with flame. I suppose I'll have to go for a longish walk now, just to do something, fill in the time; have a bath: that, I suppose, would be the most important thing to do. Cos snores again, so loud I don't know how that one didn't wake him up. I throw the rug from the back of the lounge over him and leave him there.

BERYLDA

Doubt snicks me with the tip of the blade as I stare into the night: *You can't kill Alec Howell. You can't kill anyone.*

Because I love. I love Ben Wilberry. Do I? What else is this terrible force that racks me against the clench of my hatred? This delusion that says I might have a future with him. Ben. For it is delusion, isn't it? That I could marry him. That Gret and I could fly away with him, make a home with him, and we could all live happily ever after, after all.

In hell. For what I must do to marry him will make me unfit to be loved in any way at all. I would destroy any such union, were it to ever occur. I would destroy his life, his gentleness, his happiness, by my sin. By this ultimate pollution of my soul. Cruelty's chain will never let me go.

Gret sleeps in the bed by the window, the moonlight kissing her face, a peaceful dreaming smile upon her lips. She shows no sign of the pollution in her, but it is there. The night is still now, and silent except for the croaking of a few frogs.

One more hour and I will meet him at the stables. One more hour and I will tell him that I am sorry. I have deceived him enough. What will I tell him? That I am promised to another? Tell him the truth? That my sister and I exist only as Alec Howell's whores? That is the last thing I can tell him. But I must tell him something, to turn him away. To change his mind about me.

Because I must kill Alec Howell. For revenge. For freedom. I have no choice.

And I cannot hurt Ben Wilberry. I will not hurt him any more. I will not encourage him further.

And yet my skin aches for his touch. The tick of my watch, tight in my hand, aches into my heart.

I am too evil, and yet I am not evil enough.

I will be free, and yet never free at all.

BEN

'And what are you up to, creeping about as this hour?' Cos shuffles in off the lounge and through the bedroom door, scratching his head. Impeccable timing – caught me just as I strike the match to light the lamp.

'Going to the dunny,' I say.

'My hairy arse, you are,' he grunts. 'You're going to her, aren't you. You smell like a bride's nightie fresh out of the box.'

I don't respond. I smell like soap; clean people do. I find my trousers folded over the end of the bed and as I pull them on he repeats his warning: 'Be careful, Ben.'

I don't respond to that either. On my long walk around the town in the dark just a few hours ago, with only the moon and an inordinate number of feral goats to consult, I came to the most likely theory to explain his attitude: he's jealous. Put out that his hopeless friend might well be hopeless no longer. In the history of our friendship, I've always been the awkward one with women, and generally socially inept. The one who the pitiable one might pity. This, and Susan has his nose out of joint with the twins taking her attention from him; together with his perennial frustrations at not having his genius recognised simply by imagining that it should be. And presto: he can't stand that I might actually have stumbled across some sort of happiness – with someone as beautiful and brilliant as Berylda Jones. It must be killing him. Let it kill him, until it doesn't. He'll get over it.

I take the lamp out through the saloon and across the yard, but hardly need it to find my way, the waxing moon is high now and blazing tonight.

And in the dark of the stables, I find her first by her perfume, that fragrance of rosemary and –

'Ben?' she whispers, from above.

'Yes.' I raise the lamp, the light falling first across the horses dozing in the stalls, catching the black polish of the rounded back of the buggy, the peeling red paint of Wheeler's heavy cart, the tack hung around the walls. And now Berylda's small white porcelain face looking down the ladder from the loft.

I suppose I scale it in three steps.

'You're here,' she says softly, taking the lamp from me.

'I am.'

And she is naked, but for her nightgown falling from her shoulders, her dark hair falling all around her.

And she is waiting for me.

BERYLDA

'You must be cold,' he says.

'Not now,' I say to him, and I have no more words for him. No sorrow and no shame. The lamplight caresses his fair lashes and his lashes caress my cheek as buttons are rent furiously through canvas, through calico. And I look at him: his body is superb: he is da Vinci's Proportions of Man. He is precisely what a man should be. I touch his face; I touch his chest; I touch the firmness of him and I am the lightning. I crack and open to him. The brittle shell of me shatters; I am ripped from my carapace. Skin upon skin, I guide him to me, I guide him over me, and then as nature would have him fill me, he does, and the further he fills me, the more I swell and shore around him.

Until we are one. In exaltation, and in pain. I have never known such pain, nor such a longing for it to remain. I hold him deeper and deeper to me; I am filled with stone; I am filled fire; I am filled with light. His kiss swallows my cry. We two were designed in every detail to be together in this way.

He holds me cupped in his arms and he trembles over me; he trembles into me, through me.

'Ah!' he cries out, and I feel his pulse within me; I feel the surge of a great wave; I fly into the heart of this pain.

And I hold him closer and closer as he subsides. I don't ever want to let him go; I don't want him to leave me.

He eclipses all malignance from me, hiding me under his too-long hair, under his body. He holds me as if I am precious, as if I am unbroken. He is my boat; I am the sailor and the sea.

I tremble now too. I tremble gently in his arms, and I grieve.

BEN

'Have I hurt you?' Please, no.

'No.' Her eyes are closed but she shakes her head, rustling the hay under the blanket beneath us. She holds my face in her hands, and whispers: 'I've never been so still. So quiet ...'

'Oh good.' Is that good? It must be. It has to be. There is no other goodness like this one that has just revealed itself to me. I am in awe of her; of us; of this. Holding her.

I am at some edge of thought aware that my elbows are beginning to suffer a little as I continue to keep my weight from her, but I can't move from her, and she doesn't seem to want me to. She pushes her hips against mine, pushing inside her quiet stillness so that I'm almost hard again. I don't want to ever stop seeing her, here in my arms, above this stable, in this cool-warm summer air, on this perfect night, in this lamplight, frowning as she pushes against me, in some pleasure that is all her own, until she really is quiet, and still. I will never stop seeing her here, for as long as I am alive.

'Berylda.' I say her name, to somehow mark upon the rafters that we are here; mark it upon the air.

'Hm?' A faint smile but her eyes remain closed.

'I love your name,' I say, because I do. 'Berylda. It's a song. A spell.'

'I love my name too.' She smiles again, more fully, but she will not open her eyes, as though she is holding herself in some reverie, some spell she doesn't want to break, as she tells me: 'My parents invented it – Papa found a piece of beryl stone on one of his licences, out at Ophir, just as Mother wished me into existence. My sister's named after a whole mine, though – little place called Greta in the Hunter coalfields, where Papa was born, before he ran away to make his first fortune in mountain shale – Shhhh, don't tell anyone that either, will you? Rags to riches. Isn't that romantic? A mineral love story, of daring Welsh prospectors and pretty China girls ...'

I kiss her forehead, and her loss, and her luck at having parents who evidently loved each other and their children, as I tell her: 'I'd like to see that piece of beryl. I bet it's –'

'You can't.' She flinches, and the frown sweeps across her face again; she holds her eyelids tight shut in it, and I hold her tighter in my arms. 'Mother had it made into a pendant, oval-shaped, a cloudy sea-green, scallop-edged with gold. But it disappeared, with the rest of her jewellery box, after ...'

'Shhh.' I kiss her again. 'Don't leave sweet dreams.' I don't want her to think of him – this thief, the uncle, their guardian; I will help her reclaim what she can of her parents' estate from him, engage a solicitor – as I shall probably have to on my own account at some near time, to claim what's mine of Mama's. But now, I only promise her what I must: everything. 'I will always be here for you. I will never disappear.' I wonder if that sounds a bit dramatic and so I add: 'Unless, of course, you'd ever want me to.'

She laughs through her dream at me, the sweetest mockery. A tear tracks across her cheek and I kiss it away; taste its salt. But her smile stays with me, and not with me, as though she is listening to some melody only she can hear; I want to hear it too.

'Where have you gone?' I ask her.

'Over the chimney pots and far away,' she murmurs. 'Hm ... a land of admiration and respect ...'

Her face tilts a little towards the lamplight. I am a giant holding a small, beautiful world in my hands, and I do believe that she has fallen fast asleep.

BERYLDA

I gulp blindly at the blackness, the chain iron-heavy across my ribs, a massive link constricting my lungs as I fight to drag in the air. What? But the chain is warm, soft. Flesh: an arm wound around my waist. I am sleeping? No. How did I allow myself to sleep? Is it dawn? No. My eyes are open, but it is still dark. Just: grey light creeping in from somewhere below. A lone bird chirps; the crushers are not yet thumping. Panic engulfs me.

'Berylda?' he rouses, confused, as I push his arm from me. 'It's all right. I'm here.'

It's not all right. I scrabble amongst the hay for my nightgown and throw it over my sinfulness, my vast and unfolding sinfulness, my wailing guilt. I find the ladder and I am down it and across the yard, cold slap of dew against the soles of my feet. I fell asleep? How did I fall asleep?

What have I done? In the few moments it takes to reach the verandah, sense returns enough for me to answer that question with the cold-slapping facts: I have allowed myself to love Ben Wilberry, I have allowed him to love me, and none of this can ever be. Because of what I must do today. Today.

Today, there is no God, and I am a murderess.

'Wait – *wait*,' he whispers after me across the yard, his breath at my back, his stride quaking the earth, breaking the earth in two, for me.

311

But he can't rescue me, us, and I can't wait. Can I? Can I? Can I? The answer returns and returns and returns: no. The blackness is greying faster and brighter with my every step and I dare not look behind me. My heart is screaming each way, along the future and the past, as I turn the handle of the bedroom door.

To hear my sister moan, right into the centre of now: 'Ryldy? Ryl, please, is that you?' A gasping sob ragged as my mind.

'What's wrong?' I rush to her side and as I do I smell the sick in the pot on the floor at my feet. 'Oh, Gret. Greta, I'm so sorry.'

'Where were you?' She is warm to the touch; her face clammy with sweat. This is not merely yesterday's overindulgence of ginger beer, and I can't answer her. She cries: 'I'm the one who's sorry, Ryldy. I'm sorry that I am ill.'

'Don't be so silly,' I say. 'We'll find out what's wrong, and we'll fix it.' And still I cannot tell her what I suspect this is; what I know this is: the seed that grows inside her, the germ twisting into life. But how? Why is it hurting her so?

'I just want to go now, back to Bellevue – I just want my bed, my own bed,' she sobs as I check under the bedclothes here, now, under her nightdress, for blood: none. She cries out at my touch to her abdomen now, though, pushing me away: 'Don't – please!' But I persist. The injury is plain and raw within her hips as I continue to prod, yet even so there is nothing I can feel of it under my hand. What should I feel? What do I know? What *is* it? Could it be an infection after all? Or – what is that condition where the child in embryo strikes in the wrong place, before it reaches the womb? I can't remember the word. But I know the consequence: haemorrhage and death. It kills hundreds of women every year. She needs a doctor, a hospital – a surgeon, possibly. And not the doctor in this town – *slothful and incompetent*, Uncle Alec called him, just an ordinary country physician. She needs an experienced surgeon. And one who is not also her abuser. Dr Weston, it will have to be – he's mostly retired from those more arduous duties but there is no other choice. We must leave for Bathurst immediately.

'Berylda, please.' Ben is at the verandah door; beyond the lace, his head is pressed against the glass. 'What's happened? Is everything all right.'

'No.' I let him in; I have no choice. 'Nothing is all right. My sister is dangerously ill.'

'Ryl – please. It's not so bad as that,' Greta sits up in protest, or attempts to, clutching at her side. 'I just want to go to my own bed, my own pillow. Truly. I will be all right.'

'Greta!' I scream at her. 'You are *not* all right!'

I wake the house, 'Please! Please!' making my way towards the kitchen and finding Mrs Wheeler already arrived there from her apartment, already reaching for pots and knives in her cap and nightgown.

I will never know what I scream at her now, but she replies, 'Yes, yes.' Nodding, making noises of assurance, 'I know, I know,' wrapping sandwiches and stirring porridge, but her eyes hold terror: *Don't let your sister die here.* Ruin the reputation of her already near invisible business. God forbid.

Buckley appears behind her, from another door beside the pantry, yawning and scratching his stubble but reliable as ever, already on the road and instructing: 'Don't worry, Miss Berylda. We'll take the way through Turondale – it's the longer way but faster. We'll get there – we'll be right.' And he follows me back across the saloon.

Where he takes me by the wrist before he leaves for the stables. I gasp at him, this leather-skinned old gardener – *You don't touch me.* But he does, and roughly. His eyes full of care and warning. Roo Buckley, my ally, my friend.

His brick dust scrapes into me: 'Miss Berylda, slow down for a minute,' he rasps, a whispering growl, not letting me go. 'You need to listen to me. Stop right now and listen. I run into George Conroy last night, over at Kitty's – you know, that bloke who Ah Ling done that miracle job on? He's got two arms on him, all right. The Chinaman's medicine does what it says, and I know what Howell has done to Miss Greta. I heard you talking to Ah Ling, yesterday, in his hut. I heard it all – every bit. I heard one of yous crying out in the night New Year's Eve too. I shoulda come into the house there and then.' He tightens his hold on my wrist: 'I'm an old man. Let me do it for you, girl. I'll get rid of him for you. Don't matter if I hang.'

'No!' I shriek it at him, ripping my arm from his grasp, as Greta emerges from the door to our room. She is stooped, lost, frightened, and the dark shadows under her eyes are frightening me.

'Ryl, I can't find my boots,' she says, as if that's her fault too.

I turn back to Buckley before I go to her. 'No,' I hiss it though my teeth. 'Whatever it is you heard, you heard it wrongly.'

If I have one atom of decency left to me, one power left to me, it is this: I will avenge myself and my sister. No one else will do it for us. No other will make this payment to hell. This evil, this poison, stops here: with me. Today.

REQUITE

The worst enemy you can meet will always be yourself;
you lie in wait for yourself in caverns and forests.

Thus Spake Zarathustra

BEN

'Greta Jones seemed in fine form yesterday,' Cos continues packing only his pipe. 'Sweet as a pea, that one, in every way. Nothing wrong with her.'

'Well, she's not in a good way now,' I tell him again, throwing his clothes on the end of his bed. 'Just get dressed, will you, please?'

'What did bitter little kitty witch do to her?' he says at my back as I turn away to pick up our bags, and he's pushed this once too far.

I look across at him. 'What did you say?'

'You heard me.' He strikes a match. 'No wonder Greta gets ill. You know, she does want to see what I can do to help her sell her illustrations, she asked me again yesterday, and I do know someone who might well be interested. Greta herself is *very* interested in earning some pocket money – no doubt to get away. Get a life. Spread her wings. And her sister could not be less interested.'

'You've got no idea what you're talking about,' I tell him, with no intention of talking about what I know of the girls' situation, that it's Berylda's intention to support them both, to get away together; it's not yet my business to tell. 'Just get up and get dressed.'

He continues to lie there, puffing. 'And now kitty's got her little witchy claws hooked right into you, too.'

I pull him up by the front of his nightshirt and tell him right into his face: 'Get dressed, get outside, get back on that horse, or I will throw you through this fucking wall to save time.' I shove him up against the liner boards. And then I let him go as quickly at the sound of my father's voice that has just shot out of me.

'Look who's a man now, then.' Cos gives me a threatening stare, but he picks up his trousers. Unlike him, I've never deliberately hit anyone or picked a fight; but at the same time, I've never been shy of a tackle or short on strength. I could probably actually throw him through this timber wall.

I give him some threatening stare back. 'Don't push me again. Soon as we get back to Bathurst, you can go – get out of my life.'

He says nothing to that – because I mean it. I don't know who he is any more, if I ever did. There's such a thing as being a difficult character, and there's such a thing as just being a nasty –

'Shit,' he says when he sees Greta Jones, as he follows after me, pulling on his boots across the back verandah. 'She's not well, is she.'

One needn't be too observant to see that the girl suffers badly. Berylda and Mrs Wheeler are half-carrying her to the stables. The girl is pale and visibly tense, keeping hold of her sister's hand all the while as though that might help to ease the pain. I run over to help them; lift her up into the buggy. She weighs less than nothing, but she is heavy with distress: 'Oh Mr Wilberry, Ben – I'm so sorry to make this terrible fuss and trouble.'

'You're no trouble at all.' I pat her awkwardly on the shoulder, wishing there was something else I could do, and Mrs Wheeler pats her on the knee: 'There, there – it will come and it will go. All things pass.' As Berylda glares at her; withering: 'Pass? What would you know?' And I look at Mrs Wheeler, who is stung, and apologise, very awkwardly: 'It's been a difficult morning for everyone.' But she is already walking away, with a Baltic curse.

Mr Wheeler is holding out reins to me, somewhat under the weather himself, and as I take them I glance up into the loft: this place where Berylda and I gave ourselves to each other only hours ago. If I couldn't see the little bed lamp still resting there I would question whether it had happened at all.

'Follow the signposts to Bathurst, east and then south, round Monkey Hill,' Buckley urges, bringing the roan out for Cos, and grim as I am about what this day might bring. 'Keep us in sight, will you?' he adds, though he needn't have, and we're away as the dawn breaks, blazing through the needles of the black cypresses that tower along this road out of the town.

My back is soon cricked from turning in the saddle every few moments to see that they stay with us, watching for Buckley to tell us to break for the mare to catch her breath, and not bothering to watch if Cos stays with us too – if he delays at all, he can find his own way back. Or not. The road is sound, fairly recently graded, and bounded each side mostly by dense stringy bark and yellow box, and I've never hated a forest more. Never hated a forest before. Or the tight bends in a road, slowing our pace as we begin to descend now through a shaded terrain of jagged cliffs that I would otherwise belt down happily, taking in the broad forever view from this vantage across these tablelands of rolling green and gold and blue. Here, I am caught between looking back for the buggy and looking forward for a rock fall, a stray branch, a crumbled bridge, but the road remains clear, empty but for us.

We pass the fork for Bathurst and Sofala, turning southwards and back across the Turon at a shallow causeway, and still Buckley doesn't signal for us to stop. I want to stop, to see how the girls are faring; each time I look behind me I see only the tops of their hats tight together and downcast so that I cannot tell them apart, never mind if they are going all right. But on and on we ride, and it's not until the sun is well above the trees, above a gully flat, before we hear the old man call out, 'Whoa there,' for a small billabong, beneath the wide rambling canopy of an apple box. The coals of a fire smoulder beside it, and an old copper pan and sifter lie discarded by the stream that trickles down into the waterhole; we've interrupted someone's prospecting, it seems.

'Where are we – how far along?' I ask Buckley as he takes the buggy past me to pull up by the water.

'Jews Creek – just over halfway,' he says. 'The road will be more or less straight from here. Give us a half-hour resting and we'll be in Bathurst about three o'clock, I'd reckon.'

'It's all right, please, gentlemen.' Greta Jones turns and looks over the back of the buggy at me, blinking as though she might have slept through the last few hours, unlikely as that would seem.

'Don't push the horses too hard on my account. Really, please. I don't feel nearly so dreadful now.'

Her cheeks are pink once more, her eyes alive and bright now she smiles. She does look much better than she did.

Cos groans behind me; I hear him slide out of the saddle and thud to the ground, muttering something or other, annoyed. Let him be. Does he think Berylda has somehow orchestrated all this just to get under him? I don't care what he thinks. But it is fairly odd, for Greta to be so ill one moment and perfectly fine the next.

I move towards Berylda as she steps down from the buggy now; I want to ask her what she thinks is going on. I want to know what has happened to last night, to us. What happened this morning: why did she run from me? Did she somehow hear her sister calling to her? Perhaps when I was still asleep?

She glances behind her, at me, and quickly moves away as I near, towards the old man at the water's edge. 'Half an hour, Buckley — half an hour and no more,' she says.

He doesn't reply, but gets on with filling the billy and muttering to himself about ghosts that can't kick their fires out. Cos stuffs his pipe; Greta settles by the water and begins sketching out the apple box tree as though indeed she had never been ill in any way. Cos says something to her about her drawing but his words are swallowed in the crash and rumble of a mail coach flying past.

I stretch and crack my aching spine. A mopoke blinks down at me from an elbow in the branches of the apple box, more tree than bird. I move towards Berylda again, and she moves away, to stand behind her sister, to stare into her pocket watch. This strange dance with her returns; what does it mean? Only hours ago, we could not have been closer; I moved inside her; I kissed a tear upon her cheek; I kissed her breasts. I harden just to think of it, and it's me now who has to look away. Does she regret what we have done? Why? Why could that be? I want to pull her shoulder round towards me, make her face me; tell me. But I can't do that. Not right at this moment.

I look over at the abandoned pan and sifter, copper greening by the billabong like weird mould. I don't know what to make of her; of this; of anything. I take a look around upstream a little way, looking for more *beryldii*, in the dappled shade, where they'd best be found. Didn't Buckley say they were abundant round this Monkey Hill way? They might well be, but I see none.

BERYLDA

Mr Thompson is saying something to me, from where he sits on the ground beside Greta, but I don't hear him. He won't stop looking at me with his cool grey eyes, though, with his overfed conceit, so I ask him: 'What?'

'I said would you like a sandwich?' He has unwrapped one and is holding it up to me, the waxed paper beneath it fluttering limply in the breeze.

'Oh. No. Thank you.' I look at my watch again; the hands swim, as if their gold is melting in the heat of my palm. From my rage. This rage that grows by the minute within me, so that if I slipped my harness now, I might kick out, I might kick the sandwich from his hand, kick my boot into his fat complacent face as the face of Alec Howell's proxy, tear off his too-neat beard, his vanity, as he lounges here by my sister, tear down the tree before them, tear down the hills and the sky.

'Ryldy suffers such terrible anxiety on my account,' Gret explains to him fondly, lightly, and I walk away to hurry Buckley up again.

My sister appears to have rallied, yes, but the condition persists. What else can it be now but some severe case of morning sickness? A lost line of newsprint returns to me from somewhere, some passing joke: *'Morning sickness?' I asked the Doc. 'But I must be having triplets then, for it comes to me morning, noon and night.'* And with this severity which Greta is experiencing, logic

322

from somewhere else tells me that the pregnancy might be further advanced than I had presumed. *When did your last menses come?* I asked her on New Year's Eve, when she told me she was only so tender and sore because her whatsits were late. *Oh three weeks, maybe four …* My own ignorance scalds; that I do not know my own body either. Does it come for me next with Ben Wilberry's seed? How stupid have I been? Wilfully stupid.

'Miss Berylda,' Buckley addresses me as I approach him, standing by the fire with his mug of tea and his cigarette. 'Don't do this,' he tells me in his low growl, glancing up the little rocky stream towards Ben, who is searching the grass there. I look down at the ground; I cannot let my rage fall upon him. 'Don't go off on your own this time,' Buckley says. 'Let me help –'

'No. You cannot,' I tell the mat of dead grey leaves at my feet, dead grey dust. 'There is nothing you must help me with.'

'I can go to the police with what I know,' he says, bending across me to poke the coals with a stick. 'And I know Miss Greta ain't the only –'

'Ha!' Contempt snarls through rage and warns him in return: no policeman would believe the word of an old convict labourer against the word of the district surgeon, the treasurer of the Liberal League, a captain in the corps. All that would achieve is our ignominy.

I glance up again, at Ben; he waves as he sees me, stepping down the gentle slope, stepping across the stream. I shrink from his warmth now, from this picture of the future that should be ours, and can't be. What would I say to him if I could? How would I break things off? Tell him that I cannot allow him to be any further corrupted by me, because that is true, and I am devastated, utterly devastated, that I will never know his breath upon my lips again. This pain drives a black rat hole of despair into my chest.

I look back at Buckley and my voice is death as I tell him: 'It's time to go.'

I return to Gret: 'Come on, pack up.'

'Oh, but I just want to fin –'

'Finish it back at Bellevue – in bed. You are not as well as you think you are.'

Her eyes beg me to calm down; mine beg her to do as I ask. 'Greta, please don't argue with me.'

'Oh all right.' She tosses her pencils back into her case, but she snaps the lid shut, exasperated with me. Perhaps I am pulling her too sharply from her denial; perhaps she doesn't want to know what this strange illness is, or perhaps she has guessed; I don't know.

But I must remind her: 'This morning you were so violently ill, you frightened me into thinking you might not survive this journey back to Bathurst. To lose you would be to lose all meaning to my own life. So you can be as cross with my impatience as you like – all right?'

'All right,' she sighs heavily but she smiles. 'I am a bit tired, I'll admit.'

I am. And not least because I need you safely, blamelessly in bed, my sister, while I do all that must be done this afternoon.

Mr Thompson continues to stare at me with his cool complacency, calculating perhaps what gibe he might serve to me next. But whatever it is, he keeps it to himself, which is possibly wise. For I am busily calculating too, beneath all the violence coursing through me, wave upon wave; as Greta stands up, still bent with pencil case and book in hand, I bend with her and whisper: 'I'll call for Mrs Weston when we get in – have her look at you first, before any doctor. All right? I'll make sure *he* doesn't come near, I promise you.'

Greta nods, clasping her shame to her breast with her pencils. 'Yes.' And there is something in that look that makes me sure she knows now: she knows something is very wrong inside her, something that grows worse daily. If the shame must be exposed, better that Mrs Weston be the one to discover it. She may be outraged, but that outrage will soon be confused by the sudden demise of Alec Howell. She won't broadcast the transgressions of a dead man around town; she is too decent a woman for that sort of moral gloating; there will be no side to take in grief but ours. And even if she did shun us afterwards, what would it matter then? We will be free of him. We will be free. In a matter of hours.

And I can't wait one second more than I must. The time is now, or this storm in me will pass; I will lose my nerve.

I squeeze Gret's hand with all my addled love and cunning. 'Don't tell Mrs Weston anything you don't want to, darling. But you must let her examine you, please – I need to know you're all right.'

With any luck, Mrs Weston won't find out about any of this at all. She won't ever suspect that Greta's unwellness was anything more than some menstrual anomaly, once I've found and administered the cure myself, and the child is gone from her. But of more pressing concern, I must somehow arrange the timing of things precisely so that Mrs Weston will be with my sister this evening, all evening, should anything happen to me. Should I be –

No, I will not be caught.

I keep my eyes fixed to the road ahead.

Step after step, there is nothing but the road ahead.

BEN

'Suppose that's it then, old matey. I'll walk back to the pub, get the next train out of your life. See you in some other realm sometime,' Cos says to me when we reach the stables.

'Righteo. Do that then.' I don't care what he does; I don't look away from unsaddling Jack, or bother asking Cos to help with the roan, Rebel. He wouldn't know how, not that I'd want to put the martyr through any further ordeal anyway. I'll do it myself; there's no boy here at Bellevue to do it. No one but Buckley, who's busy with the mare and the vehicle. And Berylda, who's taken Greta directly into the house and is clearly making a point of not speaking to me; couldn't get away fast enough at first sight of the front door. So Cos can go and stuff himself, for all –

'I reckon it'd be a good idea if yous'd stay with us here for a bit, if you can,' the old man says behind me.

'Stay? Why?' I ask as I lift the saddle. So that Berylda can demoralise and humiliate me some more? It's not as though I asked her to kiss me, not as though I slipped a note under her door asking for a midnight rendezvous. That's all my doing, is it? Women are evidently not for me, or this one certainly isn't: I should have listened to Cos in the first place, shouldn't I. Oh well, Mama, at least I got a new species to show for the trouble – unless I'm completely wrong about that too, and pink *macranthums* are endemic across this whole bloody district and I'm the only one who didn't know about them. Probably. But when I turn to Buckley and see his face, I see a great deal more trouble than that. His eyes nail me with something that looks like dread. I immediately think that Greta is more dangerously ill than she appears. 'What? You think we should go on to the hospital, after all? Or do you want me to go and get a doctor to come here?'

The man seems torn in his conscience somehow, raising a fist to his head as he wrestles with whatever this is that he does not want to say.

'What – what is it? Why should we stay?'

'It's Miss Berylda,' he finally says. 'She's the one not well, not right in her mind – she intends to …'

'She intends what?'

'She intends to harm Mr Howell, her uncle,' he tells me. 'She got some – she got something from the Chinaman yesterday, something to see him off. You gotta stop her – someone's gotta. Get her off this path. She won't listen to me.'

For a moment I don't understand what he has said.

Cos groans, incredulous. 'Oh for the love of Delilah, you can't be seri –'

'You don't say nothing against her.' Buckley cuts him off with a threat as brutal as it is righteous. 'That bastard Howell deserves it, like no one ever has.'

'Why? What has he done?' I ask him; I must know. Berylda intends to what? Howell does what?

'Oh Jesus.' The old man looks up at the rafters, still struggling with this betrayal.

'You must tell me.'

And now he does: 'He hurts Miss Greta,' Buckley tells me. 'He hurts her in a way that's not right, against her will, and she has got the worst for it. You know what I mean.'

Strike me blind, I think I do. And everything makes sense now. Sickening sense.

'She ain't the only one either,' Buckley says. 'A while back, maybe six or seven years, some girls went missing over a time – three, maybe four. Then another one, couple of weeks back. Only put it together last night, from something the Chinaman said, and talking to Wheeler and some other fellers at Kitty's about what they'd heard. All of 'em Chinese girls. One from Tambaroora, two around Mudgee way. Maybe one at Gulgong as well. No one ever seen 'em again, except the little one from Tambaroora – they found her just before Christmas, off the Mudgee Road, like she'd been chucked off the back of a cart. Can't prove it, but I reckon Howell had his way and done 'em all in, one way or another.'

That chills: because I have no trouble believing him capable of such things. Greta's haunting pictures, the bruise on Berylda's hand, her sadness, her frown, her charging disquiet: the slug trail that is Alec Howell.

'What do you want me to do?' Cos says beside me and I almost tell him to go and fill himself a sock full of shit before he ever opens his mouth again, but when I turn to him his face is full of care. He shrugs and says: 'I was wrong. Mea culpa. Sue me later. But now, tell me what I can do.'

One day I will no doubt consider this a defining moment in our shared history, but now I can only tell him, 'I don't know,' as I run past him and up to the house, where I bang on the back door, until the housekeeper's face appears at the kitchen window: 'Who is it?'

'Ben Wilberry – I must see Miss Jones – Berylda Jones. Let me in, please.'

The housekeeper looks at me warily, as though I'm mad. 'Why do you want to come in, sir?'

The staghound, Prince, bounds up to me along the verandah, but he doesn't launch himself at me; he starts barking beside me, his paws planted on the boards facing the housekeeper, as though he is insisting she let me in, too. I tell her: 'Miss Berylda is expecting me.'

'I doubt that very much, sir.' The housekeeper is doubtful to the point of being rude; a bit above herself. 'She's with her sister. Miss Berylda just now came to the kitchen for a plate of my passionfruit custard puffs and then she went back to Miss Greta and she said they were not to be disturbed for any reason.' The housekeeper glares sourly at the dog: 'Will you be quiet.'

No. Prince continues to bark, and I agree: bugger your passionfruit bloody custard puffs. I ask her: 'Is Mr Howell at home, then?'

'No, sir. He is at the hospital, of course. He is a very busy man.'

Good, I suppose. He's not here, at least. I can talk to Berylda freely, plead with her to talk to me, and I plead with the housekeeper now: 'Please, madam. Please, let me in.'

'Oh.' She shakes her head, clicks her tongue, nettled but resigned that she will not be getting rid of me. 'Wait there.'

Like a dog at the back door. I wait with Prince. A small forever. What is taking her so long? I attempt to collect my thoughts as I stand here; assemble and reassemble the elements of all that Buckley has just told me. Berylda intends to poison Alec Howell? Her sister is molested and made pregnant by him? Chinese girls have gone missing from the old goldfields over the years, presumed murdered, and Buckley suspects Howell? The master of this chocolate box dollhouse. Howell. What else has he done is the question that comes next for me, and it is me that wants to kill him. I will kill him with my bare hands. I look at my hands now. These hands. Shaking with fury.

'Strange.' The housekeeper returns to the window, sour mouth turned further down in wonder. 'Miss Berylda isn't here. Miss Greta says that she's gone into town to fetch Mrs Weston, but I sent Lucy to do that not ten minutes ago, first thing Miss Berylda asked of me when she got in, though Miss Greta might be mistaken, mind – she's a bit tired, she's not well, you know.'

I don't need to wonder a second longer. I know where Berylda has gone. But how?

'Horse!' I call up to the stables as I run back, and bless Cos for his uselessness for once as he's not halfway to unfastening the saddle straps on the roan when I get there. In fact, he's now rethreading the strap he just undid and asking me: 'Do you want me to come with you?'

'No.' I don't know what I'm going to do but I'll be doing it alone. I take the reins of the roan from him.

And he grabs my wrist as I do. 'I'll be here,' he tells me, old matey returned at the eleventh. 'Whatever happens, I'll be waiting for you here. Doesn't matter what you do – do whatever you must. I'll have your back however I can.'

I don't know what he might do for me at my back or otherwise, but I take some heart at the thought as I mount and turn the horse towards the stable doors, to find Buckley searching the landscape for some sign of her.

'I'd guess she'll have gone as the crow flies,' the old man supposes, 'up through the scrub, round the back of Glynarthen, the property next door. Two mile that way.' He nods in the direction of the town.

And I look across the bald expanse of this property here with him: nothing but tussocky wire grass and a few wind-beaten wattles all the way to that distant stand of candlebark. She must have flown. And so shall I. I've got to head her off – stop her. She can't go through with this, no matter what Howell might deserve. It can't happen at her hand. I can't let it.

BERYLDA

Glances of the sentinel turrets guide me through the bush. I glance at my watch, only twenty-one minutes gone and I am almost there. My lungs are scorched with every breath, the muscles in my legs wail as the hill climbs more steeply now, and my left shin stings from the lashing of blackberry thorns that snagged up under my skirt, but I don't stop. Not until I see the tin sheds of the dairy at West Street do I stop. I place my basket on the ground for a moment, smooth and pin my hair, check to see there are no tears in my stockings, as if anyone might see them if there were; there are a few burrs caught in the edges of my skirt, though, and I pick them off. I am tidy. I tidy the tea towel that covers my basket too, tuck in the red and green stripes all around to make them straight, and then I walk up the lane by the dairy and into the grounds of the hospital.

Along the sweep of the drive, I close my eyes, afternoon sun blasting over my shoulders, steadying my breath and the pounding of my heart. When I open my eyes again, the arched colonnades that run top and bottom from sentinel to sentinel are gaping mouths condemning my every step. I walk past them. I turn their iron to marzipan. I turn into the passageway between the east wing and the central building, to take the rear staircase to Alec Howell's private consulting room.

'May I help you?' A nurse stops me on the stairs. Her voice is low, reverent, and poised to deter me, a small wall of starched white pinafore. I am approaching a doctors-only quarter here, not that I have visited these halls very many times myself to know them with any great familiarity; only on a handful of occasions, at his command, have I been summoned here for tea with his colleagues, for him to boast of my academic results as so many reflections of himself. I barely know these steps I take, and I don't recognise this nurse at all.

I inform her: 'I am Berylda Jones. I am Mr Howell's niece. I must see him immediately, on an urgent medical matter. There is an illness in the family.' And you will not block my path.

'Oh?' she replies and looks up the deserted corridor behind her and back to me. 'Mr Howell is not in his private room at present.' As if she might have eyes that see around corners and through walls. Admiring and protective of him, as his handmaidens invariably are, she adds: 'He has many matters of importance to attend to.'

'Where is he?' I demand. 'On rounds?'

'No. Er.' I have her as swiftly ruffled. 'Mr Howell is still downstairs, in the operating theatre, I imagine. It's been a – hm. A difficult afternoon.'

I manage not to smile: how excellent. He will be ruffled then, and therefore more easily suggestible, more vulnerable to my manipulations. My game. This final game between us. I inform the nurse: 'I will wait for him in his consulting room. Please make him aware that I am there.'

Her forehead twitches a little in dismay but she does not stop me.

A detail missed almost stops my heart, however: Neddy, our workhorse – Alec would almost certainly have ridden him here – he can't be left uncared for overnight; he's old, and I don't want him to be out in the paddock alone. I look back down at the nurse upon the stair and inform her further: 'Oh, and should we leave together by cab, as I suppose we might, please see to it that Mr Howell's horse is stabled and brought out to Bellevue tomorrow – yes?'

She says, 'Hm. Yes,' and continues on her way down the stairs, as I continue upwards.

I open the door to his room. I take the cake tin from my basket and set it on his desk, remove the cover: four pastries here in all, and I set one in the very centre of a plate, in the very centre of the desk, for him; and an empty plate near the cake tin for me, with napkins placed upon it, as if I have been interrupted at the arrangement. I take the bottle of poison next, from its snug wadding of tea towels in the bottom of the basket, unstop it gently, carefully, with my handkerchief around the rubber seal, and I inject whatever is in the dropper into the centre of the custard puff. It will be more than the three drops Ah Ling instructed; it will do what is required. I open the door to the balcony and tip the remainder of the bottle into the potted palm there; it's half dead anyway. Its withered fronds shiver in the warm breeze; it will be wholly dead soon, I suppose. I drop the bottle over the edge of the balcony rail, and it vanishes into the dense hedge below, just an empty, carelessly discarded phial amongst hundreds, thousands, should it ever be found at all. One shot. One shot I have, here inside a pastry on a picnic plate, a surprise afternoon tea treat for the one I am promised to. Let it find its mark.

Beyond the desk, the bookshelves stare down at me from the case against the wall opposite. The key to this case will be mine tomorrow. No one will deny me his books when I ask; who would deny a grieving medical student all this knowledge? This is almost too-sweet a revenge, that I should steal his books as I steal back my sister's life. As I wait for him, I smile amongst the titles, amongst the jumble of gold lettering along the spines, searching for the one that will tell me how to safely and efficiently induce an abortion. I will find it. A German text swims out at me immediately, *Medizinische Gynäkologie*, and another *The Obstetric Armamentarium*. I will find it quickly. Tomorrow. One step at a time. Today there is only one task that must be completed.

The gold spines blur and swirl around the pastries reflected in the glass. The blue hills roll and roll away beyond the balcony door. I unbutton my blouse to the top of the yoke, turn out the collar like the little slut I am, revealing just a hint of my camisole lace, and I am ready for him. I am ready to end him.

At this moment, so calm and so fixed upon this singular resolve, I frighten myself.

BEN

'Mr Wilberry, isn't it?'

Is it? I'm not sure I know that, either. But it's that German fellow from the dinner the other night, the chemist, asking me, here in this hallway, or wherever I am in this impenetrable warren of a place.

'Gebhardt, we met at Mr Howell's abode, on New Year's Eve, you remember.' He is extending his hand.

'Yes. Mr Gebhardt.' Of course you are, I shake his hand, looking over his shoulder for some sign to direct me to the District Medical Officer's secretary, of whom I've been told I might best enquire after Mr Howell's whereabouts.

'Doctor, I am a doctor. I am a pharmacist, actually,' the German corrects me. 'What brings you here this afternoon?'

'Ah, I'm looking for …' And now I see him, Howell, making his way across the landing at the top of this staircase, right above us. 'Um – Howell. I'm here to see Mr –' I point up the staircase.

The German is not letting go of the handshake; he is saying: 'It was a wonderful evening, don't you think so? The fireworks were magnificent. Our Mr Howell puts on a jolly good show, ja!'

'Ja – yes. But I really must –'

'Oh? You are in a hurry to find him today? What is the reason? A happy reason, I hope.' The twit lets go of my hand but he does not stand aside to allow me to take the stairs. He is looking me over from head to toe, the way only a German can. I am filthy from the road and ill-attired, yes, and unquestionably mad: what I am going to do when I confront Howell, when I confront Berylda, I have not the slightest idea. I should not be here at all. The fathomless intricacies of Berylda's deceit – a deceit that I am beginning to suspect has in no small part brought me precisely here – should turn any sensible man away, but I can't turn away. I can't turn away from her suffering, whatever her suffering at his hands might be; nor her sister's. And I can't let her kill him, either.

Unaccustomed to deceit myself, though, I let the German have the first garbled load that comes out of my mouth: 'I have made a discovery – a new plant. I really must – ah. Share the good news with – My apologies –'

I push past his next exclamation of, 'Well, well – congratulations to you!' and belt up the stairs.

Into an empty hallway. But the door is easy enough to find, with MR A. M. HOWELL, DISTRICT SURGEON stencilled on it.

My knuckles meet the polished surface of the timber, but I hesitate before I knock.

I hear Berylda's laughter, those cascading stars of her laughter: 'Oh, Alec, my darling Alec – can't a clever girl change her mind? Come to her senses? Of course I'll marry you.'

BERYLDA

'**R**ight then.' He is so pleased, beyond all my hopes and expectations. So very pleased that I am here, perched upon his desk, giving him the smile he demanded I find for him. Giving him everything. He folds his arms, regarding me with triumph. His wolf grin glimmers. 'This is a fine way to end a long day, I'll say. I should let you traipse around the countryside more often, I suppose.'

'I suppose you should.' I nod, lowering my face to look up at him with some sort of coquettish admonishment and I gesture at the pastries: 'I've called for tea.' I've done no such thing. 'A little afternoon toast, to us.' I beckon him: 'Come here, come to me. Let me practise, let me be wifely. Tell me, why has your day been so long?'

The wolf and his grin steps back to snib the lock on the door, and he begins loosening his tie, unbuttoning his collar, preparing to take whatever he wants; and still, I know no fear of him. Not now. 'Yes,' he says. 'It has been a long three days, without you, thinking about you and what our life will be. How I've been hoping you'd come around to the idea. Just as you are. Aren't you capital, girl. Just capital.'

'But you've been so busy, Alec, I'm sure. You haven't been thinking only about me all that while.' I pout; I moisten my lips, a promise that I will surely let him kiss me now without resistance. Or maybe not. 'How did your Federation speech go? I'll bet it was outstanding. How was the town hall ceremony?'

'Ridiculous,' he groans and I laugh, playing with him: winning. 'Anyone of note was in Sydney, of course. The rest, you know, intellectual midgets round here. Oh God, Berylda. Insufferable bunch, I can't begin to tell you. I need you by my side at these things … Together we will be the shining pair.' His face edges ever close to mine. 'Confined to Bathurst for a time, perhaps four, five years. And then it's Sydney for us. Macquarie Street – consulting rooms there and a seat on the Legislative Council. Then who knows? The world is ours.'

'Oh dear, what plans you have.' I turn my face from his abruptly, shocked at the breadth of his ambition. What will he crave next: the prime ministership? My eyes fall straight upon the pastries, though, steering me back on course as surely. 'I think we should eat something first, before we embark on conquering the world, don't you?' I say: 'Look what Mary made. Mm. I think they might even be your favourite?'

'You little vixen.' He laughs, shaking his head once more at my change of heart, of mind. 'I'll never know quite what you're up to, will I?'

'Possibly not.' I smile for him again. 'That's why you adore me, is it not?'

He laughs again. He is a handsome man, it's true, when he smiles naturally like this. Smiling at a custard puff, smiling at a witty to and fro. A mirage of the future he offers shimmers through my mind: the surgeon's wife, the parliamentarian's wife, the captain's wife, the mother of four or five, a doctor in her own right. What a picture. Who wouldn't want that picture? But that I don't exist inside it. It is not me he sees when he looks at me; it is something else altogether. A cipher, perhaps, for what he thinks a woman is. A little China girl to have, to hold, to break. I do not ever care to know how his mind has constructed me; or any of us.

'Can't say I'm very hungry myself.' He rubs his temples now over a weary yawn. 'Really, the past few days have been hellish here.'

'Oh? Do tell me.' What is hell for you? And then let me stuff that cake into your mouth by all and any force I might muster. He is not leaving this room until he has eaten it.

'Hm.' He grunts, bored to speak of his tribulations. 'Mining accident yesterday, dead on the table, blast wound to the neck, couldn't stop the bleeding, hours at it – stop, start, miserable thing couldn't decide whether to stay or go. And today a boy under a timber dray out at Kelso, waste of a day altogether.'

As if the miner and the boy besmirch his reputation. The impudence of them.

'Well, you can let it all go now,' I say. I pick up the plate and hand it to him: 'Eat. Restore your strength. I want to watch you eat your pastry. And then ...' I dare to play my highest card: 'Then I want to begin our congress now. Here. I want you to take me for your own on this desk.'

'Do you now?' He grunts again, with rather more vitality, and bites into the pastry. 'Mm. That is good.'

'Good.' My voice quavers under a flooding of disgust as he chews and swallows. That it is done, and I have done it. A sprinkling of tiny pastry flakes in his beard as he takes another bite, and a tremor in my hand as I take a cake for myself. The black curtain billows across my eyes. I move to the balcony door and stare through the shifting shrouds and shrouds of black. Stare until the world reappears. The hills. The white clouds that streak the sky. The coal cart coming up the drive. A nurse wheeling a patient into the sun. And a horse tethered in the shade of a tree: it looks like Rebel. Fear throttles at this close whispering of the familiar: this world is real. This act is real. What do I do now? Tonight. Tomorrow. I will be a murderess for all time, from this moment forward. How do I return to the world? Return to Gret this afternoon, return to my studies in a matter of weeks, return to Flo at Women's, as if nothing more remarkable has happened but a summer holiday? How do I become a murderess in the world? How do I clean vengeance from me? It is now tattooed.

'You're not watching me eat.' Alec Howell pretends a complaint, but it is in fact a demand: 'I'm finished. Now I want to watch you eat. On your knees.'

'On my knees?' What does he want me to do? Pray to him?

'Yes.' The wolf nods. 'That's how we begin our congress.'

'I'm sure I don't know what you mean.' And I don't, except that I know it will be a humiliation. I can hear it in his voice: that twist of sadism. A twist of power that confuses and erodes confidence, saps all defences and forces one into bondage; as he has done to my sister, so he shall do to me. Carry every second of her pain with me now, against fear, and against guilt.

'I know you don't know what I mean,' he says. 'But you will learn. You are a clever girl, my clever girl.'

He takes off his jacket and waistcoat; hangs them on the back of the door, brushing a piece of lint from a sleeve. And now he steps towards me again, shaking off his suspenders, undoing his fly buttons.

Whatever will be, will be, I steel myself for what comes next. I must hold my nerve. Take whatever it is that comes, and regardless know that I will never have to do again. I babble as he nears: 'Wonder where our tea's got to. Hm?'

He ignores me; he says: 'I will test your obedience to me now.'

'Test me?' He must hear my fraud, surely. He must hear my heart begin to crash and crash. He grasps the front of my blouse in his fist and I think he will throw me to my knees. I scramble and scramble to regather the game. 'But you have our whole life together to test me. Love me now. Please. Love me sweetly.'

That seems to stop him: he lets go of my blouse and looks at me curiously for a moment. He sighs, heavily, and moves away from me, looking down at the desk, and now he rests against its edge with both hands splayed, and he does look weary. He says: 'You are quite right. I had intended to wait those few weeks longer, and so we must. Keep with the correct order of things.'

'Must we?'

'Yes.' He terrifies me even as he sighs again, squinting contemplatively as he informs the blue hills: 'There is something I must tell you. Something that must be attended to before we commence our own relations. I had hoped to have it dealt with once you were back at the university, but now – well, your sister, I believe, may be pregnant, you might as well know. Don't be alarmed by this, however.' He raises a hand to quash any concern. 'It will be taken care of, regardless of whether she has in fact conceived in this instance or not. I will perform the sterilisation myself. Removal of the uterus will be best for her, so that the problem is resolved completely.'

I can hardly hear my voice over my terror: 'Sterilisation?'

'Naturally.' He nods, as if we might be discussing the fate of a cow, and now he looks directly at me, into my eyes. 'This can't be allowed to happen again.'

My mind races against my blood. '*Again?* But you will not need Greta any more. We will be married. You will not –'

'Berylda.' He rubs his eyes at the absurdity of my suggestion. 'Is this what your visit here today is about? Is *this* why you come to me with your professed change of heart? Your deviousness is so transparent, it always is. You want me to keep away from Greta? What do you expect me to do when you are at the university? Or when you are with child?'

'I expect you to control yourself,' I say, but not to him. How long has he preyed upon my sister in this way? Weeks? Months? Years? How many times has he raped her? When did he begin? Only one thing I know: he will never stop.

He is as vicious and as calculating as he is insane, this animal whose every desire is his entitlement. He says: 'You do not make demands upon me, girl.' Shaking his head at the ceiling lamp, a disbelieving chuckle. 'You are as stubborn as Libby ever was. It's the yellow tramp in you, I suppose.'

It can only be the long habit of terror that restrains me from attacking him with the rage of all the yellow tramps he's violated. How many? How many of us have you destroyed? And Aunt Libby the best of them, the gentlest; she bent to whomever asked her to bend; stubborn she was not. She sacrificed her own happiness to look after our grandfather; she would have done anything for us, for those she loved; her smile so warm I feel it still. And I will be terrified no longer. I let my hatred cry out at him with my grief: 'She worshipped you.'

'But not enough.' He presses his lips into a dubious sneer, and he's pleased that he has me upset. He is so pleased that he wins his game again, and again, and again. 'Will *you* worship me enough, Berylda?'

'We'll have to see about that, won't we,' I reply. I am the blade today; not you. 'I am yet to learn how much adoration a man might need, aren't I. Tell me, Alec, darling, what did Aunt Libby ever deny you?'

'She denied my will,' he says, still smiling inside his sneer, measuring me inside his squint. Always measuring. 'She denied my authority.'

'What? How?' He must be lying; he is lying.

'Libby was not the saintly angel you imagine, Berylda,' he says, dispassionate, regretful. 'She sought to cheat and manipulate me, too. She was ungrateful, conniving.'

'*How?*' I demand.

'There is much you don't know, isn't there? You really are little more than a child.' He is all revolted condescension. 'You don't know what your aunt did after I took you and your sister into my home, do you? You don't know how she repaid my kindness. Well, let me tell you. She took it upon herself to consult with a solicitor, to ask that your parents' estate be held in trust until your majority. That is what she did.'

I blink at this; uncomprehending. 'And how is that unreasonable?'

'Let me count the ways,' he says, counting them out on his fingers: 'She did not ask my permission. She spoke of my business to another man. She sought to deny me the estate that the law makes rightfully mine.' He holds three fingers in front of my face, shaking them at me, threatening to strike me.

I tell them: 'My parents' estate is rightfully Greta's and mine – it is not yours.'

'Ah, now doesn't that sound familiar.' He scoffs: 'That's just what Libby said to me. And she would not relent. As if you were not going to be looked after adequately by me. She was so ungrateful.'

'And so ...?' My blood is dead cold as I delve now, all my senses dulling as I move closer and closer to the truth. 'What did you do to Libby?'

The sneer falls away and he is cruelty pure and plain. Remorseless. 'Never push me too far, Berylda,' he warns. 'Libby pushed me too far. Be a good girl and you will be looked after.

Well looked after. If you are not a good girl, then ...' He grabs at my left breast through my camisole; he pinches and twists my nipple.

I stand rigid inside this screeching stab of pain. 'Tell me some more,' I say. 'What poison did you use to kill my aunt?'

'Poison?' His reptile eyes don't move from mine, but his hand is cast from me as if he touches the lightning I have become. He licks his lips; I have him unnerved. I am so close, this may as well be his confession. He takes a step back, rubs his sternum with his fist, masking the action as consideration of his next words, but I hope with all the ragged hope left to me that some acid burns there, snaking its way through his body. He says: 'Typhoid was Libby's punishment, you know that. She was punished by God.'

'And so shall you be,' I tell him, I promise him, as I move past him, as I unsnib the lock and leave.

BEN

'**B**en?' Her eyes are wild: a small creature captured in flight.
Howell looks at me through the open door, just for
second, a blank, unknowable stare, before I take Berylda by the
waist and down the hall, down the staircase, away from him, down
through the foyer that is now quiet as a tomb. I tell her only: 'I
know now what you have suffered. I know what your sister has
suffered by him.'

She says nothing. She seems dazed, in a dream, as I carry her
along with me, her feet barely touching the floor. I am barely here
myself, after all that I have just heard. Who *is* Alec Howell? What
man does these things? And what for? He meant to compel her
into marriage to him? If only she had told me. Why didn't she tell
me? But how could she have told me? All questions leading back
to his blank, unknowable stare. A creature unidentifiable, in form
or purpose.

As we step through the main doors and onto the portico outside,
I look back to see if he follows. But there is no one, apart from
a dustman sweeping the tiles behind us. The roan waits on the
lawn across the drive, where I left him under the cedar there. The
western sky is slashed amber and vermillion, a flock of sulfur-
crested cockatoos sailing through it, calling out the end of the day.

'Rebel, it is you,' she says from her trance as we walk towards
the horse, towards the road; she says to me: 'I left my basket in
his room.'

I ask her: 'Does it matter?' I will retrieve it for her now if it's important that she have it.

'No. I don't suppose it does matter.' Her reply is a whisper; and then she asks the sky: 'Do you know what I have done?'

'Yes,' I tell her. I know that she has done it; I know from all that I heard through the keyhole of the door, I know it somehow by holding her, too, as I am still holding her beside me now, and even in the cold shock of it all, what she has done seems somehow only natural. Horrifying. Harrowing. But natural. A logical correction of order. She has sought to crush a catastrophic force that by some trick of chance shaped itself into the figure of a man, one that would probably struggle to exist at all if women were considered to be equally worthy of life themselves; if Orientals were considered to be human at all. How can I blame her for what she has done? How could anyone blame her? What blame is there in nature? I tell her: 'I don't judge you for it. I never will.'

'I did not ever mean for you … I did not want …' Her voice drifts away. She looks out over the field of tall wallaby grass that stretches alongside the road below us here, her blue eyes searching the blond river, her face washed of any colour it had, and now she clutches my hand at her waist, fingernails sharp in my palm, her words barely breath at all: 'But I want to see him die.'

I never want to see him again; his stare remains with me: the stare of nothing; no one.

She says into this nothing, her voice returned: 'Sometime tonight I will see him die. I have to.'

'Yes,' I tell her. I am her accomplice now; I will not leave her side.

I am the road for Berylda Jones.

BERYLDA

We might be any two friends, walking on a Thursday afternoon, along the cartway at the back of Glynarthen. I look into the faces of the dairy cows at the fence line; they are brown cows, russet in this sunset light; their grass is bright; they chew contentedly. And I shall see Alec Howell die tonight, if anything like luck allows.

I must keep myself from running back towards the hospital, to hover, to watch and wait. I must keep myself from shouting out with triumph what I have done – at last. Remind myself a thousand times inside each step that it is crucial I remain contained, that I walk along this cartway with Ben Wilberry as if nothing else on earth is occurring.

Ben Wilberry walks with me. I can scarcely believe that he does, and yet I do believe it. Now. Would it have made a difference to today if I had believed in him yesterday? Had I understood the bargain we two had already made? Perhaps, but then love might have robbed me of this reckoning; this revenge. It sings through me. I look up at Ben as we walk, my hand resting in the crook of his arm, taking strength from him even now, and I want to thank him: without him, without his having wandered up to Bellevue on New Year's Eve, I would not have been able to get away to Hill End, I would not have found the means to end Alec Howell. I would not have found the courage. But how can I possibly thank him for this? For helping me to damnation, and bringing himself with me. He might change his mind about me, regret his involvement yet.

That is, if Alec Howell dies. Panic takes me. How do I know I have poisoned him at all? How do I know Ah Ling didn't give me a bottle of snake oil? Dragon tears. What is that? Nothing more than castor oil; the worthless word of a Chinaman.

I clutch Ben's arm reflexively, and he bends to me: 'Don't worry. Please, Berylda. I will never betray you. I'm sorry you felt you had no other choice. I'm sorry you felt you couldn't tell me what he was doing to you. Whatever happens now, I will stand beside you. In fact, I insist on doing so. You're not alone with this any more, hm? It's the worst shame that you ever were.'

'Hm.' How does one thank another for that? When I have stepped far enough away from this black place, I will find the words. I will marvel at this moment, at this plain fact of love for me, this loyalty, but now it is all I can do to continue to put one foot in front of the other.

'You must be tired,' he says. 'Why don't you get up on Rebel and I'll lead you the rest of the way?'

Tired as I know I must be, I shake my head. The beat of my boots upon the ground is all that is left of my resolve. I am suspended somewhere above fatigue, above time. Nothing else will happen until Alec Howell is dead.

He must die: he killed Libby.

He killed Libby?

I can scarcely believe this, either. But it is true. I will see the way he recoiled from me at the question for all that is left to me of life: it is true. As true as it is that I am his murderer now – *please*. Let every footstep make it so. I am his killer, and I am glad.

And careful. Across these final hours and all that is left to me of life, every word and every action must conceal what I have done. Not for my sake – I would take the noose proudly – but for Gret, for Ben, I cannot make one slip. No one will pay for this but me. I feel the stones beneath my boots: feel the dimensions of every one. Make every step a step towards the light.

Bellevue is lit up like a city when we see it; lit up like a fat cigar forbidding the fall of night. My stomach lurches. How I hate this house. But my hatred is a dull, slow thing. Now.

I break away from Ben as we approach the yard, and I make my voice ask him: 'Could you have Buckley ready Sal with the buggy again, please? I will need it again. Soon. Don't let him argue with you.'

I cannot make my voice explain my rationale: if things go as expected, I will need the buggy in order to return to the hospital when I am informed that Alec Howell ails there, or to take him there myself after a collapse at home, however things might unfold tonight. And yet Ben nods his understanding.

'Don't worry,' he assures again. 'Whatever you need, it will be done.'

I glance back at him as we part, as he heads off towards the stable drive with Rebel. How is it possible that we are such friends? I must keep myself from running to him, from shouting out my gratitude.

I step up the front path, across the verandah of this place of misery, but just as I reach the door, it's flung wide and Cosmo Thompson is before me, grinning: 'Come in, come in from the cold, would you? I've just got a fire going. I don't know how you live here at all – midsummer and it's bloody freezing.'

I follow him down the east hallway, unsure if I have stepped into a dream.

He turns back to me as he strides on up the hall: 'Hungry? Whether you are or not, I think I might force you to have a bite of something. You didn't eat your lunch.'

I would ask him why he is suddenly being so oddly nice to me, but I suppose it is at Ben's insistence; I must suppose Cosmo Thompson also knows something of what I have done. Either that, or Lewis Carroll has devised a new and macabre fabulation just for me. I lose my sense of direction; confusion spins around me, as he continues past my bedroom, and Gret's, and out to the rear parlour.

Where Mrs Weston leaps up from the settee there, rushing at me, and confusion spins again. I am relieved to see her here, of course, as was my plan – that she be fetched for Gret. But does she know

347

whatever Mr Thompson knows, too? I can't imagine what my face must look like as I fight down each of my emotions all at once.

'Berylda. Oh my dear girl,' she is saying. 'Where have you been?' Her lavender velvet embracing me, I watch a rose petal fall to the floor from the vase behind her, a little white boat floating down onto the timber zigzags of the parquet floor. 'I was beginning to worry. Greta, too. Where did you go, my dear? You didn't go into town looking for me, did you? I came as soon as your maid –'

'No.' I sigh; I have to look away, to swallow this wave of relief: Mrs Weston does not know a thing. I pretend some exasperation with my sister: 'Poor Greta, she's as muddled as a box of old buttons at the moment, or she must have misheard me. I only went into the hospital, to let Uncle Alec know we'd arrived back and –'

'Poor dear Greta,' Mr Thompson interjects and I hold my breath for what might issue from that wild tongue next. 'Mad. That girl has been completely mad all day,' he says authoritatively. 'I suspect she is mostly mad most of the time – judging from her work. I've spent the afternoon going through her drawings out here, in the chest.' He points to the cane trunk she keeps her favourite pieces in, under the table tennis set and quoits that never get used. 'She said I could – to look for a portfolio amongst them all – and it is my considered opinion that your sister is one hundred and three percent off her sweet little kadoova. It is the creative's prerogative, and all kadoovaishness is relative to goodness, isn't it? She is rather good, isn't she? Don't you agree, Mrs Weston?'

Mrs Weston blinks at him askance; I'm sure I do too. She takes me by the arm a little way back up the hall, and keeps her voice low: 'Greta, I'm certain, is perfectly good – she is in fine health. She explained everything to me.'

'Did she?' I had counted on her saying nothing. Oh God. Mrs Weston must feel my juddering.

'Yes. Particularly your high level of concern.' She smiles in that reassuring, forthright way of the midwife. 'Berylda, your care for your sister is admirable, wonderful. I wish I had a sister just like you. But a late monthly flow is nothing out of the ordinary, really – or even one missed entirely. Hysterical irregularities are as common as they are mysterious.' She clicks her tongue. 'Young women shouldn't have to go to medical school to learn these things. It should be taught at Sunday school, if you ask me, spoken about frankly and openly amongst the sisterhood, but I despair that it never will be.'

I am embarrassed, thank you, Greta, and all the same relieved once more: she has told Mrs Weston nothing of the truth; the most obvious culprit of absent menses having been thoroughly overlooked. There is no reason for Mrs Weston to suspect pregnancy: she knows Greta is a virtual prisoner in this house.

'I'm sure you are right,' I reply, wary of my every word. 'I should give Gret a hearty dose of Fluid of Magnesia and stop worrying, shouldn't I, but – Oh but I'm sorry to have caused such an alarm, put you out so. Please, stay with us for supper, won't you? Let me make it up to you? Having made you come all the way here.' Please, you must: you must stay here with Gret as her witness that she knows nothing of what I do.

'You would never put me out.' Mrs Weston smiles more deeply. 'I quite understand, Berylda. Your sister is so very dear to you.'

Inarguably. I will pay with my life for her, yes, if I must.

'She's just tidying herself up now.' Mrs Weston squeezes my arm. 'Let's share a meal for the pleasure of each other's company only, what do you say? Girls together. Oh, and the, er, inimitable Mr Thompson, who appears to have invited himself.' She laughs, and then she peers at me when I don't: 'Are you quite all right yourself, Berylda? You seem a little pale, to me.'

'Do I?' Even my voice is pale. 'Tired. Long day.'

'Miss Jones? Anyone there?' Ben is calling up from the back door, by the kitchen, I see him at the other end of the hall. My anchor. He clears his throat. Our eyes meet, and he nods that all is well, transport is arranged.

As Greta's face appears at the door to her room, not two yards away: 'So *there* you are. Where did you go off to, Ryl?'

'I told you – to let Uncle Alec know we were back.'

'You didn't say that. You said –'

'I *did* say that,' I tell her to shush with my eyes and glance at Mr Wilberry coming up the hall towards us as if he were the real reason for my absence – let Mrs Weston have seen that too, just to muddy these waters a little bit more. 'And I can also say Uncle Alec probably won't be in by dinner, either – they were very busy at the hospital this –'

'Oh, I know,' Mrs Weston adds. 'Donald hasn't been home in time for dinner for I don't remember how long. I'm sure they have a private club upstairs there, don't you?'

'Mrs Weston, ah, good evening.' Ben is here; right here. Taking Mrs Weston's hand.

As Cosmo Thompson bounds in from the rear parlour. 'Wilber! You dashed dashing thing. Doesn't he make you want to eat your handbag, ladies? Handbags full of words. Edible, all of them. Is everybody hungry! I am so starving I could eat a shipload.'

'So, am I allowed out of my room now, sister?' Gret raises her eyebrows at me, brushing past me: 'Cosmo, did you find what you were looking for?'

I follow the sounds and the movements, by some automatic instinct. Greta pushing her shoulder playfully against Mr Thompson: 'Let's be radical and have supper out in the rear parlour, shall we?' The edge of Mrs Weston's steady broadcloth hem brushing the skirting boards: 'It really is lovely to see you again, Mr Wilberry. I feel we didn't have a chance to meet properly the other night. How did you find the excursion to the Hill?' A cry of delight when he tells her of his discovery of a flower by the river. I watch him return her smiles and queries tiredly, thoughtfully, tucking his too-long hair behind his ears. I wonder again if I might have waited, if there might have been another way, if I might have found the courage to confide the truth in Ben and had him go to the police for us; he would have been believed. And I discount the thought again as quickly: Alec Howell would never hang for his crimes, regardless of what son of a cattle king spoke against him. What man today is ever hanged for rape? What man can be hanged for a murder that can't be proved? None.

I eat creamed potato soup and crisp fried croutons, and I pray that there is justice; that he is dying now.

Is he?

In pain. He deserves to die in pain. He killed Libby. The shock comes for me again and again, with the terror of the truth beneath: I *knew* this all along. Somewhere inside my scrambling through the signs of the fever, looking for rose spots that weren't there on her lovely skin: I knew he killed her then. But I was only a child; I was only fifteen; I couldn't grasp how, or why anyone would do such a thing. He poisoned our Aunt Libby, possibly with some combination of organic chemical similar to that which I have given him; and he killed her for money: for our grandparents' estate, and then the unexpected windfall of Papa's. He killed her because she questioned his authority. Because she was a yellow tramp.

Oh my dear God.

And so I must witness his death, if God will not. Please. I look at my watch: *Hurry up, hurry up*. It's only ten past seven; eleven minutes past. I stare out into the hills disappearing into the sky outside. I watch the stars begin to prick through each of the three-inch squared mullioned panes.

'What's wrong? Ryl – tell me,' Greta whispers beside me beneath some wide-flung loudness of Mr Thompson; she is still wondering what happened when I went to the hospital, she is asking again, concerned. She knows something has happened; something is happening. She knows I have lied to her somewhere this evening.

'Oh I might be a bit annoyed you made a fool of me,' I whisper back, 'pretending to Mrs Weston that there's nothing wrong with you.' I attempt to roll my eyes, but they barely move in my head. I am silently, calmly petrified.

'There *is* nothing wrong with me.' Greta touches my knee under the table. 'Not now. Truly. Believe me.'

Prince barks out the back on his chain, and a clattering of footsteps on the front verandah interrupts our meal, an urgent ringing of the bell. Mary is calling for Lucy, then thumping up the east hallway herself, muttering: 'Suppose I have to do everything at once, since there's three of me.'

It's a boy from the hospital at the door, raced up on a pony, and jabbering at Mary: 'It's Mr Howell – tell the Miss Joneses – he's been taken ill. He's got some stomach trouble and it's got him something bad. Tell the Miss Joneses! Them doctors said it was real bad.'

Time clatters and leaps against exclamations and assurances; of course Mrs Weston will wait with Greta here, and Mr Thompson will wait here too, while Mr Wilberry and I return to the hospital, and Greta says nothing of her thoughts. Only her eyes ask: *What have you done?* And I look away.

'Oh my dear, my dear, what a day this is turning out to be for you.' Mrs Weston clasps my hand as we are leaving. 'It never rains but it pours, doesn't it? My love goes with you,' she sighs us back out to the stables and into the gathering night.

Where Buckley is waiting with Sally and the buggy, as Ben has instructed him to do. But Buckley cannot look at me as I dash out towards him now. Let him condemn me. Let him be my judge. Let him be the only one.

BEN

'She! She! She!' he screams at her when we enter the room. 'She poisons me!'

He is tied to the bed with leather belts, and thrashing against them, almost lifting the bed from the floor. He is livid and streaming sweat, eyes bloodshot and shaking in his head, a demon trapped.

'It's the delirium,' Dr Weston says between us, and he takes Berylda's hand, cupping it in both of his to assure her. 'Ignore the outbursts. Typhoid fever, of course – unmistakeable case. No rash as yet but the rest is self-evident. Possibly contracted from a patient, possibly before Christmas, there were a few cases out at Magpie early in December – you know how giving of his time he has always been with the troubles of the poor. Not so considerate of him.' Dr Weston exhales a gust of misplaced esteem, overlaying the stench of sickly dysenteric excrement with a sharp vapour of Scotch.

'Was there no clue, no warning?' Berylda asks him, and her voice is small but assertive.

'She murders me!' Howell screams again and writhes ever more violently.

Dr Weston flinches but otherwise ignores the accusation, answering Berylda: 'Perhaps there was a hint. He has seemed weary, distracted the past few days, agitated, I suppose. But therein lies the benefit of hindsight, yes? I would hazard a guess that he has ignored the signs himself, as most men would, too busy to bother with being unwell, and now it's come on remarkably strong – and fast.

Most awful.' Weston looks now to me, regretful: 'You know his wife perished of the same infection. Almost exactly five years ago.' He pats Berylda's hand again. 'But your uncle is physically fit, my dear, in his prime. They do not come fitter than Alec Howell, do they? He is fastidious in his health if ever anyone was. Typhoid takes only the weak.' He says that last as though he decides it.

But of course, Alec Howell does not have typhoid fever. And I am mesmerised by Berylda yet again and more. She knows so precisely what she does. Her recourse is not admirable, no. But she is. That she can stand here before this foulness without baulking. If I didn't have her to regard, I would have difficulty keeping my stomach where it belongs. She is a rock of will.

Dr Weston says to her: 'This must be terribly distressing for you. Now you have seen him as you wished, it is best that you go – go up to his private room, make a cup of tea, I'll find you there. Leave us to tend him. All will be well if I have my way.'

'No.' She will not be moved. 'No thank you, Dr Weston. I will care for Uncle Alec. Please.'

'Oh? Well.' The man is nonplussed, but perhaps his desire for another Scotch sways him, and he is quick to yield: 'As you wish, my dear, I suppose. As you wish.'

As Weston leaves the room, leaving us alone with Howell, Berylda goes to the basin in the corner. She soaks a cloth there and places it in a bowl, takes it over to the night stand by the bed, and then she shifts a chair to sit beside the man who has robbed and defiled all that she loves. He is disgusting in every way. The teeth are bared, moiling to gouge her. But he can do nothing except dare her to draw nearer.

'There, there, Alec darling ...' She continues her deception and her truth, holding the cloth by him, as though waiting for him to settle for long enough that she might be able to wipe the bile from his mouth. But she does not touch him. She looks into his eyes, she holds him in her eyes, as he raves at her.

'It's hell for you, slut! Hell, I say!'

He spits at her and she does not look away. He bawls at her, over and over, the longest notes of helpless anguish.

'Listen to me!' he begs me blindly. 'Listen to me, please.'

I feel only the need of a pistol, and the chill that compulsion brings.

He rails and spews for almost two hours before the bile turns to blood and Weston is in the room again, grave now, declaring the infection fatal. 'I am so sorry, my dear. It would seem there is nothing to be done, after all. The sepsis has its way. It will be finished soon, however. There will be mercy soon. You need not –'

'Thank you, Dr Weston, but I shall stay.' She is stoic; hers is the face made perfect with reflected venom. She is the rare and solitary trigger flower that lashes and consumes the bee. Immaculate.

Howell soon lapses into a shivering silence. The reverend is called for. Drs Weston and Gebhardt bicker in the hall, the German adamant about hand-washing and the spread of germs or some other trivial thing. And Berylda chooses her moment now to lean close to Howell and whisper in his ear.

BERYLDA

'Give my regards to Lucifer,' I say to him, and that is enough. Perhaps, if there is no God to have answered my ceaseless prayers for justice, there is no Devil to punish us either. There is no hell other than the flames of hatred we ignite and fan ourselves. I don't know what justice, what retribution will come for me in time, but I want no more of this revenge now. It is done.

I stand and there is Ben, behind me, as he has been throughout this night. My witness. I say to him: 'I should like to go home now.'

I am senseless with relief and hollowing with every step as hatred begins to drain from me, as Alec Howell ends. Straining for his final breath, unsated for all time, the everlasting vision in my mind. Hell enough. I am spent. It is twenty minutes to midnight. I don't see Dr Weston or Buckley or anyone else as I leave the hospital. There is only Ben's hand over mine, and an owl on a low branch over the drive, gold eyes caught in the swaying lamp of the buggy. The air is damp and cool and black.

And in the house, I am guided to my sister's room along a hush of lavender sympathy: 'My dear, dear girl. My poor dear girl. Greta is in her bed – go to her. Be with your sister, take comfort with each other now.'

Yes.

'Ryldy?' she asks me through the dark, and I curl around her.

I say to her only: 'He is gone.'

356

She turns in my arms, her forehead pressed to mine. She says: 'Good. I'm glad.' I breathe in her sweet peppermint breath and she tells me: 'I used to wish that he would be thrown off Jack and trampled by him; I used to wish that all the time. I'm happy he's dead, Ryl. It's wrong, but I'm happy. You don't need to tell me another thing about it.'

A strange rushing in begins to fill me. My skin is raw and tender and yearning all over, my sister's absolution encircling me.

Clean your heart, Ah Ling's words come back and back to me. *Clean your heart.*

Vengeance has come. And so it must be made gone, too. Somehow.

'All things pass.' Greta kisses my forehead. 'At least that's Mrs Wheeler's philosophy on life and death. And we're all sinners – that's my pennyworth, and it happens to be a fact. Ryldy, we're sinners together, you and me.'

I look at my sister: she is silver with moonlight. I say to her: 'You've never done anything sinful, Gret – ever.'

'Haven't I?' She strokes my cheek and tells me: 'My whatsits finally came, while you were out. I got something from Mrs Wheeler, yesterday, when you were out visiting that Ah Ling man; something to bring them on. A whole load of Bates' Bitter Apple, it was – God, I was sick from those pills. I'm so sorry to have worried you like that. I didn't want to tell you, not at all, but I think we both know what was wrong with me. Uncle Alec did it to me, and it's all gone now. All of it. You don't have to think about any of that any more.

'Oh Ryl.' She holds me tight. 'I can tell you now, I was so happy when you said on New Year's Eve that we'd be going to the Hill – didn't you see my jaw drop? I could barely believe what you were saying. You see, I'd wanted to get help from Mrs Wheeler about this. I was going to ask you all along if we could go to Hill End while you were home. I'd overheard some gossip at Mrs Hatfield's salon, when I was getting pinned up for my Christmas dress, that Clara Bidwell – you know, from church, the vet's elder daughter? – had to go off to Mrs Wheeler, in September. She'd got into trouble with the fellow she was engaged to, Bradley Piper, who by that time had gone off to the war in Africa. Mrs Wheeler helps a lot of women and girls in the same sorts of predicaments, thank heavens. It cost a bit, though – one whole pound. And I stole that from Uncle Alec's desk, when you were arguing with him on New Year's morning, just before we left – that's how I came to forget the jam, in all my sneaking about. So sinner I am, through and through.'

She kisses me again. 'But really, fate was always going to come round to our side one day, so long as we kept wishing for the same thing. We did. We always have. And now we are free.'

So we are, for whatever freedom might be, for us. And now I begin to cry. I course and flood and burst with every unshed tear.

RETURNING

Now I fly, now I see myself under myself,
now a god dances within me.

Thus Spake Zarathustra

BEN

Amazement slips into some kind of anaesthetised abeyance of everything I might have known, or thought I did, before this day. Too remote to respond to Mrs Weston's insistence that Cos and I stay overnight here in this house, and too close to Berylda's sobbing to hear it as anything but pain convulsing from the very heart of the world. The world is wounded, and I can't move from the door. Her door. Closed once more.

'Mr Wilberry.' Mrs Weston's hand is on my shoulder now; firmly: 'Please.'

I can't stand here all night, her plea implies. Why shouldn't I stand here all night, I could ask. Where else might I be? But as I turn, I see Mrs Weston is accompanied by the little dollhouse maid, who carries a tea tray, toast and cocoa on it, for the girls; and Cos is behind them, saying: 'Come on, old matey. Let's go for a ramble – you're always up for that.'

Yes, that's probably a good idea.

We leave via the rear door, and I hear the housekeeper whimpering softly in the kitchen as we step across the verandah. We walk in silence, towards the town, and I am spiritless, worn as a length of old rope. We pass the hospital, invisible now except for a gas lamp lit on the hill; the moon is an electric eye above us.

Did any of this happen? This day; these past three days – three weeks? Am I here, or am I still in Brisbane, drinking at the Swamp, avoiding Pater after Mama's burial?

'Hang on a sec.' Cos stops to light up: some yellow devil's face above the match.

I say, to probe reality: 'She killed him.'

He drags in his smoke and says: 'Yes. I assumed as much.'

I tell him: 'She killed him so that it appears the death was from typhoid fever – no one suspects anything else. Weston declared it himself.'

'Sensational,' says Cos.

'You don't find that disturbing?' Last time we walked this way he didn't think much of her at all; why has he changed his mind so completely? Because what she has done is justified by what Howell did himself?

'Yes, and no,' Cos says now. 'Most disturbing is that I could have been so wrong about her. All that she and Greta must have endured makes me … I don't know. I can't say anything about it except that I'm sorry. Head too far up my own arse, for a change.' He laughs at himself. 'I think she's probably something of a Super Girl, as it turns out – one creature Nietzsche neglected to mention. A cut above the usual anyway; a cut above good and bad, yes and no, black and white. She's certainly got some balls. Exemplary balls. Terrifying, to be honest.'

'Yep.' I nod. She has more courage than any man I know.

He says: 'All balls considered, I should probably make an attempt to find my own pair, get home to Susan and the children. You're right, I have been a bit of a bastard lately, or more so than usual. I'll make arrangements in the morning, get out of your way, unless you want me to stay around with you and … Do you?'

'No, I don't think so.' I imagine him becoming drunk and bragging of murder to the local sergeant; I'm sure he wouldn't, but trust is beaten a little thin between us right now. I let him know this as I add: 'You wouldn't want to stay around to watch me beg for scraps from her high table, now would you – because I'd say that's just about all I'll be doing until I know where I stand.'

'Yes, well.' He laughs again, but I can hear some deeper apology in it, and some regret for more than his misreading of her as he says: 'You don't need my assistance there. You never have needed me, you know.'

'I need you,' I tell him as we sight the town and the pub. 'I need you to get quickly arseless with me – right now. I will always need that from time to time. But if you breathe one word about –'

'Jesus, Ben,' he cuts off the thought. 'Believe me, please – she has my admiration, respect. My awe. I was only ever looking out for you, shit poor as I am at it. But things will work out between you, despite me, I'm sure. I understand it now – you and Kitty Cat are as well made for each other as Susie and I are. Two halves somehow.'

Are we? I don't know about that. I don't know that someone as extraordinary as Berylda Jones was made for anyone.

BERYLDA

'You'll get housemaid's knee doing that,' Greta chides me as she returns from town with supplies and the last of the mail.

'Oh well.' I shrug. I am scrubbing the boards in the study, as I have scrubbed the boards of every room of this house, taking the brush into every groove, ridding the timbers of every trace of him. All around the walls I've been, and into each corner of bookshelf, drawer, windowsill, skirting board. Some self-imposed punishment, I suppose, of me, and of him: by his total removal. Every last hair, sliver of fingernail, flake of skin, every ex-libris label torn out from every book and burned: gone. The monster is no longer here, unless I allow it. And I don't. It's taken me almost three weeks, I am being so fanatical about it, and why shouldn't I be? It's so very nearly done. I have stopped listening for his footsteps up the hall, the squeak of the boards, the snap of a command. Almost.

'Big news today,' Greta drops the *Bathurst Free Press* on the floor in front of me. 'Queen Victoria is dead.'

'Oh?' I sit back on my heels and stare at the newsprint.

'Black armbands all around town. Mrs Wardell and Mrs Hatfield standing on the street dabbing hankies. I'm not sure what that sort of mourning is all about,' says Gret. 'Bit of a show, isn't it? All that public weeping. I mean, she was eighty-one, wasn't she? What do people expect? That she'd really turn into a thousand statues and live forever?'

364

'Probably ten thousand statues. The end of an era,' I say vaguely, still staring at the paper. An old queen has passed peacefully away in her bed, a million lives from here, taking nothing with her but her soul, if such things as souls exist. Just another human, when it's all said and done. Oh well. But when I look up at Gret again, she is positively vibrant: her soul fills every scrubbed clean space around me. My sister has returned to me and she is never disappearing again. She's so alive, so here, she's even thrown out all of her old paint tubes and pencil stubs – drawers and boxes full of them, I never knew she hoarded so many, stuffed into her chiffonier, as if each one held a wish that couldn't be discarded, until now.

'Mr McLean up at the grocers was funny,' she chatters on. 'He said we can get on with being Australians now without feeling guilty, you know, about Federation. Isn't that a strange thing to say? But Buckley was even funnier in his reply – he said now, when our boys win Olympic championship medals for swimming, they'll be ours and not belong to Britain. He said that's all Federation is about for the man on the street.' She imitates his gravel rasp: 'Wavin' flags.'

For boys winning medals, and boys going off to war. That's right: they are all Australians now, under the one flag – when the squabbling has ceased as to what flag that'll be. We don't seem old enough to be a country somehow, grown up enough; but then I remember Mrs Wheeler's story of the French and German miners wrecking her front saloon over Alsace in the seventies, and wonder what country ever is grown up. The postcard I received from Clive last week, hoping my holidays are going well as he rides out from Cape Town, says they are all just boys. I feel so old; older than nations. I close my eyes for a moment and see Clive galloping across the veld, and I pray that he is surviving all the bullets and camp-life diseases and everything else that pursuing Boers for a dead queen has to offer. I pray that he comes home safely, not too scarred by murder, to find a nice girl, as if my prayers mean anything much.

'Oh, and Flo sent a telegram – see.' Gret flashes the crumpled telegram at me from under an armful of parcels from Milford's stationers in town, and I smile at her and the telegram both. My sister is buying up enough paint and paper and card to last us through some sort of Armageddon, replacing one form of hoarding with another, and not sparing any expense. We will need the proceeds from this house to pay for it all. Or some substantial royalty from the illustrations she has been asked to complete for a serial collection of bush fairytales. That incorrigible Cosmo Thompson came through, after all, with a recommendation to an editor, someone called Felix Craft, somehow associated with *The Worker* magazine out of Brisbane. The only monsters she'll ever have to consider now will be the bunyips she will create in pen and ink – fabulous.

I take the telegram from her and some glimpse of my own happiness flits through me with the words:

ARRIVE ON MORNING TRAIN. GET TO KATOOMBA 10.45 FRI 25 JAN.

That's the day after tomorrow. This is our last night in this house, this hated house, Bellevue. Tomorrow we're going home, to Echo Point. For all Alec Howell's meticulousness, he never amended his will on Libby's death, and so, as wills go, it remained in favour of wife, Elisabeth Flora Pemberton Howell, and after her her heirs, in order of the eldest male child first, and so on down the line to me and to Gret. An oversight or perhaps there simply was no one else to leave it all to? Whatever the case, while the estate is being examined for probate, the solicitor has found no bar to us moving back into our mountain home. Tomorrow. And I couldn't think of a better person to share our first new full day there with than Flo McFee. I'm so glad she's been able to get away, to spend some holiday time with me, to meet my sister. But fear follows any sense of joy, for what Flo might see in me, for what I have done. Do I wear some mark of it on me somehow? How can I go about in the world as the murderer I am?

'I saw Ben in Durham Street, too, on his way to the bank. He said he'd come and take Jack when he was finished there. I said that would be all right.'

Gret clomps away across the entrance hall with her parcels, leaving me to my thoughts of Ben, the fear and joy I find in him. I stand up and face the daisies, his daisies that Greta placed in the brass vase on the plinth by the drawing room doors for all to see as they called to pay their respects, though for all I remember of those two days between death and burial it might only have been Mrs Weston who came to the house, holding me under her wing. And Ben, always somewhere beside me. And these daisies, my one answered prayer: *Please help us*, I asked them in the night; my desperate prayer to the shadow of a stranger, the small half of a wishbone held tight. Twenty-four days ago. Their drabness is crisp-dried now, their flowers sepia-scorched, and they only grow more lovely to me. They are dead but alive, these *Helichrysum elatum*, and I will carry them with me always, work them firmly into the hole where my hatred used to lie. I touch their feathery petals now, or rays as I have learned they are properly called, and they are papery indeed, fragile but strong, and I cherish them as I have cherished nothing else. They don't call them everlastings for nothing, do they?

I turn and look out of the open front door now, to look for him, but I see only the northern hills, and the smoke cloud smudged above them from this summer's bushfires. The blazes have cut a path of destruction across Tambaroora from the west this year, heading for Sofala, taking tobacco plantations and joss houses and poppies with them. And Tiger Sam, too, who stayed at the farm to try to protect his crop. Dr Ah Ling and his young niece escaped along the Mudgee Road towards Hargraves, and Buckley heard they've since got on a boat back to Shanghai. I see them out on the waves of the blue hills somewhere, a little lacquer-haired girl quietly playing peg dolls beneath paper sails. I am cleaning my heart, I tell the hills, I tell her, I tell Ah Ling, I am cleaning my heart. I am reconstructing it with paper daisies, and with gratitude. And I will succeed. Eventually.

I touch the pendant at my neck: my mother's pendant of beryl, which my father had made for her from his prospect at Ophir, wishing for me. I look at it in my hand: it is home, there in my hand. The rough-cut stone barely polished, the inferior rose gold – it's not as beautiful as I remembered it. It's far, far more beautiful. It looks like Papa had a go at making the piece himself, it is so amateurishly wrought, the loops of the scalloped edge uneven and the casing oddly bowed down one side. Absolutely worthless but to us, to me.

I clutch it to my throat with the reverberating shock that it was ever denied us. Why? Why did you take it from me, Alec Howell? Why did he shut it up in a safe deposit box at the Australasia Bank? All of Mother's and Aunt Libby's trinkets – hair combs, paste jewels, a string of pearls with a broken clasp – kept from us. The questions I will never escape no matter how many other things I might stuff into my mind to ward them off.

How is such a monster made? How is a monster measured? Such questions might drive me perhaps to consider investigating psychiatry one day as an area of study. When he is far enough away. When he is merely bones and the headstone is so overgrown I cannot read his name. But the mind surely is a strange beast, isn't it? Mine as strange as anyone's. Not least that I mourned without pretence at his funeral. I overheard Justice Wardell and J.C. Dunning discussing him outside in the churchyard, the one telling the other that there was no chance the Free Traders would have chosen him as their candidate anyway. He'd made quite a terrible hash of his Federation speech, saying some pompous thing about fixed grain and wool prices being part of a socialist plot to destroy the Commonwealth economy, insulting every farmer there, hardening their resolve to vote for the Protectionists – who are indeed now in bed with the Labor Party on the issues. God forbid. The sadness of it overwhelmed me; the pointlessness: to work so hard and for it to come to nothing. To be so endlessly, insatiably in want. And ultimately unwanted. Hated. The response to the *Notice of Death* cable sent to Barnstaple via London, to the father's address, was swift and brief, a reply from, presumably, a brother: *With regret, we inform you that we have no interest in this matter.* As if he had ceased to be long ago. Even at the hospital his absence has barely been felt. A locum has come out from Sydney to take over as surgeon until a permanent replacement is found. While my sister appears to have tossed him out with a box of old paint tubes. Life goes on. Life goes round and round.

'Miss.' Buckley tips his hat as he passes on his way across the front garden with a barrow full of tools to move onto the dray at the gate. He still won't look me in the eye. I suppose he maintains that I should have let him hang for us. Or perhaps he sees the monster in me. But every time he avoids meeting my gaze, a dread falls over me: I can't continue with Ben: I can't allow him to love this monster.

Prince begins to bark, bounding around manically from the stables, and leaping back and forth either side of the path, as if all four legs are being pulled hither and thither by rubber bands. I can't help smiling at that: Prince hasn't so much as growled since the master left the premises. He is such a happy hound today. Wonderfully silly, bouncing hound.

Greta yells up the east hallway, yelling at the top of her lungs because she can: 'Well, that'll be Ben now!' And I can't help laughing to myself, and a little out aloud, at the fact of that. Perhaps this bush fairytale won't end precisely as Greta planned it for me; but maybe, given time, it will come close.

I see the afternoon light in his hair first, sunshine spilling out from under his Huckleberry hat, his loping strides taking the rise of the hill as if he owns it, because he rightfully should, and darkness is blasted from me. A thankfulness that sparks and soars. In every practical sense, he has been invaluable to us over these past few weeks, accompanying us to the solicitors' office to attend to the probate application and all the necessities of the circumstances, using the Wilberry name to expedite things; using his own cash to provide generous payments to Mary and Lucy, to send them off with equally generous references, for I cannot bear to have others too near. Shielding me in every public situation, and there haven't been too many of those, as I have preferred to scrub boards alone. And now here he is walking up to the house, on his way to take Jack, on his way to Manildra to look for another flower, his mother's flower at Mandagery Creek, after which he will return to Melbourne, because he must return to his work.

And I don't want him to go. I want to run to him, across this field between us and into his arms. But still I can't. My knees are locked. I am not yet ready, not yet so unchained. I am not far enough away from here; I am not yet truly home.

'You look a bit lost,' he says, smiling up the path at me, smiling at the washerwoman splotches on my skirt, my rolled sleeves, my headscarf. I'm sure I've never looked more an actual gypsy.

'I am,' I admit to him. 'But not for too much longer, I hope.'

I stand on the top step of the verandah, to meet him eye to eye. I hold his necessary, sunshine face in my hands, to invite him to kiss me, for the first time since we came together rushing with strange fever in a stable loft, and when his lips touch mine now, his gentleness, his fearlessness breathes new faith into me. The quiet power held in his shoulders, the salt taste of his cheek, the softness of his beard on my skin; we kiss for the first time all over again. I love him. He replenishes me. He heals me. But I have so much healing yet to do. A life I must spend restoring life, every moment, for the one I took.

Can I dare to believe that this life begins for me, for us, here inside this kiss?

BEN

This will not be the last time I kiss Berylda Jones at her door; nor the last time we say farewell.

'Will you stay with me when you bring Jack back to Echo Point?' she asks me, whispering against my ear. 'Will you love me then?'

'Yes.' And I will ask her to marry me then, too, when I have worked out how I might move to Sydney, and when. As much as I would grab at any chance of getting out from under Dubois, I owe Professor Jepson the completion of my main work, with the Board of Agriculture, and the expansion of the department into that field. Perhaps a year; might take as long to pack up my potting shed of a house. And a few excuses contrived to come up to explore the New South Wales botanical record in the interim. The curator at the Gardens must be due for retirement, elderly fellow – perhaps I'll drop in and have a word to him. I tell Berylda: 'I will love you every second until then and forever beyond it.'

'How long do you think you'll be at Manildra?' she asks me, although I've already told her. She asks everything two or three times as though testing the veracity of this weird place we move through.

'A week at the most,' I tell her. 'I've really got to get back to Melbourne.' And I'm not sure why I'm going out to Mandagery Creek now. A week is not nearly long enough for a decent exploration, by the time I get there, et cetera – I don't expect to find anything. I suppose I'm only going to honour that promise to Mama. If I move to Sydney, there'll be plenty of other opportunities to come out here to look for mythical red daisies, though I suspect with all manner of confidence that Mama might have decided I've already found what she wanted me to look for. I tell Berylda: 'I'll try to stay two nights in the mountains with you. At least.'

She kisses me again, and I'd better go, or I might be compelled to love her right now. Just the feel of her hands on my face is a reawakening I don't know that I can step away from. But I have to; it's too soon for that, today. And not here. There is no love of this kind to be found in this house.

'Enjoy your going home,' I say as I step down from her.

She smiles: 'Oh I think I will. I will make every effort to.'

And I leave her for the stables, to go and saddle up Jack. I take him out across Glynarthen, stretch him out to the distant candlebarks, and he'd be happy to keep on going but I've got to get my swag from the hotel. I'm not setting out until the morning, either – it'll be a full day's ride tomorrow, and I'm looking forward to it. It'll be good to get out of the fishbowl of Bathurst. For all that it is a pretty town, even the parks, with their tightly set conifers and their iron lace fences, are claustrophobic here. Brass dirges play in every bandstand of every town for the old queen.

The publican of the Royal catches me round at the stables at the back of the hotel: 'Some mail turned up for you. Something from Melbourne. Just put it under your door.'

'Righteo – thank you.' I go up to the room, thinking it will be a note from Professor Jepson – a happy receipt of the *beryldii* specimen I sent him a fortnight ago, along with a firm assurance of my impending return and much improved spirits.

But it's not from Jepson. It's mail originally addressed to me at the university, sent on, possibly by Gregham, and I recognise the hand as soon as I open it: Pater's blunt, thick strokes of the pen. I imagine it will inform me that he has commenced the fight over Mama's estate, to attempt to disinherit me, but it doesn't say that at all. He tells me:

Dear Son,

It is no good to either of us that we remain on such bad terms.

I was too harsh in what I said to you before you left Brisbane last. I am a harsh man but I do not want to drive you away. Your Mother would not want that. You are no coward. You have a different streak of stubbornness from mine but you are no less an unyielding bastard.

I hope to see you at Jericho on your winter break, if you were thinking of coming home then as you usually do. If not, you know where to find me. I would like to know you better.

Your Father

John Wilberry

Now *that's* extraordinary. I wonder first if there is some ulterior motive: does he need something from me? Something from Mama's estate? No, possibly not. As difficult as the new Commonwealth arrangements might make things for Queensland cattle and cane farmers with the price of labour increasing and the protection of tariffs decreasing, Pater, like the Thompsons, only stands to win: buying up cheaply the land of those battlers who'll be forced to the wall. He'll make a killing. And one day it will all be mine, it only occurs to me now as I stand here. I don't even know how much land we have as it is. I don't know what to do with that thought, or with Pater's olive branch. What would I do with fifteen thousand shorthorn? Turn them loose? It's not a conversation I can ever have with him: cattle just don't belong on that land, and somehow I don't quite belong to John Wilberry, either. Then again, grief does work some baffling wonders on us, doesn't it?

I fold the letter away into my satchel, in the front pocket, something to think about later, and as I do I see the one I received from Cos last week, sticking out of the top of my notebook, reread a few times now to test its own revelation of wonder. He tells me of his gladness at re-ensconcement at the Swamp, and that it appears his balls were in fine working order all along as Susie is pregnant again. He's thinking of moving them to the West Indies, to Barbados, where his grandfather has some cane investments that need the occasional Thompson signature, and where he and Susie can be themselves in a shack on the beach, where it's not so out of the ordinary to have brown-skinned babies, and where they also have cricket – all year round. Could be the most sensible thing that Cos has ever done. I hope he gets off his lazy arse and does it. I'd like to get drunk with him in Barbados one day.

But now, the brass funeral march starts moving along the street outside the pub, and I have to get out of here, I realise. I can't wait until tomorrow. I have to get out, into the air. I grab my swag from my luggage and Jack from the stable and I am gone. I'll find somewhere to camp along the way. It's a beautiful afternoon. The sky is blue, huge, still, warm.

I head west, out along the Mitchell stock road, and on the edge of this side of the town the great hulking edifice of Bathurst Gaol imposes itself over the road like the last bastion of the law before the wilderness. Not for the first time I wonder if the felons in there are the least of those amongst us. Not for the first time I wonder if I shouldn't be in there myself for my part in the murder of Alec Howell.

Before I recall that in killing him Berylda did the only thing she could, however wrong the Crimes Act might deem it. She stopped him. Someone had to. In the absence, in the silence of the law, she did the just thing, the courageous and self-sacrificing thing, and she pays, every moment, for having done so. She pays as no hanging judge or executioner ever would.

I feel her sadness as I ride towards the lowering sun, feel the weight of that conscience she carries with her. I will never be able to relieve her of it, as much as I might want to, but one day she might see it as I do: a part of her, no less vital than any other. No one is sinless, spotless. Just as in nature there is always a blemish: a knot, an asymmetry, a fissure, the line of a frown between the brows – the shapes of difficulties overcome, of struggles worth fighting for, and won. All perfections in themselves. Striving to be who you are.

Who is she? She is perfect, in every way, to me.

BERYLDA

I look up and down the platform of Katoomba Station, my heart racing crazily with every emotion. This is the first time I have been out in the world on my own, since – shush. It's high holiday season and there are people everywhere – half of Sydney has come up to the mountains to retreat from the humidity; the other half is waiting for the train, for friends to join them – and I am so jangled and raw I imagine they can all hear my thoughts.

The whistle blows and I jump; I see the steam from the engine puffing around the curve of the tracks from Leura, and Flo is nearly here. A screech of the brakes, a surge of summer hats and parasols. And she *is* here, running up the platform towards me. She is impossible to miss, wearing that great big splashy hat she got from the Grace Brothers sale – which would seem to have happened several lifetimes ago. Has it only been six weeks? Yes. And, massed with extravagantly pink and yellow roses, this hat is even more hideous than I remember. It is marvellous and I am up on my toes, waving. My whole being is a grin – bracing for the impact.

'Bryl! Happy twentieth century, comrade!' All ringlets swinging under that ridiculous awning of tulle.

I can barely reply, wiping tears from my eyes – of happiness. Everything is possible and promising in her sparkling green eyes. 'God, it's good to see you.' I squeeze her tight.

'You too, duckie.' She just about squeezes the breath out of me back, and barely takes one herself before hoisting me along with her: 'You'll never guess what happened to me these holidays – utterly, deliriously shocking. I've been dying – just *dying* – to tell you.'

I can't stop laughing – with relief. My knees are shaking with this relief. I signal to Buckley, over by the ticket window, to pick up Flo's bags and call to him through the crowd: 'We'll walk through the town – see you at the house.'

He tips his hat over a nod; he smiles at me – at last. What does he smile at? My release? My return to myself? I am returning. I am. Every atom trembles and glistens with the excitement of it.

'I've had a proposal.' Flo strides on, out of the station. 'A proposal of the marriage type.'

'What – from a boy? You have not,' I say to her, and I am shocked. 'What sort of brave boy is that?'

'Not a boy exactly. A man.' She blushes: Flo McFee is blushing – I don't believe it. 'Lawrence Moverley,' she says. 'Believe it. Larry – he went to school with Bruce.' Her eldest brother. 'He called in on us at Woy Woy. Stockbroker – he's awfully nice. Not quite as progressive as Old Mac might choose for me. I scandalised him by swimming overarm stroke and beating him in a race across the bay, as if the mixed bathing in broad daylight wasn't enough to do him in, and then dear old Dad scandalised him some more by insisting I beat him at downing a pint of beer. Poor Larry didn't know if he was Arthur or Martha by the end of his visit. But I'm thinking about it, Bryl – I'm seriously considering it.'

'Are you? Why?' I am having trouble understanding this turn in any way; the Flo I know is far too blue-stocking for any such thing. She swims at the beach in blithe contempt of anti-sea-bathing decrees, never mind in mixed company; she doesn't do anything by the book. Except her studies. 'Will he let you continue at Law?'

'Oh yes, I should think so.' She nods assuredly. 'Most definitely. Bruce and Chas and Hoddy all agree that he's desperately in love with me – Larry would do anything I told him to. And he's thoroughly petrified of Old Mac. He's also got family in San Francisco and mentioned the possibility of one day relocating across the Pacific – something to do with the gold trade. "Would it be attractive to you to travel to California at some time in the future?" he asked me, and I said, "Would it what!" Bryl – don't you see? Women can practise law in California. They might not have the vote, but they can darn well practise freely at their professions. They can even bathe in the ocean at times of their choosing – wearing bangles and bows, if they wish.' She winks, all vim and mischief. 'It could all work out for me fabulously well. Besides, I like Larry – he's good and kind. A safe pair of hands, I suppose you might say. That's not very romantic, though, is it?'

'Oh I don't know,' I say, feeling Ben's hand holding mine, as if he is here with me, because he is. 'Safe can be a very romantic word,' I tell Flo. 'Safety is a very precious thing.' And I blush, for all that safety means to me, for all that I can never tell Flo.

'You sound like you know what you're talking about.' She leans in conspiratorially. 'What's going on? What have you been up to on your break? Come on – out with it.'

'Oh, this and that.' I flutter a hand dismissively over the idea that I could possibly have been up to anything whatsoever, and I tell her the only truth I may: 'I might have met a man myself. A man called Ben. Ben Wilberry – you'll meet him in a few days.'

'Wilberry?' Now Flo is shocked. 'As in the Wilberrys of Queensland?'

'Hm.'

'No!' She is scandalised.

'Yes.'

'Really,' she says, intrigued and suspicious. 'But aren't they Anti-Socialist Protectionists?'

'Ben's not.' I smile with my best secrets. 'He's not like anyone. He's good and kind and just himself. *And* he's a vegetarian.'

'No!'

'Yes.' I laugh, but the sound is too loud. I hear it cut through the bustle of Katoomba Street, clattering along the verandah poles and through the spokes of cartwheels. How dare I pretend that Ben is mine; and yet he is. 'I'll tell you all about him when we get to the house,' I say to Flo, and I look away, down the steep decent towards Echo Point, out across the cracks and crags of the mountaintops that pave forever. Where do I begin?

'Oh dear,' Flo sighs beside me, tucking my hand under her arm. 'But I do go on and on, don't I? I haven't even given you the slightest commiseration in respect of your uncle – I'm so sorry to have heard. When you wrote of the circumstances of your change of address –'

'It's all right,' I tell the mountaintops some truth again. 'We weren't very close. He didn't much care for Greta and me.' My voice is not steady but all the same it's surprisingly easy to say.

'Oh.' She shrugs. 'Well it's a strange one that wouldn't care for you.'

'Strange. Yes. He was.'

And Flo McFee is not the slightest bit interested in discussing the subject further. As we reach the bottom of the hill, the pines of Katoomba towering above us and all the little miners' cottages that dot the way to the cliff edge – to home, almost there – Flo resumes her whirl of news and views.

'You can't have everything you wish for tied up in a neat bow, can you?' she muses as we walk on. 'Or certainly not all at once, as you would want it. I'm beginning to learn something about compromise, I think, comrade. Speaking of such, Old Mac doesn't think the legislation for the New South Wales Women's Vote will go through this year at all – they're going to leave it to occur in conjunction with the Federal Act, and that won't be until next year in all likelihood. Ooooh, but this makes me itch. Why do the wheels have to turn so slowly for us? Still, we'll be ahead of Melbourne most probably, and our full enfranchisement must come – it will come. It's simply inevitable. *Even* in Melbourne.'

'It will be if you have any say in it.' I nudge her playfully, but I don't share anything like her certainty. It took Federation itself a decade to come from Sir Henry Parkes's call for it and it could all unravel at any moment. Even if we do get the vote it can be snatched away as quickly, and will be if and when it suits the men who decide how we should live our lives. Still, I tell Flo, and I almost believe it too: 'One day, you will make a run for parliament. One day, you will be our first female prime minister.'

'Heavens, I'll take that wish for my own,' she says up into the furthest boughs of the pines, and she's already writing her acceptance speech.

I look up too. How many times I have looked into these pines from the train and felt only cool, dark dread in the sight of them. Huge, looming black monsters of loss. But now they stand at the entrance to my sanctuary, love and memory whispering through every needle on the breeze.

The rusty gate squeaks as I lift the latch.

'Oh my word! Is this the house?' Flo squeaks in reply. 'How very beautiful – I'm so glad I overdressed.'

The ivy is rampant right up to the front door and there are jungles of blackberry and jasmine strangling every camellia, engulfing entire flowerbeds, but its wide weatherboards are still a merry white against all the deep greens of the garden, its portico posts still gorgeously turned – *Just like your mother's ankles,* Papa used to wink.

Greta waves from the bay window of the front parlour. She is up on a ladder, curtain rod in hand. Prince is leaping up and down below her, his silly face bobbing over the high sill, ears flapping. He still can't believe he's allowed inside.

'Jumping Jezebels,' Flo exclaims, looking down to her right at the path that snakes towards the low wall at the cliff, pointing out at the vista. 'You've got the Three Sisters in your front yard.'

'We do.' I am all grin again. 'And in a moment we shall be three sisters having tea on the terrace.'

I hunt about for the key in my pocket. I jiggle it into the door and feel the click as the metal gives: the liberty that is so dear to me. Greta shouting out down the hall: 'Hello! Hello!'

I look over my shoulder at Flo and my heart is racing crazily again: because I am home. Finally, home.

My spirit flies out across the gorge and back to me.

BEN

Even the wire grass is battling to hang on in this paddock, set just off the tablelands where the hills become plains. It's been turned over exclusively to sheep now for twenty-five years or more, with plans to soon put it all under wheat. But I am here, Mama. I made it.

I look around her old family selection, which once was the Trentons' and now is the Bentleys', and the pair of them combined have just about completed the destruction of whatever indigenous ecology was here before them. Even the creek seems to be drying off at this point – exhausted – exposing the roots of the native sandalwood scrub on the banks: thirsty.

Jack snorts: What did you bring us out here for?

That's a very good question.

But there's a lonely old tree up ahead, just the other side of the creek. It looks like a bimble box, with its slender trunk and vertical branches, the high sun playing glassy on the leaves. It reminds me of Mama, of riding out to the billabongs of the Jordan with her; making mud pies out there as a boy, making her smile. I'll go and pay my respects and then let's call it a day – let's call it three days with Berylda in Katoomba instead of two, making her smile. I will when I tell her I left her for nothing but a brief chat with a bimble box. There really is little else here. Sheep bleat at me as I walk through them, dimly annoyed at the interruption; they are saying: That's right, we ate every last daisy that ever was in this place, and they were delicious.

The tree is not a bimble box, though, I see as I get closer; we're possibly too far south to see them here anyway. I think it's just a young ghost gum then, tall but not yet filled out, the shine on the leaves just a trick of the light. I walk across the creek for a closer look at the bark to identify it, and the water is deeper than it appears – I'm soaked up past the knees at halfway. But when I get to the opposite bank, I see under the dappled shade of the tree, a cluster of low woody stipes – greenish-brown. You could easily mistake them for a twiggy hand of gum leaves fallen from above; I could easily have trodden on it.

The leaves are long, lanceolate and few; the flocculence almost prickly to the touch. Three plants – no, four. The bracts are russet globes, still shut tight yet. One's about to go, though – and I can just see the first of the rays are red. This is it. These are Mama's everlastings.

I look around at Jack and laugh.

This bloom will be fully opened come the morning.

AUTHOR NOTE

Paper Daisies, like the three novels before her, is a fiction inspired by the history of the country I call home, a quest to uncover what threads of the past remain woven through our present. This time there was one great cracking spark that set this particular quest in train: Prime Minister Julia Gillard's now infamous misogyny speech, delivered in October 2012, and the various reactions to it. In some shock at the most critical interpretations of the speech, namely that Gillard was cynically 'playing the gender card' and that there was no substance to the issues she raised, I began writing this novel, and what began as an exploration of what misogyny means quickly evolved into expression of the grief that sexual denigration, control and abuse causes, and an allegory of how it has not only affected me personally but also the lives of many women I love.

In real life, for the women I know, being raped and otherwise brutalised, terrorised and sneered at for another's gratification is not as pleasure-inducing as some fashionable contemporary erotic literature would have us believe, and my quest for some truth about the sickness that is misogyny became more urgent as the legal cases surrounding the murders of Jill Meagher, Lisa Harnum and Allison Baden-Clay unfolded across my writing days. And amongst all of this, when a schoolgirl in Pakistan, Malala Yousafzai, was shot in the head for campaigning for female education in her country, some commentators in this country pointed at her assailants, the

Taliban, and cried: 'See look, real misogynists! We don't have any misogynists here!' Of course not.

But one of the quieter and more insidious reasonable-sounding attitudes coming from the sisterhood today is that we don't need feminism in this country because women have all of the opportunities they need. The ignorance of this view chills me. We only have the opportunities we have as women *because* of feminism, and by the support of good men who believe in the benefits of sexual equality – men who still predominantly control our world.

There is one historical fact here, though, of which Australians can be justly proud. Contrary to my Berylda Jones's doubts, Australian women received the right to vote in federal elections and to stand for office the following year, in June 1902. It took nineteen attempts for the legislation to be passed, and decades of work by the suffragists to see it happen; this franchise bill also excluded Aboriginal and all non-White people from voting, and not all states granted the women's vote at that time, but the bill was still a world leader, second only to New Zealand in the granting of universal, national suffrage. Women in the United Kingdom wouldn't win the right to vote in their general elections until 1928.

Sadly, though, it seems to me that we are only ever a breath away from returning to a time where the rights of women are secondary to those of men, or nonexistent. It remains a fact that a majority of women are economically and physically more vulnerable than men. It remains a fact, too, that a woman is most likely to be raped or otherwise physically abused or murdered by someone she knows, most often her partner or a close family member or friend, and that the abuse will most likely go unreported. According to White Ribbon research, in 2013 forty percent of Australian women over the age of fifteen had experienced an incident of physical or sexual violence; currently, on average, one woman per week is killed by a male partner, or ex-partner. Given this, it seems to me that it can never be wrong to talk about violence against women, or their denigration, or the challenges they face simply by being women in our society. It can never be wrong to 'play the gender card', or 'the race card', or 'the victim card', or whatever card the bullies want to wave about contemptuously at anyone who criticises them. Justice is a whole house made of cards, and it is one we all live very much inside. We have to maintain it wisely and carefully, for all our sakes.

But *Paper Daisies* is, I must stress, fiction. In real life, I would never condone a resort to murder for any reason. Such murders of violent bullies occur of course, and women are still occasionally gaoled for them, but I've only killed some demons here, an exercise I highly recommend to anyone seeking restitution where no other kind but the imaginary might be found.

I must stress, too, that all of the characters in this novel are also fictional. There was no such Queensland Minister for Agriculture called John Wilberry; and nor was anyone called Alec Howell treasurer of the Liberal League, or member of the Free Trade Party, or District Surgeon of Bathurst Hospital. As for the mythical daisies that Ben finds along the way, they are inventions for him alone – but then again, perhaps they are still waiting to be found.

I would like to acknowledge here the invaluable treasure that is the Australian literature collection of the Mary Elizabeth Byrnes Memorial Library, Orange. It is wonderful to have such an incredible resource sitting in the middle of the New South Wales Central West, not far from where I live. And of course, as libraries go, I can't do anything or go anywhere without Trove, the National Library of Australia's database of newspapers, books and photographs.

The quotes at the beginning of each of the parts are all taken from Friedrich Nietzsche's experimental novel, *Thus Spake Zarathustra: A Book for All and None*, first published in English in 1896 – and of which the *Sydney Morning Herald*'s review of 1899 declared, 'everyone to his taste'. And the Louisa Lawson quote that opens the novel is from her 1911 poem, 'The Mount of Achievement', sourced from Elaine Zinkham's essay, 'Louisa Albury Lawson', which appears in *A Bright and Fiery Troop: Australian Women Writers of the Nineteenth Century*, edited by Debra Adelaide, 1988 – because I could not find any reference to this poem anywhere else. If this is not a prime example of our neglect of the literary heritage of our women writers, I don't know what is. Louisa Lawson was hardly a nobody – she was editor of

The Dawn, a well-known contemporary poet and journalist in her own right, and the mother of our beloved Henry. Without her, and other women of her calibre, Australian women would not have won the vote so soon, and would not have had a voice in print much beyond baking recipes and knitting patterns.

Finally, I owe thanks to Selwa Anthony, Cate Paterson, Emma Rafferty and Julia Stiles for their kind and wise guidance on the original manuscript and its first publication; to Lou Johnson for valuing the 'difficult' women in literature and for encouraging this new edition. And, last but never least, to my muse de bloke, my perennial hero and gentlest giant, Dean Brownlee: you are the best random stranger I ever met.

Take a journey through time with Kim Kelly. You've never seen Australia like this before...

JEWEL SEA

Based on the true story of the loss of the luxury steamship *Koombana* to a vicious cyclone off the coast of North-Western Australia in 1912, *Jewel Sea* is a tale of fatal desire, theft and greed – of kindred spirits searching for each other, and for redemption.

WILD CHICORY

A journey from Ireland to Australia in the early 1900s, along threads of love, family, war and peace, **Wild Chicory** is a slice of ordinary life rich in history, folklore and fairy tale, and a portrait of the precious bond between a granddaughter, Brigid, and her grandmother, Nell.

THE BLUE MILE

Against the glittering backdrop of Sydney Harbour, *The Blue Mile* is a story of the cruelties of Great Depression poverty, the wild gamble a city took to build a bridge – a wonder of the world – and the risks only the brave will take for a chance to truly live and love.

THIS RED EARTH

It's 1939 and the girl next door wants adventure before she settles down – but war gives her more than she's asked for. From Australia's sparkling coastline to her dusty, desert heart, *This Red Earth* charts a fight for home, and a quest to tell the truth about love – before it's too late.

BLACK DIAMONDS

From the foothills of the Blue Mountains to the battlefields of France, comes a story of war and coal. Told with freshness, verve and wit, **Black Diamonds** is the tale of a fierce young nation – Australia – and two fierce hearts who dare to discover what courage really means.

For links to all major retailers, please visit: kimkellyauthor.com/books/

KIM KELLY

Kim Kelly is the author of six novels exploring Australia and its history. Her stories shine a bright light on some forgotten corners of the past and tell the tales of ordinary people living through extraordinary times.

An editor and literary consultant by trade, stories fill her everyday – most nights, too – and it's love that fuels her intellectual engine. In fact, she takes love so seriously she once donated a kidney to her husband to prove it, and also to save his life.

Originally from Sydney, today Kim lives on a small rural property in central New South Wales just outside the tiny gold-rush village of Millthorpe, where the ghosts are mostly friendly and her grown sons regularly come home to graze.

CPSIA information can be obtained
at www.ICGtesting.com
Printed in the USA
LVOW11s2123170118

563096LV00002B/282/P